P9-APD-229

Acclaim for Alan Lightman's

THE DIAGNOSIS

"Lightman is a highly original and imaginative thinker. We realize with some alarm that Chalmers's world is not that far removed from our own. . . . [*The Diagnosis*] forcefully captures the great confluence of our times: information overload, unimaginable prosperity and spiritual bankruptcy." —*The New York Times Book Review*

"A darkly allegorical novel about the human costs of a meaningless, high-tech work world run amok. . . . A black-comic, surreal descent into the maelstrom." —*The Boston Globe*

"A modern-day 'Metamorphosis.'" —*The Baltimore Sun*

"A work of vivid sensuousness, sparkling intelligence, and poignant beauty." —*Booklist*

"Mordantly comic. . . . Lightman's diagnosis of our culture's ills is right on the mark." —*The Seattle Times*

"Dark, deadpan, and decidedly Kafkaesque. . . . *The Diagnosis* offers a robust indictment of a time-crunched, information-glutted world." —*Entertainment Weekly*

"A grueling, funny, Kafkaesque fable."   *—Newsday*

"This is humor based on the precarious, a humor of brinkmanship as a character fights for his own soul."
—Los Angeles Times

"A chilling portrait of contemporary American culture and its obsession with convenience, speed, and social status."
—The Hartford Courant

"Lightman has taken on the fast-paced, keenly competitive world of modern business and technology with a wicked, grim sense of humor."   *—The Atlanta Journal-Constitution*

"In a world gone largely wrong, Alan Lightman continues to do something right. The prognosis is good."
—The Brookline Tab (Needham, MA)

"The vision that animates this book is frightening, unforgettable, and only too true."   *—The Times* (Trenton, NJ)

"A mindblower of a novel. . . . Vitally important in its subject matter, truly tough to put down, impossible to forget once finished."   *—The Commercial Appeal*

"The story is a mix of dark comedy . . . and urban horror that proves both satisfying and unsettling."
—Wyoming Tribune-Eagle

"A disturbing novel. . . . *The Diagnosis* paints the definitive picture of the hapless, helpless human cog in the wheel of the information society."   *—The Chapel Hill News*

"A brilliant allegory of the fast life. . . . The author's beautiful, descriptive writing style is mesmerizing, and the problems encountered along the way are immensely thought provoking."   —*Deseret News* (Salt Lake City)

"A powerful critique of a barbarously accelerated society. Lightman's understated style . . . gives the book gravity and lucidity, and creates an unexpectedly haunting effect."
                    —*The Times Literary Supplement*

"A hard-hitting satire with a profoundly human core."
                    —*The Sunday Telegraph*

ALAN LIGHTMAN

THE DIAGNOSIS

Alan Lightman was born in Memphis, Tennessee, in 1948, and educated at Princeton University and at the California Institute of Technology. His previous books include two novels, *Einstein's Dreams* and *Good Benito*; a collection of essays and fables, *Dance for Two*; and several books on science, *Origins: The Lives and Worlds of Modern Cosmologists, Ancient Light, Great Ideas in Physics,* and *Time for the Stars.* He is an adjunct professor at the Massachusetts Institute of Technology (MIT).

ALSO BY ALAN LIGHTMAN

Einstein's Dreams

Good Benito

Dance for Two: Selected Essays

THE DIAGNOSIS

THE
DIAGNOSIS

❖

ALAN LIGHTMAN

VINTAGE CONTEMPORARIES
Vintage Books
A Division of Random House, Inc.
New York

FIRST VINTAGE CONTEMPORARIES EDITION, JANUARY 2002

Copyright © 2000 by Alan Lightman

All rights reserved under International and Pan-American Copyright Con-
ventions. Published in the United States by Vintage Books, a division of
Random House, Inc., New York, and simultaneously in Canada by
Random House of Canada Limited, Toronto. Originally published in hard-
cover in the United States by Pantheon Books, a division of Random
House, Inc., New York, in 2000.

Vintage is a registered trademark and Vintage Contemporaries and
colophon are trademarks of Random House, Inc.

The Library of Congress has catalogued the Pantheon edition as follows:
Lightman, Alan P., 1948–
The diagnosis / Alan Lightman.
p. cm.
ISBN 0-679-43615-4
1. Executives—Fiction. I. Title.
PS3562.I45397 D5 2000
813'.54—dc21 00-024543

Vintage ISBN: 0-375-72550-4

Author photograph © Jean Lightman
Book design by M. Kristen Bearse

www.vintagebooks.com

Printed in the United States of America
10 9 8 7 6

IN MEMORY OF
JEANNE GARRETSON LIGHTMAN

AND FOR
JEAN, ELYSE, AND KARA

THE DIAGNOSIS

ON THE SUBWAY

People must have been in a great hurry, for no one noticed anything wrong with Bill Chalmers as he dashed from his automobile one fine summer morning. Earnest and dressed in a blue cotton suit, he was immediately swept up by the mass of commuters also galloping from their cars toward the elevators and down to the trains of the Alewife Station, a cavernous structure of concrete and crisscrossed steel struts, one end of the Red Line through Boston. At the ground floor, Chalmers presented his pass and rushed through the turnstile. He was halfway down the stairs to the platform when he heard the taut string of electronic beeps and the doors began sliding on train Number One. A woman groaned. Another commuter, a tall nervous man with squeaky shoes, lunged ahead and ran alongside the train, shouting and slapping his magazine against the red paneled doors. But the train was already in motion, its steel wheels scraping and squealing so fiercely that several people had to turn up their head sets. The tall man swiveled and shot Chalmers an accusing stare, as if his lack of sufficient speed through the turnstile had caused a half-dozen people to miss their trains. What a jerk, Chalmers thought to himself and looked down at his watch. It was 8:22. Twenty-three minutes to his stop, a nine-minute walk to his building, two minutes on the elevator, and he'd be sitting at his desk by 9:00. Assuming the train on Track Two arrived and departed within four minutes, as it should. With some satisfaction he reminded himself that, unlike the ridiculously agitated man with the magazine, he had calculated his morning commute so that he could miss the first train and still arrive at the office on time. Abruptly, he began worrying that the train on Track Two might be late. Never had that happened when he'd missed train Number One, but it was certainly a possibility. Stroking his mustache, he continued down the stairs and looked again at his watch. He mustn't waste the four minutes. However, he slowed his descent to drop fifty cents into the cup of a homeless woman sprawled on the edge of the stairs. She looked disturbingly like his old piano teacher. "Thank you, kind sir," she said. "Please don't thank me," he answered, embarrassed. "I thank everyone who is more fortunate than me," she called to him as he hurried down to the platform. Waves of people flowed around him, jostling and crushing from all sides, shoving each other to gain an advantage for the next arriving train. Gulped down in seconds were muffins and rolls, hard-boiled eggs, bananas, coffee, and crackers. Some commuters tried to unfold newspapers in the cramped space but gave up and contented themselves with staring at the digital sign on the kiosk, where bits of news and the correct time scrolled by in bright glowing dots. The dozens of upturned faces were waxy and yellow beneath the underground fluorescent bulbs.

Even in that pale yellow light, if any of those waiting had looked carefully into Chalmers's eyes, they might have observed a faint petrifaction, a solidification, some sign that all was not well. But they did not, occupied with their own busy schedules and the marching dots on the sign. Chalmers himself felt perfectly fit, aside from the normal stresses and aches of a man just past forty, arguably overweight but by no means fat. He glanced at his watch, 8:23, and forged a path to the kiosk. Above his head, the digital sign flickered and hummed and something clattered repeatedly against the high concrete ceiling and the air sagged with the burnt smell of hot brake fluid. Several radios blared, jumbling their throbbing bass notes in competing rhythms. Huddled against the kiosk as if battling a strong wind, a woman in a smart linen suit was delivering instructions into a cellular telephone. Chalmers couldn't help noticing that her phone was a new model, considerably smaller and sleeker than his. He took out his own phone from his briefcase. As he began dialing, he found that he was still shaken by the poor woman on the stairs. Her misery had cast a gloom over him, which he tried to forget by pushing the tiny buttons as fast as he could. First, he called Jenkins, to make sure that the proper documents would be ready for his 9:15 meeting. All was in order. He hung up and stood on his toes, peering down the dark tunnel of Track Two. Over the track, hundreds of glowing red neon tubes dangled down from the ceiling, one of them broken and blinking like a Christmas tree light. His telephone rang. Two men reached inside their briefcases, thinking it theirs. "Mr. Chalmers, this is Robert again. You didn't tell me if you wanted the Lehman file for the meeting." "No. Thank you, Robert." "Just checking to make sure everything is in order, Mr. Chalmers. We're set for TEM at ten-thirty." That Jenkins was an excellent young man, Chalmers said to himself. He would remember to compliment him when he arrived at the office. People didn't compliment each other nearly enough. Everyone was too quick to criticize. Chalmers looked at his watch and dialed his voicemail. As the connection was being relayed through space or wherever—who knew exactly where cellular transmissions were at any one instant?—he twisted his neck and gazed up at the digital sign: "8:24 . . . Introducing a new feature of Providential Services: Providential Online . . . Get stock quotations on your pager, minute by minute . . . Think of Providential Online as 'Work wherever, whenever'™ . . . PO@Provins.com . . . 8:24." Chalmers fumbled with a pencil and hurriedly copied down the e-mail address before it fled from the screen while a feminine voice crooned from his telephone receiver, "The Plymouth voicemail system will be disabled for twelve hours, beginning at midnight on June 26, while Telecom performs an upgrade of the system. At Telecom, progress is our business. You have three messages." Which must have arrived in the previous twenty minutes, since Chalmers last checked his voicemail. A dog barked. What were dogs doing down here? he wondered. People should be more considerate. Last week he had come within inches of stepping in dog poop. He retrieved his first message. "Jasper Olswanger calling. I need to talk—hold it a moment, please. . . . Sorry, that was call waiting. I need to talk to you as soon as possible. You've got my number." Someone was shouting Chalmers's name over the roiling of voices and music and dogs. He removed his ear from the receiver and went up on his toes. Twenty feet away he spotted the shouter, now waving and grinning. "Yes," Chalmers answered, trying to make out the man's head in the ocean of pale, fluorescent faces. Gradually he recognized the sunken eyes of Tim Cotter, his neighbor across the street. He didn't know Cotter very well. Cotter worked in a small bank somewhere downtown and came home late every night to the loud reprisals of his wife. Chalmers waved back good-naturedly and started to retrieve his second message. Someone elbowed him, shoving the phone into the side of his head. The neighbor continued waving and shouting "Bill, Bill," with a definite note of urgency, as if there was something he needed to tell him that moment. "What?" Chalmers shouted back, still standing on his toes. His neighbor didn't seem to hear him, then removed one of his earphones and yelled, "What did you say?" "I thought you wanted to tell me something,"

Chalmers shouted back, realizing at once that he had used far too many words under the circumstances. "Lower your voice," yelled a cheeky college boy standing next to him. "You're destroying my eardrums." The student made a face and slapped his hands over his ears. Chalmers glanced at his watch. He had only two minutes or less to retrieve his messages. With a sigh, he began working his way through the concrete thick crowd toward his neighbor. Cotter shouted something else, which Chalmers didn't hear, and refastened his headphones. Now Chalmers could see that his neighbor was sitting on some kind of fancy foldable chair, like a beach chair or a country lawn chair. He made a mental note that he should get one for himself. "Guess what I'm doing," said Cotter, keeping one of the earphones pressed against his ear so that he could listen and talk at the same time. His fingers tapped on his briefcase. "I don't know. What are you doing?" "I'm reading," said Cotter, grinning broadly. He paused, to let the announcement sink in. "Books on Tape. *The Bridges of Madison County.*" Chalmers made a thumbs-up sign. For the first time, he realized how much he disliked Cotter. In a hundred little ways, Cotter always tried to make him feel like a slacker. Cotter was just envious of anyone seriously engaged in their profession. It was Cotter who was the slacker. The dog was barking again and Chalmers began coughing, having inhaled an invisible cloud of the burnt brake-fluid air. In addition, the morning's usual indigestion had just slammed into his stomach. "Nice to talk to you," said Cotter. "I haven't seen you since Phil's thing." He put his second earphone back on. At that instant, with a high shriek of metal on metal, the train on Track Two arrived. Chalmers looked at his watch, 8:26, and surged forward with the torrent. By the time he had squeezed through the doors and been shoved to a spot in the middle of the car, the seats were long gone. The upright commuters, pressed hard against each other, clutched their coffee cups and muffins close to their bodies and searched in vain for handrails to grasp. Chalmers began brooding over his unretrieved messages. Maybe one of his appointments had been rescheduled. He could have an important call from New York. Those people got to their desks early. As he was considering the various possibilities and their dark implications, with the knowledge that he would be incommunicado for the next several minutes, an extremely loud alarm bell rang, then the series of electronic beeps, the doors slid together, and the train jolted into motion.

It was between Harvard and Central that Chalmers forgot where he was going. This realization did not arrive suddenly but seemed to trickle up slowly into his consciousness, like a trapped bubble of air rising from the bottom of a deep pond. At first, he was calm. He was most likely suffering from a momentary lapse of memory, as when he'd forgotten Morla's name at the last New Year's party.

He took a long breath and maneuvered himself between bodies to the front of the car, where he could read the list of stops on the wall. They were all familiar, but he could not remember which one was his. He pronounced the name of each stop softly, so as not to draw attention to himself, and ran his fingers through his thinning brown hair. When the train screeched to a halt at Central Square, he peered out the window and studied the token booth and the passageways and the stairs. Commuters hurried forcefully in every direction. Could this be where I get off? he asked himself, trying to jog his memory. He couldn't decide. The doors slid shut and the train was in motion again. He looked at his watch. It was 8:39. If he didn't straighten himself out soon he'd be late. But he was not late yet. No, he was not late yet. If he could just remember his stop before he reached it, no time would be lost. With that logical deduction, he seemed to relax slightly and gazed out the window into the black tunnel flying by. He remembered that he was due at his office at 9:00, that he had appointments at 9:15, 10:30, and noon. Then, with alarm, he became aware that he couldn't recollect precisely where he had to be at 9:00, or who he was meeting. The meetings, the meetings. He strained to remember. They were probably important. In fact, it was quite possible that his meetings were critical, that a great deal hung in the balance. His grip tightened on the overhead rail. Nothing like this had ever happened before. He had worked in his office a long time, he was certain of that, and he had always met his responsibilities with efficiency and speed. In a sickening premonition, he imagined the vice president smiling sympathetically at him and then quietly transferring away his better accounts. A sweat broke out on his cheeks and the palms of his hands.

So distraught was Chalmers by this time that he didn't think to open his briefcase, which contained, among other items, his appointment book and dozens of letters and office memoranda bearing the name of his company and its address. Instead, he looked anxiously into the faces of the two men standing on each side of him. One sported a faint smile, as if amused by the crush of humanity around him, and was dictating something into a tiny recorder. The other had lightly closed his eyes, possibly engaged in one of those new business visualization techniques. The two seemed so confident and self-assured in their plans for the day. He could not bring himself to ask them for help. Maybe he could locate his neighbor. Standing on his toes again, he looked in both directions without success. Then he noticed that a man in a green plaid suit, occupying one of the scarce seats on the car, was gazing intently at him through the thicket of torsos and arms. As soon as the seated man saw that his gaze was returned, he quickly went back to typing on a computer in his lap. He

seemed vaguely familiar. Perhaps he was a professional colleague, or possibly an employee. His computer screen was
tilted at such a wide angle that Chalmers could see some kind
of spreadsheet, with a colored graph shimmering at the top.
After a few seconds of purposeful typing, the man looked
up again, apparently to verify that Chalmers still saw him
profitably at work, then returned with a smirk to his computer. Looking about, Chalmers noticed that other people,
even those standing, were reading reports, making memos,
checking off columns of figures and lists. Everyone was busy
at work. He took a piece of paper from his pocket and began
thinking of something to write on it. Immediately, the man in
the green plaid suit craned his neck nearly out of his collar to
see what Chalmers was doing. This unwelcome surveillance
made Chalmers even more upset and moist.

Avoiding eye contact with the green-suited man but feeling
his gaze, Chalmers once more pushed to the front of the car
to ponder the list of stops. This time he pronounced the name
of each stop out loud. "Do you have a problem?" said a huge
woman with blue frizzy hair and two silver rings in her nose.
She looked him up and down, her chin remaining hidden in
the rolls of fat around her neck, then offered him some of
her blueberry muffin. The train pulled into another station.
People raced off, people raced on. There were still twice as
many commuters as seats. Without recognition Chalmers
gaped at the fluorescent terrain. Men and women fled toward
the exits at both ends of the station. Between the tracks hung
long silver chimes, and an enamel map of some kind covered
the wall. He was beginning to feel nauseous. Could this be
my stop? he said to himself, again trying to shake loose his
memory. A sign on the wall said "MIT." MIT? Could he possibly work at MIT? He examined his clothes and tried to
recite some school math formulas to himself.

It now occurred to him to look in his briefcase. "My briefcase," he shrieked when he realized that it was not in his hand. At his exclamation, people rotated their heads to stare at him. When he succeeded in groping his way back to the middle of the car, his briefcase was gone. And with it, all identification, since he routinely carried his wallet in his briefcase on the advice of his chiropractor. For the last several years, he had been told that his tight muscles and little pains were caused by his wallet pressing against certain cartilages and nerves. "Has anyone seen a leather briefcase?" he shouted without thinking. The train lurched forward and he grabbed for a hold bar. "Has anyone seen a briefcase?" he repeated more softly. The commuters nearest him glanced down at the tiny bit of bare floor and shrugged. Two briefcases were discussed, but they belonged to other people. A woman wearing a blue running suit and a black beaded cap took off her headphones and asked Chalmers what he was saying. He looked at his watch. It was 8:42.

Chalmers glanced at the faces of the other commuters. He'd made a fool of himself. Only people totally out of control lost briefcases. Were they all mocking him behind their self-satisfied activities? Who were they, to mock him? he thought angrily. Although he could not at the moment remember exactly his job, he knew that he was somebody important, a specialist of some kind. Slowly, he made his way down the car, searching for his briefcase. The other commuters grudgingly moved aside, momentarily folding up their memos and pads of papers. At several points he stooped down to survey the floor and was thrown into backpacks and purses and knees as the train swayed from one side to the other. Then the train was suddenly above ground, in the bright sunlight, traveling over a river. He blinked in the light and looked out the window. The view was not unfamiliar. On either side of the bridge stood ancient stone towers, shaped like salt and pepper shakers, beyond which dozens of sailing masts huddled in a curved inlet in the distance. A little boat-house with an orange roof. Tiny figures on rollerblades slid along the shore. Behind the boathouse, an angular tower gleamed blue in the early morning sun, and next to it some office building. On the side of the river they were leaving, two massive triangular buildings like pyramids, and two white domes on either side of an edifice with a spire. He felt that he knew these sights well, he must have passed this way often. The train pulled into another station, high above the streets of Boston. Charles/MGH, Massachusetts General Hospital. Chalmers looked down at the busy street and the rush-hour traffic, then toward the hospital. Hospital, hospital, he said to himself and searched his pockets. No stethoscopes or hospital things to be found. He did produce car keys, a "to do" list, some coins, his subway pass, and a Post-it note that said "Call Mary Lancaster." He finished with his inventory just in time to see the green-suited man hurrying off the train with his computer and down the metal stairs to the street. For an instant, the man peered over his shoulder and then disappeared. The wheels screeched and the train dove underground.

Chalmers was now obsessed with finding his briefcase. It struck him that perhaps he had left it on a neighboring car. At a previous stop he might have gotten off briefly to study the station and could have reboarded a different car. Next stop, as his train pulled into the station, a pulsating beat blasted him like a cannonball. A group of wiry-haired musicians was installing itself and its amplifiers on the platform between the outgoing and incoming tracks. Chalmers leaped off the car and hurried onto the one behind it. "Coming through," he heard himself shout. A mass of people huddled in the aisle of the new car. He was sweating pretty heavily now and wiped the perspiration from his face. Over the door, a sign in red letters read: "IN CASE OF EMERGENCY PLEASE FOLLOW

DIRECTIONS OF THE TRAIN CREW." "I'll report my missing briefcase to the train crew," he said out loud. He glanced out the window and noticed a sign pointing to the direction of transfer to the Green Line. Green Line, Green Line, he repeated to himself, without recognition.

As the train left the station, he miraculously sighted his neighbor, standing at the end of the new car. "Tim," he shouted. Cotter took off one earphone and waved. Chalmers gasped with relief and began pushing his way down the aisle. He felt like throwing his arms around Cotter, but of course he could never do such a thing. "I've lost my briefcase," he blurted out. "Gosh. I'm sorry," Cotter said and turned off his headset completely. "On the train?" "Yes," said Chalmers, "I'm almost certain that I had it when I got on at . . ." "I'm so sorry," repeated the neighbor. "You look terrible. Need anything?" Tears came to Chalmers's eyes, and he quickly looked away, into a woman's sunburned back. He began rehearsing to himself how he could describe his predicament. Then, unexpectedly, he had a vision of being laughed at. After that, he couldn't get any words out. With a sudden stab of shame and anger at himself, he wished he had said nothing to Cotter. He had never confided anything to his neighbor before, he didn't at all care for the man, and here he was making an idiot of himself. God knows who Cotter would tell about the lost briefcase. The train rolled into the next station, and Chalmers looked out the window. Downtown Crossing. "Well, this is my stop," said Cotter, checking the time on his watch. "Got to go. You should report your briefcase to somebody. Bummer." He patted Chalmers on the shoulder, turned his headphones back on, and bolted off the train. Chalmers stared at Cotter as he raced down one of the hallways and disappeared around a corner.

At the next station, which reeked strongly of urine, more people got off than got on. As the train flew away, Chalmers looked at his watch. 8:48. Almost certainly now he would be late for his 9:15 appointment. He remembered that he was to meet a man and a woman at 9:15. He'd met them before. The woman had blond hair and wore scarves and took notes on a laptop during meetings. He began imagining various scenarios. In scenario one, the visitors would show up and be asked to wait until he arrived. When he didn't, the appointment would be rescheduled, possibly after lunch. What was on his agenda today after lunch? He would worry about that later. In scenario two, the president would ask that cocky Harvard fellow to fill in for him. There would be an unpleasant scene and some posturing the following day. In scenario three, the visitors would express their annoyance by taking their business elsewhere, bringing down on Chalmers the wrath of the entire company. And who could blame them? Their time was valuable. Time was money. Chalmers struggled to remember the nature of the meeting. The phrase "the maximum information in the minimum time" suddenly came to him. It was the motto of his company. His company. He strained to remember its name, pulling at his mustache. What was happening? What was happening to his mind? Was he having a nervous breakdown? Frantically, he glanced at the people around him, complacently going about their business of the day. He was feeling more and more ill and needed to sit down, but no seats were available. With a groan he took out his handkerchief and held it to his mouth. Then, he saw with astonishment that he had been carrying his cellular phone all of this time. "Oh, thank you, thank you, cellular phone," he said out loud, to the stares of other commuters around him. Forgetting that his phone was inoperative in the tunnels, he pushed the power button. A red light reading "No Serv" flashed on the digital display. He wiped his sweating hands with his handkerchief and began to push other buttons, but the red "No Serv" light continued to flash and the receiver whined like a miniature police siren.

"Doesn't work underground," said a man wearing chino pants and a Red Sox cap. Chalmers remembered who the Red Sox were—he had even attended some games—and he clung to this small bit of recognition as he slammed his No Serv phone shut. The man in the Red Sox cap proceeded to swallow a hot dog in two gulps. "They're coming out with one that works anywhere," he said, wiping his mouth. "I think it's fiber optics, or ultrasound." He paused, looking at Chalmers. "Here, take my seat, bud, you look wiped." Chalmers smiled weakly and sat down, his hands shaking. He began going over what he knew of the morning. He remembered arriving at Alewife at 8:20. He remembered billboards with fish and cottontail rabbits. He remembered making a telephone call to Jenkins, who spoke in a high-voltage, caffeine voice. In fact, he could even see Jenkins, a nervous young man, prematurely bald, with a carefully tended two-day beard. What was Jenkins's first name? He began running down possible names and matching them with Jenkins. Abandoning this line, he attempted to focus on his appointments. One was at 9:15—he was certain of that—one at 10:30, and one at noon. A man and a woman were to meet him at 9:15. He stared outside the window at the darkness flying past. Every few seconds, a smattering of light from a fluorescent tube. What was happening to him? He gazed at the man in the Red Sox hat, who was mindlessly turning the pages of a magazine. The train coasted to a stop, and Chalmers had the prickly sensation that he might be starting to remember things. He squinted at the walls of the station. A "Wanted" poster showed a man in two profiles. Another said: "Socrates? Plato? Why not? At Metropolitan College Online." It was 8:50. With a whoosh, the train left the station.

After the next stop, which Chalmers didn't recall ever having seen in his life, the crowd on the train diminished substantially. Now there were only a dozen people in his car. He examined each seat and its occupant, as if somehow hoping to uncover a clue to his identity. In one sat a man with braided dreadlocks, listening to music on a portable CD player and counting subway tokens. In another, a skinny young mother with a phosphorescent blue-green halter top sipped on a Diet Coke and fed some of it with a straw to her baby. An older woman, wearing a black leather coat despite the heat, gazed absently out the black window and rocked back and forth in her seat. The train vibrated and twisted down the tracks. Chalmers searched for the man in the Red Sox cap, but he was not on the car. Two pimply teenage girls with beach towels, dark glasses, a radio. An elderly man and woman, both with long white hair and canes, were arguing about something while eating Egg McMuffins. Their voices were thin and breathy and faint, wind moving through dry reeds.

Suddenly, the train lit up with sunlight and was again above ground. Trees flew by like flailing arms. Beyond the vegetation, a mixture of residential and commercial buildings, parked cars, telephone poles, a brown building, a Burger King. The train stopped and several young people darted off, carrying books. They must have been students. Chalmers peered at the sign on the wall. JFK/UMass. The train was now far from the downtown area, heading farther from Boston. Chalmers remembered his cellular phone. He extended its antenna and pushed buttons: 617-567- . . . He couldn't remember what came next. Continents of memory had been lost. He began dialing random numbers, hoping to connect with someone. In the process, he accidentally entered the security code that prevented the phone from sending or receiving further calls. A "Phone Lock" sign began flashing. He stared at the useless instrument. "Good God, I can't remember any telephone numbers," he said out loud. "I can't remember my name." One of the passengers glanced quickly at him, then returned to her magazine. Sweat streaming down his face, Chalmers closed up his phone. Railroad tracks fluttered by like matchsticks. Trees, white and gray clapboard houses with paint peeling off, junkyards with stacks of flaccid tires and crumbling cars, four-story apartment buildings with children playing in the narrow alleys between, laundry hanging from windows. An expressway looped in from somewhere, flying alongside the train, cars shot by in both directions. After the next stop, they passed water, a bay, a huge cylinder with red and yellow stripes. Suddenly the train entered some small town and stopped under a green awning. Along the concrete sidewalks, pedestrians floated, cars stood at red lights, everything seemed frozen. A few passengers embarked and the train was in motion. Leafy green trees, then the light dimmed two octaves and the train had again flown below ground, blackness outside. At the next station, which said Shawmut, a strange silence. No one got on or off. Then a woman's voice singing, *You're gonna want me* . . . A voice on a speaker said, "Next stop, Ashmont. End of the line. Ashmont. Thank you for riding the T. Don't forget your belongings." Shortly thereafter, the train pulled into Ashmont Station and stopped.

Chalmers sat dazed in his seat, holding his handkerchief to his mouth. The train was empty and silent. In the distance, an automobile groaned, sliding its sound into the muffled hum of the station. After a few moments, an attendant walked over, stood glaring down, and said, "No passengers beyond this point. You'll have to get off." It was 9:09 by a giant white clock in the station.

Wobbly on his legs, Chalmers walked out of the train and sat on a bench. It felt hard after the padded seat. Ashmont

Station, bottom end of the Red Line. The station, at street level, opened to real air. Pigeons flew in, just under the arched roof, swooped down to the brick floor, and pecked for food. Peanuts, scraps of sandwich meat, pieces of bread. He gazed at the birds as they jerked their heads right and left. On the other side of the station, a bus whined and exhaled a tuft of acrid gray smoke. A woman in a blue beach hat got on. Chalmers looked at his watch. There was no doubt now that he would lose a good part of the morning. Unconsciously, he began panting in rapid, shallow breaths. Closing his eyes, he tried to visualize the place where he was going, he pictured office buildings, shops, department stores, corporate campuses, any place he might possibly be employed. Various people that he had met flickered in his mind. His hands trembled and he couldn't keep from rocking like the woman on the train. Still shaking, he spotted the stairway to the train in the opposite direction, back through Boston. Immediately, he flung himself from the bench and hurried up the stairs. "I'm going to put an end to this craziness," he said out loud, taking a deep breath of bus exhaust. "People are waiting. I won't allow myself to get further behind. Go. Go." He slammed his hand against the rough concrete wall. On the second time around, he would recognize his stop, he would remember, he would have to remember where he was going, he would remember.

At the beginning of the return trip through Boston, Chalmers regarded each stop even more intently than before. At two stations, he leaped from the train and paced the platform, hoping to feel some glimmer of memory in the concrete and brick. The train was now about half full with people, who appeared to be shoppers and tourists and college students going to midmorning summer classes. Someone giggled at the far end of the train, where a man in unlaced hiking boots was embracing a woman. At Charles Street, Chalmers threw up.

"Are you all right?" asked a spectacled college girl sitting across from him. He looked at her blankly. She moved a few seats away. Grimacing, he lay down across three seats, then sat up when the train went over the river. Now sailboats dotted the water, their white sails fluttering and curved in the wind. In the distance, a line of cars, bumper to bumper, oozed across a bridge. Kendall Square/MIT. Central. Harvard. Porter Square. Davis Square. Chalmers no longer got out of the train at each stop. He would simply sit up and peer out for a few seconds, then lie down again. "What's happened to me?" he mumbled, over and over. He held up his hands and examined the veins near the surface, fragile and faint like the strings of a puppet. "What's happened to me?"

Then he was at Alewife, the end of the line, where he vaguely remembered starting that morning. Mercifully, no attendant told him he had to get out of the train. He could just remain lying down in his three seats, wait until he started moving in the opposite direction, back toward the station with the swooping pigeons. With a half-dozen people in his car, the train began once more flying south. It was just after eleven o'clock on the morning of June 25.

Unaccountably, he felt like walking. He had a noon appointment. He had a noon appointment. With a grunt, he sat up and wandered down the car, holding on to the overhead rail and gazing idly at the signs on the wall. Outside, the darkness flew past in black streams. By now, his demeanor was attracting attention. His hair was matted with sweat, his tie dangled loosely around his neck, his shirt was soggy and stained. He didn't know where his suit jacket was. "What's happening to me?" he said to anyone who would look at him for longer than a second. He had now grown accustomed to stares. Yet he could not bring himself to ask any of those faces where he was going, where he was supposed to be. A man with a baseball cap on backwards began mimicking him:

"What is happening to me? Like, what's happening, man? To me. What's up, Doc?" The man followed Chalmers to the end of the car and began inspecting his cellular phone. Chalmers tightened his grip on the phone and hastened toward the other end of the car. A young man and woman were holding hands and laughing. When they saw him, they turned and began whispering. Newspapers and food wrappers covered the floor. The fluorescent light hammered. Two men in identical headphones and identical gray silk shirts looked at him curiously. "What's happening to me?" he asked them. They shrugged. From behind, someone tapped him on the shoulder. He turned. A woman, middle-aged, green light in her eyes. She handed him a green dollar bill and walked away. He let his tie fall to the floor. "My briefcase," he said. At the next stop, he changed to a neighboring car. "DO NOT LEAN AGAINST DOORS." He looked down and saw that his shoes had become untied. They were becoming a nuisance. With a flick of his ankles, he kicked off his shoes and left them behind. The train braked sharply around a turn and he was thrown to the floor, his cheek landing hard against a fresh wad of gum. "You should sit down, please sit down," came a voice. He got up and continued walking, cooler now without his shoes and socks. He took off his shirt and tossed it onto a seat. A woman's face dissolved. There was shouting. He hurried up the aisle of the car.

When the police boarded the train at South Station, they found him curled up on the floor in a fetal position, clasping his phone to his bare chest.

IN THE HOSPITAL

"Pretty foxy-looking cell phone—eh, Matt?" said the younger patrolman as he and his partner rolled Chalmers over on the floor of the train and covered him up with a dirty blanket. "What do we charge him with? Doing it with a c-phone in public?"

The older officer just frowned. He turned to the cluster of former passengers who stood on the platform, twittering and gaping into the train. "What are you people gawking at?" he shouted and waved his cap. "Give the man some dignity. Step back." The crowd didn't budge. "Pervert!" someone yelled. "Arrest the son-of-a-bitch!"

"What time is it?" asked Chalmers from the floor. "Something happened to my watch." He sat up and blinked at the empty seats and at the two police officers leaning over him. The older of the two had a big rubbery face, with more skin than necessary, and a sympathetic smile. The younger held a pair of handcuffs, twirling them impatiently. His eyes darted about like a small animal's. Both men wore short-sleeved blue shirts soaked with sweat.

"You don't need a watch, mister," said the officer with the darting eyes. "What's your name and address?"

Chalmers became aware of the stink of the blanket. He leaned his head back on the seat. Slowly, he remembered that he was late for the office. "What time is it?" he repeated. "I've got a twelve-o'clock appointment."

The younger officer snickered. "Hear that, Matt, he's got a twelve-o'clock appointment."

"Cut it, Ernie," said the policeman named Matt. He turned to Chalmers and asked in a gentle voice, "What's your name?"

Chalmers closed his eyes, trying to find some light in his head. He could feel the train vibrating. He could feel his veins pulsing. With appalling clarity, he suddenly remembered stripping off his clothes in the train. What had he done? He began sweating and feeling nauseous all over again. He pinched his arm fiercely, grimaced with the pain, then glanced at the faces on the platform. Who had witnessed him making a fool of himself? Did he know anyone there? With a shudder, he turned away from the gawkers and pulled the filthy blanket more tightly around himself.

The police cruiser didn't stop at the main entrance to Boston City Hospital but drove straight to the Emergency Room area on Albany Street, which was aging and ugly like a condemned office building. A thick yellow steam duct protruded from the second-floor brick wall and out across the street.

"Why are you bringing me here?" Chalmers asked from the backseat of the car. The cruiser was boiling, the dirty blanket was already drenched with his sweat. "Are you going to help me?" The officers said nothing and eased their car next to a couple of ambulances parked with their engines running. Underneath the angled concrete awning, three orderlies were horsing around, smoking and slapping each other on the back and passing around a plastic gallon of Dr Pepper. When they saw the police, they giggled, then became silent. The patrolmen escorted Chalmers past the gaping orderlies, through the sliding glass doors, and up to a massive curved desk. Behind the railing sat a receptionist. More precisely, she hunched over and pecked at a keyboard below the rail, making herself invisible while people with minor emergencies stood about on the other side of the rail waiting to see her.

At the arrival of the patrolmen, the receptionist stuck her head up. Her hair appeared first, piled in a bun and dyed the same salmon color as the tiles on the floor. She glanced at the officers, then at Chalmers in his dirty blanket. "What you guys brought me today?" she said, chewing gum while she spoke. She looked at Chalmers again. "You got a flasher?"

"Close," said the policeman named Ernie. He grinned at the receptionist. "Mister was ninety-five percent through his strip show on the T, fondling a cell phone."

"I see," the receptionist said and raised her upper lip with disgust.

Chalmers cringed against the railing, his hands shaking. He could sense the jeering gaze of a dozen people behind him. The odor of antiseptic and rubbing alcohol floated down the corridor. Fragments of memories. A noon appointment with a young woman in data systems analysis. Tokyo.

A telephone rang behind the giant desk. Something electronic buzzed, and the receptionist swatted it like a fly. "Ten minutes ago," she said looking up at the officers, "some guy come in here with a camera wanting to take pictures. Nervy. Can you believe? I told the bugger no pictures. This is a hospital, not a frigging museum. Am I right? Now, you got papers for me?"

"We're putting a hold on him, until CID comes up with an ID," said Matt.

The receptionist nodded. A nurse began shouting to someone and waving a clipboard. "Mary Ann," said the receptionist without explanation. "Can you believe?" she said. It was not clear who she was speaking to. "What do they think I am, a person with three heads? Leila, answer the phone. Leila, check people in. Leila, update the files on the frigging computer. And by the way, Leila, your lunch break has been downsized to thirty minutes. Like I had time to eat lunch. I'm frigging overloaded. This whole place is frigging overloaded."

Two physicians in blue scrubs raced down the corridor, stuffing down sandwiches and talking between bites. It must be lunchtime, or past, Chalmers thought, recalling a doughnut he had eaten a century ago. "What time is it?" he asked.

The receptionist regarded him as if stunned that he could talk. With an inch-long salmon-colored fingernail she pointed to the clock on the wall. "It's never right," she said. "I'm extremely busy." To emphasize her point, she waved toward the people standing beyond her desk. Then she bent down and disappeared again below the railing.

"Are we done yet, Mr. Matt?" said Ernie. He was leaning against the desk, crumpling up blank registration forms one by one. "I'm awful hungry. I want some of that good barbecue on Mass Ave."

"Done," said Matt.

"He goes through the double doors on your right to get checked, before Psychiatric," said an invisible voice from behind the railing. A hospital security guard took Chalmers's arm. One of the policemen unfastened the handcuffs.

"Yessiree," said Ernie. "Goodbye, sweetheart." He turned to Chalmers. "Have a nice day." The two patrolmen started to leave.

Chalmers reached out and tapped Matt on the shoulder. "Are they going to help me?" he asked.

"Sure," said Matt. He left with his partner through the sliding glass doors.

———

The triage room was barely larger than a walk-in closet. Two chairs, an intercom on the wall, a sink, a table with digital equipment registering Chalmers's vital statistics in illuminated numbers. Temperature, pulse rate, blood pressure. "How are we doing today?" said the nurse brightly. She received no reply.

Chalmers sat confused and uncomfortable in his flimsy blue hospital gown and white booties. He had been treated badly, he understood. Now his fear and humiliation were turning to anger. He was not being helped. He had to get back to his office, wherever it was. Suddenly, he had a desperate vision of paper emerging out of a fax machine and fluttering helplessly to the floor. Where was a telephone? His eyes roamed around the room. The intercom didn't look like a real telephone.

"What's your name?" he said finally.

"Nurse Higley." The nurse bent over her chart. Chalmers guessed that she was in her early thirties. Her hair fell just to her slender shoulders.

"Could you please tell me what time it is?"

"One-fifteen."

Oddly, with this little bit of information Chalmers felt a slight relief. Now he knew at least one definite thing. It was 1:15. He stared longingly at the pale white band on his left wrist where a watch had once been.

"Not much of a job, is it," he said to the nurse as she wrote.

"What?"

"Not much of a job, checking out every Tom, Dick, and Harry who walks in off the street."

"You get used to it," she said without looking up. "It's a job. It's not half bad." She was copying down numbers from the instruments.

"They think I'm crazy, don't they. Do you think I'm crazy?"

"No," said the nurse. "No crazier than anybody else." She put down her pen and smiled. "We're almost finished." She placed her fingertips lightly on his cheeks and felt the glands in his neck. Abruptly Chalmers slipped his hands around her wrists and kissed her. He was as startled as Nurse Higley, who uttered a small cry and began backing toward the door.

"I'm extremely sorry," stammered Chalmers. "I don't know why I did that, I've never done anything like that before."

The nurse remained standing by the doorway. "Why do I do this?" she said, suddenly looking exhausted. "I can have an orderly here in one second."

"Don't call the orderly," said Chalmers. "I promise I won't touch you again. I don't know what came over me. Please."

Nurse Higley, all of the good cheer sapped from her face, walked slowly back toward the chair where Chalmers was sitting. "I'm almost finished," she said without any expression in her voice. She shined a light into his eyes.

"Oh," she said after examining his eyes, and she stepped back from his chair. She looked again, this time longer. Pursing her lips, she placed the instrument down on the table.

"What is it?" asked Chalmers.

"I don't know," she said. "Probably nothing. Anyway, we have doctors to make diagnoses. I'll just have Dr. Barthelme take a look." She left the room for a few minutes and returned with the doctor.

"How are we today?" Dr. Barthelme said sleepily. He was young and gaunt, like a marathon runner, and barely awake, as if in the last hour of a twenty-four-hour shift. "I'll just take a quick peek at your eyes."

Nurse Higley closed the door. Immediately, another nurse knocked, opened the door a crack, and whispered to Dr. Barthelme that he was needed urgently to consult with Dr. Chase.

Dr. Barthelme sighed, brushing his thin blond hair out of his face. "Tell Dr. Chase I'll be there momentarily," he said and shut the door.

He examined Chalmers's eyes, then frowned and sagged, as if he scarcely had the energy to express an emotion. "How do you feel?" he asked Chalmers.

"Fine," said Chalmers guardedly.

"No headaches? No dizziness?"

Chalmers shook his head no. "Do you know what's wrong with me?"

"Your eyes don't look right. Something." He turned to Nurse Higley. "Nurse, I'd like a CAT scan." He wrote down some specifications on a yellow slip of paper.

"Can I have something to eat?" said Chalmers. "I'm starving."

"Certainly," said Barthelme. He turned again to Nurse Higley. "Ask an orderly to get him a box lunch at the cafeteria. Get one for me as well. And black coffee. They're trying to kill me here. And please notify Dr. Chase and myself as soon as the CT is ready." He looked at his watch and hurried out of the tiny room.

Forty-five minutes later, the two doctors stood at the CT console examining the pictures. They spoke in hushed voices. On the computer screen in front of them trembled a digitized X-ray of Chalmers's brain, a broad cross section passing through the cerebellum, the third ventricle, and the cerebral cortex.

Chalmers himself lay on the longitudinal positioning board across the room, his head in the hole of the doughnut-shaped X-ray scanner. Over the last twenty minutes, lying within the machine, he had been trying to get a grip on himself. Most likely, he decided, he had suffered some kind of nervous breakdown. But the worst was probably behind him. His memory would return. He needed to be calm. He needed to close his eyes, breathe slowly. He vaguely recalled a television show on meditation, and he focused on his breath. A slow outward breath, a slow inward breath, a slow outward breath, a slow inward breath. To see if he was calming himself, he tried to feel his pulse. He was certainly alert, invigorated by the corned-beef sandwich in his stomach, and, despite the doctors' low voices, heard everything they said.

"I'm not sure what this is," whispered Dr. Chase, who was dressed in a green Polo shirt and slacks.

"You're not sure?" whispered Barthelme.

"Well, I'm sure, yes, of course I'm sure," said Chase, "but we may need more information." A dozen numbers glowed along the top of the screen. The senior physician took a mechanical pencil out of his pants pocket and began gnawing mindlessly on its lead point. "Show me another section, Doctor."

Barthelme's skinny fingers fidgeted on the keys. "I'm examining the edges," whispered Chase. "Just at the periphery, just the outer few millimeters. Let's check the Hounsfield unit."

"You're the radiologist."

"There must be something here."

Dr. Barthelme yawned and sat down in a chair.

A beeper began squawking and Chase shut it off with a slap. "I want to do a microbiopsy," he said.

"Shouldn't we do an MR follow-up?" yawned Barthelme.

Someone was knocking on the closed door. "Ten minutes," yelled Chase.

"We can't do a biopsy," whispered Barthelme. "We don't have authorization."

"Shit," said Chase, looking with irritation at his junior colleague. "Authorization? From whom? Wake up, Frank. This man doesn't know who he is. Who are you going to get authorization from?"

"Sooner or later, maybe tomorrow, they'll find out who he is. Then he'll have relatives and we'll need authorization. I'm not breaking the law."

"Goddamn," said Chase. "I don't want people swarming around me like goddamn Japanese beetles. Listen. We have an opportunity here, Frank, a real opportunity. Now, in a room down the hall, is the brand-new computer-guided aspirator."

Barthelme, whose head had been slowly sinking in his chair, popped open his eyes. "I've been wondering how Boston City got that CGA."

"Never mind," said Chase. "That's business. We've got one, and I want to use it. I got checked out on it last week. I've been waiting to use it. Delay until this guy is identified, and cousins and aunts will be withholding authorizations, who knows what, and the hospital bureaucracy will be telling our asses what we can't do." He paused, as if thinking the situation over to himself. "This will be for the patient's good as well as for ours."

"You're full of it," said Barthelme. "I don't like this one bit. I don't like anything that's happened here." He yawned and looked at his watch. "In ten minutes I'm out of here."

"Don't be such a baby starched shirt," said Chase. "Just come with me and take a look at this machine. It's state of the art. It's beautiful. It's a goddamned miracle." Chase's beeper began beeping again. He tossed it into the desk and closed the drawer.

"What's that about authorization?" Chalmers interjected.

At the patient's surprising and unwelcome outburst, the two doctors ceased talking to themselves. "We won't be needing anybody's authorization for anything because we're not doing anything," said Dr. Barthelme, addressing himself to the torso protruding from the CT machine.

"Of course not," said Chase. "We're just going to take you next door for a few minutes and then your examination is finished."

A disheveled nurse appeared and began working on Chalmers. He felt a needle go into his arm. Then, the sound of wheels on the floor. Someone was shouting about an overdue shipment of rubber gloves. A heavy door opened and closed.

Silence. The air was dim and thick and pale blue, like at the bottom of a swimming pool. Chalmers found himself propped up in a hospital bed, conscious but unable to speak. Slowly, his eyes adjusted to the faint bluish light. After a few moments, he could make out a dim table to his right on which sat a Sun workstation, bathed in its own blue-green emanations. On the wall, an oval silhouette of dials and regulators of some kind. Other objects were shadows in corners. A console, a desk, a chair. The two doctors stood near the door. In the middle of the dimly lit room, arched majestically over an operating table like a surgeon who never grew tired, was the computer-guided aspirator. It hummed softly. It glowed. It was the size of a man. Even in its dormant condition at this moment, the instrument projected silent blue guide beams down at the operating table and up at the ceiling, so that it appeared to hover in space, suspended from above and below by its own turquoise filigree. Extending down from the bent head of the thing was its single moving part, a syringe with a needle. Electrical cables slithered down from the legs of the instrument like nerve endings, winding their way along the floor to control panels and computers.

"Jesus H. Christ," whispered Barthelme, his face reflecting the gauzy blue light. He sat down on the floor, completely awake.

"Yes," said Dr. Chase. "Yes." Smiling, he walked to the machine. He reached out to touch it, then withdrew as if committing a sacrilege, then reached out again and permitted his fingertips to rest lightly on the curved arch. His hand, blue in the blue guide beams, slowly stroked down the back. "I wanted to be an engineer," he said softly. "Didn't have the math." He paused, letting his hand travel cautiously to the titanium mounting. "The needle can be guided to one-hundredth of a millimeter. Made in America, Frank. Made in America. Our country is damn good." The machine purred, as if waiting.

"I don't know what to say," whispered Barthelme. "It's beautiful."

The voices grew more and more distant. Chalmers felt like he was falling. When he awoke, he found his head completely immobile. Something in his mouth tasted like sharp lemon juice and tingled his tongue. Out of the corner of his eye, he could see a ceramic arch and a needle poised over him, blue beams of light. He screamed, but no sound came from his mouth.

"Ready?" asked Dr. Chase. The positioning icon of the syringe and a contoured map of Chalmers's head glowed on the computer screen.

"Ready," said Dr. Barthelme excitedly from the Sun station. "Jesus. Oh, Jesus. I can't believe we're doing this."

The needle descended. There was a grinding sound, like a fine chisel working on rock. After that, the room was silent again, save for the soft purr of the machine. Lights began blinking on the central console.

Chase hesitantly left the console and stood, confused, in the middle of the room. He stared toward the lowered syringe of the instrument, turned back toward the flashing lights on the console. "What the devil? I don't understand," he muttered and cast a questioning look at Barthelme. "I followed the protocol. I know that I followed the protocol."

Dr. Barthelme abandoned his post by the Sun workstation

to make his own observation. He bent over the speechless but fully conscious patient, careful not to touch the machine.

"Something has gone wrong," said Dr. Chase, frowning and walking slowly around the room. "Nothing seems to have been aspirated. The protection lock has shut the CGA down. Something has gone wrong."

"Shit, shit, shit," said Barthelme. "We shouldn't have done this. I knew we shouldn't have done this. I hope he's okay."

"He's okay," said Chase, still pacing the room. "I'll examine him later. But something's wrong with the machine. I can't believe it. I followed the protocol. This is a brand-new machine." The older doctor suddenly seemed to become aware of his consternation. "We'll have to think hard about this," he said. Dr. Barthelme nodded. "You go on home," said Chase. "I'll have him stitched up and sent to Psychiatric."

In the middle of the night, Bill Chalmers awoke from a dream about a pretty auburn-haired woman who was massaging his forehead. He was terribly disappointed to find himself alone in a narrow bed, smelling milk of magnesia instead of her soft skin. His head hurt. He had to escape. In the low light, he could look out of his doorless room into the central service area and beyond. Across the ward, five other patients lay asleep in their doorless rooms, breathing quietly. A nurse sat at the central desk; a guard read in the corner. He waited. After a half-hour, the guard apparently decided that he could risk leaving the outer door unlocked for two minutes while he made one of his trips to the cafeteria for coffee. Immediately, Chalmers placed a pillow under his blanket and eased himself out of his bed. Where were his pants? He moved silently to the bed of another patient, a large man snoring on his back. Chalmers found the man's bag and put on his pants. The nurse at the desk didn't notice as he tiptoed out of the ward.

Another night nurse, who should have questioned him, trundled groggily on her way to answer a call. Halfway down the hall, a laundry cart provided cover until he could pad in his booties to the stairwell and down to the ground floor. After several tries, he found a door leading to the basement, where he discovered a back stairwell smelling of turpentine. A door opened to the street, locking behind him. Miraculously, he was outside. He was free. Outside, the night air hung humid and warm, and the license plates of parked cars gleamed with the reflection of the moon. Across the street, a feeble light flickered in a window. And Bill Chalmers, wearing a hospital shirt and a pair of pants three sizes too large, chose a direction and walked.

EARLIER THAT AFTERNOON

<Cider Girl: It's so hot here. It muyst be cooler
where you are. Do we have until 4:45? Please say that
we do.>
<Prof: I wish we did, but a sutdent is coming by at
3:30, my time. I tried to reschedule her later.>
<Cider Girl: I'm disappointed. We have so little
time.>
<Prof: I know, It makes me sick.>
<Cider Girl: It's not your fault. So we've got 45
minutes, no 43 minutes now.>
<Prof: Let's try to forget aoubt the time. Tell me
what you did after we talked yesterday.>

In the warm dark of the room, with day turned to night by the
thick damask drapes, Melissa Chalmers was only a dim form
in the small light of her screen. Her face faintly glowed.
Almost invisible were the chairs and divan, the little French
country writing desk and its antique tin-box lamp, her husband's bureau. A thin wire ran from a telephone jack to the
bed, where she reclined in her silk robe, her fingers fluttering
on the keyboard.

Although she'd never met her correspondent, although her
correspondent had not seen her once in their two years

together, she always fixed herself up for their afternoon com-
munions, and today was no exception. After coming home
from her shop thirty-five minutes away, she had showered
quickly, drunk a glass of lemonade while watching the clock
on the bathroom counter, then allowed herself a few minutes
at her chintz-covered vanity, carefully reapplying skin creams,
lipstick, mascara. She smiled at herself nervously in the mirror. Even at age forty, her slightly upturned nose and mouth
remained delicate and precious, like the features of a doll,
and her waist was still twenty-four inches. She much regretted the shadows under her eyes, caused by insomnia as
much as by age, and she worked at them intently until they
vanished. With two minutes to spare, she succeeded in restoring herself to the youthful appearance she felt she
deserved, after which she turned off the lights, let down
the Scalamandre damask drapes, and curled up on the dark
canopied bed with her laptop. Ocean waves flowed from the
sound synthesizer by her bed. At 3:44 she logged on. Soon she
was adrift, at great distance from the mumble of the television downstairs, the muffled shouts of children across the
street, the clicking of keys.

<Prof: I was thinking about you.>
<Cider Girl: What about me.>
<Prof: I was thinking that I juest wanted to hold
you.>
<Cider Girl: Uhmm, that's nice. What are you wearing?>
<Prof: Khaki pants, a button down white shirt, a red
and white tie with silly trinagles. The proper college
professor. Let me guess what you're wearing. It's hot,
so you've taken off your work clothes. You're in your
robe. Am I right?>
<Cider Girl: You know me well.>
<Prof: I wish I was there with yuou right now.>

<Cider Girl: You are. It's so good to talk to you Tom. What happed with Martin Barbeau? Professor Creep.>
<Prof: You gave me good advice about Professor Martin Barbeau. I bit my lip and went to the Dean.>
<Cider Girl: What did he say?>
<Prof: The Dean said that no way was Martin Barbeau going to teach my honors calculus class next semester.>
<Cider Girl: HURRAY! Good for you, darling. When was that? You were going on yesterday afternoon weren't you? Or was it this morning?>
<Prof: Yuesday. Yesterday.>
<Cider Girl: Yesterday I was thinking of my mother. I don't know why.>
<Prof: You havent' mentioned your mother in a long time.>
<Cider Girl: I miss her.>
<Prof: Did you get your VCR fixed? You really should chuck your Panasonic and get a Toshiba. It has six heads/ That's my excellent advice for the day. ANd no need to go to the dean. Now we're even. How was the shop today?>
<Cider Girl: Busy. A woman in a Donna Karan outfit strode in, from CT, and bought my old stoneware jug lamps. Tom wait a sec. Gerty wants to come in. She's scratching the door.>

Melissa cracked her bedroom door, letting a sliver of light into the dark room, and in leaped a huge Labrador retriever, dirty and dripping unashamedly. Gerty had returned from her afternoon romp through the neighborhood, careening through lawn sprinklers, chasing squirrels past the sugar maples on both sides of the street. Immediately, the dog began barking happily, then wriggled on the floral hooked rug, jumped over the blanket chest at the foot of the bed, and flopped

on the cushioned divan near the vanity. The unruly appearance of Gerty contrasted strongly with the rest of the room,
which looked like an antique dealer's display. In a fashion it
was, for Melissa Chalmers was constantly buying new furniture for her house and sending what she had tired of to her
retail shop in Littleton.

"What a mess you are, Gerty girl," said Melissa, futilely
picking up hairs from the part of the rug she could see. "I
don't know why I keep you. Do you love Mama? Yes, you do.
Yes. Yes." She stroked the creature under the neck. "Now, be
a good Gerty girl and you can stay." She closed her door
gently and the room became dark once again.

<Prof: Melissa are you there?>
<Prof: Melissa? Where are you?>
<Cider Girl: I'm back, in my bed.>
<Prof: Your and Bill's bed you mean.>
<Cider Girl: Please, Tom, This is my private place when
we talk. this is where I like to talk to you.>

>>> MAIL 50.02.04 <<< From: Fred at Noplace.Com
==> Received: from RING.AOL.COM by AOL.COM with GOTP
Orlando Vacation Give Aways, Fred@Noplace.Com

<Cider Girl: Oh no, here comes the junk mail.>
<Prof: We've got 36 minhtes left. I just looked at my
watch.>
<Cider Girl: I was looking at mine too. It goes by so
fast. Everythig does. I haven't had time to get in my
garden for two months. I don't even remember the
forsythias blooming. This time we have together is
precious to me Tom. It's pure.>

<Prof: It's pure all right.>
<Cider Girl: This may sound silly, but sometims, when
we're not together, I imagine talking to you and I see
the keyboard in my mind. I can feel my fingers moving on
the keys, typing the things I want to say to you. I can
feel my fingers moving, honetsly.>
<Prof: Let's go to Paris together.>
<Cider Girl: I would rather go with you to Florece.>
<Prof: OK Florence. To the Ponte Vecchio.>
<Cider Girl: With the peeling ochre arches and the
shadows in the water. And the l itlel jewelers' shops
along the sides of the bridge>
<Prof: We'll buty some fresh pasta and a bottle of dry
Orvieto and walk slowly acaross the bridge. No one will
hassle us, no one will know we're there. We can walk as
s lowly as we want. All I wnat is 24 hours. Wow, my
typos are awful today.>
<Cider Girl: You'll have your arm around me.>
<Prof: Then we'll sit on the bank of the river and
watch the little skiffs go by and eat our psta and
drink our wine.>

>>> MAIL 50.02.04 <<< From: MT at TX.ORG
==> Received: from RING.AOL.COM by AOL.COM with GOTP
id AQ06498; Wed, 25 Jun 15:56:52 EDT
for MCHALM@AOL.COM; Wed, 25 Jun 15:57:03 -0400
Press * for message

<Cider Girl: A message has come in for me.>
<Prof: Three have come for me. Don't look at it.>
<Cider Girl: You don't need to say that. You know that
I never lok at my messages wile I'm talking to you.>

<Prof: Except for Alexander's.>

<Cider Girl: I answer him as quickly as I can.>

<Prof: He just tries to bug you. Is Alexander home at this minute?>

<Cider Girl: Probably. I haven't heard the phone ring for awhile, so he's probably on the other line using thw internet. He's started fencing lessons. At 5:30 I have to take him to get new shoes. He knows not to open my door when it's closed.>

<Prof: So he broods in his room and sends you e-mail instead.>

<Cider Girl: Please don't talk about my son like that Tom.>

<Prof: I'm so rry. I guess I'm not in a very good mood today. Where were we?>

<Cider Girl: Florence. I want you to buy me a tiny gold wtering can I saw at one of the shops on the Ponte Vecchio. The size of a dime. I've been thinking about tht little watering can for ten years. You can put it on a necklace around my ncek. Then I want to walk with you in the Boboli Garden. We can go there after lunch and lie in the grass, and I'll oput my head in your lap.>

>>> MAIL 50.02.04 <<< From: Unknown at Unknown.Com
==> Received: from RING.AOL.COM by AOL.COM with GOTP
Make Big $$$ Online, Cowboys on Computers
Unknown@Unknown.Com

<Prof: Everybody in TravelChat has been to Florence.>

<Cider Girl: I don't keep up with those people anyjore. They're so BORING.>

<Prof: Except that I met you.>
<Cider Girl: Yes. I didn't tell you that I got a haircut.>
<Prof: When?>
<Cider Girl: On Saturday.>
<Prof: Why didn't you tell me?>
<Cider Girl: I forgot. I 'm sorry.>
<Cider Girl: Gerty is barking like crazy. Someboyd must be ringing the front doorbell downstairs. I can't hear it over the television and my sound machine.>
<Prof: Don't leave.>
<Cider Girl: Let me klisten. I hear noise downstairs. Merde, I forgot, soeone was supposed to pick up a rug for cleaning this afternooon. I can't stand the chaos in this house. It might be the architect. I to ld him not to come until 5, but he ame an hour early last time. That man is stuffed with himself.>
<Prof: Architect?>
<Cider Girl: W're putting in bay windows in the study downstiars. I want curves in the house.>

>>> MAIL 50.02.04 <<< From: ACHALM at AOL.COM
==> Received: from RING.AOL.COM by AOL.COM with GOTP
id AQ06498; Wed, 25 Jun 16:04:33 EDT
for MCHALM@AOL.COM; Wed, 25 Jun 16:04:52 -0400
MESSAGE LOCK OVERRIDE
>>> MAIL 50.02.04 <<< From: Alexander at AOL.COM
There is a rude man dowwnstairs who has invaded my domain. He carries secret papers and shouts vile demands. Also, He woldn't fence with me. I dn't think he could handle a sword anywya. Should we send him to the dungeon?

What's for dinner? And when's Dad coming home? He
promised to fence with me tnight.
_____

_____

To: Alexander Chalmers <ACHALM@AOL.COM>
From: Melissa Chalmers <MCHALM@AOL.COM>
Subject: Re: Your message
Hi sweetie. I put a pizza in the microwave for you.
That's Mr. Turgis, the architect downstairs. Please
don't put him in the dungeon. I'll be down in a few
minutes.
_____

<Cider Girl: Alexander is home.>
<Prof: What does you new haircut look like?>
<Cider Girl: It just touches my shoulders.>
<Prof: Sounds lovely. What did Bill say? Scratch that,
I fogot. But I'll bet he didnt' even notice.>
<Cider Girl: What men noatice their wives' haircuts
Tom.>
<Prof: What does he notice?>
<Cider Girl: You're not going to bait me into talking
about Bill.>
<Prof: I'm not trying to bait you. But I know that you
don't tlak about him because it makes you less guilty
about you and me. You can pat yourself on the back for
not talkingabout him.>
<Cider Girl: You shouldn't say that Tom.>
<Prof: I didn't mean it.>
<Cider Girl: You typed it.>
<Prof: I didn't mean it. I didn;t mean to send that
remark. I was going to delete it.>
<Prof: I'm sorry. I respect your guilt. But I don;t

feel a particle of guilt. We have nothing to feel guilty about. Havae we ever touched each other? We have one shitty hour a day on these machines. One hour. And now we've got only 16 minutes.>
<Cider Girl: I don't tlk to you aout Rosalind.>
<Prof: Let's change the subject shall we. You win. You win.>
<Cider Girl: I don't want to win. I need you Tom.I love you.>
<Prof: I love you too. You know that.>
<Prof: P leas send me a photo so I can see your new haircut. Will you do that?>
<Cider Girl: Yes.>
<Prof: Do you promise me?>
<Cider Girl: Yes, I promise.>

>>> MAIL 50.02.04 <<< From: Dolores at PLYM.COM
==> Received: from RING.AOL.COM by AOL.COM with GOTP id AQ06498; Wed, 25 Jun 16:16:26 EDT
for MCHALM@AOL.COM; Wed, 25 Jun 16:16:50 -0400
Press * for message

<Cider Girl: Another message has come in for me.>
<Prof: So?>
<Cider Girl: It's from Bill's office. Plymouth never e-mails me. There might be a proble. I'm going to look at it. Wait a sec Tom.>

>>> MAIL 50.02.04 <<< From: Dolores at PLYM.COM
Dear Ms. Chalmers,
Do you know where your husband is? He didn't come to

the office today. At 3:45 pm, we received a call that
his briefcase had been found in a trash can at Sixth
and Thorndike in Cambridge. That's all we know. We've
called the police.

<Prof: What is it Melissa?>
<Prof: Melissa, are you there?>
<Cider Girl: Tom, I've got to go. Something terible has
happened to Bill.>
<Prof: What's happened?>
<Prof: What happened? Please Melissa tell me.>
<Cider Girl: I don'tknow. I've got to go Tom.>
<Prof: Will you be online tomorrow? P lease. Please
don't do this to me. I love you.>
MCHALM@AOL.COM logged off Wed, 25 Jun 16:19:05 -0400

Melissa moved in slow motion. At first, she remained
sprawled on her bed, gazing at the computer. It flickered and
hummed.

"Oh my God," she moaned softly. Gertrude began whimpering and licking her feet. "Never never again, I won't ever
again. Just let Bill be all right. Oh God. Bill, I love you. I love
you. Please be all right."

The telephones began ringing, all of them, the telephone
on the writing desk with its muted chisel, the telephone in
the family room like a shrill hyena laugh full of teeth, the
hammering telephone in the kitchen. It was George Mitrakis,
the president of Plymouth, calling from his car. He'd been
calling every two minutes, he said, getting a busy or the tape.
He was fifteen minutes away and wanted her to wait for him.

She stared at the laptop. From across the room it looked so
small, like a grin. Using all her strength, she tried to twist off
its screen. Failing this, she shoved the machine over the side

of the bed. It landed with a soft thud on the rug and continued to hum from the floor.

The air was suffocating. Melissa pulled open the damask drapes, flooding the room with the full summer light, and its heat. Reeling back from the window, she went to the walk-in closet and hurriedly began dressing. "Bill, I'm sorry, I'm so sorry," she whispered as she threw on a pale yellow sundress. She sat down on a stool and began crying.

The telephones were ringing again. Numbly, she let them ring. Then, she ran for the phone on her desk, but the caller had hung up even before the tape machine kicked in. When the telephones stopped, in the silence after the ringing, she listened to the computer humming from the floor. She stood up and looked at herself in the mirror. Her eyes were swollen and puffy. She was perspiring and she dabbed a handkerchief under her arms. Uncontrollably, her fingers began twitching and tapping on the desk. <Cider Girl: What should I do? Shouldn't I call the police? He could be lying bleeding in an alley somewhere. And the hospitals, maybe he's in a hospital. I'll call the hospitals, and the police. I've ruined everything. What will happen to me? I've got nothing. Don't you understand? Nothing. No, I can't think of myself. Bill could be dying somewhere. I've ruined it for all of us. I'll be damp and pathetic when George Mitrakis gets here.>

The humming grew louder and louder, overwhelming the waves from the ocean, the thoughts in her mind.

ESCAPE

After his clandestine departure from Boston City Hospital, Chalmers began walking northwest along Massachusetts Avenue. The air felt hot and thick against his skin, especially after the cool of the hospital ward, and he began sweating almost immediately. Something hummed overhead. Looking up, he saw dozens of wires hung between poles like dark nooses waiting to be drawn taut, wires for telephones and electricity and cable TV. In the distance a police siren warbled and wailed. He hurried away from the hospital, staying far from the streetlamps and their yellow cocoons of light. The siren continued screaming. Surely, his escape could not have been reported so soon. Was he now a common criminal, to be hunted down by the police? To the contrary, he was a professional of some kind, an accomplished professional, he was certain of that. A wave of anger surged through him and settled like sewage in his stomach. He had been violated and soiled. But to whom should he direct his anger?

He ran under a dark overpass. Bits of sandwiches, plastic wrappers, and metallic soda cans crunched painfully under his feet. He could smell the odor of soot and automobile exhaust. Beyond the overpass, on the right, rose a stone office building in ruins, cradled by iron scaffolding and illuminated by the neon sign of a funeral parlor next door. He peered inside the glass windows, searching for a telephone, but all he could see were dark rows of desks and chairs. He must find a telephone, he thought to himself, although he could not remember who he should call. And a reliable wristwatch. Again, his thoughts dwelled on what had happened to him. How had it happened? How had it happened? He must think. He must not panic. Now he needed a telephone. He was wasting time. His cellular phone, where was it?

An automobile honked at him. Startled, he leaped to the sidewalk, tripping over a bottle. It rolled over the curb and shattered on the street. Disturbed from his thoughts, he now became aware that cars were thundering past on the wide avenue, one after another, their windows rolled down in the heat, their radios forcing loud music into the warm evening air. "Need a do?" someone in a tank top yelled from the window of a passing car. The automobile slowed as it slid past Chalmers and examined him, then accelerated with a blast when another car behind it began honking.

Smells of urine and stale beer jumped up from the sidewalk. Chalmers swooned. He covered his nose with a shirtsleeve and slumped against a streetlamp, afraid to look down at the filth. Something mushy and foul had started to seep through his thin hospital booties. In the yellow light of the streetlamp he was clearly visible to all passersby. A group of teenagers drove by in a convertible with the top down, gawking at him. "What do we have here?" they yelled out and laughed. "Look at this asshole."

Chalmers let go of the streetlamp and ran for the shadows. Continuing along the broad avenue, he came to a curving wall of apartments three stories high, red brick in the lamplight, with stone steps and iron handrails leading up to each doorway. Half-eaten pizzas and beer bottles littered the sidewalks in front. As he passed, fragments of TV commercials and voices escaped through the open windows, drowsy arguments over money, small cries of love and jealousy, magnified by the undulating acoustics of the building and the hot stench of trash in the narrow alleys below. Some of the residents had wandered down from their baking rooms and sprawled on their front steps, half naked in undershirts and nightgowns. They sighed as they rubbed ice cubes on their faces, they scratched their panting dogs and cats, and from time to time they shouted back at their children to shut up and go to bed. Could he possibly borrow a telephone? With amusement they stared at him. "What did you trade for those duds you got on?" someone hollered. "You lost, or what?" When he turned his steps toward one of the doorways, the couple in front began whispering and then fled inside of the building, locking the door behind them.

Just beyond the row of red brick apartments an illuminated sign revolved on a pole, advertising hats. "Elegance For All Occasions. You Need A Bateson Hat." Chalmers could see a row of hats, dimly lit, behind glass. Instinctively, he put his hand to his bare head, wondering whether he should buy a hat. The fingers of his left hand tingled and felt slightly numb.

"There he is. It's the asshole again," shouted the carload of teenagers. Apparently with nothing to do on a hot Wednesday night they had returned to taunt Chalmers. They crept beside him in their automobile, ignoring the loud honking of horns. One of the young men pulled his pants down and mooned Chalmers. Roaring with laughter, they sped away. "Punks!" Chalmers shouted at their vanishing car.

How long had he been walking? A mile, two miles. At the intersection of Mass Ave. and Columbus he spotted Al's City Diner, gigantically lit up with green blinking lights above its glass entrance. It was locked. Also locked was the beauty supply store next door, with wigs and perfumes in its windows. Two men stood motionless in the asphalt parking lot and stared at Chalmers as he tried the two doors. He turned and walked along Columbus Avenue, almost empty of people and cars but with nicer shops and tall buildings in the distance.

A name appeared in his mind. George Mitrakis. A bear of a man with a neck reeking of cologne. Bill could see disjointed images of his office: his desk, a computer terminal, a beige carpet. George Mitrakis. With that recollection, he shouted with happiness and began walking more purposefully. His memory was returning, and its return forced a pleasant gush of blood through his veins. Thank God, his memory was coming back. Immediately he heard footsteps and glanced over his shoulder. The two men from the beauty parking lot followed, walking at an easy gait and talking in low voices to each other. Behind them, on Massachusetts Avenue, cars flew by in a thin yellow haze of automobile exhaust and the Al's City Diner sign rotated red and gold against the dark sky like an airplane about to make a night landing and the glass of shop windows glittered in the neon lights. Chalmers wiped the sweat from his face and walked faster. So did the two men. Were they pursuing him? He broke into a run, bringing agony to his feet, for the hospital shoes had already begun to shred and fall apart. The steps behind him turned into an ugly rhythm of drumbeats, racing to catch up with him, louder. His feet burned and he heard the panting breaths of the men. A sweaty arm threw him down to the ground.

"We ain't hurting you," said one of the men, standing over him and wheezing. "We just want your wallet. Give us your wallet."

"I don't have a wallet," said Chalmers. He screamed for help.

"Shut the fuck up," said the other man, gripping Chalmers around the neck. He roughly went through Chalmers's pockets, finding a quarter, a button. "What kind of shit is this," he growled and threw all of it into the darkness. "You some kind of weirdo? You playing with us?" The two men walked away unhurriedly, turned down a side street, and were gone.

Laughter and music floated in the warm sticky air. How long had he been sitting on the sidewalk? Even without touching his body he knew that he was unhurt, but he could still feel the sweaty clasp of the thief, and he trembled. The music again, something familiar about it, a sweetness and warmth, like small bits of sunlight.

CHURCH

Somewhere, a churchbell began chiming. Twelve chimes, midnight. Days, it seemed, since he had escaped from the hospital and the chewy odor of milk of magnesia. He stood up in his sagging pants and walked in the direction of the bells, passing apartments and shops, a brightly lit parking lot with Volkswagens, old Fords, Mercedes sedans, a forest-green Jaguar. Then there appeared the unmistakable towers and arches of a church, its stained-glass windows pulsing in the blinking light of a nail-care salon next door. Voices and laughter grew louder and merrier, and he realized that they poured from the great open doors of the church. Open arms waiting to hold and comfort him. Impulsively, he walked up the stone stairway and entered.

Inside were hundreds of people, drinking and eating. To Bill's surprise, they were playing bingo. It was an enormous space, with chandeliers and fans dangling from the vaulted ceiling and massive arched windows on the side walls. At the front of the church, on a raised stage, a young woman picked colored balls from a giant bowl while a sweating man stood at the pulpit and blurted out the numbers into a microphone. His voice could barely be heard over the general commotion and the music from *Oklahoma* booming out of the balcony.

Chalmers stood in confusion at the entrance. Within

moments, an older woman, heavily rouged and swathed in blue satin from head to toe, approached him and insisted that he be her good luck charm. "You. Sadie wants you." Other people had brought their own trinkets and charms, rabbit paws and yellowed teeth, foreign coins and curled photographs, all of which they had laid out in the pews and stroked before each pick of a numbered ball.

Chalmers recoiled at the woman's alcoholic breath, but she seized his arm with her damp hand and led him to her seat. "I've been waiting for you, sweetie," she said, fanning her face with her bingo card. "Sadie is going to get rich tonight. You'll see." She smiled behind a blue veil of cigarette smoke. The room felt like it was a hundred degrees. "You just sit right here beside me, sweetie. Would you like something to eat?" Chalmers stared at her without being able to talk. Regarding this response as a yes, Sadie stood up and shouted and waved a twenty-dollar bill in the air. A man sprinting up and down the aisles with a food cart brought sandwiches and beer. Although hungry, Chalmers was too dazed to eat. He sat down in the fog of smoke and mindlessly began unwrapping a sandwich. Sadie rattled her bracelets in satisfaction.

"I 17," shouted the man at the pulpit. His voice drowned in the hot sea of music and voices. "Louder," cried someone in the back. There were hollers and laughter. As Chalmers looked about, he was overwhelmed by the squirming mass around him, people in business suits, people in dark service uniforms, in summer sundresses and casual shirts and trousers, attorneys, doctors, bankers, schoolteachers, computer programmers. All were constantly in motion, hopping up and down in their seats, dashing back and forth between the pews, negotiating deals to buy and sell other people's partly filled cards, then flying back to their own seats before the next number was called. Scattered altercations broke out like small fires in a parched forest. Far in the back, a gallery of children sat glassy-eyed and lethargic in front of a row of television sets.

"I 17," the sweating man on the stage screamed again. "Fifty dollars for a card, up to five thousand to win." "I 17," someone shouted from the pews. The room boiled and Chalmers was dripping into his uneaten ham sandwich. The whirling fans succeeded only in circulating the hot smoke of a hundred cigarettes, while song flooded out of the choir balcony: *I'm jist a girl who cain't say no, I'm in a turrible fix.*

Chalmers staggered to his feet and looked for the door. Immediately, a well-dressed man began waving to him and smiling from across the smoky room. Chalmers peered at him from behind his napkin. Riley Appleson. Like the name of George Mitrakis, the name came to him in a sudden wave of recognition. Riley Appleson. Where did he know Appleson? He could remember seeing him on an elevator, the smell of wood polish. Appleson clearly recognized him as well, for he had begun to make his way down an aisle, still waving at Bill. Could Appleson be a friend? Or a business associate? He seemed like a business associate, moving forcefully and carrying a briefcase. Chalmers ducked down and into the next pew. What should he do? His head was spinning in confusion, he was not sure where he was, he could be imagining this entire smoke-filled room. Was Appleson real, or a dream? He longed to talk to him, to get help and memory. But he could not bear to let the other man see him at this moment in his absurd hospital booties and oversized pants. Or perhaps he was imagining that as well. What should he do? Keeping low, he looked around and found himself crouching next to a puffy-faced fellow wearing a ragged sweater in spite of the heat, alone and talking to no one. The floor under his feet was covered with cigarette butts. Just then a new number was announced and the puffy-faced man began analyzing his four bingo cards, twirling his fingers over the columns and rows. When he could not make a match, he threw his cigarette to the floor and sank back in his seat as if he'd been kicked in the stomach. Chalmers could see his small, frightened eyes and felt pity. He moved closer and started to speak, but the man glanced suspiciously at Chalmers and slid a few seats away. Now Chalmers poked his head up and saw that Appleson was still advancing in his direction, zigzagging across pews and down aisles, waving all the while. When Appleson got near the stage, however, his attention was diverted by the beautiful brunette at the bowl. Indeed, a half-dozen men lingered there, glancing appreciatively at the young woman as she swayed back and forth in her fringed cowgirl skirt, rhinestone-studded boots, and halter top. Chalmers stared at her in a daze, he could see the white flashing of her body. "Fifty dollars to play, up to five thousand to win," she murmured to the men at the edge of the stage, while wives and girlfriends angrily waved them back to their seats. More people streamed into the church, clutching cushions and battery-operated fans and wallets of money, and Appleson temporarily disappeared in the crowd.

Appleson. Appleson. It was possible that Chalmers's identity, his entire life, was only fifty feet away. What should I do? he thought to himself. Should I go to Appleson? What will he tell me about myself? What kind of man am I? I could be a fraud. Or the president of a bank. I could be a slacker. Could I be a slacker? Who am I? Who am I? Chalmers stared at his hands, pale and porcelain, almost feminine. As he glanced again with uncertainty toward where Appleson had been, he heard an odd chattering behind him. Turning, he saw two middle-aged women with hands clasped as if in prayer. Both wore dull flowered dresses and stunning hats. Although he had no interest in the two women, Chalmers strained to hear what they were saying, for they seemed to be talking to him. After a few moments, one of the women motioned for him to join them. No, he shook his head. Her companion gestured again and smiled, then pointed with much significance at the ceiling. Chalmers craned his neck up but couldn't see anything unusual overhead, aside from the great painted dome and stone buttresses. "Come here," she mouthed with her lips, throwing him a look of urgency.

The two women seemed friendly and harmless; perhaps they could help him. As he made his way to where they were sitting, he could hear their hoarse mutterings:

Blessed be the God and Father of our Lord Jesus Christ,
The Father of mercies and God of all comfort,
Who comforteth us in all our affliction,
That we may be able to comfort them that are in any
*   affliction,*
Through the comfort wherewith we ourselves are
*   comforted of Jesus.*

"It's comforted of God," said one of the women to her companion.

"That's what I said."

"No, you said comforted of Jesus."

"You say comforted of God, I'll say comforted of Jesus. I've been saying the Corinthians for decades."

"You're losing your mind, Blanche."

"Don't tell me I'm losing my mind. My mind is as sharp as a cat's claw."

The women scowled at each other and resumed their prayer:

For as the sufferings of Christ abound unto us,
Even so our comfort also aboundeth through Christ.

"Gracious, you've come to pray with us," one of the women said to Chalmers. She surveyed his trousers and shoes. "I'm Blanche. This is Marcia." They moved over in the pews and offered him a seat.

"I didn't come to pray with you," Chalmers said and released a sigh of fatigue.

"Oh. In that case we apologize for disturbing you," said Marcia pleasantly. "Please forgive us. Prayer should never be insinuated on people. It's such a personal thing." She was interrupted by shouts and cheers as the announcer called out a new number. "We just thought that you wanted to join us, the way you were staring at us."

"I'm sorry, I didn't realize I was staring at you," replied Chalmers.

"Yes, you were," said Blanche, dabbing at her face with a pink handkerchief. "But that's all right. You don't have to stay. You can go back to that other woman you were with." She patted him on the hand. He barely felt her touch and realized that his left hand was numb. His other hand had begun tingling as well.

"They shouldn't allow alcohol in here," said Marcia to Chalmers. "What do you think? I hope they all get sick."

"They allow it because the church gets fifteen percent of the pot," said Blanche. "We should go to Newfaith, I keep telling you. They don't allow alcohol at Newfaith."

"I'm not going to a Presbyterian church," said Marcia. "I don't feel comfortable in a Presbyterian church." She turned again to Chalmers. "What denomination are you?"

Chalmers shook his shoulders. He couldn't remember what he was, or whether he was anything at all. "Do you mind if I sit with you for just a minute?" he asked. He was feeling shaky on his feet. "Not to pray, just to sit." The women nodded and again smiled. Chalmers sank into the pew and slung back his head like a heavy sack. He closed his

eyes. He was struggling for more memory, he needed to remember. George Mitrakis, he mumbled. Riley Appleson.
George Mitrakis.

"You must be wondering why we come here to pray in
the middle of the night," said Marcia. "I think people wonder,
but you can never ascertain for sure what's in other people's
heads. It's because we're too busy on Sunday. We both work
on Sunday. Blanche works at Bubby's Delicatessen in New-
ton, and I work in the office of a certified public accountant.
He pays overtime on Sunday."

"Oh," said Chalmers. "I believe that I'm sick." He opened
his eyes and looked at Blanche, whose beautiful maroon hat
was cocked back on her head and pinned to her hair. "I think
I need a doctor."

"Gracious," said Blanche. For a while, the two women
didn't say anything. They sat and dabbed at their perspiring
faces with their handkerchiefs. Marcia adjusted her hat.
"Would you excuse us just a moment?" said Blanche. They
gathered their purses and moved to the aisle and down several rows, whispering to each other and casting occasional
glances back at Chalmers. After a few moments, Marcia
walked over and said, "Blanche wanted me to tell you that we
are happy to have met you and you should go see a doctor."
With that, the two women hurried away, just as a new
number was shouted through the hot, smoky air.

Suddenly, a great agitation erupted in one part of the
room. Chalmers leaned forward to see what was the matter.
People were hollering and arguing and herding toward one
of the pews. Someone raced down to the stage. At this
point, a man whom Chalmers had not seen before appeared
with much authority on the stage. He huddled with the announcer, the two of them gesticulating, waving clipboards,
and receiving instructions from an invisible third party.

"Bingo! Bingo!" screamed a woman. "Bingo!" A number of onlookers leaped to the stage and began shouting. Making his way through the waving arms and legs, the announcer got to his microphone and shouted, "We have a winner, ladies and gentlemen, we have a winner, the second bingo of the night." Although no one could hear his exact words, their meaning was unmistakable, setting off an immediate frenzy of clapping and more shouting and stampeding toward the front to buy cards for the next round.

"Everyone, please return to your seats for the cash booth," the announcer shouted with futility into his microphone. There was more screaming and applause. "Please return to your seats." "The cash booth," someone cried. "Give her her money." "She deserves her money." "Would everyone please return to their seats," shouted the announcer. He turned up the volume of his amplifier, causing all of the loudspeakers to begin screeching in a torrent of electronic feedback. "Everyone please return to your seats," he shouted. "It's time for the cash booth." Chalmers could see a couple of men at the side of the stage, struggling with what looked like a glass telephone booth. Wires and tubes trailed along behind it. As soon as the men had placed the cash booth out on the stage, there was a new round of screaming and shouting, and people fumbled to get back into their seats. "It's the cash booth!" someone yelled.

All at once the lights went off, leaving a single spotlight beamed at the cash booth onstage. In the near darkness, the great stained-glass windows suddenly burst out of the night, demanding attention, throbbing on and off with the neon lights of the nail-care salon next door. Leaning over a disciple was a pulsating Jesus, exhausted and bored.

Onstage, the winner had entered the cash booth. The crowd began screaming with fresh energy. "Quiet," someone shouted. "We love you, Susan," someone else hollered. Susan, from her spotlighted position within the cash booth, made the V-for-victory sign with both hands.

"Quiet," yelled the announcer. The crowd's intensity diminished slightly. "Five thousand bucks, ladies and gentlemen. Two hundred and fifty twenty-dollar bills, each engraved with a picture of the honorable Andrew Jackson, seventh president of the United States of America. The lady keeps as many as she can hold on to." "Shut up," someone hollered, "and give her the money."

Twenty-dollar bills began fluttering down from the ceiling of the cash booth. The audience screamed in ecstasy. Completely visible through the glass walls of the booth, with the spotlight pounding upon her, the woman twisted this way and that, stabbing at the air, trying to grab bills and stuff them into her pockets. Most of the bills slipped around her hands to the bottom of the booth, where they were sucked up by a vacuum cleaner–like hose. Some of the woman's supporters, against the announcer's protests, had come to the edge of the stage to coach her. "Lower, Susan." "No, higher." "There." "There, got that one." "Don't move so fast, wait for them."

Chalmers's head began pounding. What kind of place was this? Everyone was out of control. He wanted to lie down, but he continued to stare at the woman in the glass booth. He was repelled and attracted at the same time.

By now the entire audience was on its feet, egging the winner on. "Go, Susan." "Grab them." "You can do it." The pockets of her blue jeans were bulging with captured bills, her shirtsleeve had become ripped and it flapped at each turn, her cheeks flushed red with the heat and the anxiety and the fury. She spun, she swiped, she slammed into the glass. When the bills finally stopped dropping, she was led from the stage in a daze, amid shouts and screams from the spectators.

"Where have you been?" said the lady in the blue satin

dress. She stood in the aisle glowering at Chalmers. "I've been looking for you. How do you expect me to win without my good luck charm? Wasn't she sensational, that woman? And so attractive. I won't ask you where you've been, just come back and sit beside me. I've bought a new card, and I feel lucky. Oh, I feel lucky."

Chalmers felt too weary to argue. He followed her back to her seat and laid his head down, oblivious to everyone around him, oblivious even to Mr. Appleson, wherever he might be. Let him come. Let him jeer. Let him say what he wanted. Chalmers wanted only to rest. His eyes closed. Gradually, the laughter and shouting trailed off to distant movements of air. He dreamed that he was walking through the narrow halls of his high school, on his way to an examination. Looking down, he saw the black and white squares of the linoleum floor, scuffed with the marks of ten thousand shoes. The dark hallways were illuminated only by light coming through windows at the far ends, so that as he turned each corner he had the sensation of entering a long tilted tube. Down hallway after hallway in the dim light, other faceless students glided past him like mannequins on a conveyor belt. A big clock on the wall informed him that he was late. The hallways had emptied. Now he was alone. He began running, flying past the grim metal lockers on both sides of the corridor. The tilted tubes went on and on, twisting and rotating. At last, just at the door of the room where he was to take his exam, he realized with horror that he had forgotten to study. So diligently had he taken notes during the classes, but somehow he'd forgotten to read through them the previous night. He could imagine his pages of notes, the ink marks and words. With a sickening feeling, he peered through the glass window of the closed door and saw the other students sitting at their desks, filling in the answers to the exam. Quickly, he had to study. Another clock on the wall announced that he had already missed twenty minutes. Throwing his hands in the air, he ran back down the hallways toward the library, where he might find what he needed to know. Through half-open doors he saw other students grinning at him in mockery. Now he'd forgotten where the library was. Did anyone know where the library was? People were shouting. What did they want? His teacher was yelling at him to come to class, come to class, then she was laughing.

People were shouting. Sadie was laughing. When Chalmers opened his eyes, half of her card shone with red. It seemed that every number of the new round had landed on her card, the red buttons had proliferated and multiplied. She clapped, she sang, she ordered more food and beer. She stood up and sat down and kissed Chalmers on his head. He dozed off again, this time a shallow, half-waking sleep. A seashore, green ocean, the flickering of light. There was more shouting. Then, in one last throttle of excitement and palpitation, she screamed "Bingo!" "She's got bingo," someone beside her shouted. "Another woman has bingo." The man in the ragged sweater stared with incomprehension at his impotent cards and buttons.

"I can't stand it," gushed Sadie. "I knew I was going to win." Chalmers looked at her groggily. People were screaming all around them. A man whisked away her card and flew down to the stage. "You must go into the cash booth for me," she said to Chalmers.

"No, no, I couldn't do that," he muttered.

"Yes you can, yes you can," she shouted. "You're young, you can catch far more than I can. You're my good luck charm. Sadie will give you a hundred dollars, how about that? Oh, I can't stand it. I knew I was lucky tonight." "The cash booth," someone screamed. "Bring out the cash booth."

By this point, Chalmers and the woman were both on their feet, and others had joined in the discussion. "Go take the money," someone yelled at him, "help the old lady out." "Doesn't he want the money?" another person shouted. "Put that guy in the cash booth."

Chalmers felt hands pushing him along like oars through the smoky sea of the room, against his wishes, down to the front and up on the stage. People clapped and shouted. "There he is, the guy who didn't want the money." "Look at his shoes, look at his shoes." There were roars of laughter. "Give him a chance."

The lights went out and Chalmers found himself standing inside the cash booth, squinting in the hot floodlights. The floodlights stormed and boiled in his face. His body was on fire. He stared out into the vast room but could see nothing. "You're blinding him," someone yelled, and the spotlight lowered its hot beam. Now he could see the stained-glass windows on the side of the room, the leaning Jesus beating on and off. The announcer made his little speech while the spectators screamed and cheered.

Chalmers was trapped. He began banging his fists against the glass walls. He wanted to break them into thousands of pieces. The glass was thick, it felt smooth and cool against his forehead, like rock underwater. He kicked, but his shoes were too soft. He spun around looking for something to swing with, something to smash with, he wanted to murder the announcer.

Then the bills started to fall. The bills plunged without warning into his tiny glass world, droppings of green from the church and the hot greed of voyeurs whose screams he could no longer hear. He dodged the bills. He spit at them. They were green and crisp. They were immaculate. They fluttered down, flashing like leaves from a prematurely aging tree, and were sucked away by the earth god below. Some swirled as if caught by a breeze. How many had fallen? They twirled and they floated. It was a leaf-fall of money. One fell on his head.

Another lightly touched his cheek, like the brush of a dead leaf, then like the fingertips of a woman. He could hear the breathy sucking of the vacuum cleaner near his feet, almost gurgling. Then it too became silent. Now there was no sound at all. Only the money. The money was fresh, even beautiful. In the spotlight, in the silence, he could see the filigree script in the corners of each bill, the delicate lines like veins in a leaf, all tumbling in light. Silk. It was a flood of green silk. And as the bills continued to fall, so thin and so perfect, he realized that he wanted them. It was he who should have the money, not to spend, but just because he should have it. Now he wanted the money more than anything in the world. But he would not flail like the woman before him. With a twist of his body, he turned away from the voyeurs so that all they could see was his back, and he began snatching the bills with small, hidden movements. He was much better at it than the woman before him. She had panicked. He would not panic. Everything seemed like it was moving in slow motion. The bills floated. His hands floated. One inch at a time, each bill sank through the shining white air. He grabbed with one hand and stuffed with the other, all in short, controlled movements, invisible movements. The bills came to him. He wanted them all. Now he was going well, he was getting every single bill that dropped, he was getting every one, every one, every one, he would have a hundred in his pockets before it was over, two hundred, two or three thousand dollars.

The slow leaf-fall stopped. "Bill Chalmers!" a man shouted. Chalmers found himself on the main floor, at the edge of the stage, surrounded by people, the woman in the blue satin dress, the announcer, someone else shoving closer to meet him.

"That was quite a performance, Mr. Chalmers," said a

man who laughed and held out his hand. "Quite an excellent performance. You're a crowd pleaser. And that outfit." He laughed again. "Riley Appleson, from Stokes International. We're on the fifteenth floor of the Marbleworth. You're on the forty-second, aren't you? Never seen you here before. Let me buy you a drink. Or maybe you should be buying."

HOMECOMING

Bill ran, ran from the church, ran into the street, remembering everything in an avalanche, his head pounding, remembering too much. A strange sensation of awareness went through him, as if that moment were the first moment of his life, the feeling of the air on his skin, the precise placement of cars in the street, lampposts, the hum of a neon sign. With a sudden rush of new consciousness, he could feel the difference between life and death, he could feel the long nothingness of death, and beside it this tingle of awareness as if he had been born at this moment, an unpleasant sinking sensation, the slender closeness of death one inch away, and the nothingness.

Remembering everything. No, remembering nothing. Details had shifted imperceptibly. After Appleson dropped him off at the Alewife Station, Bill recalled having programmed his son's birthday to unlock the door of his car, but after several minutes of running through all the meaningful numbers in his life, all remembered with frightening veracity, he discovered that the door was opened by his personal computer password at Plymouth. Did the former world still exist in this new razor consciousness of his mind? Getting into his car, he found himself obsessed with tiny details. The precise curve of the dashboard, the elliptical bevel of the turn-signal lever, the scratch on the right side of the ignition switch. His blue slacks, dry cleaned and packaged in plastic, were draped over the backseat, as he remembered. Or had they been hung from the coat hook? He put the pants on, breathed in and out gauging the fit. In the glove compartment, the extra key.

The road out of the station swung around to the right, as he recalled, becoming instantly entangled in the absurd convergence of eight streets at the corner. As he squinted through his headlights to confirm this last recollection, a heavy rain began to fall. The rain hammered the roof of his car and lifted great clouds of steam from the pavement. Driving felt uncomfortable, odd. Both of his hands were completely numb, so that the steering wheel seemed to float in midair, unattached to his body, moving this way and that by pure thought. He watched the traffic light silently change colors. Then, with a swish of his tires and an uneasy dread of the world, he started up Route 2 toward Lexington. It was 2:15 a.m., according to the digital clock on his dashboard. By 2:40 he would be home.

His mind was back. He was in control now. His hands trembled on the wheel. The smell of the car was familiar, a remembered faint odor of carbolic acid. That was good, every car had its own smell. That was good. He was on his way home to see Alex and Melissa. He felt them in his body, a warmth came over him and spread from his face to his chest to his legs. The night that he and Alex had stayed up pumping air into Alex's fish tank with a bicycle pump because the electricity had gone off, whispering to each other for hours in the dark. Alex's fish tank and his wall covered with matchbook covers and the shy way that he expressed affection to Bill, looking away with his dark, dewy eyes. Alex would be devastated to learn that his father had gone cuckoo on the subway. No, Bill could not possibly tell him that. He would tell Alex that he'd been mugged.

The rain had diminished to a smooth hiss, practically merging with the stillness of woods on both sides of the road. It was a silence that Bill had rarely experienced and that now amplified his anxiety. He turned on the radio loud, loud enough so that he could see his stale morning coffee vibrating in its cup on the dashboard. That was better. *Is love so fragile, and the heart so hard, to shatter with words?*

His mind was beginning to settle, he was feeling better. He was on his way home, driving his car on Route 2. It now struck him that he had panicked excessively. First thing in the morning, he would be back at his office. In actuality, he would have lost only a single day of work, almost as if he had taken a day of vacation. Jenkins could reschedule B&B for a lunch meeting, not at the office but at the Ritz Carlton Hotel. That should compensate even the aloof Christine Johnson. Some of tomorrow's originally scheduled business, which pertained to a 20-gigabyte review of the Trague Group, could be moved to the weekend. All of these items were in his head in the most minute detail. Nothing had been lost, nothing had been lost. *Now is the time to stock up on all of those summer items you need. Call the king of walking beams, R. L. Davis and Company, 1-800-101-3748. Get your truck in by 8 in the morning and you'll be back on the road and making money by noon.*

He pictured Melissa lying on the sofa downstairs, where she went when she couldn't sleep, letting the television play all night. How he wanted to put his arms around her and kiss her. In his mind, he was brushing her hair as she liked him to do. He imagined her closing her eyes while he brushed up and down. But she would have suffered terribly not knowing his whereabouts. She would be weeping and sleepless. He wanted to talk to her, to tell her what was going through his mind. But how could he tell her about all that had happened, especially his humiliating behavior on the subway, without causing her more pain? Maybe he would tell her some now, some later. He wanted to tell her, he needed to tell her, but he could not hear the words coming from his mouth.

Then he thought of his mother, pacing by her bedroom window, wearing her monogrammed driving gloves and scarf even though she was not allowed to go out. He wanted to tell her, too, about the terrible events of this day. And then have her hold him. But she would not remember, she would barely know who he was. Tears came to his eyes.

Suddenly, a car with a disabled windshield wiper whooshed by, dangerously close, possibly at seventy-five miles per hour or more. Bill honked his horn. In reply, the other car slammed its own horn and accelerated, its trailing red lights vanishing in the rain. Tufts of fog hung over the highway. Bill began worrying again about what to say to Melissa. Sometimes he couldn't understand her reactions to things. Sometimes her emotions would flare up when he was being so calm and reasonable and responsible. What should he say to her now, without upsetting her more? What should he say?

While Bill was pondering these disturbing questions and uncertainties, his automobile, almost with a mind of its own, traveled Route 2, found its way along Waltham Street into Lexington, and made a right onto Kendall, sleeping and dark. Bill glided slowly past Max Pedersky's crumbling Victorian, an embarrassment to the neighborhood even in the dark; the Allison house, with a tiny light in the upstairs window, perhaps Jane's bedroom. Jane's BMW in the driveway. In the Terris driveway Bill could see a Toyota Camry, out-of-state plates. That meant Marty, Sam and Gloria's married son, must be visiting. From Pennsylvania. Bill nodded in satisfaction at each of these confirmed recollections. Bob and Silvia Tournaby's house and garden. The Cotters. Then he pulled into his own driveway. Clicked off the radio. For a moment, he remained in his car, calming himself and verifying the placement of small things. The outside lamp glowed famil-iarly on its tall cedar post. Three steps up to the front door. The brass letter box just below the doorbell, the recent gash on the right side of the garage. The rain had slackened to a fine silvery mist and shone on the leaves of the rhododen-dron, precisely where it should be. He let out a small sigh of gratitude and eased himself out of his car, walking quietly up the steps. As he crouched before the front door, searching with numb fingers for the spare key under the ledge, a dog suddenly exploded in wild yips and squeals. It was Philippe, a raw nerve of a little dog belonging to Melissa's sister, and the creature's presence in his house meant that Virginia and her two young children and dog had come for the night. Now Philippe's little claws were frantically scratching the other side of the door. Lights went on.

Later, Alex came softly into his parents' bedroom and lay across Bill's chest.

A DAY OF REST

When Bill awoke the next morning, the tingling and numbness had progressed up his arms. This condition he ignored for the time being, concentrating instead on the pleasant damp of Melissa's head against his shoulder. She had clung to him in the bed without letting go, dropping off to sleep only after the dawn. For a few moments, he kept his eyes closed, listening to her shallow breathing. His first waking vision was the illuminated dial of the clock on the vanity. In the dim light, he could barely discriminate between the clock and its reverse image, reflected in the mirror beside it, so that he saw two clocks. Sleepily, he watched the two second hands rotating in opposite directions and wondered what the world would be like if it ran backwards, whether progress also would run backwards, with modern automobiles dissassembling themselves into Model T's, and those into horses and buggies, everyone becoming dumber and dumber. Then he noticed the time. It was 10:26. With a shriek, he leaped out of bed, switched on a lamp, and began pulling drawers from his dresser. A clean shirt.

"What are you doing?" Melissa moaned and sat up. Her eyes were puffy with exhaustion. "Come back to bed."

"I've got meetings," Bill shouted. He struggled to insert buttons into buttonholes with his numb fingers. In his mind, he was already recalculating his day's activities based on a late arrival. He would telephone Jenkins immediately. "I'm leaving."

"You can't," said Melissa. She got out of bed and wrapped her arms around his waist and pressed her head into the small of his back. "You need to rest," she mumbled. "You've been bashed in the head. And I need to rest. I want you here with me." Bill pleaded, but she would not release her grip, her fingers dug into his skin. He turned around and kissed her on the forehead, then on the lips. She began sobbing.

"Melissa."

"Don't make me beg you."

"You're up," Virginia hollered suddenly, just outside their bedroom door. Bill could hear her heavy body bumping against the closed door. She began knocking brightly. "We're so relieved that you're okay. All of us are so relieved." Then she released her goose-honk laugh, which both Bill and Melissa felt had contributed to the departure of her husband.

The knocking continued and Melissa walked unsteadily to her closet, where she put on the cotton trousers and short-sleeved beige shirt that she wore on days home in the summer. As she dressed, she called out instructions to her sister. Janie would need to be told that Melissa wasn't opening the shop today. Janie would also need to delay a delivery of cane chairs from an auction in Salem and reschedule an appointment at Friar's of Boston. Already, Melissa had slipped into the southern drawl that she used with her sister.

"Janie has already called twice," said Virginia through the door. "She wants to know if she can come by and pick up the keys from you. For just a few minutes. She needs to get something she left at the shop."

"Ask her to wait until tomorrow. I'll be going in tomorrow."

"You have three other messages. A woman at the Concord

library wants you to give a talk about eighteenth-century New England furniture. She heard you speak somewhere else. And two messages for Bill."

"Who called me?" Bill shouted and hurried toward the closed door in his pajama shorts. "Did you write them down?"

"They're on the tape."

"Are you sure there were only two?" He began hunting in the writing desk for paper and pen.

"I'm not sure," said Virginia from the other side of the door. "You'll have to listen to the tape."

Melissa, now dressed, glanced at herself in the vanity mirror. "I look awful," she whispered. "Don't I."

"You just need some sleep," said Bill. He went to the window and pulled back the damask drapes.

For a few seconds, Melissa worked at her face at the vanity. Then, with a weary toss of her arm, she swept the little bottles and jars clattering into the drawer and slammed it shut. Swaying on her feet, she opened the door.

Virginia plunged in immediately, huge and stubby, her loose summer dress lagging behind her. "Give him some warm oatmeal with milk," she said to her sister, referring to Bill in the third person even though he sat on the edge of the bed. "Do you have any oatmeal? That used to calm Frank down." She peered behind herself, into the hallway and over the banister. "Remember to be gentle," she called to her children, Jennifer and Todd, who were downstairs riding Gerty like a horse.

Melissa sighed and sat down on the bed with Bill and clenched his hand. "Virginia, you ought to run on now," she said. "You've been a help. I can make the calls."

Virginia stood her ground in the doorway. She plucked a handkerchief from under her sleeve and dabbed her damp face. "I don't know why they don't have air conditioning up here," she said. "It's just as beastly hot as it is in Fayetteville." She paused and stared at her sister, her eyes moving from Melissa's face to her slender arms and waist. "But you never sweated that much, Missy."

Melissa started to say something but began rubbing her swollen eyes. "Before you go," she said to Virginia, "mum's the word on all of this. Absolutely mum, and I mean it. You haven't talked to Janet, have you?"

"Janet is visiting her latest loser in Cincinnati. With her kids."

The telephones began ringing. By reflex, Bill and Melissa both lunged for the remote phone on the blanket chest. "Hi, Marlene . . . I'm not feeling too well this morning . . . No, I can't do it . . . Maybe tomorrow . . . Yes . . . Tomorrow." There were screams from downstairs and Gerty came scrambling up the stairs and crept behind the washing machine in the utility room. Melissa suddenly stood up, as if something downstairs demanded her attention, and walked to the doorway. She would not let go of Bill's hand and pulled him with her.

"When's Dad getting up?" called Alexander from his room at the other end of the hall. "Isn't he up by now?" Alexander's door opened a crack, letting fly a torrent of rap from a Puff Daddy CD. Jennifer and Todd began battling over the TV downstairs, and the door to Alexander's room slammed shut, sending the red "DANGER" sign crashing to the floor. A few moments later, Alexander threw open his door wide, with a shout of "En garde!" He was outfitted in a steel-mesh face mask, white jacket, white glove, and white shoes, all purchased within the week, and he brandished a foil. "Sir," he called down the hall to his father. "Would you care to fence with me? You can find an extra weapon and mask in the mud room of the castle."

"Doesn't Alex look handsome in his new outfit?" said Melissa. "He's been waiting to fence with you."

"You do look very handsome, Alex," said Bill.

"Sir, appearances do not concern me," said Alex, who was small like his mother and had the bony, off-center head of his father. "I'm a fighting man. Now, to your weapon. Quarte." The boy flipped his sword hand over and gripped the foil handle from the top. He retreated a step, advanced down the hallway, leaped into the air, and with a deft thrust of his sword knocked over a stack of the week's *New York Times,* still rolled up in their blue plastic wrappers. The telephones began ringing.

"Did the guy who mugged you have a weapon?" asked Alexander. "A knife? Or a pistol?"

"I don't know," said Bill. "Maybe a pistol."

"Then they can get him for assault with a deadly weapon. What did he look like?"

Unprepared for this line of questioning, Bill shrugged his shoulders.

Alexander had taken off his face mask and was staring steadily at his father. Something was not right about him, Alex seemed to sense that. He hesitated, then went back into his room and closed the door.

There was more screaming downstairs, from the kitchen area this time, and the doorbell rang. From nowhere, Philippe launched himself into the hallway and skittered down the stairs, with Virginia running after him. The musical voice of Doris, the cleaning lady, boomed into the house. "Everybody's home." Doris stood at the bottom of the steps by her vacuum cleaner, straining to hear what Melissa was saying to the police on the telephone. "It'll take me an extra two hours today," said Doris. "You know what I'm saying? You've had guests, haven't you. And everyone is home. What is Bill doing home in the middle of the day? He should at least hide his car. Bill, can you hear me?" She started her vacuum cleaner.

Bill looked at his watch again. It was 10:45. Communications would be coming in from the West Coast. He threw on a bathrobe and hurried down to the kitchen. "Where's the bread?" he shouted. There was no time for breakfast. He slammed the refrigerator door closed. Notes and memos rained to the floor, notices of meetings, claim slips and receipts, chiropractor and podiatrist appointments, calls to return from the answering machine.

Upstairs, Bill sat at the French country writing desk in his bedroom, eating airline crackers that he had saved from a business trip and staring at the screen of his laptop. Messages from Plymouth were already stacked up and arriving.

>>> MAIL 50.02.04 <<< From: MITRAK at PLYM.COM
====> Received: from BUSTER.INTER.COM by INTER.COM with NIO
id AQ06498; Thur, 26 Jun 9:46:36 EDT
for WCHALM@PLYM.COM; Thur, 26 Jun 9:46:42 -0400
Press * for message

>>> MAIL 50.02.04 <<< From: MITRAK at PLYM.COM
Dear Bill,
Having learned from Robert this morning of your
ordeal, in which, ultimately, that is to say,
sometime last night I presume, you got home not too
badly bruised, I was overjoyed and gratified to
learn the same. Mugged!!!! Where are you? We've
been worried like hell about you. Regards,
George

To: George Mitrakis <MITRAK@PLYM.COM>
From: Bill Chalmers <WCHALM@PLYM.COM>
Subject: Re: Your message

Hello George. Thannks for your E-mail. I'm working at
home today. Melissa insisted. I'm fine. I'm going to
reschedule the B & B and the TEM meetings. I've already
been in touche with Kurt Hendredon and Christine
Johnson. Please let Harv know the B & B account is on
track. I beleive can get everything I need for the
Trague review today.

_____

_____

>>> MAIL 50.02.04 <<< From: Unknown at Unknown.Com
==> Received: from RING.AOL.COM by AOL.COM with GOTP
Make Big $$$ Online, Publishers on Computers
Unknown@Unknown.Com

_____

_____

>>> MAIL 50.02.04 <<< From: Theroux at PLYM.COM
====> Received: from BUSTER.INTER.COM by INTER.COM with
NIO
id AQ06498; Thur, 26 Jun 9:50:12 EDT
for WCHALM@PLYM.COM; Thur, 26 Jun 9:50:38 -0400
Press * for message

>>> MAIL 50.02.04 <<< From: Theroux at PLYM.COM
Dear Bill,
We're alll glad to herr th at yo're OK. Robert played
your message over the intercom this morning. I'd like
you to do me a favor. You know Mike Gaffey better than
I do. He was supposed to send me twenty megabytes by
9am today and he sent only ten. that man is a male

chauvanist pig and I don;t want to soil myself with him
again. Cank you send the asshole a message and tell him
he gets 10 more megs to me or I'm cancelling his
accoutn. Thanks.
Lisa

_____

_____

>>> MAIL 50.02.04 <<< From: MITRAK at PLYM.COM
====> Received: from BUSTER.INTER.COM by INTER.COM with
NIO
id AQ06498; Thur, 26 Jun 10:52:42 EDT
for WCHALM@PLYM.COM; Thur, 26 Jun 10:52:52 -0400
Press * for message

>>> MAIL 50.02.04 <<< From: MITRAK at PLYM.COM
Dear Bill,
If I were you, I would not kill one's self working
today. In regard to the Trague review, furthermore,
that is not to be worried about. Everything at the
office, and with most particularity the Trague review,
is here at the office being managed satisfactorily. Take
the day off.
Regards, George

_____

_____

To: Robert Jenkins <JENKINS@PLYM.COM>
From: Bill Chalmers <WCHALM@PLYM.COM>
Subject: The Trague Group Review
Robert, pleae have Dolores E-mail me Trag.dat1. It may
not all fit into my machine here. I think I can hold
about 100 megs. Trag.dat1 was 3 gigabytes the last time
I checked on Moidnay It may have grown since then. Is
there anyway we can swap 100 megs at a time in and out
of my machine? Thanks for evrything.

Has Harvey Stumm said anyhng about my missing the B&B appointment yesterday?

_____

_____

>>> MAIL 50.02.04 <<< From: Rossbane at PLYM.COM
====> Received: from BUSTER.INTER.COM by INTER.COM with NIO
id AQ06498; Thur, 26 Jun 10:52:31 EDT
for WCHALM@PLYM.COM; Thur, 26 Jun 10:52:35 -0400
Press * for message

>>> MAIL 50.02.04 <<< From: Rossbane at PLYM.COM
Dear Bill,
I was worried about you. We're very glad you're back.
You are back, aren't you? Your office looked dark the
last time I passed. Diane

_____

_____

>>> MAIL 50.02.04 <<< From: Jenkins at PLYM.COM
====> Received: from BUSTER.INTER.COM by INTER.COM with NIO
id AQ06498; Thur, 26 Jun 10:53:06 EDT
for WCHALM@PLYM.COM; Thur, 26 Jun 10:53:17 -0400
Press * for message

>>> MAIL 50.02.04 <<< From: Jenkins at PLYM.COM
Dear Mr. Chalmers,
Mr. Stumm hasn't said anything about your missingi the
meeitng yesterday. But then he wouldn't. I'd be
careful. Please delete this message. Robert

_____

Bill was having difficulty at the keyboard. He could not feel the keys. Two keys at once. Missed keys. Faster, he needed to go faster, he had so much to do. And he was so far behind. How could he go faster? He regarded his numb hands and arms with a strange disconnection, almost a contempt. They were dead limbs protruding from the trunk of a tree. Every few minutes, a wave of tingling would surge down his arms from his shoulders, prickle in his fingertips, and then flow up again. Otherwise, there was no sensation, no heat, no cold, no quivering of blood, no pressure inside or out. He scraped the point of a paperclip across the skin of his forearm, making white lines in his flesh, and felt nothing. What an ugly marvel that his fingers and hands could move without feeling, like remote-control toys on the other side of the room. Press a button here, they jump and twirl there.

>>> MAIL 50.02.04 <<< From: JOLSW at OLS.COM
==> Received: from RING.AOL.COM by AOL.COM with GOTP
id AQ06498; Thur, 26 Jun 10:55:29 EDT
for WCHALM@PLYM.COM; Thur, 26 Jun 10:55:32 -0400
Press * for message

>>> MAIL 50.02.04 <<< From: Olswanger at OLS.COM
Dear Bill Chalmers,
I've been leving you voice-mail messages since yesterday,
without any response, so I thought I'd try this. Did you
know about the expected merger of Teneco and ChicagoCorp?
They're opening a new products line, but they knowless
than nothing about patterns of consumption This could be
very lucrative. I know that you've had ealings with
Teneco in the past. Do you want to play? Plymouth would
love you for this, and so would I. We need to make thema
proposal by 4 pm EST. (I'm in Los Angeles today.)
Jasper Olswanger

```
>>> MAIL 50.02.04 <<< From: BERT at BAZEN.ATS.COM
==> Received: from RING.AOL.COM by AOL.COM with GOTP
id AQ06498; Thur, 26 Jun 11:01:19 EDT
for WCHALM@PLYM.COM; Thur, 26 Jun 11:01:42 -0400
Press * for message

>>> MAIL 50.02.04 <<< From: Bertolazzi at
BAZEN.ATS.COM
Dear Mr. Chalmers,
Regarding that argumant we were having about candy bars
last week, I looked it up on the internet
(MarsInc.com). Milky Ways do not have nutts. Almond
Joys, Snickers, and Baby Ruths have nuts.
Best wishes, Bruno Bertolazzi
```

Melissa hurried into the room, closed the door behind her, and went into the bathroom. "Virginia is driving me crazy," she whispered. "She says she might stay until lunch." Melissa came out of the bathroom and slumped across the bed. "I just wish I could sleep." She let out a groan of exhaustion. "Silvia Tournaby came over and asked me for Ralph Turgis's telephone number. She wanted to know how much he was charging us for the bay windows. She brought some fish that Bob caught last weekend, a present for us. And the Cambridge police called and said that someone can pick up your briefcase at the station. But they need you to fill out a report."

"Can they e-mail the report to me?"

"I don't know. Why are you hunching over like that? Do you need more light?" She got up and moved the tin-box lamp closer to the keyboard. "Doris wants to know when she can get in here to vacuum." Even at that moment, the vacuum cleaner was revving impatiently in the hall. "Bill."

"I can't think about that now, Melissa."

"I'll tell Doris to hold off a half-hour. A half-hour, okay? That should be eleven-thirty." Melissa left again and closed the door.

```
>>> MAIL 50.02.04 <<< From: ACHALM at AOL.COM
==> Received: from RING.AOL.COM by AOL.COM with GOTP
id AQ06498; Thur, 26 Jun 11:02:36 EDT
for WCHALM@PLYM.COM; Thur, 26 Jun 11:02:49 -0400
MESSAGE LOCK OVERRIDE
>>> MAIL 50.02.04 <<< From: Alexander at AOL.COM
Do you know what the guy who mugged you looked like?
They ahave artists who can do drawings and put them on
the net, like wanted posters. Were you scared? Also,
when will you fence with me? Ive learned a bunch of
stuff.
Love, Alex
```

```
To: Alexander Chalmers <ACHALM@AOL.COM>
From: Bill Chalmers <WCHALM@PLYM.COM>
Subject: Re: Your message

Just a few minutes, Alex. I'm in the middle of some
things. I do want to fence with you.
```

Bill had just managed to link up through the Internet to the online *Encyclopedia of Medicine* of the American Medical Association. He looked at the clock on the vanity. He would allow himself ten minutes to research his symptoms. Tingling.

Tingling. Alternative term: Pins and Needles. Symptom
chart.
Symptom chart. Numbness and Tingling. Did you notice
the numbness AND/OR tingling after sitting in one
position for a long time or after waking from a deep
sleep? No.
Are only your hands affected? No.
Does the numbness AND/OR tingling affect only one side
of your body? No.

>>> MAIL 50.02.04 <<< From: Jenkins at PLYM.COM
====> Received: from BUSTER.INTER.COM by INTER.COM
with NIO
id AQ06498; Thur, 26 Jun 11:03:27 EDT
for WCHALM@PLYM.COM; Thur, 26 Jun 11:03:38 -0400
Press * for message

>>> MAIL 50.02.04 <<< From: Jenkins at PLYM.COM
Dear Mr. Chalmers,
Dolores is about to send over 100 megabytes from
the Trag.dat1 file. She wants to know whwther it
matters which 100 megs she sends. Also, I've
reschehdueld the TEM meeting for 11:15 tomorrow
morning, right afteryour teleconference with New York.
Robert

Do your fingers or toes get numb and turn blue in cold
weather, and then become red and painful as feeling
returns? No.
If you are unable to make a diagnosis from this chart,
consult your physician. Thanks alot.

Tingling. Alternative term: Pins and Needles. Symptom
chart.
Tingling: See pins and needles sensation.

>>> MAIL 50.02.04 <<< From: ACHALM at AOL.COM
==> Received: from RING.AOL.COM by AOL.COM with GOTP
id AQ06498; Thur, 26 Jun 11:05:03 EDT
for WCHALM@PLYM.COM; Thur, 26 Jun 11:05:07 -0400
MESSAGE LOCK OVERRIDE
>>> MAIL 50.02.04 <<< From: Alexander at AOL.COM
Dad, there's a really cool college course I want take
on the Internet. Brad did it. It costs $90, but yotu
don;t have tot pay for the whole thing if you don't do
the whole thing. Brad did $50 worth. Can I do it,
please? Mom saidd to ask you. I don't have anything
else to do today.

To: Alexander Chalmers <ACHALM@AOL.COM>
From: Bill Chalmers <WCHALM@PLYM.COM>
Subject: Re: The College Course

What's it on?

>>> MAIL 50.02.04 <<< From: ACHALM at AOL.COM
==> Received: from RING.AOL.COM by AOL.COM with GOTP
id AQ06498; Thur, 26 Jun 11:06:13 EDT
for WCHALM@PLYM.COM; Thur, 26 Jun 11:06:19 -0400
MESSAGE LOCK OVERRIDE
>>> MAIL 50.02.04 <<< From: Alexander at AOL.COM
Plato. I know that sounds boring, but Brad said it

was really cool, with lots of interactive stuff.
Please.

_____

_____

To: Alexander Chalmers <ACHALM@AOL.COM>
From: Bill Chalmers <WCHALM@PLYM.COM>
Subject: Re: The College Course

OK. Try out $10 worth and see how you like it.

_____

Pins and needles sensation: Persistent pins and needles
sensation may be caused by neuropathy (a group of nerve
disorders).
Neuropathy: Disease, inflammation, or damage to the
peripheral nerves, which connect the central nervous
system or CNS (brain and spinal cord) to the sense
organs, muscles, glands, and internal organs. Most
nerve cell axons are insulated within a sheath of fatty
substance called myelin, but some are unmyelinated.
Most neuropathies arise from damage or irritation
either to the axons or to their myeline sheaths.
Causes. In some cases of neuropathy there is no obvious
cause. Among the many specific causes are diabetes
mellitus, dietary deficiencies (particularly of B
vitamins), persistent and excessive alcohol
consumption, and metabolic upsets such as uremia.
Other causes include leprosy, lead poisoning, or
poisoning by drugs. Nerves may become acutely
inflamed. This often occurs after a viral infection (for
example, in Guillain-Barré syndrome). Neuropathies may
result from autoimmune disorders such as rheumatoid
arthritis, systemic lupus erythematosus, or

periarteritis nodosa. Neuropathies may occur
secondarily to malignant tumors.

Bill began searching for a discussion of pain. Or, more precisely, its absence, since he did not feel the slightest pain in
connection with the tingling and numbness that enveloped
his hands and arms. Surely, the absence of pain must mean
something?

The experience of pain may be reduced by arousal
(e.g., an injury sustained during competitive
sport or on the battlefield may go unnoticed in
the heat of the moment); strong emotion can also
block pain.

>>> MAIL 50.02.04 <<< From: Loeser at TEM.COM
==> Received: from RING.AOL.COM by AOL.COM with GOTP
id AQ06498; Thur, 26 Jun 11:16:36 EDT
for WCHALM@PLYM.CM; Thur, 26 Jun 11:16:42 -0400
Press * for message

>>> MAIL 50.02.04 <<< From: Loeser at TEM.COM
Dear Mr. Chalmers,
In pe3pration for our rescheduled meeting tomorrow
at 11:15, I'm sending you an attached file about our
recent project with Stanford University ("Total
Efficiency Mangemtnent and Stanford in the New
Millenium"). Would it be possible for you to take a
look atit and review it with me before 3 pm today?
Thank you in advance.
Fred Loeser

There was a knocking at the bedroom door. "I'm sorry to disturb you, Bill," said Doris. "May I come in? I'll just be a minute." Doris eased open the door with the hose of her vacuum cleaner. "It's so dusty in here. Doesn't this dust bother you? It would bother me. You know what I mean?" Doris, in her late fifties, stood four feet eleven inches tall and had curly dyed red hair. Immediately, Jennifer and Todd burst into the bedroom, chasing Gerty.

"I thought you weren't coming in here until eleven-thirty," said Bill.

"Oh," said Doris, looking perplexed, "isn't it eleven-thirty now?" She stood just outside the door waiting for definite instructions. "That's a cute poster of Elvis in Alex's room," she said. "I loved Elvis. I loved his gyrations."

"Jennifer and Todd, you come out of there," shouted Virginia. "You're disturbing Uncle Bill." Virginia pushed into the bedroom holding a magazine she'd been reading. "You come out right now, or you'll have no sweets after lunch." Gerty barked from under the bed, then shot from the room with the children in pursuit.

For a moment Virginia stood gazing at Bill at his desk, then she sat down on the bed. She began crying. "I'm nothing but a nuisance to everybody," she said. "I'm a selfish nuisance. I got all of my good qualities from Frank, and he took them with him when he left."

Bill stopped his typing and turned unhappily to his sister-in-law. "Oh, Virginia," he sighed. A new e-mail message had just come in from David Hamilton and another one from Jasper Olswanger. He rose from his chair and walked to the canopied bed, where Virginia was buried in the cottony blue panels of her dress. "You have a good heart, Virginia. No one can take that away from you." She looked up at him and rubbed her eyes and smiled weakly.

"I think of all those dinners when Melissa was sick," said Bill.

"Oh, that was easy for me," she mumbled, still dabbing at her eyes. "I like to cook."

"Stay with us another night."

At the other end of the hall, behind his closed door, Alexander's fingers were jumping like minnows over his keyboard. His fingers moved even more rapidly since he had reprogrammed his keyboard to correspond to his study of the most optimal location of the keys. Just in the last month, Alex had created his own Internet links to the Federal Aviation Authority (to keep abreast of the latest investigations of plane crashes), to the summer tour schedule of Tuff Girls, to the personal web page of Alicia Silverstone (courtesy of International Artistic Management), to Virtual Master Tennis, and, yesterday, to Fencing on the Web. Today, Metropolitan College Online.

To: Brad Serano <BSERANO@AOL.COM>
From: Alexander Chalmers <ACHALM@AOL.COM>
Subject: Re: MCO

Mr. Bradford. Are you awake yet? I'm doing the Plato thing. I'll wait 60 for you, then I'm starting. A.

>>> MAIL 50.02.04 <<< From: BSERANO at AOL.COM
==> Received: from RING.AOL.COM by AOL.COM with GOTP
id AQ06498; Thur, 26 Jun 12:03:26 EDT
for ACHALM@AOL.COM; Thur, 26 Jun 12:03:29 -0400
Press * for message

>>> MAIL 50.02.04 <<< From: Brad at AOL.COM
Whoa!!! Hold onto your nads, Mr. Big, that's all
I can say. You should DEFINITELY do Crito first.
Cretin Crito. Wait, an urhgent message is beaming
down from Jocko. Do you want to come over
later? B.

_____

_____

To: Brad Serano <BSERANO@AOL.COM>
From: Alexander Chalmers <ACHALM@AOL.COM>
Subject: Re: Regarding

Thanks, but my dad is home today. I think I'll hang
here. A.

_____

Alexander pounded his chest, Tarzan-style, and did some
warm-up exercises with his fingers. He felt cramped. For
today's bold exploration in cyberspace, he would need a major
cube of clear air. With a sweep of his arm, he flung everything extraneous off his desk, including his fencing mask, a
good spool of number 30 copper wire, some Snickers bars,
and a framed photograph of his father at twenty years old.
Launch.

Welcome, Alexander Chalmers, to Metropolitan College
Online.

This session's course is PLATO ONLINE™, at a
cost of only $90, charged through your America
Online account. PLATO ONLINE™ includes condensed
forms of the original Dialogues of Plato, by
special arrangement with Oxford University
Press.

"Alexander!" His mother was shouting to him through his closed door. "You have a fencing lesson today at three-thirty, and a Longine festival rehearsal after that. Remember? It's a little after twelve now. Please be ready at three-fifteen. Okay?"

"Okay."

"Okay? I can't hear you over that music. Three-fifteen. Look at your watch."

"Yes. Okay. I'll glue my watch to the ceiling."

```
To begin, select a condensed Dialogue from the
following menu: Protagoras/ Crito/ Meno/ Anytus/
Sophist/ Apology/ Euthyphro/ Parmenides/ Phaedo/
Gorgias/ Symposium/ Theaetetus.
Anytus

Time: Archonship of Laches = 399 BC
  15th day of Elaphebolion = early spring
  Dawn.
```

There was screaming from outside Alex's door. "I'm bleeding," Todd bawled. "Oh, my God," shouted Virginia. "Missy, I need your help." "It's only a scrape," said Doris.

"Can you guys be quiet out there?" yelled Alex. "I'm taking a college course in here. Show a little respect." He turned up the volume of his amplifier.

```
Press return for the first line of Anytus. Then press
return for each successive paragraph. Questions follow
at the conclusion of each section. Return


  Just after dawn on the fifteenth day of the month of
Elaphebolion, in the archonship of Laches, two men sat
silently in the little Portico of Artemis, a stone's
throw from the northeast edge of the city. . . .
```

ANYTUS

Just after dawn on the fifteenth day of the month of Elaphebolion, in the archonship of Laches, two men sat silently in the little Portico of Artemis, a stone's throw from the northeast edge of the city. The first was Anytus, wealthy tanner of Athens. Anytus, wearing a white mantle with a fine vermilion border, slumped moodily beneath the roofed colonnade upon a white marble bench. He was no more than a shape in the faint early light. The second in the portico was Pyrrhias, favorite and most devoted of Anytus's fifteen slaves. Pyrrhias squatted on the stone floor twenty feet from his master, quietly scratching the large mole on his neck. Every few moments, he would look up and study the slumped form on the bench, trying to read thoughts and desires from a crossing or uncrossing of legs, a slight shift in the shoulders, a sigh. For the last hour or more there had been little movement. Yet Pyrrhias understood that his master was troubled.

Anytus, in fact, was contemplating his present political position. The sophist. While it was true that the precise words of the accusations against the old sophist had been formulated by Lycon, and that the case had been argued in front of the court by Meletus, reeking of one of his cheap fragrances, it was common knowledge that the conception and driving force of the charges gushed directly from himself, distinguished citizen of Athens, former general in the war against Sparta, leader of the new democracy returned out of exile—the same who now sat in the little portico, fingering his olive-oiled but still scraggly beard. He should be pleased. Had he not rid the city of a self-righteous worm, which was slowly digesting the foundations of the democracy? More importantly, he was at last to gain personal revenge.

Anytus had been sitting on the marble bench now since before dawn, brooding in the dark silence, watching from the corner of his eye as the first rays of sunlight streamed through the east colonnade and cast long turquoise shadows across the floor and up the back wall onto the painted mural of the Battle of Marathon. A breakfast of fresh bread, figs, and wine lay uneaten on a tray at his feet. A roll of papyrus for the day's instructions to the manager of his tannery lay untouched at his side. The only motion for the past hour had been the fragile wings of a ringdove, which flew into the little open-air portico, fluttered noiselessly between the white columns, and then perched on the dim marble statue of Artemis just outside the south façade. Most of the city still lay sleeping and silent. So silent that Anytus could hear the minute scratchings of a cicada crawling across the limestone floor, and another tiny murmur of air that may have been a breeze moving through the olive groves past the Northeast Gate. The air fluttered and ruffled and blended with his slow breathing, liquid and small.

Anytus's skull was beginning to pound. He gingerly massaged his temples, gazing absently at the patterns of shadow on the floor, then shrieked as a wave of pain surged through his head. At the cry, like cymbals crashing, Pyrrhias lumbered heavily to his feet, nearly tripping over his tunic. "Master, please," he whispered. "Please let me help you. I know what you need." Pyrrhias had a face as honest and vulnerable as a peeled fruit. He leaned over his master and began rubbing Anytus's forehead.

Anytus moaned softly and closed his eyes. "You do care about me, don't you, Pyrrhias."

"Yes, Master."

The tanner leaned back on his elbows and tried to let his muscles go slack.

"I am making you feel better, aren't I?" said the slave.

Anytus sat up and opened his eyes. "Thank you, Pyrrhias, that is sufficient." He waved the slave back to his spot on the floor.

"It is a quiet morning, Master," said the wide, squatting man, "a good time for thinking."

"Thinking has given me a roaring headache," said Anytus. He continued rubbing his temples, holding his head as motionless as possible. To make his suffering worse, the myrtles had started to bloom, the spring's yearly curse. Somewhere he knew there were myrtles, not among the shrubs and lilies in the octagonal garden outside the portico, but somewhere, throwing up their nauseous white flowers and oily capsules. Anytus's nose dripped like a fountain, his eyes had turned red-veined and swollen. I am being punished, he said to himself. So be it. So be it.

Gloomily, he raised his head and peered out of the portico. The city was still drowsy, the narrow passageways of the Skambonidai almost empty. In the soft and utterly transparent Athenian air, every stone seemed an arm's length away. Along the squalid, unpaved roads, barely wide enough for a cart, he could see weeds hanging from cracks in the stuccoed walls of the houses. In the middle of the Leather Makers' Road, a slave emerged from one of the windowless, flat-roofed houses, dumped fish bones into the street, and went back inside. At a neighboring house, two slaves who had been guarding the front door during the night rolled over in the road, then sat up snorting and yawning from their deep slumber. In the distance, just inside the great wall of limestone and brick that circled the city, an old woman sat silently beside one of the rough shanty huts built hastily and in fear during the War.

Bad omens everywhere, Anytus thought to himself. Three slaves spotted in the street at first light. Three times the ring-dove had circled the portico before landing. The wealthy tanner groaned and began counting cracks in the wooden ceiling over his head, then counted again, trying to reconcile numbers.

The counting was interrupted by the soft clapping of sandals on limestone. Anytus turned to find his son stumbling toward him from the other side of the portico. Prodicus's face was bloated and pink, his frog-green mantle dragged ridiculously at his feet.

"What is this place?" shouted the young man. "I had a hell of a time finding you. What are you doing here sulking with your fat dog?"

"You're drunk," said Anytus. "It's not even opening time for the market."

"That's my business." Prodicus flopped down on the opposite side of the bench from his father, tossed off his sandals, and began devouring the bread and the figs.

"You eat like a Boeotian," Anytus said to his son.

Prodicus glared at his father, then resumed eating. His chomping and guzzling echoed off the back wall of the building. Crumbs dropped to the floor. When he had consumed all of the food and the wine, he stood up and withdrew from the folds of his tunic a piece of papyrus. He slapped it down on the bench without looking at his father. "A message for you from the King Archon, delivered to the house at dawn."

"Did the King Archon's secretary see you drunk?" asked Anytus. He sighed. "No matter." The tanner unrolled the papyrus, whose seal had already been broken, and read its contents. Scowling, he crumpled up the letter and threw it to the floor. "Callias says the Sacred Vessel has been sighted off Sunium and will arrive at the Piraeus tomorrow. He says that he cannot legally delay the execution of the old sophist any longer." Anytus laughed bitterly, showing his two missing teeth crushed by a Spartan stone in the Pylos campaign. "Why is he telling me this? The entire city knows that the ship has returned. Can't legally delay the execution! As if Callias ever lifted a finger to save Sokrates. Always the politician, that Callias. He's playing both sides."

Prodicus remained standing, glowering at his father and twirling a fig seed between his fingers. No longer did he appear intoxicated, although he had just drunk most of the wine, intended only for dipping bread.

"Is this why you came here?" asked Anytus. "To deliver this laughable message? Next time, send Pronapes or Charinades. When I want to see you, you are gone for days at a time, and when I want to be alone, as at this moment, you hound and harass me. Leave me, Prodicus. Go back to your carousing, go back to your drunken cronies. Here, here's a swallow of wine you didn't finish." Anytus kicked the silver wine cup on the floor toward his son. The shallow vessel fell over and slid across the smooth stone, trailing a thin line of red liquid, reached the edge of the north façade, and clanged down the limestone steps one at a time to the street. Then the little portico became silent again.

If only that stillness would last, thought Anytus. If only I could be left alone and in silence. I am tired of talking and of being talked to. I am tired of thinking. Anytus closed his eyes and once more began massaging his poor head. Despite his wishes, a low buzz was now rising from the direction of the market, the comingled rustlings and mutterings of perfume hawkers and olive farmers, oakum sellers and lampmakers, charcoal vendors and fishmongers all setting up their cloth-covered stalls, money changers testing out the day's rates, the tin and grain merchants, cobblers laughing disdainfully at the shoes of the first passersby. Much closer, the squeals of a pig being chased down a street, a child bawling. The City of the Owl was awakening.

Still standing in front of his father, hands on his hips in a defiant posture, Prodicus said, "How does it feel to be responsible for the death decree of the wisest and best citizen that Athens has produced? Tomorrow, you will become famous forever, at last the important man you always wanted to be."

"Leave me, Prodicus," said Anytus, his eyes still closed.

"How does it feel, Father? Father! I would rather have been sired by a goat."

"By Zeus, leave me. Pyrrhias. Pyrrhias." Anytus opened his eyes and beckoned to his servant. "Pyrrhias, please take my son out of here. Give him some drachmas and take him to the market. Take him to the cockfights. Just get him away."

Pyrrhias, who had once been forced to swallow a fistful of worms by Prodicus, took one step toward the green tunic but no more. He looked nervously at the son, then the father. As if somehow satisfying Anytus's command by mere motion, he held up his arms and stretched out his hand in front of the bright sun, which now flooded headlong into the portico and created great pools of light on the smooth limestone floor.

"I will be delighted to leave," said Prodicus to his father, "and without your dirty money. But first I want you to know something about the man you have condemned."

Anytus sighed, his tunic readjusting itself over his middle-aged paunch. "I know a great deal about your self-anointed wise man," he said softly, so as not to jostle his head more than he had to, "and he is as dangerous now as he was twenty-five years ago, before you were born. He is a rabble-rouser."

"You know little about him. This I will tell you, but only because Crito sat on me. On the walls of his prison cell, he has drawn a pictorial history of the human soul. With charcoal. I have seen it. There are thirty-nine panels, one completed each night that he has been caged in that smell hole, waiting to drink the hemlock."

"I see that I cannot prevent you from consorting with him in prison any more than I could when he was at large in the city," sighed Anytus.

"The jailor lets in anyone who wants to see him," said Prodicus tauntingly. Anytus made a mental note that he would talk to the Eleven about prison security.

"Tell me what you have seen on the walls of his cell," said the tanner, closing his eyes and resigning himself to more insults before his son would at last disappear.

"I'll tell you, but you won't understand. Sokrates has drawn what he is too modest to speak. He has revealed his true self and the selves of us all. On the floor of his cell are the gods, the cities and sea vessels of men, the battles and love affairs, the fluted adventures. A wild jumble of lines is Chaos, the origin of the world. Laughing Hephaestus splits open the headachy skull of Zeus with his bronze ax to unleash Athena, her eyes shining, her javelin ready. Our Athena, the goddess of our city." Prodicus stopped here and shot his father a look of disgust. "And to think that one of your phony charges against him was godlessness. In other panels, Prometheus mixes the soil with his tears to make the first man. Then the great Ages—the Gold, in which men were happy in their festivals and died as if slipping into sleep; the Silver, in which men became timid farmers, obeying their mothers like sheep; the Bronze, which turned men into soldiers, constantly cutting each other's throats. And finally the Iron, in which men respect neither vows nor justice nor virtue. There are lean sailors from Corinth founding the city of Syracuse, beautiful women seducing men beside rivers, gowned maidens picnicking in the shade of plane trees, colossal temples overlooking olive groves in Gela, Metapontum, Sybaris, Selinus, and other places I don't recognize. Ships carrying tin and silver from Spain, artisans sculpting from white marble. The beginning of the Great Peloponnesian War and our disgraceful Athenian defeat."

Several citizens strolled by the octagonal garden outside the portico, vaguely on their way to the market. Pausing, the young man in the green tunic looked toward them, then toward the southwest. The sun was just starting to glint off the Great Temple high on the Acropolis, at this distance a striated white pearl hovering above the rooftops of the city.

"Are you still listening?" asked Prodicus. "As splendid as it is, all that lies on the floor pales beside what resides on the ceiling. On the ceiling of the cell, standing on the shoulders of his friends to reach it, he has portrayed the souls. The great human soul, out of which all individual souls radiate and return, is a giant myrtle plant. It floats above every small and faded episode of earthly existence. It holds within its leaves the absolute good, the absolute virtue, the absolute beauty, the absolute truth. In the gradual unfolding of time, the myrtle occasionally sends a slender vine down the wall to make contact with mortal flesh, then to return. These tender shoots are the single souls of individual men. But mortal flesh can know nothing. As human events take place on the floor below, the great myrtle-soul on the ceiling barely changes. It gently sways, as if caught in some mild Elysian breeze. It beams and contains and sings like soft trumpets."

Anytus sneezed and his head resumed pounding. What were these strange words from the mouth of his crocked son?

He was startled as much by his son's extraordinary oration as by the prisoner's drawings themselves. The situation was worse than he had believed. Prodicus did not merely follow the old sophist through the dirty streets of the city. He was deeply under his spell.

"Let me ask you something," said Prodicus. "Do you believe in anything?"

"I believe in democracy."

"Democracy! Democracy? Is destroying the greatest thinker in our city democracy? No, you're not just destroying a man. You're destroying the world."

Anytus looked up from the floor, looked at his son, taller than himself by half a foot. Unexpectedly, his red itchy eyes saw not a twenty-three-year-old man but a six-year-old boy with a favorite mutt that followed him everywhere. It was a particular day, before the Sicilian Catastrophe, before the blockade. Summer. He and Pasiclea and Prodicus had gone down to the Piraeus to escape the savage heat of the city, leaving all of their servants behind. They had found a quiet cove away from the harbor, they could just see the tops of a few masts in the distance. Pasiclea prepared lunch under the shade of a plane tree, and he and his son stripped naked and dove into the water for a swim. Prodicus laughed in the coolness, then hit his head on a submerged ship's plank and went under. Suddenly, the ocean stopped, turned to stone. Anytus, wailing, pulled his child from the stone sea and carried him up the hill, cradled him unconscious in his lap, kissed his blue cheeks. An unmeasurable time later, Prodicus miraculously opened his eyes. He looked into the eyes of his father and whispered weakly, "Father, are you angry at me?" At that moment, forever etched in Anytus's mind, the sad notes of a cithara floated over from the harbor. Where had time gone? Where was that son?

Prodicus had finished speaking. He put on his sandals to leave, gathered up his drooping tunic, and threw a one-obol coin in the direction of Pyrrhias.

Anytus felt drained. He felt limp. He slowly stood up and reached toward his son. The wetness in his eyes could easily have sprung from his allergies. "Come sit here beside me," he said softly. "Your mother and I are planning a pleasure trip to Aegina next month. Will you come with us?" He looked away. "The wine is good in Aegina."

"I am occupied," said Prodicus. "Besides, the world ends tomorrow."

"Sit here with me, my son," repeated Anytus. "Please. I am your father. Haven't I taught you anything?" The tanner's head was pounding, but he ignored the pain.

For a fleeting moment, Prodicus hesitated, as if remembering something. Then his muscles tightened, the corners of his mouth became hard again. "Yes, you have taught me," he said. "You have taught me drinking and whoring."

"Can't you see what that old man has been doing to you?" Anytus shouted, his head ripping open. "He doesn't care about you. He's using you."

"He is planning an escape," said Prodicus. "And I will help him." Without uttering another word, the young man departed through the south side of the portico. The tanner sank back on the white marble bench, which was now covered with blue morning shadows, and buried his face in his hands.

He did not look up when a buck-toothed but pretty slave girl walked by the portico with two children in tow and happened to spot Anytus's slave inside. "Pyrrhias," she whispered in surprise. "What are you doing here?" Pyrrhias heard her and became agitated, turned and put his fingers to his fat lips with a pained expression on his face. She stood for a moment and looked at him longingly through the fluted columns. Then she walked on.

"Wasn't that Iphigenia who just called you from the street?" asked Anytus, without looking up.

"What, Master?"

"The young woman who just called you from the street."

Pyrrhias hesitated. "Yes. She's nothing, Master. She's of no consequence. I'm sorry she disturbed you just now."

"She's been visiting the house for six months now. Does she make you happy?"

A perplexed look overtook the slave's face. "Happy? Sometimes, when she's not screaming at me." Pyrrhias smiled, embarrassed.

The slave leaned over and began rubbing his master's shoulders, gathering flesh and letting it go. "Your son is too full of himself," Pyrrhias said softly.

Without raising his head, Anytus wrapped his hand around the back of his slave's neck, gently but firmly, and said, "Pyrrhias, you know that you are dear to me, but don't ever speak ill of my son again, even once. Do you understand me?"

"I did not mean any ill will, Master," said Pyrrhias, shaking.

Suddenly the light fled from the portico, the pools of sun on the floor evaporated. "Great Apollo," Pyrrhias exclaimed. "Clouds at this time of year?" Indeed, stony dark clouds had abruptly appeared in the sky, blocking the sun. In the distance, the Great Temple vanished as if it had never existed. Roofs turned to black slabs. On the back wall of the portico, the prancing horses and foot soldiers in the mural of Marathon faded into darkness. The tanner stared at the vanishing figures and it seemed that he, too, was fading into darkness, headed toward the fearful place. He shuddered. He put his hand under his mantle to feel his heartbeat. "Oh, most holy Artemis," he whispered toward the gray bust outside the portico, "great goddess of the hunt and destruction, bring me prosperity, for I have always honored you." Anytus held his eyes on the statue for some time, then lowered his gaze to the floor.

"I want to see Sokrates," he said finally.

Pyrrhias smiled. "You will prevent his escape, won't you," he said.

Anytus wrote something on a piece of papyrus, squinting in the low light, and spent some moments sealing it with his sardonyx seal ring. "Please take this to Xanthias of the Eleven. You might find him at the Prytaneum after the market has closed. I have requested that Sokrates be escorted into my keeping for the rest of the day. I'll be waiting for him at the tannery. Xanthias will know how to make the arrangements. And afterwards, go back to the house and tell Pasiclea that she will not see me until dinner tonight."

"Everything will be done as you wish, Master. You can trust me." Pyrrhias took the papyrus and vigorously shook his leg, which was still stiff from squatting on the stone floor.

RED WANT

STUDY QUESTIONS
· Use the Internet to find out what a cicada is and in what climates they live.
· Why would a democracy allow some people to be slaves?
· How did people send messages and communicate with each other in ancient Greece? Compare with the methods of communication today.
· Describe how Anytus and Prodicus feel about each other.
· Is Anytus superstitious? What are the gods he believes in?
· Use the BkSp key and the @ key to rewrite the opening scene of the Dialogue so that Prodicus will be happy to see his father when he first arrives in the portico.

Congratulations, Alexander Chalmers, you have just completed the first section of Anytus, from MCO's PLATO ONLINE™. Your prorated charge for this portion is only: $8.50.

As a new student in Metropolitan College Online, Alexander Chalmers, we would like to offer you a membership in Shopping US Online, at no additional charge. SUSO provides its members with an online directory of the finest stores and shopping experiences in over 100 cities in the United States. Furthermore, many items can be ordered and purchased directly online through your Shopping US Online account, at a special discount to SUSO members. Delivery on most items is within 5 business days, by UPS. Also available for you eager beavers is a 1-day delivery service by FEDEX. Here is a micro sample of our directory:

Chicago:

Olympiad Zoom 2500 Camera. Built-in 38mm zoom lens, lightweight and compact, multi-mode "red-eye" reduction flash, film speed set automatically, automatic focus and light control, optional wireless remote control. Availability and Pricing: Tarrabys, 369 W. 55th Street, 1-800-131-5867, ChiTar@SUSO.COM, $146. Cameras and Things, 26 Halsted Street, 1-800-171-0493, ChiCT@SUSO.COM, $162. Smith and Barney, 189 Foster Avenue, 1-800-152-4068, ChiSB@SUSO.COM, $138. Unit price to SUSO members: $129. For more information on SUSO, visit our website: HTTP://WWW.SUSO.COM.

>>> MAIL 50.02.04 <<< From: Fred at Noplace.Com
==> Received: from RING.AOL.COM by AOL.COM with GOTP
Orlando Vacation Give Aways, Fred@Noplace.Com

Alexander turned from the computer screen and smiled at his ultra-high-frequency Stademeir speakers, suspended on wires from the ceiling. A new tune from Red Want was playing. *Whenever you look at me, I want to have your baby, baby.* The Stademeirs swung back and forth on their wires, propelled by the acoustical thrust of 120 decibels of sound. Alex looked at his watch. It was 1:45. Yawning, he logged off the computer and went down to the kitchen to see if his mocha frappe was still intact in the refrigerator.

That night, at dinner on the screened porch, Bill could no longer conceal his numbness. To maneuver his fork, he had to grip it so tightly that his fingers turned white.

"I want you to see a doctor tomorrow," said Melissa. Why hadn't he told her earlier? she asked. Was it related to the incident on the train? Could it be from the blow to his head? She grasped for his hands and kissed them.

He didn't know what to say and stared at the delicate thinness of her wrists.

"I need to sleep," she said. "I'm going up to bed. Will you come with me?" She moved her chair back but remained at the round wicker table, carefully folding and unfolding her napkin. Overhead, the basket of pink fuchsia swayed in a puff of evening breeze.

"Melissa."

"Listen to me. When I was in college, a woman I knew started the same way as you are now. I think she had numbness in her arms and her face. Gradually, she lost everything."

"You always get crazy over these rare cases," said Bill. "I know a dozen people who had numbness for a day or two and then were fine." He paused. "I've got to get to the office tomorrow."

"Numbness can turn into paralysis." Melissa's fingers began fluttering, as if on a keyboard. "If you aren't concerned for yourself, you should at least be concerned for your family. For Alex and me."

He cupped his hand over her shoulder and leaned around to kiss her.

"No, don't look at me. I look awful." She slowly stood up and caught a glimpse of herself reflected from the rim of the silver coffee service. "I'm going to bed."

A fine mist of water drifted into the porch as the automatic sprinklers started their evening program.

WAITING ROOM

It was with a sense of extreme frustration that Bill parked his car at the Alewife Station the next morning, on his way to the Massachusetts General Hospital instead of his office in the Marbleworth Building. Only minutes earlier, Jenkins had called with an urgent message relating to the appointments rescheduled once again. "If you're not going to be at your terminal this morning, at least stay near your phone. I'm doing everything I can for you here." Bill smacked his dashboard, feeling no sensation but minutely relieved to have expressed something.

He had arrived at the Alewife well after rush hour. Nevertheless, out of habit he ran from his car for the elevators. His recovered briefcase bulged with the entirety of the Trag.dat1 file, which to the best of anyone's knowledge had never before been printed out in hard copy. Of far less weight was the slim new cellular phone in his pocket.

The train was half empty. Taking a seat, Bill found himself trembling. The last time he had boarded the subway, the world had collapsed. With some difficulty, he wrote down "MGH, Petrov at 10:30" on three pieces of paper and put one in his briefcase, placed one in his shirt pocket, and held one tightly in his hand. This safety measure brought him a small modicum of comfort, although he was still much too anxious to work. He was also exhausted. Melissa had sat up most of the night at her vanity, sleepless, a silent silhouette every time he opened his eyes in the dim light of the room.

His gaze wandered around the train, eventually fastening on the man sitting across from him. Unexpectedly, Bill felt an odd connection to this man. He appeared to be about forty, Bill's own age, with quiet blue eyes. His skin was delicate and white, even at this time of year, as if he had affairs too important to leave for a holiday in the sun. His brown hair was neither so short as to make him seem obsessively neat nor long enough to suggest someone caught up with fashion. The subtly patterned suit that he wore, probably bought at Louis, was more expensive than Bill would ever have purchased for himself, and his shoes had those little tassels that Bill despised. Those shoes alone boasted to the world that this man had already won the Big Race, had so conquered the vicissitudes of life that he could glide to his office at 10:00 or 10:30 in the morning, and he did not want to be reminded of other people's strivings and sufferings as he now read his *Wall Street Journal* with magnificent serenity.

Bill couldn't help comparing himself to this fellow. There might he be, with a different toss of the dice. He both detested this man and wanted what he had. He knew him well, had known several men like him in school. They were the ones to whom everything came easily. They were the ones who finished their homework in half the time and then set to polishing the valves of their immaculate second-hand Porsches. This fellow, Bill felt certain, had always appeared as he did now, oblivious to the storms of the world, sailing through his professional life, marriage, and family without a ruffle in his sails. Undoubtedly, he was current on all that he needed to know, he absorbed information without effort through the pores of his pale skin. If Bill's better self, sitting there six feet away, had ever momentarily fallen behind, there was no sign of it now. If he had ever slipped or been ill, no one had known. Indeed, despite the pale white of his finely chiseled face, he seemed to exude an undeniable fitness and well-being, with a stomach considerably less prominent than Bill's. He was the best modern man, always in step with the world, the embodiment of progress.

At that moment, Bill felt an impulse to fling himself from his seat and punch the other man in the nose. The fellow deserved a good vicious wallop. Maybe after being struck he would stand up and begin shouting, his delicate white skin turning pink. Then he would drop his newspaper to the dirty floor. That would be a satisfying spectacle. Bill's impulse electrified his body and stiffened his muscles, but he remained quietly in his seat, merely staring at his alter self, twisting the universe around in his mind until the train reached his stop and he had to disembark.

With a last glance over his shoulder, thinking again that he should have walloped the other man on the train, he hurried down the hot metal stairs to the street and toward the Ambulatory Care Building, which housed the offices of his physician, Dr. Armand Petrov. At 10:28, two minutes ahead of schedule, he arrived in the waiting room.

It was the same dull and miserable little room that he remembered from his visit two years ago. Saccharine arrangements of Beatles songs dripped from the corner speakers, a Xerox machine hummed behind the receptionist's desk. Only the wallpaper had changed, from a faded pale orange to a thicket of blue and green triangles. He presented his hospital card to the receptionist, who hardly glanced up from her keyboard, and claimed the one empty seat.

Bill made a quick examination of his fellow patients. One typed nervously at her laptop, another two scribbled on documents in manila folders, a man in the corner leaned over some massive report and muttered into his cell phone. Aside from one young woman, flushed and feverish, no one appeared clearly ill. However, none seemed altogether well, either, and a vague unwholesomeness hung in the air. There were half a dozen people in the room. At fifteen minutes each, that would total up to an hour and a half! Was it conceivable that they were all ahead of him? No, that couldn't be possible. In any event, he could not afford to lose time. He emptied his briefcase and began arranging his material in two piles on the floor. A woman glanced at him disapprovingly, then returned to her magazine. Most likely she was the one who stank of the acrid musk perfume. Bill pinched his nose and inspected his watch. It was 10:33.

Despite the aggressive air conditioning, the room felt stuffy and tense. At 10:35, a man leaped out of his chair and advanced upon the receptionist. "I can't wait any longer," he said. "It's ten thirty-five. I've been waiting since ten. My appointment was at ten." The receptionist nodded implacably. "I can show you," he said. With that, he yanked the appointment book away from her and stabbed his pen on the line with his name. "Does Petrov think he is the only one whose time is valuable? I've got crucial other business this morning. I want to see Dr. Petrov immediately."

The receptionist retreated a few paces and whispered something to an assistant behind her. "I'm sorry," she said, returning to the front desk. "Dr. Petrov is busy with another patient at the moment. We'll call you when it's your turn. Would you like me to reschedule your appointment?"

"Reschedule!" the man shrieked. "So that I can waste another half-day waiting?" He studied his watch. "I'll tell you what. I'm going outside in the corridor to make some telephone calls. I want to be notified when Petrov is ready for me." He strode to the door, rotated around as if recalculating his strategies, then vacated the room. His announcements created a certain added distress in the rest of Dr. Petrov's patients, who fidgeted with their papers and consulted their own timepieces.

"My appointment was also ten," ventured the woman with the laptop. She half rose from her chair, seemingly unsure about whether to press her case forward or return to her work, and she cast a quick look toward Bill as if pleading for his moral support.

"I'm sorry," said the receptionist. "Dr. Petrov is running behind this morning."

"I will have to leave at 10:45," said the woman, again examining her watch. She was dressed stylishly in a beige silk blouse, black pants, and black heels. "Can I receive a fax here while I'm waiting?"

"I'm sorry," said the receptionist. "We don't have fax service for our patients." From somewhere behind her, the assistant whispered something and the receptionist stifled a laugh.

"You are mocking me," said the woman with the laptop, and she glanced again at Bill, who could only shrug his shoulders helplessly. Why was she asking for his assistance? The fax machine was not his problem. People en route should not be dependent on fax machines. He tried to ignore her and looked down at his papers, but her outburst had upset him, and she continued talking to the receptionist, this time in a more uncertain voice. "It would not at all be unreasonable for you to offer fax service to your patients," she said, "especially when you keep us waiting so long. I happen to need some important information to continue what I am doing. Everyone else offers fax service. Hotels offer fax service."

"Maybe you should walk over to the Holiday Inn across the street," blurted the invisible assistant, and she released a loud guffaw. The receptionist was dying to laugh. Instead, she turned around and whispered a few words of admonition to the assistant.

"I know that you have a fax machine," said the woman with

the laptop. "I saw it when I came in. It's on the desk of that woman behind you."

"That machine is for the private use of the office," said the receptionist. Immediately, she walked back to the assistant's desk and turned off the fax machine.

A nurse appeared in the reception area with a handful of glass tubes. She whispered something to the receptionist, who let out a small cry and began typing rapidly on her keyboard. "What in the world! He can't really want that." "That's what I thought, but what do we know." "This is a pain." "You're telling me." The two of them stood at the receptionist's terminal, shaking their heads with annoyance. Then the nurse dashed off. A back door slammed. Abruptly, she returned and began hunting around the reception area, feeling around in drawers with her hands as if she had misplaced some small object. Again, she vanished.

"I'll be back," said the woman with the laptop, and she hurried out of the office, scowling a last time at Bill. How could he possibly work with so much commotion? He hated doctors' offices. How much time had he wasted so far? It was 10:45. He stared at his papers on the floor, dismayed to see that they'd gotten out of order, and spent several minutes rearranging the correspondence by date before beginning to read.

"Is this your first visit?" suddenly asked a short, balding man in the next seat. His blue blazer strained at its brass buttons. "I haven't seen you here before." Bill tried to ignore him, but the man seemed unusually agitated, continually adjusting his glasses and rubbing his head.

"A real operation they have here," continued the man in the blue blazer, raising his voice just enough so that everyone could overhear him. "Someone should call the AMA, or maybe the Better Business Bureau. If I were you, I'd change physicians." At that moment his telephone rang. For several

minutes, he gave instructions to some subordinate on the
other end of the line, repeatedly referring to his watch, then
shoved the instrument into his coat pocket as if it caused him
great suffering. He leaned closer, so close that Bill could
smell a trace of cleaning detergent in his shirt. "So what's
wrong with you?"

"I'd rather not say," said Bill. People were so pushy and
obnoxious in doctors' offices, he thought to himself.

"Well, I will tell you something, my friend. A word from
the wise. Today is my sixth visit in three months, and Herr
Doctor Petrov still hasn't offered me any diagnosis. Do you
have time for that? I certainly do not."

Bill put down his papers with alarm. In fact, he knew very
little about Petrov. He saw the physician once every few
years, and on those occasions only for brief routine checkups.
How had he been recommended to Petrov in the first place?
he suddenly wondered. It struck him that he should have
thoroughly investigated Petrov's credentials long ago. Bill
guardedly introduced himself.

The other man's hand was swollen and clammy. "Morton
Bineas," he said. "Let me not pry, Mr. Chalmers. Keep your
illness to yourself." Bill shifted uncomfortably in his chair,
again cursing himself for waiting so long to investigate Petrov.
Bineas smiled, observing that he had found an appreciative
audience, and continued. "On my last visit, a month ago Tuesday, Dr. Petrov hinted to me that he might be ready to proceed to a provisional diagnosis, also called the diagnosis pro
tem. But then, just when I was leaving his office, he ordered
another group of tests." Bineas began coughing strenuously,
to the uneasy glances of the other patients, and the receptionist's assistant brought him a tiny paper cup of water. He
tossed it down with a look of embarrassment and asked for
two more. After a few moments, he continued, hoarsely. "I

once heard that when Petrov was a young physician, years ago, he occasionally made definite diagnoses, and these were often quite correct. But with the vast increase in medical technology, and with it so many new considerations to take into account, he's limited himself to what I've mentioned."

"I've got to be treated right away," said Bill, becoming angry. "I was actually hoping to be treated today. I've already lost two days of work."

"Two days? Two days?" said Bineas in mock sympathy. "You should complain. I've lost two weeks. And I'm vice president of accounting at Boston Chowder." He let out a long breath and sank back into his chair. His face softened. "Since Christmas, I've been tired all the time. It has something to do with my illness. And this terrible cough."

Bill glanced gloomily around the room, wondering about the various stages of diagnoses of Dr. Petrov's other patients. Bineas seemed to read his mind, for he said, with a wave of his hand, "No one in this room has advanced to a diagnosis pro tem, let alone a final diagnosis, I can assure you. However, I have heard that some of Petrov's patients have indeed been treated, and some fraction of those have recovered completely."

At that moment, the door to the back rooms was flung open and a patient emerged, appearing forlorn. He hesitated in front of the receptionist, as if trying to remember something, and then hurried out the front door. For a second, Bill caught a brief glimpse down the inner hall. Dr. Petrov, a small man with a small red beard, could be seen dashing from the examination room to his private office, with a nurse running after him and another patient standing half-dressed and confused in the hall. Petrov's door slammed shut, answered by the door to the waiting room.

At the departure of the last patient, the receptionist sang out the name of the woman in the musk perfume, who hurled down her magazine with a loud "Finally" and followed a nurse. It was 11:09.

"That woman," said Bineas, nodding his head knowledgably, "I've seen her here before. She believes that she has intermittent cystitis, so she's been drinking gallons of cranberry juice. But she could equally well have a small bladder tumor, or possibly inflammation of the kidneys. I happen to know that she was in line for a diagnosis pro tem three weeks ago, but Petrov was unwilling to write it down on her chart. Have you ever heard of such a crock of baloney!"

"But why do you put up with all this, Mr. Bineas?"

"Good question," said Bineas, rubbing his head. "I would have kissed Petrov goodbye long ago, but my insurance would stop covering me."

"Yes, I understand," said Bill. "The insurance companies have us over a barrel." He looked again at his watch to discover that he had already invested three-quarters of an hour waiting for Dr. Petrov.

One of the nurses who had appeared earlier entered the waiting room. However, she no longer wore her white nurse's uniform but was dressed in a smart pair of khaki pants and a blue cotton blouse. "That's Genevieve," whispered Bineas. "She won't be back until after lunch. Genevieve is quite competent, but she wants to work at the Colonial Theatre. Am I boring you, Mr. Chalmers? I must be interrupting your work. I saw you working there a few minutes ago. I should be working too, I have many phone calls to make."

"No, please," said Bill. "I'm grateful for everything you've told me. I want to know what to expect. I gather that you must have a provisional diagnosis at this time?"

Bineas rolled his eyes. "That's confidential," he muttered and turned away in his chair without further comment. He took out a pen and began writing in a crimson notebook.

"I'm sorry," said Bill to the other man's back. "I shouldn't have asked." Bineas made no reply.

After a few minutes, Bineas put away his book and turned back to face Bill. "Okay," he said in a resigned voice. "I could have lupus. It's very rare in men. So far, Dr. Petrov has been willing to rule out arthritis, fibromyalgia, and polymyositis. Chronic fatigue syndrome is another possibility."

"You seem to have learned a fair amount about your illness," said Bill.

"I have, I have," said Bineas. "But not all thanks to Petrov. I've also been getting tips from another physician who I've been visiting on the side and paying out of my own pocket. He charges much less than Petrov. There's a possibility that he might see you as well. He takes calls after eight in the evening."

"Has he diagnosed you?" asked Bill.

"Twice. Neither of the diagnoses was of much help, but he's provided me with some insight, as well as with several articles to read. Here, I'll give you his name and address." Bineas scribbled down a name and telephone number on a little white slip.

"Oh," said Bineas, after noticing Chalmers's clumsiness in grasping the scrap of paper. "I see that you're having trouble with your fine motor coordination."

"My fingers are numb," Bill said. He slapped his hands viciously against the center table.

"Anything else numb?"

"Both hands and arms."

"I see," said Bineas, shaking his head gravely. "You are quite right to see a doctor."

"What do you think I have?" asked Bill.

"You could have a pinched nerve. Or possibly some kind of tumor or disease. But we laymen can only guess at these things."

Just at that moment the receptionist called out Bineas's name. He stiffened, then visibly sagged, like an animal taking a bullet. Avoiding Bill's eyes, he gathered up his papers and meekly followed the nurse.

When Bineas was gone, Bill again surveyed the room and was surprised to discover that everyone who had been waiting earlier was now gone, and a completely new group of patients sat in the dingy chairs, nervously pursuing their activities. Neither the man who had stepped outside to make calls nor the woman with the laptop had returned. Bill sighed and returned to the Trag.dat1 file, estimating that he had glanced through the first 1 percent in half an hour. Times a hundred would take fifty hours of reading.

A few minutes later, his name was called. He looked at his watch. It was 11:45. A nurse appeared with a brisk but affable manner, as if all were on schedule. "You should bring your briefcase with you, Mr. Chalmers," she chirped. "You may not be coming back through the waiting room."

"Do you realize that I've been waiting for over an hour?" said Bill angrily.

The nurse didn't reply but led Bill down the same corridor that he had glimpsed earlier. In the middle of the hall, they turned into an examination room. Here, the nurse asked him a battery of questions about his general health and recent symptoms, took his temperature, weight, height, heart rate, and blood pressure. "Very good," she suddenly said without explanation. She washed her hands quickly with some liquid that evaporated instantly. "Dr. Petrov will be with you shortly. Just slip out of your clothes so you'll be ready for the doctor."

Bill had always disliked undressing in the examination room. While waiting in his underpants, he never knew whether to sit on the examination table, like a laboratory specimen, or in a chair with his legs casually crossed, like a guest. Maybe he should simply stand barefoot on the cold floor, crouching and on guard. At any moment, the door could be thrown open, exposing him to the nurses or to other patients. Should he drape his shirt over himself? Could he work? As he was pondering this familiar quandary, his phone rang in his briefcase.

"Where are you?" said Jenkins. "I hear doctor's office music in the background."

"That's none of your business, Robert," said Bill. "Please get to the point." He was beginning to find Jenkins too cheeky for his own good. Didn't the man have any sense of propriety? Evidently, Jenkins felt he could take liberties now that Bill was in a precarious position at the office.

There was a superior silence on the other end of the line. Finally, Jenkins said: "Your appointment with Fred Loeser has been rescheduled for 2:30 this afternoon. And I thought you should know that Mr. Linden is walking around the office bragging about some kind of deal with a Mr. Olswanger that was apparently supposed to be yours."

"I can't believe it," Bill shouted into the telephone. He sat down on the red vinyl chair, which felt too cold and too intimate through his thin jockey shorts.

Jenkins's voice: "I would strongly advise that you attend Monday's staff meeting in Mr. Hamilton's office."

"Thank you for your advice, Robert." He slammed the phone shut and returned glumly to the examination table. He had to get back to the office immediately. How long had he been waiting in this awful little closet? Thirteen minutes.

Suddenly there was a knock and the door opened and closed. Dr. Petrov was in the room, flying about and talking in a blur, small silver instruments dangling from his pockets. The doctor immediately set to work hammering different parts of Bill's body. When did the numbness begin? Any weakness in the hands or arms? Had he been suffering from headaches? Any trouble with vision? Was his appetite strong? "I'll be right back." The doctor vanished.

Bill waited. After a few minutes, he rose warily from the examination table. Still grasping his cellular phone, he put his ear to the closed door. He could hear people running down the hall, a toilet flushing, some unidentifiable buzzing sound. He waited a few minutes more, then returned to the examination table. Something hissed, like gas escaping from a tank. Where was the doctor? Petrov had run from the room so very suddenly. Possibly he had been alarmed by what he had seen and needed to consult with other physicians. Bill tried to remember whether Petrov had appeared concerned. Now that he thought of it, the physician's face did seem pinched and tight. Could he have gone out to instruct the receptionist to call Melissa with bad news? Or to gather more instruments for an additional examination? Bill crossed and uncrossed his legs and began shredding the silly white paper that covered the examination table. After another few minutes, he cracked the door and poked his head out, shielding the rest of his body. The hallway was empty. Eventually, he spotted a nurse coming out of a room. "Nurse," he called down the hall. She looked up. "What happened to Dr. Petrov? He said he was coming right back."

"Dr. Petrov is waiting for you in his private office," said the nurse.

"Do you mean I can see him right now?"

"Certainly. His office is at the end of the hall."

"I should go like this, in my underwear?"

"No, of course not in your underwear. Put on your clothes first."

When Bill entered the doctor's office, it appeared empty. The room was quite still and there was no one at the desk, which was piled to the height of a man's shoulders with papers and journals. Indeed, reports of various kinds covered nearly every horizontal surface, including the three chairs, the coffee table, and the length of the baseboard heater winding around the walls. All the documents were arranged in neat stacks, each labeled with a small yellow tab, giving the appearance of an archive in the process of reorganization by a librarian. A single window looked out on a concrete parking garage across the street. Bill was just about to call again for the nurse when he heard a little cough from behind the desk. Peering around a stack of lab reports, he found himself gazing down at the head of Dr. Petrov. He gave a start, then was further surprised to comprehend, from this unusual perspective, that Petrov wore a toupee. It was immaculately combed and gave itself away only where it joined his reddish sideburns.

"I'm sorry, Doctor, I didn't see you," said Bill, quickly backing away.

"No problem," said Petrov. The doctor coughed again and swallowed a small pink pill with a glass of water. "Take a seat, Mr. Chalmers. We will talk." The doctor remained at his desk.

Bill hesitated, not certain where he should go, then cleared off one of the vinyl chairs and carefully relocated the papers on top of another stack of papers, aligning the columns of yellow tabs. Unfortunately, from this vantage Dr. Petrov was completely invisible. Bill sighed and sat down. Now he was being treated worse than a laboratory specimen—he was being ignored. He would not stand for it. Letting his eyes roam about the room, he noticed at once the various diplomas hanging prominently on the wall. He thought of his own diploma in a box in the basement, his useless degree in history from a sleepy college he chose to forget. Twisting around in his chair, he strained to read the fancy lettering of Petrov's diplomas, where the man had attended medical school, where he had taken his internship and residency. But Bill couldn't read the print and instead began counting the pharmaceutical samples on the bookshelf.

"At this point," came a hidden voice from behind the stacks, "I'm afraid to say that we understand very little about your difficulty. It could be many things, some minor, some not minor. Some illnesses disappear on their own. We'll need to run tests." A buzzer went off. "Not now, I'm with someone. . . . Yes, I'm logged on, you can do that. . . . Five or ten minutes." There was a click. "We will begin some tests."

"Are you talking to me?" said Bill. He stood up in an attempt to see over the mounds of papers.

"Yes."

"What kind of tests?"

"I will order an MRI immediately," said Petrov. "Depending on the results of those tests, we might proceed further with a CT scan, a myelogram, some blood work, or even a biopsy if it's warranted."

"What do you think the problem is?"

The doctor didn't answer. Instead, a soft clicking noise came from behind the desk, as if he were typing at his keyboard.

"Dr. Petrov?"

"Yes."

"You're doing tests for some reason. What do you think is my problem?"

"Please, Mr. Chalmers," came the invisible voice. "I would only be speculating. There is so much to learn. We should now just be gathering information and ruling things out. Your eyes are a bit glassy. You have numbness. It could be any number of things. We begin by ruling things out."

"Like what?" Petrov was silent. "What should we be ruling out?"

A sigh came from behind the desk. "You must understand," said the doctor, "that anything I say now is only a possibility.

Some possibilities have greater or lesser probability, none of which we can know at this time." He paused and coughed. "Numbness can be caused by a metabolic deficiency, such as lack of sufficient vitamin B-12. Numbness can also be caused by lead poisoning, or a viral infection. You could have something very rare, such as leprosy."

"Leprosy!" Bill shouted. Hadn't leprosy disappeared in the thirteenth century? Would he have to be quarantined, dragged from his home in Lexington to God knows where? "What's the MRI test?"

"Magnetic resonance imaging," said Petrov, his voice taking on an intensity. "MRI is a relatively recent technique that uses short bursts of powerful radio waves and magnetic fields to get the patient's hydrogen atoms to emit other radio signals. Next time you come, I'll show you some of the images from the MRI. They are really splendid. With MRI we can get high-resolution pictures of tumors or plaques in the spinal cord and brain." Now Bill could hear an unmistakable clicking from behind the desk. "You could have multiple sclerosis, which involves a disintegration of the myelin sheath around the spinal cord and nerves. Is there any history of multiple sclerosis in your family, Mr. Chalmers?"

Despite his irritation with the doctor, upon hearing for the first time a list of possible problems, all of them sounding serious, Bill grew more frightened than he'd been at any time during the past twenty-four hours. "Oh my God," he muttered.

"I believe I've unnecessarily distressed you, Mr. Chalmers. We really know practically nothing about your difficulty at this time. That is why I don't like to give possibilities. But you pressed me. Didn't you."

Papers rustled behind Petrov's desk. Perhaps he was taking notes. "I understand from your chart that the numbness began about two days ago," said the doctor, "and it was accompanied by an initial loss of memory."

"Is that significant?"

"It could be significant," said the doctor. "On the other hand, it might not be significant."

"Significant or not significant?" Bill shouted and stood up. "I've been here since ten-thirty! When can I be treated? I came here to be treated!"

"Treatment?" said Petrov, without raising his voice. "Why certainly, we will begin treatment, as soon as we have a diagnosis. We have much to learn about this illness of yours. Do you have any other questions?" There was the sound of a chair being moved. The doctor was rising. He stared for a few moments at the stack of papers that Bill had moved. Then he smiled at Bill and touched him lightly on the shoulder and mumbled something about illnesses in the abstract.

"I have to get back to my office," said Bill. "I have a wife and a son."

"Good," said the doctor. "We will work together toward your speedy recovery. Let me show you out." As Bill entered the hallway, he passed another patient, looking distraught. Muffled thumps came from the two examination rooms. "You can call tomorrow to get the exact date and time of your MRI," said Petrov. Bill ran down the hall. He did not look back, but hurried through the waiting room, to the elevator, and out to the street. It was 12:45. Not even bothering with the subway, he leaped into the first taxi at the Emergency circle and shouted to the driver to head for the Marbleworth Building.

TAXI

As the cab navigated its way around blinking ambulances, Bill made a hasty call to Plymouth, to inform Jenkins of his imminent arrival, then sat back uncomfortably in his seat. The taxi lacked air conditioning, and the sun was exploding in the sky. "Which way you want to go?" said the driver, who was soaked in sweat. "We can go direct by Cambridge Street or loop around Storrow and Ninety-three. Makes no difference to me."

"The fastest way," said Bill, squirming out of his jacket.

"You got it."

They turned onto Cambridge Street and were immediately swallowed in a thick molasses of lunch-hour traffic. At once, Bill gagged. Squinting through the bright metallic heat, he saw a cloud of soot and exhaust trapped over the stalled autos. There should be some kind of pollution control, he said to himself and inhaled through his handkerchief. The taxi came to a dead stop, then crept along for three feet, then abruptly stopped again, nudging the rear bumper of a Toyota. A hundred automobile horns screeched in the sweltering air. It was useless, but the motorists did not stop honking at each other, inching along, stopping and starting, stopping and starting, radios blaring through open windows. Bill threw his hands over his ears. A number of travelers, evidently unable to wait, had leaped from their taxis and ran along the sidewalk, clutching their briefcases and shouting into their phones. Bill considered doing the same, and he began making estimates of the time differentials. Up ahead, a woman stuck her head out of her window and yelled profanities at the vehicle in front of her. A half-eaten ice cream lay melting on the hood of her car. "Summer in the city," the taxi driver said and turned on his radio. "What did you say?" shouted Bill.

His phone rang. "I've been trying to reach you," said Melissa. "What happened? What did the doctor say?" "He doesn't know anything," Bill shouted through his handkerchief, covering one ear. "He's going to run some tests." "I can't hear you," said Melissa. "Please come home." "I can't come home, I'm on my way to Plymouth." "What? I can't hear you. I called Henry to get the names of some good neurologists." "Henry!" "I really think we could use Henry's help." "I can take care of this myself. I don't need Henry. I don't want Henry."

Bill tried to undo his tie with his numb fingers but could succeed only in loosening it. He stared at his hands, still in disbelief at the rejection by his own body. He felt betrayed. What were his hands? Were they not part of him, more muscle and nerve and flesh? With these hands he had thrown baseballs, with these hands he had held Alex when he was a baby, tied and untied his shoes. He had lived with his hands for forty years. He loved his hands. Why had they stopped loving him? He jabbed his left hand with his pen, drawing blood, and felt nothing. Let him at least feel pain, he wanted to feel pain. His hands were denying him even pain. He jabbed himself again. The blood mixed with perspiration, turned the color of rosé wine, and trickled over his palm. He blotted the blood with his handkerchief, then wiped the dripping perspiration from his face. He was only forty years old. His father had died at age sixty-eight. People were supposed to live longer and better. Wasn't that the point of medical science? He was entitled to live longer than his father, he should have at least twenty-eight years left. And his father had gone so easily, with a sudden heart attack at his office, dead by the time he had slid from his chair to the carpet. That was the way Bill wanted to go, but several decades from now. The coward Petrov, hiding behind his mountain of paper, had suggested that he might have a tumor. That miserable physician had suspected a tumor from the beginning, Bill felt sure of it. Why hadn't he said so directly? How could Bill have a tumor? No one in his family had ever had a tumor. Tumors were usually cancerous. Tumor. The word sounded ugly and blunt, like a small heavy black gun pressed against the side of his head. It now struck Bill that Petrov had asked very few questions, considering the circumstances, a good reason to dismiss anything he said.

With a nervous twitch of his arm, Bill wiped more perspiration from his face. He had to stop thinking about his medical problem, it was wasted effort until tests could be run. To get his mind on something else, he gazed purposefully out the window, to discover that his taxi had advanced to the middle of Court Street. Diners sat under the outdoor striped canopies of Maison Robert, eating and talking into their phones. Again wiping his forehead with his useless handkerchief, Bill began mentally composing a message to Jasper Olswanger, conciliatory and forceful at the same time. Yes, he would be happy to work with Olswanger on the Teneco ChicagoCorp new products line. That spiteful worm Nate Linden—trying to worm in on his projects and beat him for promotion—he would deal with later.

A new barrage of honking and shouting roused Bill from his thoughts. Peering again from his taxi, he saw that some pudgy children had managed to wrench open a fire hydrant and were dancing happily in the sudden fountain. The water gushed forth in a giant arch, splashing nearby cars and shop windows, flooding the sidewalk and street. Steam rose from the burning pavement. In the distance a fire engine started to wail. Meanwhile other children joined in, hollering and drenching themselves. Discarded shoes floated in the gutters. Passersby on the crowded sidewalk stopped for a moment, as if briefly considering that they too might fling off their shoes and jump in the water, but they hurried on. It was 1:10. As his taxi crept past the fountain, Bill held out his hand and was rewarded with a few drops.

Now, the car began squeezing through the crooked streets of the financial district, where older, three-story brick buildings alternated with modern skyscrapers and people rushed along the hot pavement with even greater urgency. Finally, Bill's taxi stopped at the corner of Milk and Pearl. There, soaring some forty-three stories into space and towering over the tiny plaza below, was the Marbleworth Building. Although huge, it curved and it hovered. Its tinted glass reflected the sky. Bill always knew when he had arrived at the Marbleworth, even without looking up, for a section of the rude concrete sidewalk in front of the building had been replaced with pink marble. That marble was scrubbed once a day by the same uniformed porter who scrupulously tended the two white mandevillas in painted fiberglass urns by the revolving glass doors.

By now, Bill was a wet rag of sweat. He dashed past the white mandevillas and into the air-conditioned lobby, where the terrible marble clock over the revolving glass doors proclaimed 1:17. So much time had been lost. Yet he was much too bedraggled to take the elevator immediately to his office on the forty-second floor. What was the quickest route to the restrooms? He quickly surveyed the crowded lobby, surprised as always by the huge portrait of Edward Marbleworth floating like a museum banner above the reception desk. Bill had never met Edward Marbleworth, who had made sixty million in the computer software trade by his thirty-fifth birthday and then turned that into three billion in the communications industry. In fact, Mr. Marbleworth had never set foot in his building. However, every Christmas, Bill and the other 326 tenants received a personally addressed e-mail greeting from him, sent over the Internet. The next moment, Bill was jostled from behind as a half-dozen executives shoved through the revolving doors and hurried to the elevators. He jumped out of the way, then walked rapidly past the marble benches to the men's room and began blotting his face and underarms with toilet paper.

AT THE OFFICE

A few minutes later, Bill stepped off the elevator at the forty-second floor and staggered back in horror. The entire Plymouth staff was gathered in an anxious knot by the elevator. Leslie, the most sentimental in the firm, immediately leaped forward and hugged him. "What?" he muttered softly to her. Dolores strode from the communications room with a bottle of champagne and a computer-printed sign that said "Welcome Back Bill, We Know You Kicked Butt." "Yes sir," someone said. "You look great, Bill." Bodies lunged forward to greet him.

In front was George Mitrakis, president of the firm, beaming among his happy family. George was a big and loose man who never quite had the air of running a company, or anything else. He swung in his new Armani suit and guffawed and patted Bill on the back. "This was all Diane's idea," he whispered, trying to give Bill a glass of chardonnay. "I believe she's in the ladies' room at the moment but will be out shortly."

"Diane?" said Bill, attempting to take stock. Was he gripping George's hand too tightly or not tightly enough? He recalled from the past that the president's handshake ended generously, with a tentative foundering at first. Bill stared ridiculously at his hand, trying to gauge pressure from the flush of his fingers. He chatted briefly with George, insensible to what he was saying. Next came Lisa Theroux, the prominent transaction specialist. Bill knew that it would be impossible to grip her hand too forcefully, as she prided herself on her level of testosterone, so he clamped down for all he was worth. She winced quietly and smiled. Milt Kramer's handshake was notoriously phlegmatic. Remembering that, Bill simply placed his hand in Milt's and let his fingers go limp. "I've never known anyone who was mugged before," said Milt with an admiring grin on his face. Milt was the firm's specialist in information acquisition and dispersal and began saying something to Bill about the new satellite hookup. Diane's was a quick nervous twitch, over before it began. She had just emerged from the ladies' room, looking brilliant and emaciated as usual. Had the mugger gotten his credit cards, she asked between swallows of crackers and Limburger cheese. No? She couldn't hide her disappointment. What a relief, she said, her credit cards had been lost once and it was like death. From near the reception area Robert pantomimed some message for Bill. What was it? Yes, the appointment with Fred Loeser at 2:30. Bill looked at his watch. It was 1:32. Milt Kramer, having disappeared momentarily to everyone's notice, was now whining to a maid in the corridor. "You didn't touch anything on my work table, did you?" "No sir." "My office is the second from the end." "Yes sir." "What's your name?" At that, the cleaning lady fled down the hallway with her bag of trash, casting a frightened look over her shoulder.

"The office hasn't been the same without you, Bill," said Harvey Stumm. The vice president was suddenly beside him, dressed in a gray pinstriped suit, smiling with his small chalky face. Stumm held a glass of red wine, untouched. "I was gone only two days," said Bill. He stiffened, as he always did with Harvey Stumm. He could feel Stumm's eyes crawling up and down his body, examining and analyzing him. "We worried about you," said Stumm. The vice president made some polite conversation and walked to the reception desk.

Bill glanced at his watch: 1:36. Astoundingly, none of his colleagues had yet returned to their offices, even though it was prime time for working the West Coast. But he could see the beginnings of strain. Milt Kramer stood near the reception desk, seemingly casual but repeatedly looking toward the fax machine in the communications room. George and Harv were talking to each other in a corner while Lisa attempted to overhear. Every few moments she reached up to smooth her Chanel suit, glancing at her watch as she did so.

The other junior partners, Diane and Nate and Sidney, huddled in a tight group by the cheese tray. As Bill's eyes fell upon them, Nate turned toward him and silently held up six fingers, with the well-understood meaning that he had slept only six hours, working the rest of the night from his modem at home. Sidney noted the gesture, snorted, and held out five fingers. What pettiness, what childishness, Bill thought to himself. And to think that just a short time ago, he was just like them, fiercely competing for promotion, obsessed with squeezing work from each minute of the day, backbiting and jealous and petty. Now, with just the mere separation of ten feet, he could see that he was not one of them at all. Larger things ruled life. Promotion was a fine thing, and he certainly wanted his promotion, but . . . In this particular instance, for example, at this moment, he must not think about the backlog of messages waiting for him at his desk. He glanced again at the clock: 1:40.

People were starting to pace now, to openly examine their watches or the clock over the elevator. David Hamilton, who had been speaking on his cellular phone for the last ten minutes, looked meaningfully at Bill and lofted his index finger in a "one minute and I'll be with you" sign. This tiny movement broke the dam. "If David's doing business," muttered Lisa, "then so am I," and she fled down the hall to her terminal. Dolores ran after her with a fax document that she had been hiding in her purse. Immediately, John, the president's secretary, delivered a slip of paper to the boss. Grimacing, George, too, disappeared around the corner to his office. Now the junior partners began heavy fidgeting and glancing. Were they expected to remain in the reception, or get back to their keyboards? Diane left first, avoiding eye contact. Nate stared down the hallway where she had vanished into her office, undoubtedly about to send important e-mails to the West Coast. He looked over at Bill. He glanced at Harvey Stumm, always impossible to read. Then at David Hamilton, still on his phone, slyly being two places at once. Suddenly Nate tossed aside his plastic wineglass and broke for his office. Sidney Wolfson, a graduate of Harvard and Wharton, followed instantly.

"We've got to talk," Milt Kramer said to David Hamilton, who had finally closed up his phone. "About the Sperry deal."

"I don't have time to talk," said Hamilton. "Send me an e-mail."

"I've been sending you e-mails all day," said Kramer.

"I've been tied up with that shithead at Grace."

"Can we talk now?" asked Kramer.

"Send me an e-mail. I've got to answer some messages from Lisa and Harv. Then I'll answer yours." Without further conversation, both men hurried off to their terminals and closed their doors behind them.

At last, the reception area was empty. It was 1:42. Bill walked rapidly down the empty hall to his office and closed the door. As he moved toward his desk, he was unexpectedly caught by a wave of brooding. Surely, in all of those dead handshakes, someone had noticed. His colleagues surely must have detected his problem. It now struck him that George had looked at him just one beat too long as they shook hands. Bill replayed the scene in his mind. The president had walked up, suntanned and beaming, said something to Leslie, laughed, patted Bill on the back. Then gazed at him straight in the eye. Yes, Bill was certain of it. George had stared at him one beat too long. He had sniffed weakness. Not only physical defect, but incapacity, an ultimate inability to catch everything thrown at him. George had perceived incapacity. And could he be blamed? Was it not his job to ensure that Plymouth operated at maximum efficiency, processed the maximum information in the minimum time? George was a bumbler, but he was shrewd. A person would have to be shrewd to have foreseen the 1994 plummet of the peso. From now on, he would be watching Bill closely, possibly promoting the other junior partners one by one until Bill was the only junior left, a zero in the office. And the president had acted so cordially, smiling and offering him a glass of wine. What a snake! Bill had always suspected that George Mitrakis was not nearly so innocent and good-natured as he seemed. In fact, he was probably even more cunning than Harvey Stumm. Harv, so careful to conceal his suspicions, had barely glanced at Bill after the first greeting and once-over. Harv would be watching him from behind his back. Even Leslie, sweet Leslie. Now that Bill thought of it, there was a peculiarity in the way she had smiled at him, an overwroughtness, a tender pity. Secretaries were like cats. Secretaries had the most acute sense of the changing vibrations in the office—who was getting ahead and who was falling behind. Leslie had known.

With a worried sigh, Bill sat down at his desk. The room had an odd unfamiliarity, as if he had been absent for months. Something seemed different. The furniture hadn't been moved, he quickly confirmed. The carpet gave easily under his feet. It wasn't a smell. No, there was something else, possibly a sound. He held very still, and he listened. Between the tiny, intermittent honks of cars far below and the occasional thumps from the health club overhead, he heard the squeals of the fax machine down the hall, voices on telephones in neighboring offices, chairs shifting. Somewhere, muffled as if deep underground, a clock ticked. No, there was some other sound, low and steady underneath. Listening more intently, crouching motionless against the wall, he could hear the wheeze of the motors in the elevator shafts, the breathy flow of the air-conditioning system. The fax machine screeched again and he waited, as if letting his eyes recover from a flash of bright light. He waited until he again heard the faint sounds of the elevator and the air. Then these, too, momentarily subsided, and he could hear beneath them even fainter sounds. The motor of the refrigerator in the communications room. The soft undulations of his computer screen, microscopic waves on a microscopic sea. He switched off the computer, held his head still and continued to listen, and he could hear the tiny whine of the fluorescent lights, like the vibrations of ten thousand minuscule tuning forks. He listened and listened, and the vibrations decelerated in his mind, going slower and slower, descending in pitch, until he could hear each one coming after the other, dissected, atoms dropping to the floor. He turned off the lights, the atoms stopped. In the dark, in the dark there was still something else, even fainter, but steady, something steady and faint. What was it? Straining to hear, he held his breath. Some dim, residual sound below everything else. A hum.

His phone rang, then stopped, picked up by Amy. Two messages marked urgent dangled from his terminal screen. "Fred Loeser at TEM has sent over a report he wants you to read before your meeting —Amy." Bill looked at his watch. 1:48. Loeser would arrive in forty-two minutes. The second message: "The new satellite feed has overloaded the commu-

nications room. None of the documents given to Leslie after 11:00 a.m. this morning have gone out. Everybody is on
his/her own for now. I'm working on it. —Milt." Bill logged
on for a quick look at his e-mail before trying to excavate the
TEM report.

```
>>> MAIL 50.02.04 <<< From: Stumm at PLYM.COM
====> Received: from BUSTER.INTER.COM by INTER.COM with
NIO
id AQ06498; Fri, 27 Jun 7:49:36 EDT
for WCHALM@PLYM.COM; Fri, 27 June 7:49:42 -0400
Press * for message
```



```
>>> MAIL 50.02.04 <<< From: Stumm at PLYM.COM
Dear Bill,
Wasn't sure when you were getting in today. Id like
your help with the Sperry situaiton. We're close to a
deal. Please find out what kind of dealings Benjamin
Lloyd has had with American pharmaceutical cpmpanies.
I'd like something by noonn Monday, if possible. Thank
you.
Harv
```

```
>>> MAIL 50.02.04 <<< From: ACHALM at AOL.COM
==> Received: from RING.NET.COM by NET.COM with GOTP
id AQ06498; Fri, 27 Jun 9:02:13 EDT
for WCHALM@PLYM.COM; Fri, 27 Jun 9:02:41 -0400
Press * for message
```

>>> MAIL 50.02.04 <<< From: Alexander at AOL.COM
Dear Lancelot du Lac and sire,
Sir Tabor said I have a natural ift with the sword and
should joust in the first levels of the Middlesex
REgiohanl tourney, on September 24. (I did not tell him
my father was Lancelot.) Can you come? Please? Besides
the art of swroadshmanship, I will need grooming in the
fineries of chivalry, so that I might honor your legend
and uphold the family name. I eave that yht you. What
time are you returning to the castle-keep this eve?
Could you return early? I have to be off with the knave
Brad at 6:30. I await tyour relply.
Your faithful son, Galahad

_____

_____

>>> MAIL 50.02.04 <<< From: JTOOTH at GWAY.COM
====> Received: from HAL.NET.COM by NET.COM with THL
id AQ06498; Fri, 27 Jun 9:12:03 EDT
for WCHALM@PLYM.COM; Fri, 27 Jun 9:12:07 -0400
Press * for message

>>> MAIL 50.02.04 <<< From: Jason at GWAY.COM
Dear William Chalmers,
We spoke last week about the new transacction
initiative at Greenway and you asked for more
information regarding terminations. I am providing that
to you now withthe understanding that this material is
highly confidential, although tentative. Please use your
security code when responding. I'm afraid that we will
need a definitte and complete reply from you by noon on
Monday. Here it is:

Privileges and Rights of participants are currently
registered under the Exchange Act. Termination of
registration of Common data blocks and associated
Rights would make certain provisions of the Exchange
Act, such as the limited data transmission provisions
of Section 16(b) and the requirement of furnishing
backup records pursuant to Section 14(a) and the
related requirement of furnishing weekly reports, no
longer applicable with respect to ownership of data
blocks. Furthermore, the ability of "affiliates" of the
Company and persons holding "restricted" blocks of
transmission privileges to dispose of those blocks
pursuant to Rule 144 under the Act, as amended, may be
impaired or eliminated.

Regards, Jason Toothaker

_____

_____

>>> MAIL 50.02.04 <<< From: JTOOTH at GWAY.COM
====> Received: from HAL.NET.COM by NET.COM with THL
id AQ06498; Fri, 27 Jun 9:47:08 EDT
for WCHALM@PLYM.COM; Fri, 27 Jun 9:47:18 -0400
Press * for message

>>> MAIL 50.02.04 <<< From: Jason at GWAY.COM
Dear William Chalmers,
Please disregard my last mesage. Sorry for any
incovencience. I'll be in touch with you again soon.
Regards, Jason Toothaker

_____

_____

INTERRUPT!! URGENT!! INTERRUPT!! URGENT!!
>>> MAIL 50.02.04 <<< From: MITRAK at PLYM.COM

```
====> Received: from BUSTER.INTER.COM by INTER.COM
with NIO
id AQ06498; Fri, 27 Jun 13:52:21 EDT
for PARTNERS@PLYM.COM; Fri, 27 Jun 13:52:42 -0400
Press * for message


>>> MAIL 50.02.04 <<< From: MITRAK at PLYM.COM
Dear Colleagues,
   With respect to our negotiations with London, the
same, that is to say, the Sperry deal, has been delayed
until we send them more data. Can anyone do anything?
What, in the interim, can we send them? George
```

Bill stared at the president's message, trying to think of some
intelligent response. Before he could enter a keystroke, his
screen filled with a flurry of opinions and recommendations
from his colleagues, all circulated by e-mail from office to
office. Diane Rossbane, who often made unkind jokes about
people in their absence, quipped from her keyboard that they
should send the vice president of Sperry a box of Godiva
chocolates. They could e-mail the new Godiva chocolatier in
Soho Square. David Hamilton informed the emaciated Ms.
Rossbane from his terminal that Ms. Rossbane could use
some chocolates herself. At which point Ms. Rossbane shot
back that she was considered quite alluring in some quarters
and, furthermore, was married, which was more than she
could say for some people. Nate Linden announced that a
large number of gigabytes, he didn't know exactly how many,
were arriving soon from Chicago and he could forward them
to Sperry himself. Several people expressed interest in Mr.
Linden's proposal. Tom McGuinness, in Paris for the week
but monitoring his e-mail, typed in that everyone was OVER-
REACTING. He personally knew Benjamin Lloyd and was sure

that Sperry was "just puffing up its cheeks." McGuinness then loudly excused himself for a late meal and some EXCELLENT FOIE GRAS, on his expense account of course. Milt Kramer whined that this delay was going to impact his pending vacation to the Cape—he didn't yet know how, but he would take bets that he and Martha wouldn't get their full week on the Cape, starting on July 27.

Bill looked at his watch and was alarmed to see that it was after 2:00 p.m. He didn't have time to participate in this electronic chatter, he didn't even have time to read the rest of his messages. The devil take them, he would get to them tonight. And he was starving, he hadn't eaten lunch. Hurriedly, he rang Amy and asked her to bring him a sandwich from the snack shop in the lobby.

Now, the stupid report from Fred Loeser. Where was it? Bill began digging, and as he did so a mass of bile sank in his stomach. So, now he knew: George was the sly one in the office. And all of this time he had been on guard against Harv. Oh, how naïve he'd been. And what a masterful performer the president was, pretending to be so innocent, pretending to be a bumbler with his clumsy e-mail messages. Indeed, George and Harv were probably in cahoots. Of course. Hadn't Bill seen them whispering together at the party? What did they care? They had made their own little bundles, they were sitting on their pretty nest eggs with their large closets of Louis suits and their Mercedes sedans and their vacation homes on the Vineyard. What did they care about straightforward dealings and old-fashioned honesty. Better to know who your true enemies are as soon as possible, Bill thought to himself. In fact, this innocent message from Harv about Benjamin Lloyd was probably a sly trick. Undoubtedly, they had calculated that he would ignore it, with his backlog of appointments, and then they would bury him with it on Monday, reassign the job to Diane or Nate or Sidney. But he

was smarter than that. He would, in fact, produce many gigabytes of information about Benjamin Lloyd's relationship to
American pharmaceutical companies. Indeed, he would start
on the project at this moment. He began typing. Precious
time had been wasted. He decided to initiate three searches
on InfoAgent, under the key words *Pharmaceuticals, Benjamin Lloyd, Multinational Corporations*, in nested links. Let
the other junior partners envy and weep. But . . . he was
shocked at how slow his typing had become. His numb fingers jammed keys together, causing repeated mistakes. Faster,
faster. One key at a time. His mind was jamming like his fingers, he couldn't think, he couldn't think. He stood up and
stared into the hallway. Dolores galloped past with a stack of
faxes, nearly colliding with Milt Kramer. Beyond, sunlight
streamed through the floor-to-ceiling hall windows, which
wrapped around Plymouth's twelve deluxe offices and afforded
a stunning view of the city.

Abruptly, Amy appeared, a flaxen-haired young woman in a
crumpled orange dress. She set down a corned-beef sandwich
with sauerkraut, potato chips, and iced tea on the edge of his
desk, careful not to disturb the piles of papers, then hurried
from the room. My God, Bill said to himself as he discovered
that he had to resort to typing with one finger. He picked up a
half-sandwich and ate half of it in one bite, typing with his
right index finger as he ate. The mouthful was only partly
chewed when he squeezed the rest of the half-sandwich in his
mouth, chewed a little, and swallowed. The bread and the
meat and the sauerkraut slid uneasily down his throat, bulk-
ing and refusing to travel the rest of the way, and he took a
swallow of tea. His stomach began burning. What time was
it? Continuing to type, so slowly, so slowly, B - e - n - j - a - m -
i - n, he grabbed a handful of potato chips and stuffed them
into his mouth. Then the other half of the sandwich, covered
with too much mustard. His mouth bulged. He swallowed,

barely chewing at all. The food stuck in his throat and he swallowed again, painfully. His stomach was churning and rumbling. He was getting hot. Why could he not type faster? Forgetting the appalling condition of his armpits, he flung off his jacket. One finger, the index finger of his right hand, roamed over the keyboard. L - l - y - o - d. With his left hand, he stuffed the rest of the potato chips in his mouth, took a big gulp of tea, and swallowed the whole thing. His chest was on fire. He finally completed instructions for the search, taking three times as long as he should, when the buzzer on his intercom whined. "Fred Loeser, vice president of Total Efficiency Management, is here to see you." "What?" said Bill in astonishment. He looked at his watch. It was 2:30.

Very shortly thereafter, Mr. Loeser appeared at the door. He was a short, goatish man, wearing a blue suit with white pinstripes and a Phi Beta Kappa key pin in his lapel. "Good afternoon, Mr. Chalmers," he said, clasping his stubby hands together in self-satisfaction. "I'm sure you are extremely busy." He glided to Bill's work table. "It's warm, warm. We're not accustomed to your hot summers in Boston," he said and laughed. "This first meeting won't take more than thirty minutes of your time."

First meeting, Bill groaned to himself. That would seem to imply subsequent meetings. In actuality, he had little desire to meet at all with Mr. Loeser and was doing so only because Harvey Stumm had suggested it. Bill had many other known urgencies.

"By now, you must be familiar with our little project at Stanford University," said Loeser, smiling beneath his coarse, scraggly beard. He continued, mentioning various news media that had covered the project, national repercussions, biographical highlights of the executives of TEM.

Bill nodded as knowingly as he could, as if to imply that he had carefully read and digested the report lying somewhere on his desk. But the boredom and impatience in his face, accentuated by the absence of any detailed comments about the project on his part, indeed the absence of any words at all, would surely have been noticed by the other man had he not been busily pulling reports and documents from his briefcase. These he spread out on Bill's work table, explaining various columns of numbers and graphs that demonstrated increased productivities. At one point, he stopped to qualify a result with another set of graphs that he had deliciously held back in reserve. "Finally," said Mr. Loeser, concealing a last, solitary piece of paper, "I will show you Stanford's consolidated total efficiency index, which we have not yet made public. Eighteen months ago, Stanford's CTEI sagged at below 0.42. Today, it stands at 0.67." He paused, to let the significance of this result be comprehended. Then he reminded Bill that what TEM could do for a great university like Stanford it could do for Plymouth Limited, casually mentioned that TEM was also having preliminary discussions with Commonwealth Enterprises, just a few floors down in this very same building, and finally clasped his hands and waited for Bill's reply.

In fact, Bill had followed the opening phases of the presentation with attention, for the prospect of increasing the total efficiency of Plymouth, and certainly his own efficiency, was not without appeal. But his attention had not lasted long. Soon he began to nod mechanically, and he resumed worrying about the nature of his numbness and the ugly machinations at work in the office. During these preoccupations, he had forgotten to express even a mild look of interest, so that by the end of the presentation he found himself slumping over, almost asleep, and staring idiotically at the monogrammed F.L. on Mr. Loeser's briefcase.

When the efficiency expert at last stopped speaking, the

sudden silence awakened Bill, and he jerked his head up with a start. He nodded again, with much seriousness, unsure what Mr. Loeser expected. Somehow, he must acquit himself honorably, as all this would undoubtedly be reported back to Stumm. He glanced at his watch. It was 2:57. He nodded and waited. Then, with unmistakable deliberation, he set his finger down on one of the graphs and frowned. Loeser jumped from his chair and examined the graph under question. Twisting the hairs in his coarse beard, he began explaining the various assumptions behind the result, the idealizations and approximations, the possible sources of error. Then he returned to the general principles of total efficiency management. "I would wonder . . ." Bill said, uttering his first words of the meeting, and he walked slowly to his desk. Loeser looked at his watch and noted that it was precisely 3:00. Expressing the hope for a further meeting in the near future, he gathered up his papers and left.

With relief, Bill turned to his computer and went to the Net. There, on the screen, was a summary of results from his InfoAgent search: 30,194 separate listings for multinational corporations, 8,758 listings for pharmaceuticals, 3,785 for Benjamin Lloyd. The cursor blinked silently, waiting for him to select one of the 42,737 Web sites. But Bill had no time for that now and instead scrolled through another dozen e-mail messages, all he could tolerate in his present condition. Amy buzzed with two phone calls. Let them wait, he told her wearily. With painful slowness, he started to peck out a message to Jasper Olswanger. Teneco ChicagoCorp. He couldn't concentrate. People were shouting outside his door and thumping down the corridor. What? Could it already be 3:30, the moment of the day when all the Plymouth partners abandoned their terminals and trooped up en masse to the Universe Health and Fitness Club for a few minutes of exercise and relaxation? Someone knocked on Bill's door. He didn't answer. Again, someone knocked. "Okay. Okay. Okay," Bill shouted. He stood up and kicked his desk.

In the Universe, the top floor of the Marbleworth Building, rock music throbbed from the ceiling. Two dozen executives from elsewhere in the building were already installed in the machines, looking wretched. Another few sipped on protein shakes while receiving ten-minute, sitting-up massages, and one man sat meditating restlessly on a pale-green Zazen cushion. Bill had never liked the Universe. Without changing clothes, he climbed onto a Stairmaster, set the speed to the pace of a turtle, and began trudging. David Hamilton emerged from the locker room wearing his customary black Umbro shorts, white T-shirt, and Reebok running shoes. Announcing that he was prepared to do two miles, at eight minutes and forty-five seconds per mile, he hurried to one of the digital treadmills, punched in his desired pace and degree of incline, and was off and running. His reflection bounced back and forth between the parallel mirrors, producing a thousand copies of himself, each slightly less determined than the one before. George Mitrakis presented himself in a sleek In Sport running suit, black nylon with purple stripes, and straddled a recumbent bike. He held up his fingers in a V-sign. Then he adjusted his headphones and began pumping. Others entered in sweatpants, gym shorts, T-shirts and sweatshirts, running shoes and tennis shoes. Diane Rossbane peered out of the women's locker-room door in a baggy set of sweats, then quickly crept across the floor and hid behind an abdominal crunch machine.

Soon, the good smell of honest sweat and productive exhaustion floated through the air. The partners were pleased with themselves. Nate Linden, almost prone in a recumbent bike, immediately popped opened his phone with one hand and rang up Clemons Manufacturing Group in Chicago, pedaling all the while. Others strained to hear. As soon as he'd pushed the end button, Mr. Linden made a back-to-back call to his secretary, one floor below, and began whispering instructions, accented with his powerful strokes on the machine. All that could be heard was "thirty-five minutes," "sixty-five thousand," "tomorrow at nine-fifteen a.m." Although starting strong, within a few minutes Mr. Linden's physical pace began slacking, a pained expression came over his face, and his voice diminished to low feeble grunts. He had recklessly set his time for seventeen minutes.

"They think of nothing but money," whispered Charles Ravenscroft, of Ravenscroft International on the eighteenth floor, to Beatrice Denault, vice president of New England Chemical on the thirty-second. The two executives were jogging on either side of Bill. "I've never seen anything like it." Ms. Denault nodded, took a labored drink from her bottled spring water, and cast a contemptuous look at Mr. Linden. "I've heard that their janitorial service is twice a day," said Ms. Denault. "What?" exclaimed Mr. Ravenscroft, staring accusingly at Bill. "I can't believe it." "I would kill for that in my office," whispered Ms. Denault. "You don't know what slobs my people are. I think they urinate in the halls." The remainder of their conversation was unintelligible, even to themselves, for someone boosted up the volume on a television suspended over their heads.

"Did Gaffey come through?" George Mitrakis called over to Lisa Theroux, who was furiously trimming her thighs on a Stairmaster.

"We need more data for Digitel," Ms. Theroux shouted back, mishearing what the president had said.

"Bill," shouted Mitrakis, "what an ordeal for you, huh. Mugged. Thank God you're all right. We were worried sick about you."

Bill looked over at George Mitrakis and managed a smile.

What was George really saying to him? Was George staring at him from the corner of his eye?

"You should take it easy for a few days," said Mitrakis. "I mean that."

"I agree," Ms. Theroux panted as she attempted to keep pace with the rhythmic groans of the air purifier machine. Her face was dripping, her mascara long gone. Her cell phone rang. "Hello, Martin," she grunted, "you got me direct. Who gave you this number?" She listened, a frown enveloping her face. "Tomorrow! You need it tomorrow? I was shooting for Monday. What time tomorrow? . . . Don't crap with me, Martin. I don't want to do that unless it's one-thousand-percent necessary. You really have to have it by two-thirty tomorrow? . . . All right. Yes, all right. Yes, I'm sure. Okay." She called her secretary. "Four-ten," she said. "Have the Dubonnet file ready. Yes, that's good." Looking over at Mitrakis, she managed a tortured smile. "Gaffey finally regurgitated," she shouted. "Gaffey is a weasel."

"Damn straight," panted David Hamilton, who was a half-mile into his two-mile run and sagging badly, his face red and puffy. "We should stop doing business with Gaffey." He paused to take a heavy swig of his bottled water and let out an exhausted groan. "Shawmut Rubber does nothing for us except give us headaches. They sit on their capital. And we have to deal with Gaffey. I say let's get out."

"Tom got us into that one," came a voice from behind the abdominal crunch machine. "It was another of his so-called long-range plans."

"Shut up, Diane," shouted David Hamilton. "We know where you are."

"Shut up yourself," shouted Ms. Rossbane.

"Blah, blah, blah," said Milt Kramer from his massage chair, where he was being pummeled by a sour-looking masseur. "I'm tired of hearing you two bicker. I'm trying to relax."

Hamilton's phone rang in his hand. "Six-thirty," he panted into the phone. "Trust me, I'll make the recital. . . . Yes, seven-thirty. Carrie knows I'm not going to miss her recital." He glanced at the digital display and noted with dismay that his pace had dropped off to nine minutes per mile. "I understand that you don't have time. . . . I'll pick up the food at six forty-five." Now his pace had plummeted to nine and a half minutes per mile. He was breathing like a locomotive. "I know about the green coat," he said, struggling for air. "Please don't start on the green coat again. Just buy it. How's your day? . . . Love you."

For the first time, Bill realized that Hamilton used his affected British accent even with his own family. Everyone was speaking in some kind of fake accent. Bill was tired of listening to people talking, he just wanted to get back to his office. He was getting a headache. What time was it? Could he stop now without being a total wimp? His white shirt flapped around his waist like a surrender flag.

By 4:00, he was back at his desk, his head pounding. Messages flickered like lightning bugs on his screen. Painstakingly, he began pecking a reply to Jasper Olswanger. His mind wandered. Petrov. Should he attempt to change physicians? The process would take weeks. But he could waste months with that coward Petrov. Pulling on his mustache, Bill telephoned his health-insurance company, Commonwealth Health. "Welcome to the Commonwealth automated service center, dedicated to helping you better and faster. If you have a touchtone phone, press 1. . . . Thank you. Please enter your group policy number, followed by the pound key, followed by your personal ID number." Bill extricated his health card from his wallet and punched in the numbers. He sighed and waited. "Press 1 if you have an emergency medical need and cannot reach your primary care physician, press 2 for questions about Commonwealth's new Healthy Lifestyles plan, press 3 for questions about subrogation and coordination of benefits, press 4 if there has been any change in your status or that of your dependents, press 5 for desired changes in your primary care physician or the primary care physician of your dependents, press 6 for a summary of covered services, press 7 for a summary of conditions of termination of coverage, press 8 for premium structures." Bill pressed 5. "You have indicated a desire to change your primary care physician or the primary care physician of your dependents. If this is incorrect, please press 1 immediately to return to the main menu. . . . Press 2 if you desire to change your own primary care physician, press 3 to change the primary care physician of one of your dependents. . . . Press 1 if you know the Commonwealth code of your primary care physician, press 2 if you do not. . . . Using your touchtone phone, enter the last name of your primary care physician, followed by the pound key. . . . . . The name you have entered is not a participating physician in Commonwealth. We are returning you to the main menu." "Damn you," shrieked Bill. He had pressed a wrong key. "I don't want to be returned to the main menu." "Press 1 if you have an emergency medical need and cannot reach your primary care physician, press 2 for questions about Commonwealth's new Healthy Lifestyles plan, press 3 for questions about subrogation and coordination of benefits, press 4 if there has been any change in your status or that of your dependents, press 5 for desired changes in your primary care physician or the primary care physician of your dependents. . . ." Groaning, Bill sank into his chair and mindlessly pressed buttons. He looked at his watch. Precious time was evaporating away. Finally: "You have indicated that your primary care physician is Dr. Armand Petrov, Suite 403 of the Ambulatory Care Building of the Massachusetts General Hospital. If this is not correct, please press 1 immediately to return to the main menu. . . . Press 2 for a list of other primary care physicians in your area, press 3 for Bulletin Board information on changing your primary care physician." Bill pressed 3 and waited. "Due to system enhancements, Bulletin Board information is not available at this time. We are returning you to the main menu." Bill slammed down the phone. It was 4:23.

With no definite purpose, he got up from his desk and opened his door. The corridor was deserted. Through the window across the hall, he could see that a moistness had drifted in from the sea, not quite fog but a thickening of the air, a translucence. A building shimmered without edges. An airplane became gauzy and disappeared in the haze. He went back to his desk and stared without interest at the screen of his computer. One of his feet prickled. After a few moments, he returned to the window in the hallway, where he stood looking out at the harbor. He saw a red barge sliding sluggishly toward a wharf. He saw a spit of land wander out, dissolving into water and haze. And further east, beyond the harbor, he saw the ocean hover and beam and glow.

BATH

It was 7:15 that evening, the heat just beginning to wane, when Bill arrived at his home in the suburbs. His shoes thudded like stones on the stairs. Still wearing his tie, lacking the energy or will even to loosen it, he slumped on the edge of the four-poster bed. He had not released his grip on his briefcase. He had not even taken off his jacket, despite the suffocating warmth of the room. For a moment he lifted his head and squinted toward the half-drawn damask drapes, which allowed a bright swath of sunlight to cut diagonally across the floor and up the back wall, illuminating the floral print above the bed.

A few feet away, Melissa sat cross-legged on the rug, sipping a scotch and watching Bill closely. She had been drinking on and off since late afternoon, and her lipstick, usually so perfect that her lips seemed like red flower petals, was now streaked and smeared. When the telephones rang, she stiffened like a cat about to leap and waited until the answering machine stopped the ringing. Several times she started to speak but instead took another drink of her liquor, dabbed at her underarms with a Kleenex, and gazed nervously at her husband.

Her husband, in fact, was barely aware of her presence.

Again, he was brooding over the events of the day. And now his feet tingled. His position at the office seemed almost hopeless, an incredible change of fortune for someone who had only a few days ago been a rising figure in the company, almost certain to be elevated to senior partner. What had happened to him he could not comprehend, even though he went over and over it in his mind. Of one thing he was certain: that he had been afflicted far beyond what he deserved. Never had he been overly ambitious, or greedy. He knew plenty of those fellows; let them have their chairmanships and awards, their closets of suits. Let them even have their health. He did not begrudge them, he truly did not. But what about him? He, who played by the rules, who was more intelligent and able than most, who wanted only a nice house in the suburbs with a family who loved him, an adequate income, an eventual senior partnership and position where he could hold his place in the world. This affliction and degradation he did not at all deserve.

As he slumped on the edge of the bed, his legs shook and twitched. He had been sitting in this manner for ten minutes now, brooding and sour, insensible to his wife's new skirts and blouses that lay strewn on the bed, some still in their shopping bags and wrapping tissues. Melissa was speaking, but her voice was drowned by the television and the sudden sputtering of an engine across the street. She waited and repeated herself, almost shouting. At last, he lifted his head and stared at her as if she were another telephone. "What, were you talking?"

"I'll give you a bath before dinner," she said. "Come."

"A bath? I don't want a bath before dinner."

"Oh, Bill. It'll be good for you. I bought a bottle of that lemon shampoo you like. I'll shampoo your hair with it." Taking the last swallow of her scotch, she stood up and swayed on her feet and beckoned. Her turquoise silk robe draped loosely from her small shoulders and shone in the late sun.

With a sigh, Bill began removing notes and things from his pockets, looking for somewhere to place them. He frowned when he discovered that his favorite repository for odds and ends, the little French country writing desk by the window, had vanished, replaced by a reddish table with curly brass drawer handles.

"I won't like the bath," he said.

"Of course you will." She looked at her watch. "It's seven thirty-five. I'll go downstairs for one minute and put the chicken in. We'll have dinner at eight."

Bill nodded, half-listening to the TV on the bureau. A man in a tennis outfit, clearly with leisure time on his hands, was being interviewed. *I said to myself, you're good at food marketing. You're particularly good at refrigerated foods. But markets change. You have to ask people what they like. If you want to sell golf balls, have you ever thought of asking people who play golf: What kind of golf balls do you want?* Golf balls, Bill said to himself, and for a moment he tried to identify exactly what it was that he sold himself, or what he had been doing at the office for the past month. Not that his work could be reduced to those terms.

With some difficulty he undressed and went into the adjoining bathroom, where he found a small pleasure in the sensation of cool tiles against his bare feet and the sound of the water flowing into the tub. The running water was especially nice, like one of those white-noise machines for sleeping, and he closed the door to shut himself off from the television and the phones. Removing the last of his clothes, he sat on the edge of the tub, so that he could feel the spray of the warm water on his back, and he gazed absently at the objects on the marble counter: an enamel soap dish from

Paris, a lavender-tinted glass bottle of perfume, talcum powder, an electric toothbrush, a clock. It was a liquid-crystal digital clock, some kind of novelty that Melissa had found, its
numbers silently appearing and melting against the background of a pond as if rising and sinking. While the bath continued at his back, he watched the numbers emerge and
dissolve, one after another, and listened to the sound of the
water. He searched the small space for a magazine to read.
He crossed and uncrossed his legs. Behind him, the hot-
water pipe began thumping. His eyes moved to the brass
water faucets at the sink, down to the olive and tan tiles on
the floor, then back to the clock with the numbers rising and
falling.

Now the clock bored him. He stood up in his towel and
peered through the open bath window. Along the comfortable graveled road below, just wide enough for two cars to
pass, clusters of sugar maples shaded the two-story clapboard
houses. Water sprinklers whooshed and spun, and the glistening lawns were so correctly green that they appeared almost blue. Across the street, Olivia Cotter was cleaning the
platform of her new deluxe-size gas grill while talking to
someone on her remote phone. He had never noticed before
how nervous she was, shifting constantly from one foot to the
other. Her three children, barefoot, raced around the yard
throwing water balloons at each other. Bill cringed at the
thought that Olivia might have heard something about his
briefcase fiasco from Tim. Olivia was the person on the street
he talked to most, it was Olivia he always went to for advice
about buying presents for Melissa. Several lots away, a tiny
Max Pedersky perched in a lawn chair in front of his peeling
and weedy Victorian. Abruptly, Bob Tournaby drove up in his
BMW and began honking his horn. His wife, wearing a wide-
brimmed sun hat and at work in the garden, serenely ignored
him and continued trimming her roses. The Allison sisters,

both teenagers, flew from another house, their black stiletto-heeled shoes clacking on the driveway. They shoved into a waiting automobile.

Oh, to be young again, Bill thought to himself. Images appeared in his mind. A tent in the cornfields, hitting a golf ball strong and easy, the broken right door of Peter's '63 Triumph. Suddenly Bill remembered with a quick stab of guilt that he had not gotten home early enough to see Alex. Nor had he answered his son's messages. Turning from the window, he began mentally listing his activities for the weekend, intent upon spending various periods with his son. Saturday morning was out. From 9:30 to noon was the Council of Boston Leadership meeting at the Hyatt Regency Hotel in Cambridge. Then, at 3:30, a tennis game with Stephen Roe at the new indoor courts in Waltham. At some point during the day he had to pick up shirts at the laundry and dog food for Gerty, get his black wingtip shoes resoled, and take the microwave for repair. Then at 6:30, he and Melissa were meeting one of her old college friends and her husband for dinner.

His deliberations were interrupted when his mental clock informed him that the bath must be full, and it was. Tufts of steam rolled off the tub and fogged the mirror above the counter. Letting his towel drop to the floor, he eased himself into the water, warm and velvety and green from the green of the enamel underneath, and he rested his head against the cool tiles of the back wall. Just as the water had settled around him, Melissa came in with the shampoo, smelling fresh and sweet-lemony, and she began working it with her fingers into his hair.

"Ah!" Bill released a long breath of air and closed his eyes. "Did you see Alex tonight?" he murmured.

"Of course I saw Alex. I made dinner for him. He went to the mall with Brad and some friend of Brad's."

Alex. Bill grunted and languidly scratched an itch on his forehead. Her fingers continued to work at his scalp. "I'm so behind at the office," he said, his eyes still closed.

"You've always managed," said Melissa. "You're about the smartest man I know. That's one of the reasons I married you." She gently kneaded his neck and his shoulders and poured the warm bath water over his head, and again, until it seemed to him that he was completely enveloped in the flow of her, in her love, and he let his body go limp and let the warm water of her love wash over him. With the scent of her so close, magnified by the warm humidity of the air, he felt a stirring of desire, and tenderness. Surely, she loved him more than anyone did. Aside from his mother, she was the first and only woman who truly loved him. Moments of their life together flickered like distant stars in his mind. A book lying in the grass, open to the poem she had been reading. The look on her face as they walked on the beach one winter afternoon, their breaths feathery in the cold air, him holding her warm hand. Her shoulders under a web of sunlight their first morning. He wondered if she, too, remembered those moments, if they still remained in her memory against the years of their perfunctory existence together. Again, her smell, so close.

Carefully, he opened his eyes in the steamy light and saw her head and hair just above him, sweat on the skin of her neck. With a soapy arm, he pushed the sleeve of her robe up to the shoulder, so that he could see the little scar under her arm. "I love this," he said, touching the place. "Can I have it?" She laughed. Then he pulled her down to him, ran his mouth along the sweat of her neck. She moaned as if she'd been wounded.

"When was the last time?" she whispered. She closed her eyes and reached for him in the water.

"I can't remember."

Her robe dropped to the floor, two drops of sweat slid between her breasts.

He began kissing her, using his tongue, starting at the neck, her shoulders, the undersides of her breasts, the soft curve of her belly, her thighs.

He flinched when she gripped his chest with her fingers, again when she bit his shoulder. "You aren't numb there," she mumbled, buried.

Then, leaning together over the bathroom counter. Sound drained from the room, the automobiles beyond the window, the telephones in the bedroom, even her panting, leaving only the digital numbers liquidly rising and falling, her nipples in the mirror. He cushioned his head on her white back.

And as he was leaning over her, happy in his brief oblivion, it occurred to him that now he could tell her everything that had happened on the train, because who could he tell if not her? And he would tell her about the way people were staring at him at the office, and about the new tingling in his feet. Yes, he could tell her everything because she truly did love him. Could she see how he struggled, how much responsibility he carried? But he was happy to take care of her, he was proud to take care of her, as long as she appreciated him. Couldn't she spare just a little time from her antiques and her meetings and her house projects to compliment him now and then? It didn't have to be every day, just now and then. Maybe now he could also tell her how he preferred not having the furniture constantly changing. It was a small thing. Did she believe that he never noticed having new tables and chairs every week? He would tell her everything, but he would do it gently and carefully, just as she had sponged him in small careful circles. Only let him think for a moment of how to begin. You have no idea of the burden I carry every day, he might say. But that was too vague and grandiose.

Then the telephones began ringing, and she slipped from

underneath him and put on her robe and left to answer. By the time she returned, partly dressed, the moment had passed.

"That was Tess," she said, helping him dry his hair. "There's a meeting of the Boston Antiques Dealers' Association tonight. I can't believe I forgot." She looked at her watch.

"You have to go."

"I don't want to go." She kissed him on his bare shoulder and laid her head against his chest.

"The secretary has to be there."

She put her arm around his waist. "Come with me."

"I hate those meetings."

She nodded and sighed. "I'll leave your dinner in the oven. Have you made an appointment with a neurologist?"

"No," he shouted, suddenly angry, surprised at his own voice. "No. And I'm not taking any suggestions from Henry. So please don't say anything more to him about me. I'll find myself a neurologist when I'm ready."

She turned and put down the towel and looked away. "Both of us are on edge."

"Do you think you can drive? I can take you."

"I'm okay. I'll be back as soon as I can."

After Melissa drove off and Bill had eaten and gone to his keyboard, he found that his anxieties had partly subsided. He could still feel the warm glow of his skin, smell the lemon shampoo in his hair, smell her on him. With an uncharacteristic impulse, he even permitted himself a half-glass of scotch. After the alcohol had filtered through his body, he felt even calmer. A pleasant breeze wafted through the open bedroom window. Then, with no further thoughts of his problem, aside from the necessity to peck with one finger, he began responding to his backlog of business from the day. So en-

grossed in his work did he become that at 9:30, when Olivia
Cotter commenced to shout at her husband across the street,
he hardly heard.

At 10:30, the letters and numbers began to dissolve on the
screen and his head drooped back in his chair. He would have
drifted off to sleep at that moment had he not been disturbed
by the sound of an automobile grumbling down the street.
Struggling to lift up his head, he squinted at the screen and
reread his last memorandum. The lamp on the table had become a bright, burning eye. Melissa would be home soon. And
Alex—did he remember his appointment tomorrow morning?
Drowsily, Bill fumbled with the keyboard and entered his electronic mailbox. He would scroll through one more message
before bed. It was from Alex, sent late that afternoon.

```
>>> MAIL 50.02.04 <<< From: ACHALM at AOL.COM
==> Received: from RING.NET.COM by NET.COM with GOTP
id AQ06498; Fri, 27 Jun 17:30:13 EDT
for WCHALM@PLYM.COM; Fri, 27 June 17:31:41 -0400
Press * for message
```

```
>>> MAIL 50.02.04 <<< From: Alexander at AOL.COM
Dear Dad,
I found a way to break the copy-protect lock of the
Plato stuff and copy it into my preonsnal file. Isnt'
that totally cool!!! Brad says I should sell it. But I
don't want togo to jail or anything. I'm sending it
just to you and Mom in the attached file. This is the
second part. So far, I'm at $16.50 worth.
Love, Alex
```

Bill began worrying whether Alex's electronic copyright violation could be traced to their home. But his worries soon disappeared in the cottony ball of sleep that was enveloping him, and his thoughts drifted to the past. He was trying to remember the very last time he had hugged Alex, the exact moment of his life when he had decided that Alex was too old to hug. The exact moment. Now it was so hard to go back.

He stared at the message from his son, trying to focus his eyes, and carried his laptop to the cushioned divan. As always, he found the divan completely uncomfortable, too short for him to lie down and too long to sit up. In the end, he collapsed in the middle with one leg sprawling over each side, the laptop resting on his stomach. His shoulders went slack, his head slumped back on the cushion. Then, with half-closed eyes, he looked sleepily at the screen.

```
Press return for the first line of the second section of
Anytus. Press return for each successive
paragraph. Return.
```

```
The uncommon grayness that swept over the city in late
morning, causing the market to close early, hung
overhead for the rest of the day, neither rupturing
into the storm that the grain merchants predicted nor
dissolving into the pellucid skies of the Aegean in
spring. . . .
```

THE TANNERY

The uncommon grayness that swept over the city in late morning, causing the market to close early, hung suspended for the rest of the day, neither rupturing into the storm that the grain merchants predicted nor dissolving into the pellucid skies of the Aegean in spring. The darkness seeped into houses like gray liquid, absorbing all brightness in its path, and the air in the crooked streets of the city became sluggish and damp. But there was no rain. Following a period of holding its breath, the City of the Owl uneasily returned to its business. Torches were fired in the Prytaneum and the Tholos, where the councilors resumed their discussions. Oil lamps were lit in the dark houses. Slaves carried their bundles of pilchards and tuna, thrushes and quail into the flickering light while constantly glancing up at the sky.

In the commercial Stonecutters Quarter, where Anytus's two-story stone tannery was crammed between private houses and shops, masons huddled in their shops waiting for rain. After no water from the sky was forthcoming, the wheels resumed grinding, filling the gray air with a fine chalky dust.

Anytus was talking to his foreman, Cleonymus, in the trimming and salting room of his tannery when Sokrates arrived. The philosopher was accompanied by two prison attendants, two Scythian archers, and a crowd of friends and admirers who had joined the leisurely procession from the prison and followed the gravel path west of the agora, past the twelve marble pilasters of the Theseum, and through the dusty streets of the Stonecutters Quarter, ending finally at Anytus's shop near the Piraic Gate. A sharp odor knifed through the air.

Upon reaching the tannery, the Scythian police set their bows on the ground, fell to their hands and knees, and pretended to choke in the great clouds of smoke emanating from the outdoor lime kiln. These antics much amused the half-dozen workmen loitering under a plane tree. After a round of mutual imitations, the archers picked up their bows and solemnly stationed themselves next to a pile of fresh sheep-skins at the front entrance.

Waving the throngs of spectators back with some uncertainty, the jailors entered the tannery with their prisoner. He was a short, balding man of about seventy, thick in the leg, with a snub nose and gnarled bulging eyes. Sokrates wore no shoes. His feet were covered with dirt up to his ankles from the long procession. Anytus noticed with disgust that the man's mantle was splotched and tattered from years of accumulated greases and lack of repair.

In the tannery the light flickered with torches and oil lamps and took on the brownish-red glow of the unburnished brick walls. Anytus kept the philosopher waiting while he unhurriedly finished his instructions to Cleonymus. The foreman, who was deaf in one ear, held the good side of his head toward his employer and struggled to catch each word above the continued shouting outside and the sounds of splashing and paddling coming from the soaking room next door. Another worker came in with some leaves of tannic sumac for Anytus to inspect, then covered his nose and went up the narrow stone stairs to the tanning room.

Finally, Anytus dismissed his foreman and looked across at the philosopher, who had remained standing near the front door. "I am sorry to disturb you," Anytus said.

"If I might first wash off my dirty feet," said Sokrates. "I do not want to soil your tannery."

"Of course," said Anytus. He waved to an attendant, who drenched the old man's feet from an earthenware vessel of water mixed with wine.

"I resent being dragged away from my friends on my next to last mortal day," said Sokrates in a soft voice. "But I was presented with a signed order from Xanthias of the Eleven, and I have always obeyed the laws of the city."

"But not the city's beliefs," said Anytus.

"Men must examine themselves and believe what their own minds and souls tell them," said Sokrates. "All else is shadow. Do you know Aesop's story about the dog and the shadow? I will tell you. A dog had a nice piece of meat in his mouth and was carrying it back to his home, when he saw his shadow in the river under the bridge. Thinking his reflection was another dog also with a tasty piece of meat, he snapped at the shadow. His own treasure fell into the water and he lost all."

"Save your stories and lessons," said Anytus. Without change of expression, he thought to himself how apt was the tale, and worth remembering. "I am not one of your admiring young men."

"I am sure you are not. What is it that you do admire, if I may ask?"

Instead of answering the old sophist's question, which he instantly decided was a clever trick, Anytus turned to stare with irritation at the two jailors. One of the them, the older of the two, had begun wandering around the perimeter of the stone floor, stopping to lick the salt cone in the corner, and was now dumbly rubbing his face against a large hog hide strung up to cure. "You will leave the prisoner here under my protection, and my honor," said Anytus. "I will speak to Xanthias if you do not understand me."

The two jailors huddled in a corner, muttered something to each other, and went slinking outside. Anytus made certain that the great door had closed well behind them. Inside the small room, the air was close and warm and smelled of salt. Anytus offered the philosopher some honey cakes and a stool. Sokrates shook his head no and remained standing. He had not moved since his arrival. In the dim light, his white beard had turned gray.

"I've heard about your prison drawings," said Anytus. "You have imagination."

"Merely the scribblings of an old man who knows nothing. This morning an attendant washed them away."

Sokrates was infuriatingly calm for a man about to die. "You place the gods on the floor of your cell, alongside mortal man," said Anytus. "What is the significance of that?" The tanner suddenly felt his head begin pounding again, his headache was not gone, and he strained to conceal the pain. He could not show any weakness.

"There was no room on the ceiling," said Sokrates quietly.

"I am boring you," said Anytus. "So I will not take up much more of your time. Let us not pretend. We despise each other." Sokrates remained expressionless, but his eyes fastened on the tanner with such concentration and stillness that Anytus could not return his gaze. "Nevertheless," said the tanner, "I want to make you a proposal. Will you listen?"

"I am here, as you see," said Sokrates and he shook the chains around his wrists. "But I am curious about this place where you work. We must go to the foulest-smelling room of your tannery. There I will listen."

What is this? Anytus thought to himself. He's toying with

me. Have I made a colossal mistake? But I must talk to him. Gods help me. Anytus studied the philosopher but could read nothing in his face. At last, he frowned and sighed. "Follow me to the soaking room."

The soaking room, adjacent to the salting and trimming room, contained four wooden barrels, each filled with several hides and a thick black liquid that had once been water. Torches burned on wooden posts. Oozing onto the floor, from an opening at the bottom of each barrel, was a brown sludge of removed hair, flesh, earth, and blood, which slowly crept along the stone floor to the corners of the room, where it congealed and began to rot. A sullen workman with a cloth around his nose went from one barrel to another paddling the hides. Every few moments, he stuck his head out of the single window in the room and gulped air like a man drowning.

Anytus began gagging as soon as he entered the soaking room and covered his nose with his mantle. Sokrates looked at Anytus in his discomfort, in the flickering light, and said quietly, "Let us talk in your bating room."

Yes, he is gaming with me, thought Anytus. But there is a limit to how much I will take. I have my dignity. "I will talk to you here," said the former general. "Please. I never go to the bating room. It is on the second floor."

"I can climb stairs," said Sokrates.

As soon as the two men began mounting the narrow stone steps to the bating room, they were met with the unmistakable stench of fresh animal manure, the dull stink of dog dung and the piercing acrid stink of bird dung. The fetid odor gained in ferocity as they ascended the stairs, one step at a time, until Anytus became nauseous. At the edge of the landing, his legs buckled beneath him and he collapsed to the floor. Then Anytus vomited into the sleeve of his mantle, which had been expertly embroidered by his wife.

Several feet away, two bald-headed Egyptian slaves, having long ago lost all sense of smell, stood at wooden barrels and paddled a putrid broth of skins and aqueous animal dung, replenishing the acid removed by the lime. Above each barrel, visible even in the dim light, floated a suffocating brown cloud of airborne manure. An oily brown film coated the floor, the walls, and the ceiling. As soon as the Egyptian slaves recognized their master, they dropped their paddles into the vats and froze in astonishment. The two slaves stood for another moment, wondering what terrible event could have summoned their master to the bating room, and fled down the limestone stairs.

As Anytus sat on the floor gasping for air, the old philosopher wordlessly offered him a stool, his chains clanking, then sat on a stool himself across from the tanner. "You wanted to make me a proposal," he said. "I am ready to listen."

Now that the bating vats were no longer paddled, the abominable stench of the room slightly diminished. After some moments, Anytus ceased retching. His face was pale yellow, he held a thick woolen cloth to his nose, and he struggled to gain control of himself. Suddenly he felt very much alone with the old man. The noise from outside the tannery had faded away, as the philosopher's retinue dispersed and the day's business in the quarter ran down. The neighborhood was now silent, except for the languid exercises of a lyre being practiced in one of the houses in late afternoon.

Anytus sat listening to the lyre. Then it, too, ceased. But he continued to listen, strained to listen. Some annoying sound. Was it his head? "Do you hear that?" he asked.

"What?"

"I hear something," said Anytus.

"I hear nothing," said the philosopher. "Except you talking. What is it you want to say to me?"

Anytus looked at Sokrates and his eyes narrowed. "I ask you to reconsider exile," he said weakly. "I can speak to Xanthias and facilitate an escape. I could further make enquiries in Chalcis or Eretria."

For the first moment since his arrival, the condemned man expressed interest, but his interest was more in Anytus than in the proposal. "I am surprised," he said. "You, more than anyone, argued for death at my trial." Sokrates paused and again gave Anytus his penetrating gaze. "Are you beginning to feel guilt?"

Anytus was silent.

"I refused exile before," said Sokrates quietly, "and I refuse it again. Nothing has changed. I have no reason to believe that I would be treated better in Chalcis than in Athens. A philosopher should be celebrated by his city, not banished from it. My life is already forfeit."

Anytus peered down the stone stairway, making sure that they were quite alone. "If you accept exile," he said in a choked whisper, "I will see that your wife and children are provided with twenty minas per year." He took a deep breath. "My offer, of course, requires the condition of secrecy."

The condemned man smiled faintly. "So this is your proposition, Anytus. I pity you."

Anytus's face felt on fire with hatred. He waited a moment before speaking. "It is a good offer," he said.

"Yes, it is a good offer," said Sokrates. "That is a great sum of money. But how do you know that I would keep secret the source of the income? Or even this conversation?"

Anytus thought for a moment about how to phrase his reply. "Although I have no fondness for you, I believe you to be an honorable man."

"Would an honorable man sell off his principles for twenty minas per year?"

Finally with enough strength to rise to his feet, Anytus

walked over to an open window and took a deep breath. "Apparently you care nothing for your own life," he said, "but what of the well-being of your family? I understand that you have two young children."

"I would not have expected you, Anytus, to express concern for a man's family," said the old philosopher.

"What do you mean?"

"I will leave it at that."

"Are you speaking of my son?"

Sokrates said nothing.

"How dare you," Anytus shouted, losing control of his voice. "You have taken my son. You have ruined him. Ruined him. You have polluted his mind."

"I have helped him to discover his own thoughts."

"What did Prodicus tell you? What? Did he say that I abandoned him during the rule of the Thirty?" Anytus found himself gripping the rough window casement so hard that the stone cut through the palm of his hand. A trickle of brown blood ran down the brown wall. He felt angry and foolish for having exposed his emotions, and he fought silently with himself, gripping the casement even more fiercely.

"Let us not argue any longer," said Sokrates. "I cannot accept your offer." The old philosopher stood up. "Do you have other business with me? Or may I return to my cell, where I have friends waiting?"

Anytus would not look at the other man. Instead, he gazed out of the window, staring at the thin silhouettes of smoke just starting to rise from the stonecutters' houses in their preparations for dinner.

"Goodbye, then," said the philosopher. "I am sorry that I cannot help you."

Sokrates went slowly down the steps to the lower room and stood by the door. Anytus followed. When he reached the first floor, he motioned for the philosopher to wait while he straightened his mantle and folded under the soiled sleeve. He rubbed water on his face, ran his hand through his hair. He brought himself up to his full height. Then he opened the door.

Outside, torches flickered in the dusky streets of the quarter. The two jailors were sitting cross-legged in a broken cart, talking to Pyrrhias. At the opening of the door, they came forward, joined by the Scythian archers.

"I am finished with him," Anytus announced. "You may take him back to the prison."

When the philosopher and his escort had disappeared into the dark, winding streets, Anytus did not go back inside his tannery. Instead, he sat down in the one-wheeled cart next to Pyrrhias. The sky was now a solid black mask, unpricked by stars.

"You allowed him to return to the prison," said Pyrrhias in a puzzled voice. "How will you prevent his escape?"

"There is no need to prevent his escape," said Anytus. "He does not want to escape. He wants to die." Anytus unfolded the sleeve of his mantle and stared at the stain and let out a weary sigh. "After tomorrow, I'll be a hated man in our city."

A child's laughter rang out from a nearby house. Then dim figures carrying torches passed along the Stonecutters Road, illuminating the brick and stuccoed walls of the houses. The figures became tiny floating lamps as they moved through the Piraic Gate and out into the dark rolling hills to the west of the city.

It was at that moment, following the small flickering lights with his eyes, that Anytus understood what he must now do. He would have to arrange for Sokrates to be killed, later that night, in a manner to suggest murder by a drunken slave rampaging through the city. He required an assassin who was superb at his work and utterly discreet. Anytus closed his eyes, straining, and remembered an outlander known as the

Twine, one of the thousands of aliens living within the city. According to rumor, the Twine had been employed by the Thirty Tyrants. However, no one was sure which of the many disappearances and drownings, the suffocations in the night, the silent strangulations in broad daylight had been his doing. Uncertainty and confusion were his specialties. Of his appearance there were conflicting reports. Some said he was a giant, light-skinned Megarian with hands the size of boulders. Others swore that he was small-boned and slight, womanly, invisible in a crowd. An aging Scythian archer claimed that the killer posed as a geometrician, surveying the city with his rods and his compasses. Or a peddler of saffron fabrics when his victims were women.

Anytus got up from the cart and looked down at the dark city. A faint glow hung over the roofs of the houses, the light from their inner courtyards open to the sky. Smell of thrushes cooking, music of flutes.

Later that night, as Anytus stood waiting under an olive grove outside the city, beyond the Acharnian Gate, a dark figure approached him. The man held his lamp low, at his waist, and his face was further hidden by a traveler's brimmed hat. Although the dark road was quite empty, the two men spoke in whispers, and the crooked olive trees hunched around them like a secret gathering of ancient old men. Finally, Anytus handed the man a heavy sack. The figure bowed his head slightly and turned his steps back toward the city.

THE MURDER

After he parted from Anytus, the man in the traveler's wide-brimmed hat extinguished his oil lamp and walked several hundred feet toward the Acharnian Gate. Then, he darted to the west, keeping the tiny flickering lights of the city to his left. He did not follow roads, preferring instead to pass through the scattered cemeteries and gardens that lay beyond the city gates. The night was soot black, the moon that would have gleamed off the brass garden fixtures and trellis endings was completely obscured by the hard clouds overhead. Occasional houses rose up from the dark rolling hills, windowless like the houses in the city.

Finally, the traveling man spotted a stone storage shed under a plane tree. There he dropped silently to the ground and held himself utterly still for perhaps half an hour, listening acutely for footsteps or breathing. The invisible crouching figure, sometimes known as Cephalus of Boeotia, or Meletus of Corinth, or Cinesias of Thebes, or the Twine, was not happy with his current assignment. The hasty arrangements, the urgent imperative for a strike within twelve hours, the absence of proper intelligence and preparations all violated his code of operations. However, he had been paid forty minas, twice his usual fee. Urgency could be bought. But he would have to be more careful than usual.

Even when Cephalus was quite sure that he had not been followed and resumed walking, he did not return to the Acharnian Gate, the shortest path back to the city. Instead, he continued southwest until reaching the Dipylon Gate and entered the city by that route, emerging into the crowded Inner Ceramicus, the Potters Quarter. Aromas of boiling sprats and copaic eel simmering in hot olive oil hovered in the air, the late dinners of the affluent and social. Cephalus was hungry, but he would not eat until much later that night, after his work was complete. He worked best with nothing in his stomach. Blood could go either to the head or to the stomach, but not both.

Blinking at a passing torch, he began slowly heading east, following one of the narrow, crooked streets only six feet in width. Houses were jammed edge to edge and flush up to both sides of the road, making the street a thin passage between two winding walls of stucco and mortar and brick. The streets of the city sickened him. They were filthy. He forced himself to look down at the filth: rotting fish heads, shards of pottery, entrails of birds, chicken bones, moldy bread, worn-out clothes, urine. He detested everything dirty. Blood was dirty. Bars of silver, like the ones in the sack on his shoulder, were clean.

At the midsection of the city, Cephalus crossed over the thin river Eridanus and into the south Kydathenaion. A single torch burned inside the marbled Shrine of Artemis like a candle flickering within a bony skull. The Twine saw no one, except for a man and woman embracing under the sculptured roof of a vestibule. He paused for a moment, staring at them, and walked on. Winding along one crooked street after another between the stuccoed walls, his sandals becoming increasingly caked in dirt and debris, Cephalus finally stopped at the doorway of a modest, one-story house made of sun-dried bricks. This residence was his, one of the two that he maintained in different parts of the city.

The Twine did not use the knocker, a ring in a lion's mouth, but instead whispered, "Hallah." He waited. After some moments, an ancient, blind man opened the door and let him into the dim entry way. At the sound of the door, a dog shot through the house. It leaped onto Cephalus, licked his face pathetically, and rolled over on its back, waiting to have its belly scratched. Despite its frenzied excitement, the animal had not let out a single bark or whine, for it had been trained to silence since birth.

"Sweet Hermes," said Cephalus, stooping to rub his dog's belly. "Did you miss me?" The dog rolled from one side to another, panting in ecstasy and wagging its tail.

"I didn't know when you were returning, Master," said the blind slave, Hallah, "but I lit the lamps as always. We have some Sicilian cheese, a manchet, and honey cakes in the kitchen."

"It's good to see you, old Hallah," said Cephalus. "I will be going out tonight, but back before dawn." The blind slave nodded.

Still standing in the entry, the Twine carefully removed his dirty shoes, hat, and mantle and placed them on a wooden bench. Then he proceeded into the small but immaculately kept court, counterclockwise around its stone altar to Zeus. Hermes followed closely, pressing his body against the legs of his master. The open court let into three small rooms, no larger than the slave's room off the entry, their entrances just openings in the wall without curtains or doors. Into one of these at the rear of the court Cephalus entered, his sleeping and bathing room, containing little more than a simple bed in a wood frame and two oil lamps hanging on chains from the ceiling. He dropped his sack heavily to the floor and stripped off the remainder of his clothes.

The money first. Money was clean but could be soiled by human hands and bodies. He removed the two bars of silver from the sack and poured water over them, began scrubbing the silver with wood ashes and a bronze scraper. The water flowed over his feet, across the stone floor, and into a drainage hole in the corner. He repeated. Water, wood ashes, more scraping. The old slave shuffled into the little room with hot water in a bronze vessel, which he gropingly placed on a brazier containing burning coals. Cephalus patted him on the shoulder in acknowledgment and continued to work on the ten-mina bars, scrubbing them, scrubbing them. When at last they shone in the lamp light, he rinsed them with olive oil and perfume. There would be two more to wash at the end of the night.

Next, himself. He poured the hot water on his body, then began scrubbing his skin with the wood ashes, scraping with the bronze tool. He scrubbed harder, he wanted to flay off his outer layer of skin, the filth and the blood of the city, he wanted to become as clean and as pure as the two bars of silver gleaming in the lamp light on his bed. Wood ashes and olive oil formed a thick paste all over his body, rising over the contours of the powerful muscles in his arms and chest. Then again the scrubbing and scouring, metal against skin, soundless. Gradually, the paste of wood ashes and olive oil became mixed with dirt and skin peelings. He doused himself with another pitcher of warm water. Now his skin was burning and raw and red, even his privates. He was becoming clean, he was becoming ready to go out again into the city, to do the work. The work was not part of his body, was outside his body. One final time, he covered his body with the paste of wood ashes and oil and went at himself with the bronze scraper, wincing in silence at the pain. When he was finished, he washed himself off with the warm water and gingerly rubbed a thin layer of olive oil and perfume on his bare body. Later, Hallah would scrub the stone floor.

It was near midnight. With Hermes hugging his side, the

Twine walked naked back to the court and into the next room. He stood thinking. On a table, maps of the city and outlying areas, documents in Greek, Egyptian, Assyrian. Neatly folded in two inlaid chests were tunics of various lengths and colors, padded vests, beards and hairpieces, clay noses, hats. He selected a clean, white tunic and mantle, thick sandals, a skullcap, dressed slowly and carefully like a man about to make a speech before the Assembly. However, he would not be in public tonight. He would work in the streets and in the prison, where it would be dark. The prison he had visited many times before, after bribing the jailors.

From a tiny and delicate stone vase, its bore hole no wider than a little finger, Cephalus removed a short length of twine. The coiled string, extraordinarily thin for its strength, he wrapped around his wrist. A small chest yielded a serrated Persian dagger. The dagger he used only when necessary, the dagger created rivulets of blood.

Cephalus placed his equipment in a purse around his neck, inside his mantle, then went out into the night. For a moment, he stood listening in the street just beyond his front door. Other houses stood against his in a continuous snake of gray stucco. The houses were dark and silent. He knew everything about his neighbors, knew their occupations, their movements in the city, their wives and children and slaves, their mistresses. They knew nothing of him. To them, he was a dim traveler and trader who quietly appeared and vanished, employed one blind slave, never had guests. The situation was identical at his other house in the city, also with its one slave and one dog.

It was raining. The heavy, charcoal sky had finally started to empty.

The Twine listened. Southwest, the distant voices of young men, drifting like a scent of pimpernel. He pulled his mantle tightly around his shoulders and headed in that direction. When he reached the Street to the Temple of Zeus, he followed it away from the temple, in a northerly direction, toward the voices. The houses were dark cliffs on each side of the road, he was hurtling through a tunnel, he was a thrown rock, making no sound, a stone unfeeling to water and rain. He moved off the main road onto a small, crooked street. Streets curled into streets like snakes in a pit. Without looking, without listening, he knew that he was not followed, that he was alone, a single dark rock moving through space. The voices were louder, were close by. He ducked into another street, crouched next to a dark public fountain, and saw them, saw their torches. Three. He could see their faces, flickering in the light of the torches. He could see their mouths and new beards. They paused at a corner and drank, passing around a curved vessel. When they resumed walking, he followed behind them, invisibly. Their torches illuminated the brick walls of houses, weeds, stones in the road, their own bodies. But none of the light fell upon him. He was a dark rock, clean and untouched by the light. He removed the twine from his purse, wrapped it around his wrist in two loose turns.

Now he was close behind the three puppies. None of their light touched him. The youths were laughing and drinking as they walked. They reeked of wine. The street was narrow, and one of the three walked a few paces behind, a bulky young man with long curls. Soundlessly Cephalus flew to him, slipped the twine over his head, pulled him against the dark wall of a house. The body slid quietly to the ground, and the assassin glided into an intersecting street. Then another, and another. The Twine was many streets distant when the other two youths discovered their companion lying still in the road and began screaming.

The prison was almost due west now, only a few stades away, but the assassin headed north and over the Eridanus. He had more work before going to the prison. He would create a random path of death, a confusion of meaning, odd angles. He was working well now, he was flowing. The houses were sleeping. A woman's voice, singing softly, floated through the streets, possibly a slave woman relaxing after her day's chores, perhaps a woman pacing a courtyard unable to sleep, or a woman serenading her lover in bed. What did it matter? Cephalus listened briefly, then for no reason turned off onto another road. Ahead, he detected the tiny risings and fallings of a dark layered mound, the form of a sleeping slave at watch over a doorway. The assassin suffocated him easily with his own mantle.

Steady rain now. The rain was good, it was clean. But the roads and passageways were thick with mud. Cephalus crossed south over the Eridanus, then headed into the agora.

The prison was three hundred feet southwest of the agora in a district of marble workshops, a one-story rectangular building. Slowly, Cephalus circled the building, avoiding the dark puddles by instinct, periodically placing his ear to the wall. After some time, he heard breathing. That there were two prisoners and a jailor within those walls he already knew. He knew also the location of the eight cells, the central corridor, the southerly courtyard, the warren of four jailors' quarters.

But he was not yet ready to enter. First he would watch and he would wait. He sat under a plane tree near the front entrance. His body merged with the trunk and vanished. He knew little of the man he was to kill inside the prison. A teacher, one of the sophists. He would be the older of the two prisoners, short and balding. The other prisoner, a Megarian, was in his twenties. Only one needed to die tonight, he would spare the Megarian if possible. The sophist would be just a dark form on a bed, a prone tangle of arms and legs, a mantle with a mouth and a throat.

He listened. Rain. A twig snapped. A dog barked. It was time. He readied his dagger, wrapped the twine around his wrist. He was working well.

Carefully, the assassin let himself into the front door, which was never bolted, and moved silently down the dark central corridor. He stood at the entrance to the jailors' quarters on his left, four small rooms. In one of the rooms a torch burned. After some moments, he could hear the jailor's breathing in the southwest quarter. The jailor was not sleeping. The assassin crept into the unlit northwest room, adjacent to where the jailor sat in a chair, and peered through the small open doorway. The jailor, his face partly lit by the flickering torch, was preoccupied with the dissection of an owl's pellet. On the table in front of him lay bits of bone, fur, chitin, and half the skeleton of a small rodent meticulously reassembled. The jailor whittled at the pellet with his knife, blew away some chitin, and worked out another small piece of bone. Cephalus took out his dagger and noiselessly moved along the wall of the room. When he had succeeded in getting behind the jailor, he put the dagger away and took out his twine. In one motion, he jumped forward, slipped the twine over the jailor's head, and strangled him.

From his purse the assassin removed a tiny oil lamp made of ivory and ignited it with the torch mounted on the wall. He returned to the central corridor. Very carefully, he unbolted the third cell on his right. A prisoner in chains lay sleeping on a bed in the corner. Cephalus approached him and dimly illumined his face with the small light from his lamp.

The assassin returned to the door, silently rebolted it, and walked to the cell of the sophist. Again, he carefully unbolted the door, letting it swing open. The cell was square, fifteen feet on a side. On the back wall, the sophist slept on his bed, an easy suffocation. His chains hung down to the floor.

Holding his lamp in one hand, the assassin approached the sleeping old man. He had covered half the distance across the stone floor when he was surprised to hear a rustle behind him and then a sudden burning pain in his back and another across his throat and warm liquid on his neck, he dropped his lamp to the floor and the floor rushed up to meet him, a dark sandaled foot, cool stone on his face, one distant gasp.

To: Alexander Chalmers <ACHALM@AOL.COM>
From: Bill Chalmers <WCHALM@PLYM.COM>
Subject: Sunday

Dear Galahad,

It's break time at a meeting I'm at in Cambridge, and
the lounge area has lots of computersj online. So I'm
doing the nerdy thing. Did you have fun at the mall
last night with Brad? Thanx for Anytus2. Socrates is a
self righteous snob, don't you think? I never knew
that. Im ipreseed that your were able to copy the
college course. How did you do it? No, better not tel
me. I've got some free time Sunday afternooon. How
about we fence?
Love, Lancelot

>>> MAIL 50.02.04 <<< From: ACHALM at AOL.COM
==> Received: from RING.AOL.COM by AOL.COM with GOTP
id AQ06498; Sat, 28 Jun 10:34:36 EDT
for WCHALM@PLYM.COM; Sat, 28 Jun 10:34:49 -0400
MESSAGE LOCK OVERRIDE
>>> MAIL 50.02.04 <<< From: Alexander at AOL.COM

THE DIAGNOSIS

Dear Sire,

Be prepareed to meet youro doom. tomorrow , next to the moat.

I didn;t know wwhere your were/. The mall last night sucked. TWo girls were supposet to meet Brad and met at Bannana Republick. We waited about two hours for them b ut they didn't show.

I'lls send yo more Plato stuff. I didn;t know I could t htat. I really liked the jailor who rubed his facce agaisnt the bull's hide and licked the salt thing. The assassin was really cool. What a sicko. I nevr expected him to get wiped out.

FYI, there are 378 tiles in the floor in fornt of Banana REpublic.

Love, Galahad

_____

FIRST TESTS

On Thursday, July 3, Bill had his MRI.

The following Wednesday, a day that the rain sliced through the air in great slanted blades and flooded his basement, Bill met with his physician to discuss the results. Petrov at once offered his opinion that the MRI examination had revealed no tumors or plaques. The films and results were apparently contained within a large manila folder, which the physician waved in the air but did not open. He could see "nothing even slightly askew" in the MRI test. Of course, the images would be subjected to further analysis. But at this stage, there were no indications. Excellent, they could advance to blood work. The numbness was still present, was it? Yes, yes. They were making progress, they would begin the next round of examinations. Subject, of course, to the approval of Bill's HMO. If Bill could please call the office in a day or two, he would be notified of the dates of the next tests.

Over the following week, Bill's feet became numb. This condition he confirmed one morning by slamming them, one at a time, into the concrete embankment at the Alewife garage. He felt nothing. That night, splotchy blue bruises appeared on his ankles and toes. Melissa regarded them with horror. "What were you doing to yourself?" she exclaimed and turned off the television. "A medical examination," said Bill.

Melissa began ransacking the medicine cabinet, looking for ointments and bandages, tossing bottles and tubes onto the floor. Liquids spilled. "Anybody can smash themselves up," she said, mopping with a towel. "What are you doing to yourself? Oh God, Bill." She started to cry. "I can't believe it's your feet now. It's getting worse. What are we going to do? . . . I want you to see a neurologist. Please see a neurologist. Please. Please." She gently dried off his feet and began applying a salve.

Melissa started a prescription of Valium to help her sleep, ten milligrams each night. In bed, under the covers, she would touch her husband all over his body, trying to ascertain for herself whether the numbness had spread or contracted. Eventually, she would doze off in a drug-induced sleep, her inhales and exhales falling across the house like a quiet, dark snow. Then he would hear a tapping, tiny at first but gaining in volume, the sound of her fingernails on the headboard.

When walking, he had the strange sensation that the ground moved while he was at rest, as if he were a fixed point in space, watching the planet slide by beneath him. No longer was he connected to the earth. He floated. Since childhood, he had wanted to float in the air like a bird. Now, he detested it.

On Friday, July 11, he had blood tests. A CAT scan July 15. On July 17, he received the results of his blood tests in the mail: CA: 9.2, PO4: 3.2, GLU: 97, BUN: 22, CREAT: 1.3, BUNICR: 17, URIC: 4.0, CHOL: 198, TRIG: 147, TP: 7.7, ALB: 4.9, GLOB: 2.8, A/G: 1.8, ALKP: 70, LDH: 122, SGOT: 26, SGPT: 15, BILI: 0.6, BILI D: 0.3, BILI I: 0.3, NA: 142, K: 4.0, CL: 102, CO2: 31, ANION: 9, FE: 109. Attached was a short note, with the Massachusetts General Hospital and Harvard Medical School logos at the top: "Dear

Mr. Chalmers, as you can see, everything is normal here, including the TSH, a very sensitive test for thyroid function. I can find no explanation in your blood for the numbness. Onwards and upwards. Sincerely, Armand Petrov, M.D."

At four o'clock on Monday, July 21, Bill went to see a neurologist. The neurologist, an obese man who muttered each sentence to himself before repeating it for the rest of the world, measured electrical currents, muscle masses and strengths. He conducted these experiments in his office, which smelled of ozone and alcohol. Along three walls of the cramped room were rubber hammers and tuning forks, needles, blood-pressure cuffs, coils of wires, electrodes, oscilloscopes and ophthalmoscopes, computers. Bill shuddered to think what fees the man charged. "Let me see you make a funny face. Let me see you make a funny face," said the neurologist, and he screwed up his own face by way of demonstration. No loss of muscular control there. He wiped tissues on Bill's cheeks, arms, and legs to test his sensations. He examined the cranial nerves and eyes. A peculiar dullness of expression was noted, but the retina appeared normal, the vision was good, the pupils responded correctly. He hammered Bill's elbows, his forearms, his knees, his hands. Next, the vibrating tuning fork. How many seconds did Bill feel the vibrations? Two? Three? The neurologist stroked pins along the fingertips to the hands, up the arms to the shoulder, down the legs to the feet. "You are completely numb in your feet, hands, and arms." It was 4:45. Then he wheeled out the electromyography machine, a pedestaled computer with a protruding arm from which hung wires and metallic disks. These he fastened to different parts of Bill's body and administered electrical shocks. "Silence," he suddenly boomed, without any muttered forewarning. Curves wobbled across the oscilloscope. The neurologist stuck small needles into different muscles of the feet and hands, gauging the feeble electrical currents. He scowled. He twisted his huge body this way and that as he studied the waveforms and graphs. Finally, with a toss of his hand, he consigned everything to his two frightened assistants. "I see nothing unusual, Mr. Chalmers." "Nothing?" said Bill miserably, rubbing at the gooey electrode gel remaining on his arms and legs. "How can you see nothing? I am numb. Numb. Numb. I have a problem. I want to be treated." The neurologist sighed and wiped a bit of dust from the corner of his eye. "Nerve conduction velocities are around fifty meters per second. Distal latencies are between three and four milliseconds at seven centimeters. Amplitudes are satisfactory." He shook his massive head without expression. "My apologies, but I cannot find any problem. My apologies, but I cannot . . ."

"Nothing?" Melissa said that evening. They were traveling to Sudbury to meet three other couples for dinner, in her car, a beige Volvo station wagon that already smelled of musty furniture even though it was only one year old. She had begun to insist that Bill do as little driving as possible. Besides, they were late, and her car was equipped with a radar detector. "How could the neurologist find nothing?"

"Something's wrong with your cigarette-lighter receptacle," said Bill as he tried to jam his cell-phone power plug into the receptacle. He leaned toward the dashboard, straining against his seat belts.

"What are you doing?" said Melissa. It was just getting dark, and the streetlights had come on, each giving off a pale golden glow. She switched on the headlights of her car.

Bill struggled with the plug, first twisting it so that it made a metallic scraping noise, then pushing it with his shoe. The green power light of the telephone refused to go on. "I can't believe this," he said and muttered about certain expected calls. Grunting, he yanked the plug out and tried to examine its prongs and connections in the dim light. "Can we use your phone?"

"I left mine at home. How could your neurologist not find anything? I don't understand. You're numb. Isn't that what neurologists do? Who is he?"

"A Dr. Kendry. He was highly recommended by Petrov." Bill stuck a pen into the receptacle.

"Bill," Melissa said, tears coming into her eyes. "What are we going to do? Please let me ask Henry for help. I don't understand anything. I'm so worried."

"I'll go to another neurologist."

"I can't drive anymore." She pulled to the side of the road and cried and squeezed his hand while headlights flew past.

At dinner at the Wayside Inn, in the old room with the warped floorboards, she had three glasses of wine in rapid succession. Then, understanding that she was drunk, she went silently to the restroom, where she remained for an hour, until the other couples had gone.

On the following Friday, Bill returned to the Massachusetts General Hospital to review the results of his tests. When he entered Dr. Petrov's private office, three young interns greeted him wordlessly at the door. "I hope you won't mind," said Petrov. "This is Dr. Sang, Dr. Hartunian, and Dr. Ewald." One by one, the interns smiled and nodded their heads. They were all properly dressed in blue scrub suits and hovered about Petrov like bridesmaids, waiting for his instructions. Into the little room had been squeezed five chairs, surrounded on all sides by steep cliffs of reports. Petrov nodded and the interns took their seats, their antiseptic rubber booties squeaking on the linoleum floor.

"The results of the CAT scans," said Dr. Petrov. He took a

folder from atop one of the white cliffs and handed it to Dr. Hartunian, a young man with unkempt blond hair who studied the folder for a few moments, whispered into his tape recorder, then passed it on to Dr. Sang. Dr. Sang made her own observations to her recorder. After the folder had circled through the interns, Dr. Petrov offered it to Bill, who stared at it without comprehension.

"Take your time, Mr. Chalmers," said the senior physician. After a few moments he said, "I believe I can confidently say that the CAT scans show no tumors of the brain. There are other tests which can be done for confirmation, but we also have the MRI." He paused, and the three interns began muttering into their machines. "However," continued Petrov, "section thirteen of the third set of films does show a slight ambiguity. I have sent this section to Dr. Millard Latanison, a specialist. He informs me that all features of the section fall within normal range." Immediately, Dr. Hartunian leaned over Bill's shoulder and peered again at the film in question. Dr. Petrov passed around another folder, then the blood results.

"What are you saying?" said Bill. The interns stopped their recording and studied him carefully.

"What am I saying? I believe, Mr. Chalmers, that for the most part we have succeeded in ruling out brain tumors, spinal tumors, multiple sclerosis, most vitamin deficiencies, and obvious neurological damage. I have seen Dr. Kendry's report from July 21." At this point, Petrov passed around a fourth folder to his students. "We are making progress. I'll order a new round of tests." The interns nodded approvingly.

Petrov stood up, immediately followed by the three interns. Bill remained in his chair, gaping at the various films and reports.

"You look as if you don't believe me, Mr. Chalmers," said Petrov, scratching his small red beard.

"But I am numb," shouted Bill. "My hands are numb, my arms are numb, my feet are numb." Now the three interns were staring at him sharply, like young crows. "There's something wrong with me."

"I'm not denying that," said the doctor. "It is just that we cannot yet say what it is. We must be patient, Mr. Chalmers. Patience. We have much more information about your condition than we did one month ago. I am in constant contact with specialists. I am quite satisfied that we are making good progress."

The doctor hesitated and let his hand rest on one of the tall stacks of reports. "Mr. Chalmers," he said, "before the next round of tests, I would like you to see a psychiatrist."

"A psychiatrist," exploded Bill. "For what? Do you think I'm imagining all this?"

"I would not be able to say that at this point in time. But we have to be as thorough as possible. I'm sure you understand."

"I will not see a psychiatrist."

"That is not a constructive attitude, Mr. Chalmers. I know you're upset. Illnesses are upsetting. But we are making progress. There are many more tests we can do, and will do, but you will first have to visit a psychiatrist. We are ruling things out. Please call my office tomorrow for a referral." He turned to his students. "Do you have anything to add, Dr. Sang? Dr. Ewald? Dr. Hartunian?"

<Prof: A psychiatrist. Well that says alot.>
<Cider Girl: I'm so relieveed Tom. I thought he had a
brain tumor or something. I've been worried sick.>
<Prof: So it's all in his head. That's amazing>
<Cider Girl: We don't kno that for sure. Bill says that
his doctor is trying to rule things out. Noone of the
tests show anything. The doctor must think it's
mental.>
<Prof: I would say so..>
<Cider Girl: I don't know what's going to happen. At
least if it's mental, it's not physical. Bill isn't in
any physical danger. Thank God he doesn't have a brain
tumor.>
<Prof: Yes, I can see what you mean.>
<Cider Girl: Do you mind me telling you all this?>
<Prof: No, of course not. I have a psychiatrist friend.
I'll tlak to him, confidentially of course. I wish I
could be there with you, or you could be here.>
<Cider Girl: I just wish it was over. Shrinks are
expensive, they're complicated. Virginia went to a
shrinkk a few years ago. They grab you and don't let
you go. Then the shrink is going to start looking at
his chidhood and his mother and his relationship with

his family. Then he's going to bring me in, and he's going to aks me about myself. I'm going to get involved, I know it.>

<Prof: Remember, you don't have to say anything to anybody that you don't want to.>

<Cider Girl: One of the telephones on the second line is ringing. I can't stand that phone, Tomorrow I'm going to replace it. It drives me crazy.>

<Prof: Don't tell that to the shrink. Sorry. I couldn't resist that.>

<Cider Girl: I've been wondering if I could be partly responsible..>

<Prof: Do you mean for the numbness? HOw could you be resposntible?>

<Cider Girl: If it's mental, then it could be anything. It could be me.>

<Prof: It's not you.>

<Cider Girl: How do you know it's not me? You don't really know anything about my reltshinship with Bill.>

<Prof: I don't know Bill, but I know you, and it couldn't be uyou. Believe me.>

THE PSYCHIATRIST

Petrov's office called to tell Bill that his appointment with the psychiatrist, a Dr. Pasternak, was scheduled for Monday, August 4, at 8:45 a.m.

On the day before the appointment, Bill stood in his walk-in closet. He would wear his best suit, look this Dr. Pasternak straight in the eye, and answer his questions calmly and rationally. Bill's gaze slid along the row of jackets and trousers. On second thought, he decided that what he wanted was not his best suit, which might convey the idea that he was trying to make an impression, but a moderately priced suit, solid and unassailable. There were five choices, and he tried each of them on before the mirror, judging his appearance from different angles. The first of the candidates was a dark cotton-wool blend with a soft gray stripe. He examined the stripe and concluded that it was too subtle. All should be out in the open, he had nothing to hide. A second suit was cut too aggressively with that tapered European look, projecting an extravagance even though he had paid only $250 for it. These shrinks were probably drowning in rich Boston Brahmins who threw money at their little neuroses. The third, a solid cotton, slightly wrinkled but not too wrinkled, hung from his body in a comfortable and modest manner. Yes, that was it. He had long since picked out a smart, button-down white shirt, but he spent another ten minutes selecting the tie, which should have a small splash of color. There were over fifty ties to choose from in his closet. Eventually, suit, shirt, and tie were laid out on the cushioned divan, with Gerty strictly forbidden in the room.

Early the next morning Bill was informed that the appointment with Dr. Pasternak was canceled. Some emergency had come up, a woman's voice on the telephone explained. However, an appointment with another psychiatrist, a colleague of Dr. Pasternak named Dr. Kripke, had been arranged as a substitute, at the same hour and day so as to offer the least inconvenience. In Somerville.

Bill hurled down his toast and flew shouting up the stairs. What was this? Who was this Kripke? He'd never heard of Kripke. How could they pressure him like this at the last minute? He looked at his watch. It was 7:36. He couldn't possibly make an 8:45 appointment, driving to some unfamiliar location in rush-hour traffic. Wasn't Somerville a rat's nest of one-way streets and cul-de-sacs? He ran into his bedroom and began throwing on clothes. From inside the closet, Melissa interrupted her telephone conversation to say that she could study a map and call him en route with directions. What time was it now? Seven-forty.

Alex stumbled into the hall, wearing his jockey shorts. "What's all the noise?" he shouted. "You've woken me up. I was planning on sleeping in. Dad." He stood outside his parents' bedroom door. "Dad, why are you doing this? I don't want you to go."

"It's just another doctor," Bill shouted through the closed door.

"No it isn't," Alex shouted back. "I don't want you to go. You don't need to go to a shrink."

Bill dashed into the bathroom and ran a comb through his hair, then flew out of his room, past Alex, and down the stairs. At 7:43, he was behind the wheel of his car and turned onto Waltham Street.

The long snake of traffic on Waltham Street stretched for two miles from Mass Ave. to Route 2 and crept along at an average speed of five miles per hour, stopping and starting, winding slowly around turns and over hills, honking at smaller snakes that attempted to intrude from side streets, shedding pieces of itself on the side of the road, excreting clouds of thin bluish exhaust. At least once a week, a car plowed into a telephone pole, its driver having been preoccupied on his phone, and to the poisonous gases and shouts were added the screams of ambulances and fire trucks pushing their way to the accident. Overheated cars died and were shoved to the side of the road and the snake pulled itself together and wiggled around and continued its slow journey to Route 2.

As soon as he'd entered the traffic, Bill's head began pounding and his stomach twisting, all so familiar that he scarcely noticed. Without thinking, he pressed buttons to raise his windows, recycle his air, and periodically spray cleaning fluid on his windshield. Then he opened the glove compartment and swallowed an aspirin and another pill for indigestion and picked up his cellular phone. Even with his windows up, the radios and horns of other cars were so loud that he had to press his telephone tightly against his ear to properly hear his voicemail messages: "Good morning. This is Peter Trangulo calling on behalf of Grant Twomey of Twomey, Davis, and Regina. Mr. Twomey is not fully satisfied with the correspondence of July 22. He says you will know what that refers to. He would like to arrange a conference call with you and Mr. Anthony Tobias on Wednesday at 8:30. Please let us know at your earliest convenience. Thank you." Bill winced as he remembered that he had sent only two sen-

tences of report to Mr. Twomey, far below his usual stan-
dards. But when did he have time to do more? The car several
feet in front of him stopped suddenly, and Bill slammed down
on his brake, throwing his body against the dashboard. No
damage done. Next message. "Ronald Heeschen here. 212-
707-9825. H-E-E-S-C-H at Bluebay dot com." Bill scrambled
to copy down the man's number before deleting the message.
Next message. "Hello, Mr. Chalmers, this is Jason Toothaker
at Greenway. You haven't replied to my e-mail, so I am leaving this telephone message. I will be sending you a new document today, between 10:30 and 10:45. As before, you should
treat the material with extreme confidentiality, and we will
need a definite and complete reply before noon on Tuesday. I
apologize for the short time frame, but you will understand
our pressures."

To hell with Jason Toothaker, Bill thought to himself as
the snake of traffic finally forced itself out onto Route 2 and
melded with another line of cars, five miles long. It was 8:06.
They were now creeping up a hill, bumper to bumper. He
began calculating. If he finished with Somerville by 10:00, he
might arrive at the Porter Square station by 10:15 or 10:20.
Assuming he could find a place for his car, he might be sitting
at his desk by 10:55 or 11:00, in time for the meeting with
Jasper Olswanger at 11:00. He passed under a bridge, beaded
with cars. It was 8:09. Over the next hill, the buildings of
Boston came into view, a child's toys in the distance, the Prudential Building, the Hancock, the stubby fingers of the
financial center. At the Alewife rotary, the traffic came to a
complete stop. A truck coughed up dark clouds of smoke,
prompting Bill to turn up the fan on his air conditioner to a
dangerous level. He had already spotted two cars that had
exceeded their cooling capacity, hissing and heaving steam,
slumped on the side of the road like spent animals. Poor

devils, he thought to himself and stared with fascination. But why was he gawking? He didn't have time to gawk. He must call back the man from New York. As he reached for his telephone, Bill looked at the scrap of paper with Mr. Heeschen's telephone number and recalled his impressively concise dispatch: "Ronald Heeschen here. 212-707-9825. H-E-E-S-C-H at Bluebay dot com." The message was deceptively simple, Bill thought to himself, not unlike other messages he frequently received. No explanations, no purpose, no times or dates. In all likelihood, Mr. Heeschen considered himself and his business so important that he didn't need to provide any additional information. He might have said, for example, "Hello, Mr. Chalmers, I'm Ronald Heeschen of the Bluebay Corporation in Manhattan. I read about your participation in the X, Y, or Z transaction and would like to discuss a similar enterprise with you." But no, simply "Ronald Heeschen here," as if "here" were the hub of the universe. Who was this Ronald Heeschen, anyway? And did he assume that Bill would call him back immediately? Evidently, human affairs would need to come to a screeching halt and the planet would need to stop rotating on its axis while Ronald Heeschen's urgent business was attended to this instant. Well, Bill was not playing. He had other things to do. For instance, he might prefer at this moment simply to look out the window. This Mr. Heeschen and his urgencies could wait until later today, or even tomorrow. Maybe Bill would elect not to call him back at all. What an astonishing thought. In a swift movement that startled even himself, Bill rolled down his window and tossed Mr. Heeschen out. The scrap of paper fluttered to the pavement and was shredded by the wheels of the next car in line.

It was 8:38 when Bill finally reached Planton Street, the address he was given for the psychiatrist. He lowered his windows and peered into the street. Expecting to find a modest office building that would instantly announce itself, with perhaps a garage for his car, Bill saw only a string of rickety and drab two-family houses, jammed close together on both sides of the road. Clotheslines crisscrossed each of the tiny lots, and more clothes and bedsheets were being tossed from the porches to half-naked children, who flung the wet garments up on the lines to dry. The ground-floor windows were wide open, so that Bill could smell bacon and coffee, as well as see into the cramped kitchens and rooms, women feeding their babies and packing lunchboxes for their husbands, elderly men in their undershirts smoking and shaving at the kitchen sink, the flickering of TVs. Every few moments, someone burst from a front door, shouting and cursing, apparently off to a job or some disagreeable assignment. Could there be another Planton Street? Bill wondered. He began searching for a parking place, but the little street was completely clogged with automobiles and trucks, most appearing as if they hadn't budged for a year. The one empty space was cordoned off with two chairs and a table. In the adjoining space, a shirtless young man drinking a Pepsi leaned over an open hood with his tools. He threw Bill a quizzical, defiant look. It was now 8:41.

Bill began circling the block, traversing one narrow street after another, crawling behind other automobiles that seemed to lack any destination. After ten minutes, he spotted a parking place on a little road called Dunby Street, littered with garbage and old tires. When he attempted to squeeze in, however, he discovered that the space was too small. Cars honked behind him. His telephone rang. It was Robert. "I won't be in until late this morning," he shouted into the phone. "I'm on my way to a meeting at Braxton International." He lied, as he'd been doing for weeks, to cover his absences for doctors' appointments and examinations, and he hated himself for lying. See what I've been driven to? he thought to himself.

"Enough, enough," he screamed at the honking motorists behind him. Without looking, he threw his car in reverse, slammed his foot on the accelerator, and backed his vehicle off the curb and into the street.

When at last he had found a questionable parking place several blocks away, run through the hodgepodge of streets trying to find his way back, and arrived, panting and sweating, at 37 Planton Street, it was 9:01. Sixteen minutes late. He groaned and wiped his face and straightened his tie.

Number 37, a peeling, two-story wood structure, differed little from the other houses in the neighborhood. A small wooden plaque beside the front door said "E. R. Kripke, M.D." As Bill stood reading this sign, catching his breath and still incredulous that a professional could meet clients in such a house, two barefoot boys ran up to him and began giggling. "Are you here to see the shrink?" one of them said. "We haven't seen you before." They scampered around the side of the house and brazenly stared into a window, then ran back to Bill. "We can't see who's in there now. Is it your turn? How much do you pay him for shrinking your head?" The boys hopped a short distance down the sidewalk, where they began whispering and throwing stones at a stray cat.

Bill was about to reprove the children when he noticed that two women were leaning out of a second-floor window and staring at him with an offensive curiosity. He glowered back and they vanished like squirrels up a tree. Dabbing his face again with his handkerchief, he hurried up the stairs and knocked on the front door. "Mister." "Sir." The two boys, now joined by a third, appeared on the stairs close behind him. "That's not where you go in," said the smallest of them, a dimpled, blond-headed boy with a mischievous smile. "We'll show you where you go in." They ran to a door on the side of the house. "This is where you go. But you don't come out here. You come out there, around the corner." "Let us go in with you," one of them pleaded.

"No, you can't come with me," Bill said, trying to wedge between the boys without seeming overly eager.

"Please. We'll be quiet. We know how to behave."

Bill looked at his watch and discovered that it was now 9:03. A radio next door began blasting with such ferocity that he put his hands to his ears. At that moment, the side door opened to reveal a rather small man, immaculately dressed in a bow tie and starched collar, with facial features so delicate and slight that they seemed ready to evaporate entirely. He took one step out of his house. "Off with you," he said to the boys and waved his arm at them. They stood gazing at him as if he were an uncle about to give them candy. "Off with you, or I'll speak to your parents."

"And what will you say?" one of the older boys retorted fearlessly.

"I'll say you're a nuisance and you should be punished," said the psychiatrist, failing to make himself sound angry. He turned to Bill and smiled sheepishly.

"You should pay us," said one of the boys. "We show people where to go. We showed him where to go."

"Your services are much appreciated," the psychiatrist said. "Now run along." The boys retreated only to the low fence at the edge of the lot.

"I apologize for those little pests," the psychiatrist whispered to Bill. "I am certain that some of my patients have stopped coming to me because of them. I hope they haven't overly insulted you."

"No, not at all," Bill whispered back. He would start off on the right foot with the psychiatrist, imperturbable.

"You are Mr. Chalmers, I presume," the psychiatrist continued. "I am Ethan Kripke. You must be disappointed to have gotten me when you were scheduled with Dr. Pasternak. Am I right?" He paused a moment and raised his eyebrows and smiled vaguely at his new patient. "But we had better get started. I'm afraid that we have only forty minutes now. Please."

As Bill entered the house, he could not resist looking back over his shoulder. The two nosy women had reappeared and stationed themselves at another window, where they could get a better view.

Bill was led through a closet-sized waiting room into another room, barely larger. Instantly, he could smell dust. Tinkertoys and magazines and old shoes littered the floor. There was a second door and a third, both closed, and a desk. On one of the outside walls a single half-shaded window admitted a slender shaft of sunlight, the only natural light in the room. Amidst the clutter, two chairs sat facing each other, heavy and dark like the walls.

"Do you prefer the sound of waterfalls, oceans, or forests?" asked the psychiatrist.

"Waterfalls," said Bill, without stopping to consider the oddity of the question.

"Good," said the psychiatrist. "Waterfalls are also my favorite. The forest is nice too. Whatever you prefer." He pressed a button and an electronic device on the wall began quietly gurgling, blocking out all noise from the street. For a moment, the psychiatrist stood listening to the sound of the waterfall, and a satisfaction touched his face.

"Do you know Armand Petrov?" asked Bill. He was monitoring himself carefully and concluded that his tone was suspicious. Abruptly, he smiled.

"I know of him," said the psychiatrist. "Certainly. A thorough physician." Dr. Kripke painstakingly removed his jacket and placed it in a dark corner. "Please," he said and gave his head a little tilt in the direction of the chairs. "I see a look of mistrust on your face, Mr. Chalmers. Am I right? Maybe you think that because of my disheveled surroundings, the toys and what not, I myself am disheveled as well. That would be a natural reaction. It happens that some of my patients are children, and I must amuse them." The psychiatrist waited, his hands clasped in front of him, then sat on the edge of his chair. "Please, sit down, Mr. Chalmers. I'm not going to bite you." He took out a beige notebook and glanced at the clock on the wall. "Please. Tell me what's going on."

This Dr. Kripke did not seem so forbidding, Bill thought to himself. As he began explaining his symptoms and the various medical tests, his nervousness diminished and the psychiatrist nodded sympathetically, quietly scribbling in his notebook. Apparently, he did not consider anything in Bill's presentation to be unusual or alarming. And why should he? Most likely, he saw patients with rather serious psychological conditions, people hysterical or in tears. Indeed, a box of tissues sat prominently on a table between the chairs. It would quickly become obvious that Bill's problem was physical and not mental. He was handling himself well, and he even permitted himself to let his legs twitch back and forth, as they often did, and to gaze casually around the room. In doing so, he became aware of a small red light on the desk, popping on from time to time, the telephone answering machine silently recording calls.

The psychiatrist looked up from his notebook, a distant, self-absorbed expression on his face. "I've noticed that you repeatedly refer to your numbness as a . . . problem." He studied his notebook, as if to verify his observation.

Bill nodded, unsure of the meaning of the comment. "So?"

"It might be significant," the psychiatrist said softly. He gave Bill a brief, inquisitive look and then went back to his notebook. "I don't want to make a mountain out of a mole-hill here, especially when we have barely started, but . . . Let me put it this way: a problem is generally a small thing, a difficulty that has a straightforward and rational solution. Balancing my checkbook is a problem. . . . Someone with extensive numbness for . . . How long did you say that it's been? Six weeks? Illness might be another word."

"Call it whatever you like," said Bill pleasantly. It then occurred to him that the psychiatrist had possibly hit something deep. But what was it?

"Of course, you want to be treated, you want to be well," said Dr. Kripke. "I admire your optimism. Illnesses are vague and ambiguous, omnipresent, interminable, often without any cure. But problems . . . problems are definite. Problems have beginnings and endings." He nodded thoughtfully. "I like your word problem. Let's get back to your problem, then. What's the last thing you remember before you lost your memory on the subway? Were you feeling upset or confused?"

Bill shook his head no. "It was a normal day. I know that after everything started, I panicked. I was afraid of being late for work. I had appointments that morning."

"Of course. What's the nature of your work?"

"I process information," Bill said after a long pause.

"Yes. What's the information about?" Dr. Kripke did not look up from his notebook. Bill stared at him, writing so quietly and self-assuredly, and was envious.

"All kinds of information," Bill said. "It's mostly business information. Not all."

"For whom?"

"For all kinds of people. We have dealings all over the world." This line of questioning seemed unwarranted, Bill thought to himself, and he started to protest. But he checked himself. He should not show the slightest concern about any of the psychiatrist's questions. In fact, he now stood prepared to offer any amount of random information, simply to establish his mental equilibrium. Dr. Kripke was a necessary obstacle across the road to further tests and eventual treatment. That was all.

Dr. Kripke's beeper went off, and he jumped from his chair. "I'm extremely sorry," he said, pressing buttons, "but this happens from time to time. It could be an emergency. Please excuse me." He hurried through one of the doors and carefully closed it behind him.

Bill leaned back in his chair, relieved to be alone for a few minutes, and listened to the pleasant gurgling of the waterfall. It was a soothing sound in the stillness and closeness of the room. Vacantly, he noticed a faded plaque above the psychiatrist's desk that read: "The mind is its own place. It can make a Heaven of Hell or a Hell of Heaven." Although he had intended to stand up and stretch, Bill now found himself unable to move from the chair. His eyelids began to grow heavy and he let his head drop back. The room dimmed. Far away, the tiny red light of the answering machine flickered and glowed like a firefly.

Something pinched his side. Bill found himself curled up in the chair like a dog with his eyes closed. Maybe he'd been asleep. He quickly straightened out his suit and glanced at his watch.

Shortly, the psychiatrist returned, with apologies. He peered at the clock on the wall and reviewed his beige notebook.

"Was it an emergency?" Bill asked with a little smile. He would show the shrink that, among his other worthwhile qualities, he had a sense of humor.

"I'm sorry," the psychiatrist said softly, "but I never talk about other patients. I'm sure you understand. Everything here is completely confidential."

"You had two calls while you were gone. Maybe three."

"Oh," said the psychiatrist. He stared for a moment at the answering machine. Then he returned his attention to Bill and lightly tapped his pen against his notebook. "You were telling me about your work. You analyze information. Do you also gather the information?"

"No, there are other people and companies that gather it. We don't have researchers as such." We don't have researchers as such? Bill repeated silently to himself. What an absurd comment. Was it true? No, surely he himself did research from time to time. He'd researched the Conflow deal.

"If you're only sending information from A to B, what's the value added?" asked the psychiatrist, so softly that Bill could hardly hear him over the gurgle of the waterfall. "It sounds like you're a middleman. I'm afraid I don't understand."

Now Bill felt a definite twinge of suspicion. Was Dr. Kripke intentionally insulting him, hoping that he would become angry and lose his composure? Possibly the psychiatrist was only politely suggesting that Bill's job was boring, a claim not without some validity. Now that he thought about it, Bill recalled reading somewhere that boredom could cause various neuroses. Possibly Dr. Kripke was pursuing that line of thought. Let him, if he wished. The clock was ticking.

"Is all this relevant, Doctor?" Bill said finally, using a measured tone of voice.

"I'm not sure," said the psychiatrist. He had put down his notebook and folded his hands carefully in his lap. "There's certainly a question here. If your primary physician isn't sure you have a neurological problem . . . and already it seems as if he's removed the big ones like brain tumors, MS, and so forth . . . among the repertoire of possibilities . . . If it's not neurological, then something else happened. There was a

lead up to it clearly." The red light popped on. The psychiatrist's eyes darted to his desk for a few moments, then back.
"You've already suggested that you were under stress. When
you describe what you do, I don't get the sense that you're
fully comfortable talking about it. There may be something
going on there."

To his surprise, Bill found himself agreeing with some of
what the psychiatrist said, although he did not understand it.
Something going on there, he repeated to himself. He wrinkled his face and began pondering these new aspects of his
condition.

There followed a series of questions about Bill's father
and mother and his childhood, during which the gurgling from
the waterfall seemed to gain in intensity. Bill looked at his
watch. It was 9:33. In another twelve minutes or so he could
leave. He was still conducting himself well. However, the questions about his parents had disturbed him and raised additional
considerations. With a sudden wave of guilt, Bill realized that
he hadn't yet told his mother anything. Shouldn't he tell her,
even though she would immediately forget? He was her son,
she was his mother.

"You mentioned that you always wanted brothers and
sisters as a child," said the psychiatrist, "that you hated being an only child. Then why did you have only one child
yourself?"

Bill was stunned by the question. "Alex."

"Yes. Why did you and your wife have only Alex? Why not
more children?"

Why? Bill thought to himself. It seemed like they'd always
had one child. "We never discussed it."

"You never discussed it? You never discussed having more
children?" Dr. Kripke put down his pen.

"I don't think we ever discussed it," said Bill, straining

to remember those early years of their marriage. "Maybe Melissa was too busy for another child and I didn't want the responsibility. I can't remember."

Kripke looked at Bill for a moment, nodded his head, and wrote something in his notebook. "How would you describe your relationship with your wife?" he asked without looking up.

"Good," said Bill, still thinking about why he and Melissa had only one child.

"How about sexually? . . . Are you intimate?"

"Yes, of course," Bill answered uncomfortably. "I don't know how intimate the average couple is." That was the truth. He didn't believe a word that his colleagues and friends told him.

The psychiatrist nodded. "Tell me more about your work." Now Dr. Kripke was writing very rapidly. "Have you had any problems with negative feedback at work, any clashes with people?"

"No." It was 9:44. The time was almost up.

"Do you like your work?"

Bill paused. "I'm good at what I do," he said slowly.

The psychiatrist said something so softly that it was inaudible. Then, "Are you angry at anyone?"

"No." He had answered too quickly. He'd lied. Ridiculously, he felt guilty. Why should he feel guilty? The psychiatrist had put his pen down and seemed to be waiting.

"Yes, I'm angry," Bill said.

"At whom?"

"I don't know."

"Ah," said the psychiatrist, looking up and nodding. "We will need to come back to this. And what do you do when you're angry?"

Bill shrugged his shoulders.

It was 9:48. "We're out of time," Kripke said and laid his

pen down on his notebook. "But we were interrupted. I'd like to give you some kind of summary of my impressions . . . just a few comments."

Bill was anxious to leave, but he found himself eager to hear the psychiatrist's analysis. He stood up, sat down.

Dr. Kripke studied the door to the waiting room, as if looking straight through it at the next patient in line. "I can quickly say a few things at this point," he said quietly, "although I don't yet know you very well. You're angry, that's clear. You seem to have a vague frustration that's been building over time. For some reason, you don't want to say much about your job. So there's some anxiety there. You're probably under stress. There's certainly a lot of stress out there. But it's possible to adapt to stress. We all adapt to stress. The human being is amazingly adaptive. We need to develop strategies for you to adapt. On the anger, everybody has to put their anger somewhere. Some people get diarrhea, some people get headaches. You could be putting your anger into numbness. It's interesting that you've developed precisely those symptoms that make it the most difficult for you to work."

"So you think this is mental?" said Bill, realizing that the interview had to end in this way. "You think my numbness is mental?"

Someone was knocking at the door to the waiting room, a frantic, shrill rap like a woodpecker's beak. It was 9:55, ten minutes past the official end of his session. The psychiatrist rose from his chair with a silly, blushing smile and indicated that Bill should leave by the middle door. "What you've described sounds like a complicated problem, Mr. Chalmers. I sense that we've glimpsed just the tip of the iceberg." He hurriedly wrote something down on a piece of paper and handed it to him. "Let's start you on some medication to eliminate the numbness. We'll review your progress in a couple of weeks."

Bill stood staring at the prescription in his hand. "Two weeks? Should I come back sooner?"

"That might be helpful," Kripke said softly, shepherding Bill through the door. "You can call tomorrow for another appointment if you wish."

THE FRENCH PHOTOGRAPHER

Bill had been at his office since seven in the morning, laboring through a stack of papers on his desk and sulking about Kripke and his infuriatingly soft voice. What did Kripke know about events in the world? Kripke hid in his house with his fake waterfalls and lollipops. So Bill was angry, that was the great psychiatrist's conclusion. Bill stared at his computer screen. The message prompts pulsed like African driver ants about to burst through a valley, obsessed, eating everything in sight, eating his hands at the keyboard, his body, the desk, even the computer itself, leaving nothing but white bones. He was ant food. He was weeks behind. His typing was slow. His brain was slow. Slow. He slammed his numb hand on the desk. He would have to adapt, he would have to find places to take out his anger. Isn't that what the good doctor said? He struck his hand again and marveled at the way the skin turned white and then red. And he was hot, dripping sweat. The office was boiling. Ant weather. He took off his jacket and tossed it in the direction of a chair.

Amy arrived with a new stack of documents. Was it 9:00 already? More documents? He almost yelled at her.

"Is there anything wrong, Mr. Chalmers?" said Amy, her tender face clouding over.

"No."

She stood at the door and smiled. "My mother's getting remarried on Sunday."

Bill repeated the words to himself. He looked at her standing at the door, the tilt of her in the doorway. "Amy," he said.

"My mother is getting married again. It's the first time she's been happy in seven years."

"That's wonderful." What a sweet young woman, Bill said to himself. And to think that he had almost shouted at her. He had to get hold of himself.

"I just thought I'd tell you," said Amy, appearing embarrassed. "Is there anything wrong, Mr. Chalmers?"

"No, nothing's wrong. So your mother's getting remarried." He managed a smile. Surely, Amy knew that he was far behind in his work. She was a gentle young woman who had concentrated on staying out of everyone's way ever since Jenkins had hired her straight out of high school. Could he talk to her? She might understand.

"The photographer from *Transaction* is ready, Mr. Chalmers," said Amy. "He wants everyone to come now."

"How long will this take?"

"He didn't say."

With a sigh, Bill picked up his jacket and went to the reception area, where several of his colleagues paced back and forth on the burgundy rug. The photographer and his assistant bustled about with cameras and light screens and tripods.

"I don't want the photograph now," boomed George Mitrakis, who was sitting in his shirtsleeves on the Queen Anne sofa. His face was flushed and wet with perspiration. "We've got problems now. Come back tomorrow." The photographer looked at George briefly, said nothing, and continued setting up his equipment. Next to George on the sofa was Ms. Theroux, talking to someone on her phone. She had taken off her watch and placed it prominently on the coffee table. "I thought you were ready for us," George shouted at the photographer. It seemed to Bill that everyone was in a foul mood. Possibly it was the heat. The air conditioner was blasting out warm air like it was January, and, what's worse, a rumor had drifted up from below that the air conditioners worked perfectly on floors one through thirty-six. In an effort to reduce the heat, someone had let down the white blinds on the floor-to-ceiling hall windows. The partners hardly ever noticed these windows, but so much sudden white in the halls was disorienting.

"Will we be on the cover?" asked Mr. Kramer.

"They pay me just for the shooting," answered the photographer. "You ask the wrong person." He took a small yellow handkerchief from his breast pocket and pressed it against his delicate cheeks, then returned the handkerchief to the pocket.

"This heat is a disgrace," said George from the Queen Anne. The president took off his tie and began punching buttons on his telephone.

"Where do we go?" someone said.

"He wants us standing around George. George and Lisa stay on the sofa."

"It's after nine-thirty."

Harvey Stumm appeared, so suddenly that Bill was still slumped against the reception desk, with his hands twisting in his pockets, and he just had time to tuck in his shirt to keep himself from looking as unprofessional and over-whelmed as he felt. He regretted his appearance even more when he saw that Stumm did not seem at all touched by the heat, but was fully buttoned up in a brown checkered suit, with his small white face perfectly dry. Only his tie was loosened imperceptibly.

"What an imposing group," said Stumm.

"Thank you, Harv."

"It's hot," said Stumm. "Nobody can think in this heat. I can't think in this heat."

"I've called down to Mr. Kelly to get the air conditioner fixed right away," said George.

"Good," said Stumm. "That's good." He stepped carefully over the electrical cords and stood behind George. Bill was on the vice president's left, Diane Rossbane on his right. David Hamilton, Nate Linden, and Milt Kramer crouched unhappily in front of the sofa. Lisa Theroux had mysteriously vanished.

A light exploded prematurely under the reflection tent, then again. *"Merde,"* the photographer said and glowered at his assistant. On the floor, some kind of transformer hummed and buzzed.

Stumm leaned over the Queen Anne and began talking quietly to the president. "While I'm here, George, let me mention one thing about the Sperry deal."

"The Sperry deal is under control," said George.

"I'm sure it is. One thing. You don't want to be talking to Lancaster in this final stage. Lancaster won't be able to keep up. You want to be talking to Benjamin Lloyd."

"I like Bertram Lancaster," said the president defensively.

"Of course you do," said Stumm. "But that's not the point." George sighed and nodded.

One picture had been taken. When could they leave? Bill was baking in his jacket, he felt like he was going to faint. Someone came in with a call from the West Coast. Bill opened his eyes and looked at his watch. It was already 9:42.

Later that morning, there was a knock on Bill's door. The sound seemed to come from another planet. Harvey Stumm entered, a rare visit. "Good morning again," the vice president said and smiled. Bill snapped out of his trance and turned off his monitor.

Stumm unbuttoned his jacket and leaned against the edge of Bill's work table. "A nuisance, that photographer. Came up from New York." Stumm paused, letting his eyes quickly roam over the minor commendations framed on the wall. "Alex must be what now? Thirteen? Fourteen?"

"Fourteen."

"Yes." The vice president paused. "I thought I'd see how things with Digitel are coming along."

"Okay."

Stumm pursed his small lips and ran his fingers through his thinning hair. "Digitel is an important account," he said softly. He was staring at Bill.

Then the ants exploded out of the screen. Bill could feel them climbing, biting. Ant food.

"You did a fine job setting that up last year," said Stumm. He paused and glanced at a document on Bill's work table. "Still. We're getting some complaints. Do you need any help?"

"Excuse me," Bill heard himself saying. He went to the rest room, where he poured water on his face and pressed himself against the cool of the tiles.

MARCELLO'S

In the middle of the week, Bill started on Prozac, at twenty milligrams per day. The capsules were a muted green and yellow.

"Finally," said Melissa that evening as she sat at the vanity and gingerly dabbed her face with skin toner. The cotton balls were like snow against the red of her scrubbed face. She glanced at Bill in her mirror, then dipped a Q-tip into a jar of cream, transferred the cream to her fingertips, and rubbed it under her eyes. A different cream, beige colored, filled the cracked lines around her mouth. "It's too hot to cook," she mumbled. "Why don't we get some Chinese. Or Marcello's."

"Finally what?" asked Bill, holding a handkerchief to his nose. A fine gray dust hung in the air from the grouting of the new bay windows downstairs.

"Finally we're getting some treatment for you."

Bill detected in her voice that familiar tone that meant she thought she'd been wronged. Perhaps she was just irritated by the heat, or her reflection in the mirror. "The doctor didn't say—" The telephones rang, the nearest in the bathroom, its chisel transformed into grating reverbations by the hard tiles and glass. Melissa flinched. "I've got it," Bill blurted. "Hello. . . . Hello, David. . . . I can't." Bill squinted at his watch, trying to read it in the half light of the bathroom:

7:03. "I know it's Tuesday. . . . I don't have time tonight, I'm sorry. . . . Fax? Our fax machine is broken. Yes. I'll come by your office tomorrow. . . . Nine. . . . Yes, I can e-mail you. Goodbye. No. Goodbye, David."

Bill returned to the blanket chest at the foot of the bed, where he had been sorting through the past few days' worth of magazines and catalogues. One by one, they thudded as he tossed them into a cardboard box. Every few minutes he squeezed his hands to see if the numbness had lessened, but the only effect of the Prozac so far was to make him nauseous. Two boxes full now. *Herrington, Signals, Peruvian Connection, House Beautiful, Sharper Image, Newsweek, Eddie Bauer, Fabrications, Lands' End, Time, InfoAge, House and Antiques, Lifestyle Fascination, Downeast, Architectural Digest, Antique World, Country Living, Business Week, Gardener's Eden, Trafalgar, Victoria, Horse and Rider, Ballard Design, MacWorld, Illuminations, Tech and Spec.* "Fabrications has sent us two catalogues this week." "We're big customers." "Did they give us a refund for that comforter?" "I don't know. Look on the last Visa statement." "There wouldn't be time for it to appear on the last statement. Didn't they give you a slip or something when you sent it back?" "No. I never really liked that comforter. We shouldn't have bought it." "What do you mean? We talked about it. We both loved it." "I don't think I ever liked it." "Then we should tell them to stop sending us the catalogue." "That's impossible. They'll keep sending us the catalogue until we're dead. Even after. Helen Wolfe got catalogues in her name for a year after she'd died." "Did you look at the Eddie Bauer?"

"Stop," shouted Melissa. "Stop. If you don't stop I'm going to scream."

"I'm finished."

She began rubbing her moist face with powder to take away the shine. "I feel like our life has been on hold since the middle of June," she said. "When was it? June twenty-fourth? June twenty-fifth? It was a Wednesday, I think. Wednesday, June twenty-fifth. It's been over six weeks." Her voice wavered, and he looked over at her and saw tears in the mirror. She dabbed at them quickly. Then, with her little finger, she spread a small quantity of ochre paste beneath her eyes to conceal the dark shadows. "Let's go on a trip. When you're well. That would be good for us. We need a trip. Please let's go on a trip."

"Shh," Bill whispered, "I don't want Alex to hear any of this." He cracked open their bedroom door and peered down the hall. A thin layer of gray dust lay on the banister leading to Alex's closed door. On the television, the muscular voice of an anchorman—*funds for the refurbishment of the Mammal Hall of the Smithsonian* . . .

"Why shouldn't Alex hear this?" said Melissa. "He's your son. He's worried about you. He should know what's going on with you. Do you know what's going on with him? You hardly see him. He's stopped fencing. Now he's playing chess. He's got all the games between Kasyski, or whatever his name is, and that computer on his computer." She paused and put a spray of pink blush on her cheeks. "You should play with him. Do you know anything about chess? You should play with him."

"I don't know how to play chess. I knew when I was much younger."

"What?"

"I'll learn chess. I was just getting the hang of fencing."

"You funny man," she said suddenly, laughing and throwing her arms in the air. Her face softened. "Since when did you learn fencing? Go get some pizza. And take Alex with you. He needs to get out of that room."

"No one has said that the numbness will stop," said Bill,

facing his wife's back at the vanity. "Nobody has said it's psychiatric. You sound like you think it's all in my head." He waited for her to reply, but she began massaging her eyes. "Dr. Petrov is running more tests. I talked to his office today. So it's probably not psychiatric." Bill hurled his jacket onto the divan and walked to the window. The damask drapes were half drawn, and he began wrapping the cord around his left index finger, tightly, watching the tip of the finger turn red. How odd, he thought, that there could be blood with no feeling. Behind him, the remote clicked and the television became silent.

"That television was making me deaf," said Melissa. She took a deep breath, he could hear the air sucking. "I'm just glad you're taking the Prozac. That's all."

"The shrink is trying it out," he shot back. "He doesn't know. I don't know. Maybe something will happen. I don't know." He turned from the window and saw that she was sitting up very straight now, despite her exhaustion, and was staring at him through the mirror. Their eyes met in reflection.

"So what if it's mental," she said softly. "What difference does it make what it is, as long as you can get over it."

"I know what you're trying to do. I should get another doctor. A good neurologist. That's what I should do. I'll get another doctor tomorrow. These doctors don't tell you anything." He sneezed. Damn those bay windows, he thought to himself.

She continued to gaze at him through her vanity mirror. "Bill." Now her voice was careful, as if she were handling porcelain in her shop. "I'm beginning to think that you have some . . . factitious illness."

"Factitious illness?" He laughed bitterly. "You mean fictitious illness. At least get the name right."

"Factitious." She turned around on her vanity chair and looked directly at him. "It's a psychiatric condition."

"Who told you that?" Bill said. "Factitious illness. Did Henry tell you that?"

"I shouldn't have said anything."

"Have you been talking to Henry about me? I asked you not to talk to Henry about me." His face throbbed.

"Henry is my brother. And he knows about these things."

"Henry thinks he knows about everything." Bill kicked a leg of his bureau. It made a hollow sound. "I knew Henry was going to get involved in this. You might as well tell me what Henry said."

"Henry said that some people develop psychosomatic symptoms to prevent them from doing certain things."

"Bull!" Bill shouted. "Do you believe that? Henry never liked me. You know that Henry never liked me. Henry would have been happy if you'd married that college roommate of his and stayed in Fayetteville."

Then she went to him and put her arms around his waist. "I'm so sorry," she whispered. "I've made you feel worse. I don't know what to do." She kissed him on the base of his neck and put her head against his shoulder. "I promise I won't talk to Henry about you. I just want you to be well."

What was wrong with him? The thought pinched and cut in his mind as he embraced her. He took a deep breath and could smell the lavender in her skin cream. "The shrink said that I'm angry," he said, holding her close. "Do you think I'm angry?"

"A little. What else did he say?"

"He said I'm under stress. And I have to diffuse my anger."

"Yes."

He held her against his body. There was so much that he wanted to tell her, so much was twisting and tilting in his head. Nothing was the same anymore, trees, light, the sound of footsteps, air, yes, even air. "Melissa. Do I seem different to you? Since the accident?"

"Of course you're different. You're ill. What are you talking about? Is there something else?" She hesitated. "Do you still love me?"

"Yes, I love you. It's not that."

"You're sick, Bill. I just want you to be well. That's what I want."

"Melissa, look at me."

"I just want you to get well."

A bell jingled brightly as Bill and Alex opened the door to Marcello's Pizza. "Yo, Mr. C., how are you," shouted one of the girls behind the counter. "I made your pizza personally. Large mushroom and extra cheese. Maybe you should try something else next time."

"Nice suggestion," said Bill, "but you don't know my wife." His voice was drowned by the breathy groan of the refrigerator that contained the soft drinks and prepackaged salads. Bill and Alex stood just inside the door, wriggling out of their slickers and hats. It had begun to rain, but the inside of Marcello's was as hot as ever, with the two ovens burning furiously and the heat of the day still thick across the little café. All of the workers behind the counter wore bandanas around their heads to keep from dripping into the food.

"Number 89, meatball and ziti," someone yelled. A man with an umbrella pushed his way through the crowd of people waiting for their orders, slapped his money down, and hurried out with his sandwich. The doorbell jingled. He had been in such a rush that he'd collided with two of the hanging baskets of plastic flowers, which swayed after he'd gone like waves from a passing boat.

Bill sighed and looked for a place to sit down. He was mulling over his conversation with Melissa.

"Alex, Alex." A group of two boys and two girls, all with

streaked hair and jammed together in a booth, motioned for Alex to join them. One of the couples was clenched in a kiss.

"Do you want to sit with your friends?" asked Bill as he slid into an empty booth. "I won't mind."

Alex shrugged his shoulders. "No, this is okay." Alex tried to look out the window, but all of the windows had fogged up with the rain, so he contented himself with emptying the little packages of salt on the table.

A man and his two children flew through the door, the bell jingling. "It's an oven in here," he said and hurried up to the counter.

At the sound of the voice, Bill looked toward the counter and saw his friend Stephen Roe. "Stephen."

Stephen, unrecognizable in his raincoat and drooping hat, turned and grinned broadly at Bill. "Caught in the act," he said. "Don't tell Maggie you saw me here getting junk food."

"Maggie out of town?"

"Yep. She's at some academic convention in San Francisco. You up for tennis on Saturday? I've got court time."

"I'll give you a call," said Bill.

Stephen grinned again. On his way out, he said hello to Alex and patted Bill on the shoulder.

As the jingling subsided, Bill thought to himself that he should have been more friendly to Stephen. He turned to his son, his precious Alex, and smiled. "I'm glad we're sitting together. I enjoy your company." Alex nodded in acknowledgment and began to run his fingers through the mounds of salt, making designs on the Formica tabletop. Unconsciously, Bill glanced at his watch and looked toward the counter. A light sheen of rain lay on his head like a silk handkerchief and on the collar of his suit jacket, glistening in the fluorescent lights. As he brushed himself off, the rainwater smelled fragrant and cool. He felt relieved to have gotten out of the house, able for a few moments to forget about himself and his problems. "I'll check on our pizza," he said and made his way across the scuffed wooden floor to the counter.

"Number 90, small pepperoni and cheese," shouted one of the sweating workers as he lifted a pizza out of the oven on his paddle.

"Is it still raining, Mr. C.?" asked Katie, the girl who had greeted Bill earlier. She went to the oven to see if his pizza was ready. Bill found himself pleased at the way Katie referred to him and followed her with his eyes. She was a chunky, pretty girl, rosy in complexion, with strands of hay-colored hair that could not be held in by her bandana. The red glow from the ovens and the heat made her face even rosier. Bill had seen her at Marcello's for over a year, since she wore braces.

"Yes, Katie," he answered, "and the weatherman says it'll rain all evening. Which means nobody knows." It then occurred to Bill that Alex and Katie should get to know each other. They seemed about the same age. He glanced back at Alex, who was sitting alone at their table, and then at Katie. Two other teenaged girls were flying about behind the counter, sectioning pizzas and answering telephone calls, and Bill leaned toward Katie as discreetly as possible. "Tell me, Katie," he said in a low voice. He hesitated. "Do you have a boyfriend?"

"Boyfriend! Thanks but no thanks, Mr. C.," Katie answered bitterly, ignoring the snickers of the other girls. "All the guys want is to see how much they can get off you."

"Oh, of course," Bill mumbled in embarrassment. He grimaced, thinking to himself that Alex was worth a dozen of those boys at the other booth. But there was nothing he could do now, for he had clearly stuck his foot in his mouth.

"No problem," said Katie. "Your pizza will be ready in five minutes." Bill ducked away quickly and rejoined his son at the table.

"I'm learning Chinese," said Alex, with a note of pride in his voice. He looked up from his salt drawings as if to make sure his father had heard him.

"Really," said Bill, smiling. "Really. I've never heard of anyone your age learning Chinese." Bill muttered something about how he regretted his own lack of languages and that he had once known a little French. But Chinese, that was something.

"Brad says that the Chinese will take over the world," said Alex, "and we should be ready for them." He shook his rainhat. "I'm not sure I believe him. Brad is such a liar sometimes. What do you think, Dad?"

Bill thought for a moment, grateful to be asked his opinion. "I don't think the Chinese will take over the world," he said. "But it's always good to learn a new language." He nodded approvingly. "You're really something, Alex."

"I saw on the Net that the Chinese have a population of 1.2 billion," remarked Alex, "and sixty-one attack submarines."

"Where do you find all of that stuff?" said Bill. "Sixty-one attack submarines."

Alex nodded and glanced over at the group of two boys and two girls, who were noisily leaving with their pizzas and drinks.

"Number 97, large mushroom and extra cheese," Katie shouted.

"That's us." Bill rose from the table.

"Wait, Dad," said Alex, catching his father gently by the arm. "Look at this." He pointed to one of his figures made of salt. "That means man in Chinese. See how it looks like a man. There're the two legs. There's the middle." For a moment they stood together, gazing at the figure in salt, then Alex shrugged and swept it away.

———

That night, Prozac in his brain, Bill woke up a half-dozen times, with piercing dreams in between. In one, he was receiving a piano lesson from his old music teacher in her dark little room, barely large enough for the piano and the standing brass lamp and her chair. Utter stillness, the smell of camphor and old clothes. The sound of a clock. He could see the thin skin on her temple, throbbing as she bent over him on the bench. "Listen," she said, smiling with that angelic smile of hers, and she played the Chopin prelude for him, slowly, slowly. Each note was a lifetime. "Do you hear the sorrow?" She said that he should think of a funeral procession. But he had never been to a funeral. "Listen." He closed his eyes, dreaming within his dream, and listened to the languid notes of the music. Faces appeared, his mother, his father, his grandmother whom he'd never met. "Do you hear the sorrow?" He listened harder, strained to hear the sorrow, and said that he heard it, lying. Certainly, she would know that he had not heard it, she would know. Yet he wanted so much to please her. Her angelic smile, her round face, her bigness beside him.

```
>> MAIL 50.02.04 << From: Petrov at MGH.HARVARD.EDU
====> Received: from TAR.HARVARD.EDU by HARVARD.EDU
with BFP
id AQ74078; Wed, 6 Aug 9:13:36 EDT
for WCHALM@PLYM.COM; Wed, 6 Aug 9:13:52 -0400
Press * for message


>>> MAIL 50.02.04 <<< From: Petrov at MGH.HARVARD.EDU
Dear Mr. Chalmers,
Tej attahed file contains an ectremely interesting
article from the New England Journal of Medicine that
may relate to your illness. Note graph VI in
particular.
We proceed on all frontts.
Sincerely, Armand Petrov, M.D.


>>> MAIL 50.02.04 <<< From: ACHALM at AOL.COM
==> Received: from RING.AOL.COM by AOL.COM with GOTP
id AQ06498; Wed, 6 Aug 11:02:27 EDT
for WCHALM@PLYM.COM; Wed, 6 Aug 11:02:49 -0400
MESSAGE LOCK OVERRIDE
>>> MAIL 50.02.04 <<< From: Alexander at AOL.COM
```

Dear Dad,

I figured out that there are 20 possibilities for the
first move of each chess player. I almost fogot the
knights. That means there are 20 × 20 = 400 different
ways the board can be afater the first move on both
sies. It's over 10,000 after the second move. Is that
stuff you're taking working?
Alex

_____

_____

>>> MAIL 50.02.04 <<< From: Fred at Noplace.Com
==> Received: from RING.AOL.COM by AOL.COM with GOTP
Orlando Vacation Give Aways, Fred@Noplace.Com

_____

_____

>> MAIL 50.02.04 << From: Petrov at MGH.HARVARD.EDU
====> Received: from TAR.HARVARD.EDU by HARVARD.EDU
with BFP
id AQ74078; Fri, 8 Aug 18:12:03 EDT
for WCHALM@PLYM.COM; Fri, 8 Aug 18:12:59 -0400
Press * for message

>>> MAIL 50.02.04 <<< From: Petrov at
MGH.HARVARD.EDU
Dear Mr. Chalmers,

Your myleogram is back, and I see nothing askew int he
reslts. We have a number of options. There is good
informatin to be gained by abiopsy, although this is an
invasive procedure and contains some risk. Also, more
blood workk would not be without reward.

   I would also like you to consider a PET scan
(Positron Emission Tomography), which is state-of-the-

art medicine and a highly sophistaicated uhion of
nuclear physics, biiochemistym and advance computer
technology. The CT and MRI can only iindicate
anatomical structures, while the PET measures metabolic
activity. MGH is one of only a handful of medical
centers in the world that have a PET facility, and I
hav jpersonaaly worked wth the machine. Most insurance
companies do nt cover PET, but I recommend it to many
of my patients. Of course, the decision must be yours.

There is no reason to come in to my office. I look
forward to hearing from you by E-mail, which is the
best way to reach me. In the meanwhlke, I atach an
intersteing article from Brain.
Sincerely, Armand Petrov, M.D.

_____

_____

>> MAIL 50.02.04 << From: Petrov at MGH.HARVARD.EDU
====> Received: from TAR.HARVARD.EDU by HARVARD.EDU
with BFP
id AQ74078; Sat, 9 Aug 11:48:22 EDT
for WCHALM@PLYM.COM; Sat, 9 Aug 11:48:39 -0400
Press * for message

>>> MAIL 50.02.04 <<< From: Petrov at
MGH.HARVARD.EDU
Dear Mr. Chalmers,
I thought you ight be intereted in seeing the attched
message from Dr. Jeffrey Soames of the Mayo Clinic. I
have taken the liberty of consulting withhim about your
case and wil kep him apprised of al future developments
and new findings.
Sincerely, Armand Petrov, M.D.
  Attached file:

RE: Case MGH 384930
Dear Dr. Petrov,
I have taken a look at the data for the above case and
concur with your analysis at this time.
Jeffrey Soames, SOAMES@MAYO.EDU

>>> MAIL 50.02.04 <<< From: ETM at MarbENT.COM
====> Received: from BUSTER.INTER.COM by INTER.COM
with NIO
id AQ74078; Sat, 9 Aug 13:02:13 EDT
for WCHALM@PLYM.COM; Sat, 9 Aug 13:02:27 -0400
Press * for message

>>> MAIL 50.02.04 <<< From: ETM at MarbENT.COM
Dear Mr. and Mrs. Chalmers,
You are cordially invited to a party at my house,
Marbopolis, on Saturday, August 16, 8pm until midnight.
The address is 1 Pastomine, Weston. Regrets only.
I look forward to seeing you.
Sincerely, Ed Marbleworth

LIFEIMAGES

"What will I wear?" exclaimed Melissa when Bill phoned her that Saturday afternoon. "Marbopolis," she repeated in disbelief. "I'm going to have to buy a dress."

"Your closet is full of dresses," said Bill, clamping the telephone against his head as he sat dazed at his computer. Since midmorning, he had been reading without comprehension the journal articles sent by Petrov over the Internet. A dozen memoranda of his own were waiting in cyberspace.

"I don't have any summer gowns," said Melissa. "I've got only winter gowns. People will be there from New York. They'll be wearing summer gowns."

"Where are you? I can hear honking. It sounds like you're in your car."

"I just left Lexington Television and Appliance. I'm on my way to Virginia's. But I'm going to call and tell her I can't come. I need to get a haircut immediately. There's just time for it to grow out. And then I'm going downtown to buy a gown. You need a new suit."

"I don't have time to get a new suit," said Bill. He took a small sip from a glass of ginger ale, which he'd been drinking for intermittent nausea caused by the Prozac. Crumbs of crackers, his only lunch, littered the floor.

"You want to hang up, don't you," said Melissa. "Please don't hang up. I want to talk. I'm on Route 2 now, I can talk."

Why had they been invited? she asked. She would bet that with one stroke of the key Edward Marbleworth had invited all of the partners at Plymouth. But what did it matter how— they were invited. For years she had wanted to see the inside of the Marbleworth mansion, and at last she could have her wish. But how would she look, compared to all of those glamorous women? They had thousands to spend on maids and face-lifts and Versace gowns. They would think she was one of those ignorant southern women. Maybe she and Bill should stay home. They could say they were ill.

"How can we not go?" Bill said, wincing at the new page of text that had just appeared on his screen. "All the VIPs will be there." And all the Plymouth people. They would certainly notice if he wasn't there, George and Harv whispering to themselves and scoring their points. Tick, one for Diane. Tick, one for Nate.

"You're always worrying about what people think of you," said Melissa. "You can't let those guys run your life."

"You're right," said Bill, "they can't run my life. Why should I let other people run my life? I've been letting those jerks run my life. Who are they, to run my life?" He stood up from his desk and began circling the small downstairs study, holding the phone against his ear. The wooden floorboards creaked under his feet. Suddenly, the light emptied from the room as a cloud passed in front of the sun, leaving the dark walls almost invisible and even more confining. He felt like he was inside a closet. "Dr. Kripke said I need to find places to let out my anger." He paused, recalling his last ambiguous session with the shrink. "I should confront them, George and Harv, confront them at the Marbleworth party. They'd be out of their element." He was angry, certainly, but exactly at whom he didn't know.

"Ohhh," Melissa said. "What do you mean, confront them? You have to be careful." A confusion of honking and engine noises came through the phone.

"I can't hear you," Bill shouted. "What did you say? Speak louder."

"You have to be careful," shouted Melissa.

"I've already been careful. I haven't said two words to them at the office." For weeks, Bill thought to himself, he had been avoiding his colleagues as much as possible. He was fairly certain that his condition was no longer unknown at the office, although he wasn't sure who knew or precisely what was known. No one had commented, yet the president and vice president surely knew something. Stumm had jabbed at Bill about falling behind, and the secretaries, so acutely aware of the ebb and flow, seemed to be giving him a wide berth in the hallway.

"I think I should let out my anger," he said loudly. "A man has to respect himself." He put his ear close to the phone, listening for Melissa's reply, but heard only a roar.

The evening of the party, Bill came downstairs immediately after dressing, his anxiety clearly making Melissa more nervous and thus delaying their departure. As he paced the entrance hall, checking his watch every few moments, he stopped in front of the mirror and winced. His rented tuxedo fit him as well as could be expected, even making him seem more slender than he actually was, but it could not conceal his nauseous condition. His skin was pale and noticeably green. His face sagged. He knew that he was not a handsome man, but now he looked positively wretched. In frustration, he stomped the floor, then reeled when a new wave of queasiness washed over him. What he hated more than anything in the world was waste, and tonight he was sure to waste a fine opportunity. Tonight, at such a gathering of the rich and the powerful, he could have made an important impression, raised himself up in the world. But with the bilious reflection he now saw in the glass, that was impossible. However, he did have his anger. His anger would serve a different end. Nauseous or not, he was prepared to confront George Mitrakis, or anyone else. Tomorrow he might even decide to have a word with Dr. Petrov, or dismiss him altogether for his impotent examinations and messages without so much as a provisional diagnosis. And the shrink, Dr. Kripke, whose only comment after the last session was that he would increase the dosage of Prozac from twenty to thirty milligrams per day. Kripke was useless. Again Bill stomped the floor, feeling better with anger. With a last adjustment of his black silk cummerbund, which he imagined he felt despite the deadness in his fingers, he turned away from the glass.

Just then his wife came down the stairs. She was gorgeously dressed in emerald and blue silk, around her neck the double strand of pearls with gold clasp that her mother had given her. Miraculously, all of the wrinkles and worry had vanished from her face, which beamed with a soft pink radiance. Bill could not remember her so lovely. "Melissa . . ." he exclaimed. She smiled triumphantly.

At that moment, watching her glide down the steps, Bill felt very much in love with his wife, and he wanted to take her in his arms and tell her so. But it was a quarter past eight. Barely stopping to leave Alex a note, they hurried out into the warm evening air and their car. Then, as he sat beside her, watching the lights along Route 128 dart over the shiny hood of the car, Bill forgot the moment on the stairs and began fretting about his intended meeting with George Mitrakis and Harvey Stumm. It would be best to engage them in some small parlor or secluded room, so that any loud noises would not disturb the rest of the guests. What would he say? Possibly, he would ask them to account for themselves. Yes, let them begin, let them attempt explanations, which he would seize upon and demolish. Bill stared again at the flickering lights. In the silence of his thoughts, with only the hum of the engine, he began to feel sad, quite sad, although he had no idea why.

In Weston, at the entrance to Marbopolis, their car eased into a line of cars, wheels crunching on the long gravel drive. As they moved slowly behind the automobile in front of them, they saw a greenhouse with its vaulted roof, the colored targets of an archery range, outdoor sculptures and statuary. Shouts and laughter came from a tennis court, burning bright like a baseball stadium at night.

Ahead, at the end of the winding drive, the main house shimmered high on a hill, its marble façade and columns brilliantly illuminated by floodlights. "No one will speak to us," whispered Melissa as they slipped out of their car, then mounted the marble steps to the house. A dozen different perfumes trailed the other guests up the stairs: jasmine, sandalwood, musk. Now Bill could hear music and see, through the open front portals, hundreds of people in the colonnaded reception hall, the women in exquisite gowns with bare arms and shoulders.

For an instant, as Bill and his wife first stepped onto the mosaic tiled floor, everyone's eyes turned toward them, and he felt a sensation he had not experienced for a long time, that of being the center of interest. The sensation, both pleasant and unpleasant, was flooded with the smell of grilled salmon cakes and shrimp. Then it was past. The crowd, having satisfied itself that no one of importance had arrived, returned to its chatter. Into the vacuum, music and light crashed from every direction.

Immediately, Bill began searching faces. Somewhere within this brilliant, jabbering mass must be Diane Rossbane, thinner than the thinnest of supermodels, and Nate Linden, who almost certainly had purchased a new tuxedo for the night. Bill would take an ironic pleasure in greeting them, but they were nothing to him, no more than the bits of rare tuna on toast that glided by on silver trays. It was Mitrakis and Stumm whom he wished to confront. A camera flashed, making him squint. Then another wave of nausea swept over him. In the bright, vibrating air, individual faces lost their features and merged with the white marble and stone. Colored gowns and tuxedos dissolved into tapestries strung from the walls. Some of the men huddled behind marble statues, undoubtedly discussing their latest financial transactions, while their wives, with spectacular cleavages, paraded nearby. Other guests reclined on cushioned benches, drinking cocktails or gaping at the digital paintings, which seemed to change every half-minute. In the middle of the hall, encircled by an onyx colonnade, couples danced in a sunken courtyard. Squinting through the distance and bright light, Bill thought he recognized the actress Catherine Butler, posing prominently in the courtyard and wearing a headdress like fireworks in feathers. How ridiculous were the people who circled her, pretending indifference. And wasn't that Senator Derek Edmundson beneath a bronze chandelier, his face flushed from alcohol and heat? Bill recalled that the senator had recently introduced a bill favorable to many of those present. Now Senator Edmundson stood expansively in full view, well aware that he was attracting attention. Around him flocked Boston and New York's most ambitious men and women, whom he allowed brief handshakes.

What pretensions, Bill thought to himself. Surely, he would find Mitrakis and Stumm in the vicinity of the senator. Peering into the crowd, he began to feel unsteady on his feet.

"You don't look well," said Melissa. "We shouldn't have come." She held her cool wineglass to his cheek, then turned to stare at a woman bound in antique crème lace with a large diamond bracelet on her wrist.

"Bill," someone shouted. Suddenly their friends David and Christine Jamison were upon them, gay and perspiring and breathless, as if they had just come from the dance floor. Both of them looked so handsome and at ease. Bill wished that he could just disappear. David talked into his phone while looking at Bill and extending his free hand.

"No, you could never do that," panted David.

"Do what?" asked Bill.

"Sorry, Harry, just a minute."

"What? Are you talking to me?"

"It's your insurance. Call me on Monday." David slapped his phone shut. "This your first time here?" he asked, implying in his tone that he had been a guest at Marbopolis many times before. Bill had always been intimidated by David Jamison's manner and said nothing. "You look under the weather," remarked David. He waited for some reply, then turned to Melissa and smiled and asked her how she was enjoying the party.

The two women were eyeing each other and exchanging compliments. Christine was much exposed, with the front of her pink chiffon gown plunging nearly down to her waist. Her dark hair pressed against the sides of her face in small, lacquered curls. "Hello," she said to Bill, leaning over and kissing him on the lips. "I've never seen so much money," she said. "Isn't it amazing." She paused to readjust the scant fabric of her dress. "And we can't even afford to redo our kitchen," she said and pouted at her husband. "Whoever said money doesn't buy happiness."

"We're very happy," snapped Melissa.

Bill looked at Christine and found his eyes drifting involuntarily to her bare chest. Abruptly, he began to feel incensed, incensed at her and her husband. The idea then occurred to him that he might be angry at everyone in this great house, the entire assemblage of pompousness and wealth and pretension.

"Oh, come off it, Melissa," said Christine. "Let's be honest here. We're in the same little boat."

"What Christine meant," said David, "was—"

"Don't tell me what I meant, dear," said Christine. "I said that we could do better. That's all. You said so yourself, just five minutes ago." She took a sip from her wine and asked if Bill and Melissa had spotted anyone and if they had come alone. There was a pause in the conversation as a waiter offered a silver platter of summer figs and honey.

"Have you seen *Gates of Air*?" asked David, licking the honey off his fingers. "A Hollywood film, like they used to make them."

"The last film we saw was . . . what was it, Bill?"

"We saw it last weekend," said Christine. "It's really a woman's movie. David was ashamed to go into the theater. Now he's talking it up."

"I don't know what you mean by that," David said to his wife. "*Gates of Air*. Go see it. It reminded me of *Witness for the Prosecution*, or *On the Waterfront*. A black-and-white kind of feel. Like *Mutiny on the Bounty*."

Christine glanced with annoyance at her husband. "Bill, what kinds of movies do you like? I used to enjoy your e-mail reviews. Quite good."

Bill shrugged his shoulders and sighed. Now, he was forced to speak. "Some interesting films have been coming out of Australia," he said, unable to remember the last time he'd seen a movie of any kind.

"Australia?" David exclaimed and gave Bill a queer look. "Australia? I can never tell when you're joking." He licked his fingers. "The problem with foreign films is that either you have to strain to read the subtitles or you have to strain to work out what they're saying. And they're all copying us, anyway. All the foreign films just copy Hollywood. They've learned it all from us. Australia!" He frowned at Bill.

The orchestra started up with a popular tune, and more couples began dancing. David and Christine joined them, disappearing in an ocean of moving bodies.

"Weren't they dreadful?" whispered Melissa. "Why do we keep seeing them? Let's not see them anymore." She took another sip of her wine and held her hand against Bill's forehead. "Introduce me to someone. There, that's somebody over there. A big editor. I've seen her picture. I can't remember her name."

Slowly, they made their way across the tiled floor, moving elbow to elbow through the glittering crowd. "I heard there's going to be a movie," said a young woman, staring straight at Bill with bloodshot eyes. Her thin dress was stained brown with sweat and stuck to her skin. "Do you know when it starts?" Bill shrugged his shoulders. "I hope it's happy," she said. "I need something to make me happy. Do you know when it starts?" She glanced again at him and hurried into a large room on the right, a theater with tiered rows of seats. A number of people sat before the dark screen.

"She needs a date," said Melissa. "Do you see anyone you know?" Bill squinted into the light. Rooms opened off both sides of the main hall. A library, its floor covered with oriental rugs, followed by an entertainment room with pool tables and electronic games, then a formal banquet hall with a dining table twenty feet long. Hundreds of people milled about in each of these other rooms, their faces flitting across television monitors, and Bill realized with dismay that it would take hours to search all the guests.

Just then, he caught a glimpse in a monitor of someone who looked very much like George Mitrakis. Within seconds, the man slid off the screen. Bill stiffened. What room was that? He peered into the television monitor, looking for tell-tale furniture or colors or angles. Possibly the banquet hall, or the far end of the reception beneath the balcony, where an orchestra pounded overhead. Taking a deep breath to steady himself, he began walking rapidly, attempting to pull his wife along. The hall churned around him.

"I'm going to freshen up," said Melissa. "Sit over there and I'll be right back."

Bill did not feel like sitting. Dizzily, he navigated around the dancers and others and continued into the banquet hall, which was thick with smells from the adjacent kitchens. The proximity to the kitchens seemed to have increased appetites because everyone was eating heavily, soft-shell crabs, stuffed mushrooms, filet mignon with potatoes au gratin, asparagus tips, other food that Bill couldn't even identify. Lemon meringue pie, cherries jubilee, chocolate cheesecake. Two middle-aged men sat on the floor with a dozen half-eaten desserts between them, sleeves rolled up and gorging themselves like college frat boys. "Waiter!" one of them shouted, his face red and puffy. "You can't order more," said the other man, "you'll be sick, I guarantee it." "Speak for yourself, John. Waiter. Waiter!"

Across the room, Bill spotted someone he thought to be George Mitrakis, in conversation with a pretty young woman. His heart pounding, Bill crept along the wall and stared at the couple from the corner of his eye. They were arguing about something. The woman had taken everything out of her purse—lipsticks, wallet, cell phone, keys, and cards—all of which she was tossing in her companion's lap one item at a time. On closer examination, Bill saw that the man was not George, he had only George's loose face. The stranger, clearly annoyed at being surveyed, turned and frowned balefully at Bill.

Bill hurried back into the reception hall, taking deep breaths of air to keep from retching. In front of him, a small crowd of people stood around a performer who was balancing a ladder on his nose. He wore tight leotards and white paste on his face. With each twist and turn, the clown guffawed and a bit of paste cracked and dropped to the floor. Then a second ladder went up, balanced on top of the first.

Staring stupidly at the crowd, Bill saw no one he knew, although he recognized more celebrities. Everyone clapped and exchanged satisfied glances and sipped from their cocktails, the men at ease in their tuxedos and the women in their gowns. What was he doing at this party? He was not one of these people. He would accomplish his business and leave. Where was Melissa?

In the entertainment room, men leaned over the pool tables, calling for the waiters to bring them more whiskey and beer. A woman sat by herself in a corner, laughing and talking into her phone. "I'm at Marbopolis!" she shouted. "And where are you?" Above her voice, Bill heard a voice so much like Harvey Stumm's that he could hardly be mistaken. "Harv!" he shouted. A fellow of Stumm's proportions darted out, into the reception hall, and was instantly swallowed in the crowd. Bill followed. Waiters swarmed like bees. No thank you, no thank you. Cherries jubilee. No thank you. Now his nausea was making him dizzy. He swooned and slumped against a marble pedestal, staring at the digital painting on its crown. A title scrolled by in glowing letters: Vermeer's *The Milkmaid*. Then, a few moments later, a new painting: Picasso's *Les Demoiselles d'Avignon*. Bill closed his eyes. He just wanted to sleep. Stumm's voice was so offensive, he thought to himself, offensive in its maddening politeness. It was not a human voice at all but the voice of a machine. Stumm was a robot of ruthless efficiency. Where was the robot now? Bill slowly opened his eyes and peered through the ferns in the courtyard and caught sight of the robot at the other end of the hall.

Shortly, Bill found himself inside a vast, empty conference room. Where had Stumm gotten to? Breathing heavily, closing his eyes again, Bill began rehearsing his speech. He would let Stumm have the first word. But of course Stumm would say nothing. I have been employed by this establishment for nine years, Bill would start, and for nine years I have dedicated myself to . . . That seemed an appropriate beginning. Stumm would respond with something polite and elusive, amused by Bill's sincerity. What is it? Stumm would say softly and curl the lips of his small white face. What is it? As if Bill were a child who had dirtied himself playing ball and needed help washing. He wanted to vomit, the Prozac was making him vomit, but he would hold down his bile until he found Stumm. I'll tell you what it is, he would say to Stumm. This establishment has diarrhea. The building has diarrhea, so does the subway. Stumm would not understand anything.

Slowly Bill stood up and cracked open a door. The adjoining room, a half level down, was evidently a communications center of some kind. Rows of people sat like mannequins in front of their computer screens. In a glance, Bill could see that Stumm was not here, but he continued peering into the room, mesmerized. Then he detected it, the sound he had heard in his office, the low steady hum, except now it was louder, far louder. Slapping his hands over his ears, he ducked away before he could be spotted.

He heard Stumm's voice again, this time near a doorway beneath the balcony. Every few seconds, the door opened and closed, releasing a small cloud of smoke. Bill ascended a winding staircase and emerged in an exercise room and sauna, where he discovered many more guests draped about the treadmills and weight benches, drinking and smoking. Some had donned bathing suits and floated limply in an oval-shaped hot tub. Above swirled a cloud of steam, merging with the thick haze of smoke. "Harv," Bill called out and began coughing. He moved slowly about the room and squinted at each drunken cluster of people, although it was hard to see anything through the smoke. Ice cubes crunched under his foot. A tiny explosion of orange as a man lit a match. "Harv," Bill said again. With new anger, he began to consider the possibility that neither Mitrakis nor Stumm had ever been in the house.

The orchestra stopped. "There's Marbleworth," a man shouted, pointing at one of the ubiquitous television monitors on the wall. Abruptly, the room fell silent. Everyone looked up at the flickering screen. There, moving easily across the floor of the reception hall, was Edward Marbleworth, lanky and balding, fifty years old. The orchestra began playing "God Bless America." Even seeing him only in the monitor, Bill felt a surge of excitement. The crowds parted as Marbleworth radiated down the middle of the hall. When he passed Derek Edmundson, the senator eagerly reached out and shook his hand.

"Welcome, welcome," said Marbleworth after he reached a podium, his voice broadcast to every monitor in the thirty-thousand-square-foot house. "Welcome to Marbopolis. Thank you for coming. I'm pleased to see all of you." There was a round of applause. In the exercise room, the crowd clapped. Marbleworth paused. "You probably know I'm not the easiest person on earth," he said, grinning. "I like to win." People laughed and clapped again. Marbleworth's wife, standing beside him with precious stones glittering in her hair, also laughed and gave him a kiss. "I want to make an announcement tonight." Cameras flashed. There was a commotion, one woman was knocked down, and attendants had to escort a handful of people out of the hall. After the assemblage had quieted down, the billionaire continued. "I wish to announce tonight the formation of a new company. It will be called LifeImages." A pause. "As our first acquisition, we have just purchased the rights to all images of every American's birth certificate, including the handwritten signature of the attending physician." It took a few moments for the words to register. The crowd gasped. Bill could feel the long-held-in bile screaming to escape from his gut. *We have just purchased the rights to all images of every American's birth certificate, including the handwritten signature of the attending physician.* The words repeated themselves in his spinning mind. What arrogance and depravity and disregard for . . . for what? What was it?

Clutching his stomach, Bill stared into the faces around him, expecting to see the same revulsion he felt. Instead, he saw admiration mixed with fear. All of these thoughts and sensations passed through his reeling mind in a microsecond. Incredibly, Marbleworth was still talking. "From now on," the billionaire said in the monitor, "there will no longer be delays in obtaining government copies of birth certificates. Through LifeImages, copies can be downloaded instantly. Birth records can be corollated with whatever other personal information the user wants. . . . This is America. I love it." Reporters, caught off guard by the announcement, began shouting questions, but the billionaire smiled and held up his hands. "At this time, I will say only one more thing. We hope to make this global." A man beside him shook his hand. Then Marbleworth disappeared, cushioned by his personal attendants and guards. After a few seconds, the orchestra started up on "New York, New York."

At that moment, it seemed to Bill that George Mitrakis and Harvey Stumm were nothing. They were the creatures of

Marbleworth. Marbleworth was the super robot, the super machine who controlled the other machines. How brilliantly he had amassed his power. How brilliantly, with one rational step after the other, inevitably, inevitably. And Bill had followed mindlessly, even adoringly. For that, he hated himself as much as he hated Edward Marbleworth. He was Marbleworth's accomplice.

Again, he gazed into the faces around him, smiles of admiration and fear, sobs of celebration amplified by the thick redness of gin and the warm billows of steam rolling off the oval-shaped tub. Everyone here was Marbleworth's accomplice.

Ignoring the stares of the other guests, ignoring the continued churning of his stomach, Bill stumbled down the stairs determined to find Edward Marbleworth. He wanted to strangle him. The reception hall was a caldron of guests, security guards, news reporters, and equipment. Flowers littered the mosaic floor. Shoving his way through the crowd, Bill began to question people near the podium. Where was Marbleworth? Who had been with him? Although Bill's voice was drowned out by the orchestra, several women turned and stared at him with curiosity. Then he sighted Marbleworth in one of the video monitors hung from the ceiling. The billionaire and his entourage had evidently relocated to one of the inner rooms of the mansion. "You can't do this!" Bill shouted at the image in the monitor. No one paid any attention to him. "Do you hear me?" he screamed at the monitor. "You can't do this. You can't do this."

DUCKS

"You are talking about your anger," said Kripke. "That is good. What do you feel right now?"

"I want to kill Edward Marbleworth."

The psychiatrist put down his pen and clasped his hands. For a few moments, he sat silently, staring at his patient. "Are you sure it's Edward Marbleworth you want to kill?"

"Yes."

The psychiatrist raised his eyebrows and again waited in silence. As he waited, waterfalls poured from the wall.

"I'm not sure. I'm angry at a lot of people."

The psychiatrist smiled faintly and began writing again in his notebook. "You're angry at everybody."

"Yes."

"So it's not Edward Marbleworth in particular."

"I guess not. It's a lot of people. No one sees anything."

"No one sees anything?" said the psychiatrist. "Really. What do you mean by that?"

"I was driving to work this morning, and I saw a mother duck on the side of the road, with six or seven babies wad-dling behind her. I slowed down to look and everybody started honking at me."

"And you think that other people should have stopped on the road to look at these ducks?"

"That's just an example."

"How is the numbness?" asked the psychiatrist.

"The same."

"We're going to increase the dosage of Prozac to forty milligrams per day. If the nausea persists, we'll switch to Paxil."

SPERRY

Amy, the receptionist at Plymouth, didn't know whether she was coming or going. Hardly had she met one visitor at the landing on the forty-first floor and brought him up in the private elevator when the red light began blinking again and she had to scramble down and escort another guest. The British accents and formality of the visiting executives frightened her, so that she avoided their eyes and said nothing, but when she met Mr. Andy Collingbourne, red-eyed and unsteady on his feet, she chatted with him amiably all the way to the reception area.

There waited David Hamilton and Lisa Theroux, smiling and joking as they strode forward to greet each of their new associates from London, inviting others who had already arrived to look through the magnificent hall windows at the skyline of Boston. A constant stream of people flowed back and forth down the hallways, through the reception, and into the conference room, where preparations were being made for the presentations.

"Good morning, Bertram . . . if I may call you that," David said to Bertram Lancaster, a tall, important-looking man with a high forehead and lantern jaw. "And how did you sleep? The Four Seasons is about the best we have, although

I've never stayed there myself. I couldn't afford it." He laughed nervously.

"Ah," said Mr. Lancaster. He stood just at the carpeted entrance to Plymouth, tapping the point of his umbrella against the elevator door. His assistant was led by Nate Linden down the bright hallway to the conference room in the back.

"Good Lord, David, don't badger the poor man with questions," said Lisa. "Let him have some coffee. I'll bet you need coffee, don't you, Mr. Lancaster. We have light-roasted hazelnut and dark Colombian." She smiled at the vice president of Sperry, who looked her up and down quickly and nodded, as if approving of her smart double-breasted suit with its ivory buttons down the front.

"Coffee is an idea, Ms. Theroux," he said pleasantly. "Yes." He looked at his watch.

"Where is Mr. Chalmers? Is Mr. Chalmers here?" whispered Mr. Benjamin Lloyd, who had been led to the Queen Anne sofa immediately upon his arrival. Mr. Lloyd, the oldest of the delegation from Sperry, was gnarled and stoop-shouldered but with eyes sharp as nails.

"Yes, I'm here," said Bill, proceeding hesitantly toward the sofa with a forced smile on his face. He had been dreading a meeting with Benjamin Lloyd. Bill wished, in fact, that he could have remained in his office until this entire inaugural affair was concluded.

"There you are indeed," said Mr. Lloyd. He stood up and toddled over to meet Bill. "You look just like your picture on the Plymouth Web page."

"Thank you," said Bill, immediately regretting the foolishness of his reply. Certainly he had not received a compliment, for his digitized photograph made him look weary and ten years older than he actually was.

Mr. Lloyd leaned his wizened head close to Bill's and said

in a low but not unfriendly voice, "Aren't you the young man who did the background check on me?"

Bill cringed. Evidently, it was not enough to be under scrutiny by his own firm, he thought to himself. Now he was being mistrusted and watched by Plymouth's new partners. His head turned stupidly toward the window as he searched for something to say.

"I wanted to compliment you," said Lloyd, peering oddly at Bill with his bright eyes. "That was—" He was interrupted by George Mitrakis, who came bounding into the reception area with viewgraphs and colored pens in his hands. "Who's minding the fax?" he shouted. He stood in the middle of the reception, appearing confused, then hurried into the communications room, where the unattended machine sat screeching and spitting paper to the floor. Poor Leslie, her eyes filling with tears, followed the president in and closed the door. In a few moments, Mitrakis emerged, again confused and preoccupied. Bill had never seen him so uneasy and out of sorts.

"The Four Seasons is splendid," suddenly boomed Andy Collingbourne. He stumbled from his place by the window, rubbing his knuckles into his left eye. "Rather like our Savoy in London. I'm delighted silly." He began telling Bill some story about his car and how it gobbled up one of its valves on a roundabout, then abruptly said, "I wondered, Mr. Chalmers, if it would be possible to have a room that faced the park? Do you handle that sort of thing, or should I speak to someone else?"

Bill stared at Mr. Collingbourne without grasping what he'd said.

"That would be a small detail," said Mr. Lloyd and he threw Andy Collingbourne a swift look of admonishment. "Andy should be quite happy with things as they stand."

Mr. Collingbourne glanced at Mr. Lloyd, then at Mr. Lancaster, who sat on the Queen Anne carefully eating a Danish pastry. His face clouded up like a child's. "Please, Mr. Chalmers," he said, practically whimpering and again rubbing his knuckles into his eye, "leave my room where it is."

"I would be happy to do what you wish," said Bill, addressing himself to Mr. Lloyd. He made a mental note to speak to Leslie about the matter and then realized that he had no idea how long the Sperry party was visiting. Junior partners were never told such things, they were treated like secretaries. How he wished he were in his office at this moment with the door closed.

"No, please, Mr. Chalmers," said Mr. Collingbourne. "I spoke out of line. I'm not a traveler, as you can probably see, and I'm afraid I had something bad to eat at a little restaurant outside the hotel last night. It seemed like a harmless little restaurant, but I should never have gone in there. I ate something that didn't agree with me. The waitress was very friendly." He turned and went back to the window.

"It's nine o'clock," announced David Hamilton.

"I had just noticed that myself," said Lancaster, rising from the couch.

Bill was at his keyboard later that day, after the Sperry group had gone, when he was buzzed by Amy. Mr. Mitrakis would like to see him. He mumbled into the phone and glanced at his watch. It was 12:17. Minute by minute, the last hour had slid down his screen, like the thousands of numbers and words scrolled away. With a sigh he closed down a file and flicked on his screen saver, stared for a moment at the colored fish swimming through a virtual pond, and plodded down the hall toward the president's office. He was drunk with exhaustion and he weaved from side to side against the walls and closed doors, and the August sun sliced through the endless glass windows and cut into his eyes. A shape that was Leslie flew past with an armload of documents to be scanned before lunch.

When he opened the president's door, Bill felt a tension in the room. Sitting uncomfortably on the white linen sofa was a man he had never seen before. Mitrakis, in wrinkled shirt-sleeves, leaned silently over his mahogany desk. It struck Bill, in that first moment, that the president was staring down at something he'd lost in the bottom of a deep well.

"Bill," Mitrakis said, looking up and smiling limply. He lumbered toward the door, huge in his white shirt, his face passing alternately from brightness to shadow as it caught the light from the silver fan blades turning slowly overhead. "Please." He motioned for Bill to come in.

The man on the sofa stood up.

"Bill," said Mitrakis, "this is Francis Scherer from Dorgan et al. He's one of Plymouth's attorneys." Mr. Scherer stood motionless by the sofa, holding a spiral notebook in one hand. He was a large man, like Mitrakis, with a head of tousled chestnut hair, and a certain sadness hung about his heavy-lidded eyes. He nodded at Bill and offered his hand.

"Sit down, Bill, sit down." Mitrakis sank heavily into the chair behind his desk. Mr. Scherer sat down also and placed a silver pen on his notebook and quietly scratched his thick neck.

"Bill," the president said with a sigh, "I'm afraid we're going to have to let you go."

Mr. Scherer had picked up his silver pen. Beyond the sofa, the inner door to the conference room was half open. One of the slide projectors from the morning's presentations had been left on, a glowing box in the dark.

"This is painful for me," said Mitrakis. He made a small,

helpless smile and became silent, as if waiting for someone else to speak. "I'm fond of you, Bill," he said and stared down at a glass paperweight on his desk. "You've been a very productive member of Plymouth for eight, nine years now. . . . But you've slipped badly in the last couple of months, since the mugging." He paused and looked up. "What a terrible thing that was, huh. We were worried like hell." He shook his head.

Mr. Scherer coughed. Mitrakis rubbed his hand back and forth on his face, which had broken out in red splotches. "Bill . . . we can't afford to keep all of our junior partners. You know that. We tell everyone. We just can't afford to. We couldn't keep Helen. Mark left two years ago. There are pressures. . . ." He lifted his head and looked miserably toward Mr. Scherer, then back down at the glass paperweight, which he began turning over and over in his palm. "You must know that you've fallen behind in your work. You know that, don't you?" He paused, turning the paperweight over and over. "The account with Transcom. Digitel says you've sent them incomplete information three different times. The Hanover-Bryce Group is already blaming their third-quarter losses on us. . . . Bill, what's happened? I don't understand. Was it the mugging? Tell me." He looked at Bill and waited for him to say something. From the conference room, the fan of the projector could be heard gasping as it circulated on and off.

For another few moments, Mitrakis sat in silence. Then he ran his hands over his splotched face again and said, "We've been keeping a record," mumbled so softly that Mr. Scherer stopped writing and cupped his hand to his ear. Mitrakis repeated himself, only slightly louder, and gestured with embarrassment to a folder next to his keyboard. He looked at Bill and pleaded with his eyes for him to say something. Then he sighed and slapped his desk a couple of times. "Ah, shit. Shit. I'm really sorry about this, Bill, I'm so sorry."

"We're all sorry," said Mr. Scherer.

Mitrakis stood up and walked heavily across the blue oriental rug. At the other side of the room, he put his hands in his pockets and stared at one of the framed commendations on the wall. A telephone rang in the secretary's office next door. With a grim expression, he moved back to his desk and picked up a brown envelope lying there. "This describes the severance package. Money, extended health insurance for six months, other things . . . We think it's generous. I think it's generous." He sighed. "Read it over . . ." The president's lips continued to move, but no words came out. The room had become empty of sound.

CIDER BARN ANTIQUES

When Bill turned off the highway into the little gravel lot of
Cider Barn Antiques, several other cars were parked there,
one with its engine running, another so close to the front
door that it nearly blocked the hand-painted sign reading "No
Restrooms." An ancient set of cross-country skis leaned pre-
cariously against the door frame of the converted two-story
red barn.

Bill remained in his hot car, dabbing his face and his neck
with a tissue. Should he go in this instant to tell Melissa he'd
just lost his job, or wait until the customers had gone? He
sighed and glanced at his watch. It was 2:17, right in the guts
of the day. Everyone on the planet was profitably at work,
except himself. But he didn't count because he was dead, and
worse, a reject. He was not a part of the world. He was a
nightmare. Go now, go later, go home—what did it matter.

Listlessly, he slumped back in his seat and stared at the
colored bottles in the shop window. There were eight of
them, three cobalt blue, two clear, and three muddy-brown
old medicine bottles. Beyond the window, he could see things
hanging from the low ceiling, people moving about. The
corner of the barn vibrated in the heat. Gradually, his head
dropped to his chest, his eyes began to close. The motor of
the running car began wheezing and trembling as if about to

expire in the heat. Out of the corner of his eye, Bill watched a woman come out of the shop with a yellow arrow-back chair and a pantry box. She carefully placed the purchases in the trunk of her car, straightened her wide-brimmed sun hat, and drove off in a spray of gravel and dust. He began coughing and raised his window until the dust had floated back into the hot gravel and the air resumed its bright, syrupy translucence at eighty-five degrees. After a few minutes, another car drove up. It was 2:29. There would be no good time to talk to his wife. Bill finished tearing one of his road maps into tiny pieces and walked slowly into the shop.

At his appearance, unexpected and vague like the ghost that he was, Melissa's eyes became very big and she put aside the washboard she'd been negotiating with a customer and came quickly to the door. "Bill," she said softly. "What are you doing here? Is it Alex?" She reached out and grasped his arm.

"Alex is fine," Bill said and released a hiss of tired air. His head dropped and he gazed at his wife's small feet on the wide-plank wood floor. "I need to talk to you."

"What?" She looked at him searchingly, holding his shirt-sleeve in her fingers. "Why aren't you at Plymouth?" she whispered. "What's happened?"

"I want to talk to you."

"Are you okay?"

He nodded.

"God, Bill, don't frighten me like that." She twisted and untwisted the collar of her beige cotton dress. "You picked a terrible time to talk. Can you wait a few minutes?"

Bill nodded without expression and watched her as she hurried back to the front desk, where one of her pickers was waiting with a collection of old brass bells to sell. The man spread the bells out on the wood counter and began jingling them one by one.

Despite the air conditioner that labored in the adjoining room, the shop was stifling and warm, and Bill searched for a shaded corner where he might wait, perhaps next to one of the cedar blanket chests or painted washstands. Twice before he had visited Melissa's shop in the summer. He remembered that pockets of cool air settled into little corners, mingling with the smells of dried tansy and sweet Annie that hung from the low ceiling beams and with the faint odor of horses remaining from the days when the building had been an apple storage barn. Years ago, he had enjoyed coming here with Alex after a snowstorm, sledding with him on the hill behind the barn. Now, he thought grimly, they would have to sell the whole place. It had never made any money. He stood facing a wall and stared blankly at an old cutting board, from which hung a kitchen strainer, a brass scale, a rolling pin, a sifter, a wooden spoon. He had been standing there for some time, dimly aware of people coming and going behind him, when Melissa tapped his shoulder.

"I have a little time now," she said in a low voice, "but not much. Someone just called about an estate sale."

She closed her eyes when he told her. "What reason did they give?" she said and leaned against the wall.

"They don't need a reason," said Bill. "I'm a junior partner." The floorboards creaked as someone walked past them.

"You're ill," whispered Melissa after a few moments. "You've been to see doctors. They can't fire you for illness. That's illegal. Have you been telling them that you're seeing doctors?" She glanced into the next room, where a customer was calling for her. "Screw her," she said under her breath. "That woman never buys anything." The woman kept calling. "Ms. Chalmers, Ms. Chalmers." Melissa sighed and said she'd be right back.

When she returned, she looked old. Bill studied her face in amazement, wondering how it had happened so quickly.

"Did they give you any . . ."

"They gave me six months' severance," said Bill.

"So what are you going to do?" she whispered. "What are we going to do?" She stared at something on a table. "Bill." She put her hands to her face. "I don't . . . Is this what you've been wanting all along? I can't believe this is happening to me."

"To you?" Bill shouted and slammed his hand against the wall. The brass scale and sifter fell to the floor. "What about me? I'm the one who has numb hands and feet. I'm the one who's been fired." Again, she put her hands to her face. "But you know something," he shouted. "You're right. Something has happened to you."

He pushed his way past the people gaping at him, out through the door with the horseshoe nailed over it.

NIGHT OFFICE

It was several days later that Bill returned to the Marbleworth Building to pack up his things, very late at night, when the offices were vacant and he might be spared the final degradation in front of his colleagues. As he walked from the all-night garage on Milk Street, he was gripped by a strange nostalgia and peered glumly at the empty storefronts and office buildings that he'd barely noticed through the years and might never see again: Prudential Securities, Milk Street Café, Commonwealth Investments, Milk Street Florists. He entered the dim lobby of the Marbleworth. Out of habit, he craned his neck up to examine the massive clock over the revolving glass doors: 12:48. By this hour, even the cleaning staff had gone, and the only sound in the deserted building was the restless rumble of the elevators, which never shut down, and the ticking of the night watchman's punch clock. The night watchman himself was almost asleep in his swivel chair behind the front desk. He snorted and sat up when Bill presented his temporary ID. "Working late, eh?" he mumbled. Bill nodded. "Fresh air coming in with you. Always like that fresh air."

Bill was passing along the dark hallway toward his office, brooding about his bleak prospects for future employment, when he saw a small light under Harvey Stumm's door. He paused, thinking that the vice president had forgotten to turn off a lamp. Then, to his astonishment, he heard someone talking. The thought came to him that Plymouth was being robbed. He had once seen a television show about corporations raiding each other's intellectual property, and he turned to creep back to the reception and telephone the police. On second thought, that course of action could possibly activate a light on Stumm's phone and thus alert the thief. As Bill stood motionless and frightened, uncertain about what he should do, he again heard a low mumble behind the closed door and this time it was distinctly the voice of a woman. Screwing up his courage to a degree surprising even to himself, he pushed slightly on the door and found that it opened.

Never before had he seen the inside of Stumm's office. Unlike the tidy place he expected, piles of rumpled documents and papers lay strewn about the tables and floor. Standing in the middle of the room was Mrs. Stumm.

"What are you doing here?" she gasped when she saw Bill.

"Mrs. Stumm . . . I didn't expect . . ." Bill stammered, equally shocked.

Something moved at the desk. Bill turned and noticed for the first time a man sitting there, peering back with a look of embarrassment and panic. His eyes were swollen and bloodshot, and he wore a drab T-shirt with some bicycle logo. For a few moments, Bill continued to stare at the man. He was Harvey Stumm. "Harv?" Bill whispered in disbelief.

Stumm flushed and looked down at the floor.

"What . . . I . . . I'm sorry," said Bill, feeling as if he'd walked in on a couple making love. He began backing out toward the door.

"Please, stay where you are, young man," said Mrs. Stumm. Her bulbous lips began quivering. "Now that you're here. Do you see what this job does to my husband? And to me, I might add. And I don't get paid. Here it is, the middle of the night, and we have to haul ourselves to this crummy office to go through the week's junk. I can't keep this up."

"Betty," protested Stumm, still staring down at the floor.

"No, Harvey," said Mrs. Stumm, "don't try to hush me up." She pushed her reading glasses up into her wiry gray hair, rubbed her eyes, and squinted into the fierce light pounding from the lamp on the desk. "Mr. Chalmers should know what he's in for. In another few years, they'll be working him as hard as they work you."

Bill started to inform Mrs. Stumm that he had been fired but decided that he would rather not engage her in conversation.

Some text marched across the computer screen on Stumm's desk, making beeps as it did so, and Mrs. Stumm frowned. "What's that?" she said to her husband. "Aren't we done with that one?"

"Not yet," Stumm said. He took in a deep breath of air, which made a hollow, sucking sound in his throat, and began rifling through the stacks of paper on his desk. "It's the McCormick file," he muttered. He looked at Bill, shaking his head, and said, "Frank McCormick buries me with corre-spondence. That's his strategy." Then he began typing rapidly at his keyboard, as if running after the words skittering off his screen. "Can you get me . . ."

"Yes," grumbled Mrs. Stumm, "I know what it is." She lumbered heavily around the room, poking one pile of papers after another. A box of half-eaten sandwiches fell to the floor. "I saw that McCormick stuff a minute ago. Now, where was it? It was on a shelf, I think." She went to the bookshelf, which held a row of burgundy leather volumes containing the Plymouth annual reports, and grabbed a handful of papers. "Here's some of it," she said and slapped the papers down on her husband's desk.

She turned to Bill, who had advanced only a single step

into the room. "You don't know the pressures he's under," she said. "It's not right what they do to him. It's not right." She swept aside a pile of memoranda and letters and sat down on the sofa. "My husband has been working for Plymouth fifteen years now, since the time it was on State Street. He has a long record of excellent service to the company. You would think that by now we would have a little time to ourselves. Bosh. Harvey hasn't taken a vacation in three years." She sighed. "Just look at all this crap." She waved her hand at a stack of papers. "What is this crap?" She began reading aloud from one of the documents: "It is anticipated that new subadvisory agreements substantially similar to the cur-rent subadvisory agreements for these segments will be pro-posed . . ." She let go of the piece of paper and it fluttered to the floor. "Useless. This stuff is useless."

"It's not useless," Stumm said angrily to his wife. Scowling, he retrieved the document from the floor. When he was again behind his desk, he said, "You shouldn't talk about things you don't know anything about."

"Useless," repeated Mrs. Stumm.

"You're always talking about things you know nothing about," said Mr. Stumm. He glanced at Bill and then again at his wife. "If you want to help me, then help me."

"I never asked to be dragged up here in the middle of the night."

"Then don't come next time."

"Ha," Mrs. Stumm shrieked and laughed wildly. "I'd like to see you go through this stuff by yourself."

Bill was so stunned by the scene that he momentarily forgot his hatred for the vice president and felt only raw sym-pathy, even a strange sense of shame. In a sickening flash of memory, he recalled a moment from childhood when he had witnessed a fellow student steal another boy's lunch money and had felt unaccountably ashamed. As if watching were doing. Yes, he watched and did nothing, he was a victim and a victimizer himself. Another pair of beeps came from Stumm's computer.

"Maybe I could help you look for the McCormick files," said Bill weakly.

"Oh, no," said Stumm.

"Harvey, let Mr. Chalmers help you," said Mrs. Stumm. "You're working yourself to the bone."

Stumm shot his wife an ugly look and continued typing at his keyboard.

"He's too wicked proud," Mrs. Stumm said and propped up her thick legs on a glass tabletop. "He doesn't want anyone to know that he gets so far behind. That's why we have to sneak up here in the middle of the night."

"Goddamn it, Betty," said Stumm. "Don't say things like that."

"I . . . I had no idea," whispered Bill. He found that he could no longer look at Harvey Stumm. When he did, he felt ashamed. He was beginning to feel ashamed of everything in his life.

"It's all true," said Mrs. Stumm. "And now Mr. Chalmers knows, don't you, Mr. Chalmers. You've caught us. Hasn't he caught us, Harvey? He's caught us." She took off her glasses and wiped them on the sleeve of her loose yellow shift. "What are you going to do, Mr. Chalmers, now that you've caught us?"

"What? I don't know," said Bill slowly. He was hardly listening anymore.

"Actually, I wouldn't mind at all if you told them," said Mrs. Stumm. "They should know that they're working my husband to the bone. And me." Her lower lip began quivering again. "We have a life. My father is sick. Look at Harvey. Look at his head. Just look at how he's losing his hair. He's only fifty-three years old. Do you know what's causing him to lose his hair, Mr. Chalmers? Stress, nothing else. His father kept his hair until the day that he died." She glanced at Bill's thinning head and nodded. "I can see it's happening to you too. I'm sorry for you."

"Betty, can you stop now?" said Stumm. He stood up, looking old and tired.

"I can stop," said Mrs. Stumm, "but that doesn't erase the fact that Mr. Chalmers has caught us."

"I've been fired," said Bill.

"Oh," said Mrs. Stumm. She looked at her husband with raised eyebrows. "Really. You didn't tell me that, Harvey. You didn't tell me that you'd just fired Mr. Chalmers. Then you have nothing to bargain with. Mr. Chalmers will blab to his heart's content."

"Bill," Stumm said in a small, pathetic voice, uttering his name for the first time since he'd arrived. "Please."

Bill would not look at the other man. "I'm not going to blab," he said. "I don't give a shit." At that, Bill turned and left the room, closing the door behind him. He was suffocating. When he got to the end of the hallway, he pressed his cheek hard against the window and looked out at the huge blackness of sky and the glittering lights of the city and the faint throat of line where the dark sky met the dark sea. If he could, he would have jumped at that moment just to have ten seconds of black air hurtling past, stuffing his mouth, cleansing his insides. How he wanted to be clean. Possibly he'd been heartless with Stumm. He'd hardly spoken while the man was stripped naked. He could have said something to Stumm, touched him. Far below, a row of streetlamps suddenly blinked on like a strand of pearls. For God's sake, what was he thinking? It was he who had been fired, not Stumm. Stumm had undoubtedly loaded the pistol. Stumm hated him.

Still shaken, Bill went to his office, turned on the light, and began numbly assembling the cardboard packing boxes on his chair. He stared at the Ralph Morgan print of three storks, as if seeing it for the first time, and wondered whether he should ship it to Lexington or just leave it for the next occupant of the office. His eyes roamed slowly around the room, moving to the desk lamp that had always irritated him, the Windsor chair that Melissa had gotten him for his thirty-fifth birthday, the rug that he had won in a college poker game. His beige Gateway computer, all of its business files having been deleted the day he was fired. With a weary sigh, he slumped in his chair.

Two hours later, when he'd emptied his desk drawers and file cabinets and bookshelves, eight numbered boxes stood stacked by the door. Halfway through, his legs had buckled under him and he'd tumbled to the floor. He was immensely tired. He took one last look around the room where he'd spent the past nine years and turned off the light. As he passed down the hall for the last time, he hesitated again outside Stumm's door. The room was silent and dark.

On the sidewalk, Bill's legs felt heavy and slow, and he found that he had to walk one tiny step at a time, like an old man. Glancing this way and that down the empty street, he was grateful that no one was watching. He had never worked this long into the night, even as a student, and he had foolishly exhausted himself. Twice he fell, without pain, his legs simply giving way. The pavement against his face smelled of burnt rubber and pumpernickel.

BAY WINDOWS

Rain on the roof. A throbbing sadness, where his sleeping and waking minds almost met in the haze of half-consciousness. A dream retreated, and he reached into the abyss. Then, slowly, he opened his eyes. It was Friday. No, Saturday. Rain. He could hear the swish of an automobile passing over a wet street. Downstairs, two men were shouting, Melissa's voice interceding, then the grind of an electric power tool, crushing the scampering little feet on the roof. "Melissa," he called, wishing that she were lying there beside him in the gray light of the room. After a few moments, he realized that he had probably only imagined her name. He could smell where she had been in the bed.

The illuminated clock on the vanity read 9:38. Nine thirty-eight, Saturday morning, the twenty-third of August, another day of nothingness. Four days since he'd been fired from his job.

With his head buzzing, as it did when he had not got sufficient sleep, he stepped out of bed and immediately fell to the floor. His legs were not working. Then he noticed the bruises, blue turning to russet to brown. What colors were real bruises, he thought bitterly, earned bruises? Now he would have more.

From his vantage on the floor, tables and chairs appeared

oddly angled, the ceiling seemed to curl away into shadows, and his eyes moved to the maple tree outside the bedroom window. How precious and alive the tree suddenly seemed to him. Raindrops clung to its leaves, magnifying the tiny veins and indentations, liquifying and heightening the blues and greens so that the surfaces flowed into each other in a delicate envelope of light. The entire tree seemed to swim in the air. For a few moments, Bill felt that he, too, was swimming among its leaves, a child again. Summer stretched ahead like the ocean. He had stripped off his clothes and was running around and around a tree in his backyard, the warm summer rain making mud that splattered his shins and knees, the tiny voice of his mother calling him to dinner.

Grunting, he dragged himself up to a kneeling position and watched the blue bulging of veins in his arms. He tried to stand. Again he fell to the floor, this time cutting his arm on an edge of the blanket chest, making a long gash with blood, painless. How could his body be failing him, so silently and politely? Let it happen savagely, all at once. Let it happen with pain. He wanted the clarity and purposefulness of pain. He stared at his useless legs, no longer part of him, stilts of a circus clown. He had surely done something terribly wrong. Yes, he would accept that now. Something wrong and foul to deserve these refusals of his body, but what was it? The thought occurred to him that people amputated useless legs. For these numb stilts, no anesthetic would be needed. He could do it now if he had a sharp knife. In the kitchen. He would cut away all that he could not trust. Only forty years old, he thought, cheated out of life at his prime. Because he was now fearful that he might be dying. He was dying a far slower death than the death of his father, who had gone so easily, dead by the time he had slipped to the floor of that dark accounting office that smelled perpetually of wood glue.

Melissa. Had he called her name or only thought it again? If he could touch her skin, he could save himself.

An invisible wave of damp air flowed through the open window, and Bill shuddered and managed to grab the bedpost and bring himself up to a sitting position on the edge of the bed. His bleeding arm streamed onto the white bedsheets. More loud voices downstairs. Mr. Turgis, the architect, was arguing about something to do with the new bay windows, something that hadn't been executed according to his plans, and there was a break in the drilling and cutting while he shouted at some other man, and then the tools started up again. The telephones began ringing, like drowning animals screaming for air.

Shortly, there were footsteps on the stairs and Melissa appeared at the bedroom door. "I didn't know if you were awake," she said. Her face was worn and drawn.

"I just got up." He could not bear to tell her about his legs.

She turned on a lamp, which shone auburn in her fine silky hair. "A Mr. Jason Toothaker just called," she said. "He says you haven't been answering his e-mails. I told him you'd contact him."

"I'm glad you came in. You look tired."

"I waited up for you last night." She went to the window and stood there looking out at the street. The rain was coming down harder now, thumping the roof and pinging on the glass of the windows. Bill wanted her to come to the bed, to touch him.

"Melissa."

"What?" she said, still gazing out the window.

"I hear Ralph Turgis downstairs," he commented dully. Would she not turn and look at him? Her slender hand held the cord to the drapes. He stared intently at her, hoping that she could read his thoughts and come to him.

"Yes, what about him?" Her voice was distant, annoyed.

"I was just wondering. Did we pay him to supervise the construction? I would rather not have that man in my house."

"We've signed a contract with him," Melissa said wearily. "He gets ten percent."

Why had they ever started the bay windows? Bill thought to himself. The new windows were just one more unnecessary project over which Melissa would drive herself into a nervous craze. And they could no longer afford them.

"I've always wanted some curves in this house," Melissa said. She sighed and leaned out of the open window, letting the rain hit her face. "It's supposed to rain through the weekend. I'm glad it's raining."

Bill looked at his wife, her face and hair damp with the rain, and he wanted terribly to hold her. If she would not come to him, he would go to her. He rose from the bed, took a step toward her, and crumpled to the floor.

"Bill." She rushed to him, bent over him.

He remained sprawled on the floor. Then he put his arm around her, drawing her to him. But she pulled back, a strange look on her face.

"Get up, Bill. Get up. Please get up."

He looked at her without speaking.

"Your arm is bleeding."

"Help me." He raised himself to his knees. Her face still strange and contorted, she helped maneuver him to the blanket-box bench at the foot of the bed. As he struggled to rise, his body twisted toward the vanity mirror and he caught an unwanted glimpse of himself, the head surprising him as always, appearing as if it didn't fit properly on his slumping shoulders, his mustache, now flecked with gray like the rest of his thinning hair, his loose, white stomach hanging over his undershorts.

Melissa stood staring at him. "Tell me."

He could not answer. Reaching out, he touched the hollow at the base of her neck. Then he took her hand and held it against his cheek.

"You can't walk, can you," she said in a voice that seemed to come not from within her but beside her, like the voice of a ventriloquist. "Bill, oh Bill." She began kissing him. "This can't happen to us. Why is this happening?" Her tears dripped down his chest and fell on his dead legs. Then something seemed to snap and she moved from his grasp. She went to the window. After a few moments, she said, "Our life is over."

"Melissa."

"Oh, oh, oh," she murmured. "I don't know if I can take it anymore, Bill. I'm not strong enough." She turned and stared at him, and the blood vessels were popping out in her face. "You're throwing everything away. Everything we've worked for. Your job, your health, our family. We'll lose the house. I don't know what will happen to us. Don't you get it, Bill? It's all in your head."

As soon as she'd uttered these last words, she looked quickly toward the hallway, as if fearing that she might have been overheard by the workers downstairs, and closed the bedroom door. Now her face was red and wild with animal rage. "You're doing this to yourself, and to me. Why are you doing this to me?"

"Melissa." Bill felt like slapping her.

"You're destroying yourself," she screamed. For a moment, she put her face in her hands. "You just can't hack it, so you're self-destructing."

"Stop."

"And poor Alex so much wants to admire you. But what does he have to admire? You've been at Plymouth for nine years now. You should have been a senior partner years ago. Larry Tarsky is running his own company. You don't see Larry tiptoeing around and waiting for something to happen. He goes out and gets what he wants. And I'll tell you something. Alex is turning into a tiptoer like his father. He has one friend, and he shuts himself up in his room all day with that stupid computer."

"Shut up. Shut up." Bill's face was on fire. His anger burned in him and rushed through him, and he lunged for the pineapple fixture atop the bedpost and broke it off with a loud crack of splitting wood and hurled it across the room. "I've had enough," he shouted. "Enough. You think only about yourself. Half the time you're drunk. So don't tell me I'm self-destructing. I hate these bay windows. I never asked for the bay windows. I want them stopped. No more money for the bay windows. Okay? No more money. And I hate having the furniture come and go every day. Did you ever think about asking me what I like? I pay the bills."

"Do you know how it makes me feel when you say that?"

For a few moments, he sat there on the blanket chest breathing heavily, his blood gushing through him. Then, he no longer felt angry at her, but angry at himself. With a terrible vividness, he recalled the image he had seen in the mirror. Wasn't he a flabby half-man as Melissa had said? Hadn't he allowed himself to be squashed by the senior partners at Plymouth, squashed by Edward Marbleworth, squashed by the world?

"I was thinking I should go to the hospital," he said.

One of the workmen downstairs called up with some kind of emergency. Melissa disappeared for a while, then returned with the remote telephone from the kitchen and handed it to Bill. On the line was Dr. Petrov's weekend receptionist. "No, I'm not taking Prozac anymore," Bill shouted into the phone. "Dr. Petrov knows I'm not on Prozac. I'm on Paxil now." The receptionist explained that she would contact Dr. Petrov as soon as possible. Could his wife get him to the Emergency Room? Could he take any steps at all? Was he in pain? "I have no pain," he screamed into the telephone. "I can't feel anything. Can you hear that? I can't feel anything."

Melissa flung herself across the bed, sobbing. He looked at her lying there, her small shoulders rising and falling, and he realized that he had always known she was dissatisfied with him. His eyes moved slowly from the bed to his trousers and shirt on the floor, her nightgown folded over a chair, the bureau where the photograph of her mother receded into shadow.

Then, his need for her returned stronger than before, now a sharp, sexual need. He pulled himself over the footrail of the bed and lay beside her and put his arm over her bare shoulders. "Melissa," he whispered to her. He leaned into her and began caressing her neck with the palm of his hand. "Melissa." She stopped crying but remained face down on the bed. "Let's make love," he whispered.

"Oh, Bill," she said, releasing a groan of exhaustion. "What are we going to do?"

He grasped the top button of her cotton sundress.

"What are we going to do?"

The hospital smelled of rubbing alcohol.

NATIONAL PARALYSIS
ASSOCIATION

When Alex came home that evening and saw his father in a
wheelchair, he turned pale and covered his face and ran to
his room. Bill rolled down the hallway, banging awkwardly
into walls and banisters, and knocked on his son's door.
"Alex, talk to me. Open the door." "No." "Please open the
door, Alex." "What's wrong with you?" "The doctors don't
know yet." "You're going to die, aren't you." "I'm not going
to die. I'm okay. Open the door. Please, Alex, open the
door." "No."

_____

To: Brad Serano <BSERANO@AOL.COM>
From: Alexander Chalmers <ACHALM@AOL.COM>
Subject: Re: Regarding

Mr. Bradford. My father's in a wheelchair. He can't
walk. A.

_____

_____

>>> MAIL 50.02.04 <<< From: ACHALM at AOL.COM
==> Received: from RING.AOL.COM by AOL.COM with GOTP
id AQ06498; Sat, 23 Aug 22:13:36 EDT
for WCHALM@AOL.COM; Sat, 23 Aug 22:14:01 -0400

MESSAGE LOCK OVERRIDE
>>> MAIL 50.02.04 <<< From: Alexander at AOL.COM
Dear Dad,
  I did an Infoseek searhc o n the net and found some
st uff about paralysis. Is that what you have? I copied
it onto the attached file.
Love, Alex.

Paralysis → Health: Diseases and Conditions:
Organizations → **National Paralysis Association** → Cure.

Number of documents found: 10

NPA Events Navigation Bar
Exploring a Cure for Paralysis
NPA Events Calendar
Christopher Reeve Foundation
Run for a Cure @ The NYC Marathon
NPA News
Preparations for Fall Wine Tasting
Rise to the Occasion
Harvest Soiree
Feathers and Shuttle

→ Exploring a Cure for Paralysis
Before an injury, spinal cord nerves can convey signals
from the brain to the rest of the body. After an
injury, nerves begin to atrophy. The signals can no
longer travel.
Because of research supported by the NPA and others,
there has been great progress in restoring nerve
function after spinal cord injury and paralysis. We are
now living in a most exciting time in the

neurosciences. The purpose of the NPA Home Page is to share recent progress and breakthroughs in the treatment of paralysis.

The spinal cord is a thin and delicate combination of nerve cells and nerve fibers connecting the electrical activity of the brain to muscles in the body. Trauma to these nerves can cause severe damage, resulting in a breakdown of the nervous impulses and paralysis. Some axons degenerate and others die.

However, scientists have discovered some measures to aid in nerve regeneration after injury. These studies show that nerve fibers can regenerate. Dr. Martin Schwab at the University of Zurich in Switzerland has developed an antibody called IN-1 which neutralizes the inhibitory protein in the spinal cord. Combining IN-1 with the nerve growth factor NT-3 has been found to cause nerve fiber regeneration in the spinal cord of rats.

>> MAIL 50.02.04 << From: Petrov at MGH.HARVARD.EDU
====> Received: from TAR.HARVARD.EDU by HARVARD.EDU with BFP
id AQ74078; Mon, 25 Aug 9:18:27 EDT
for WCHALM@AOL.COM; Mon, 25 Aug 9:18:39 -0400
Press * for message

>>> MAIL 50.02.04 <<< From: Petrov at MGH.HARVARD.EDU
Dear Mr. Chalmers,
Im very sorry abut the wrosening of your condition, but I am still hopeful. (1) I will reserve some time on the cyclotron so that we can do a PET scan. (2) YOu sould of course return to Dr, Kendry for another neurology

examination and my office will schedule that. (3) As you
know, I've been in touch with Dr. Jeffrey Soames at
Mayo, who is department head of Autoimmune Diseases and
president of the Autoimmne Diseases Asociation of
America. Commonwealth Health has refused to authorize
his consultations, but he has taken a personal interest
in your case. Dr. Soames now recommends some
internventions enven though we don;t yet have a
diagnosis So, I'm scheduling a plasmapheresis, which
will replace all of the plasma in your blood, and a
steroid program. (4) Finally, the really good news! By
a stroke of luck, Dr. Soames is flying thorugh Boston
next wek on his way to a confernce in London an has
agreed to stay over a few hours to see you. WE wil try
to shedule theplasmapheresis at this time, to save you
an extra trip to the hospital.
With good wishes, Armand Petrov, M.D.

\>>> MAIL 50.02.04 <<< From: Harnden at PENN.MED.EDU
==> Received: from RING.AOL.COM by AOL.COM with BFP
id MS84093; Mon, 25 Aug 15:23:49 EDT
for WCHALM@AOL.COM; Mon, 25 Aug 15:24:13 -0400
Press * for message

\>>> MAIL 50.02.04 <<< From: Harnden at PENN.MED.EDU
Dear Bill,
    I was shocked to get your message. Why didn't you
tell me earlier about what's been going on? You've got
the best doctors in the world there, but I'm going to
talk to some people I know here in Philly and the med
school if you don't mind. Contact me immediately if
there is anything I can do. I'd like to come see you if
you're taking visitors. Let me know. I can be there in

6 hours. If you don't ask me to come in the next few
weeks, I'm coming anyway.
Peter

_____

_____

>>> MAIL 50.02.04 <<< From: Roe at WELLES1.COM
==> Received: from RING.AOL.COM by AOL.COM with BFP
id JC49705; Tues, 26 Aug 14:01:19 EDT
for WCHALM@AOL.COM; Tues, 26 Aug 14:01:57 -0400
Press * for message

>>> MAIL 50.02.04 <<< From: Roe at WELLES1.COM
Dear Bill,
   Maggie and I were very sorry to hear that you're in a
wheelchair. Please let us know if there is anything we
can do. Our thoughts are with you.
Stephen

_____

A vase of flowers with a note arrived from Amy. And e-mails
from George Mitrakis and David Hamilton, carefully worded,
expressing regrets.

That evening, as Bill slumped in his wheelchair and ate his
dinner from a tray, Melissa suddenly began talking about her
mother, how she looked at different times, trips they had
taken together when the family was young. "We used to go to
a place in Florida, before we lost the store and everything.
You could see the ocean from the front window. You could
smell the salt in the air. We ate breakfast on a little porch,
and she used to ask me for words for her crossword puzzles."
   "Harriet liked the ocean."
   "You were so sweet with her, Bill." Melissa stood up, her

eyes teary. "Thank you for that. Nothing's fair, is it. Daddy told me nothing was fair, and he was right."

She stooped and gathered up the spilled food on the rug and picked up his tray. "What else can I do for you right now? Have I done enough?" She leaned against the bedpost and closed her eyes. "I'd like to go out for a few minutes."

"Do you hate helping me?"

She moved toward the door. He knew she was going to the liquor store. He couldn't blame her. "Now they think I've got an autoimmune disease."

"Well, well," she said. "That's good to know. I'll be back in a few minutes. We should sue Plymouth. If you don't, I will. The disability insurance, even if we get it, is nothing."

As he heard her car pull out of the driveway, the telephones began ringing. Instinctively, Bill wheeled himself to the writing table but saw that the phone had been removed from its base. He turned and listened. Was it coming from the closet? "Alex," he shouted, "get the phone!" The telephone continued to ring, and he wheeled himself bumping across the floor to various corners of the room, to the closet, and yanked open the door. Melissa shouldn't have left the phone in here, he thought angrily to himself. She was always taking the phones off someplace. Who could it be on the phone? It could be anybody. "Alex," he screamed. Without thinking, he had been counting since the phone started ringing. Thirteen, fourteen. He bent down in his chair and flung clothes aside. The ringing was coming from somewhere in the back of the closet. Sixteen. By now, the answering machine should have picked up, but it hadn't. The answering machine must be broken. Eighteen. Why was he chasing the goddamned phone? Let it ring. Let the stupid thing ring. He slammed his hand against the wheelchair. Where was the phone? He shoved himself further into the closet. Shoes got under his wheels, he swung at hanging dresses and suits.

PLASMAPHERESIS

The cell separator looked like a portable washing machine. A clear plastic tube, red with flowing blood, looped away from the needle in Bill's right forearm and into the machine. Another tube returned cleansed and reconstituted blood into the left arm. Bare plasma, stripped of its red and white cells, was the color of straw. It tasted like seawater. Even his blood was no longer his own, Bill thought to himself. He was a part of the machine, one giant circulatory system. Veins connected to tubes connected to veins. One pint of blood at a time, ten pints in two hours. The thumping of the pump sounded like a human gulping for air. Or was it his heart?

He lay on his side and stared at a photograph on the drab plaster wall, "MGH Nursing Staff 1911." A hundred nurses posed in front of the old stone hospital, each identically dressed in a white cap like an inverted flowerpot, a white collar encircling the neck, a dark, long-sleeve shirt buttoned up to the collar, and over that an apron-like white top that concluded in a flowing white skirt. All clasped their hands purposefully in their laps and looked straight ahead at the camera. Tears came to his eyes.

Melissa sat beside his hospital bed and was saying something about getting Alex ready to start back at school. Thursday. High on the wall, a television droned.

He could hear Dr. Soames's assistant, who had arrived in advance to make all necessary preparations for the examination. The assistant was searching about the cramped hospital room for a telephone jack into which he could plug his modem and laptop. He rolled Bill's bed away from the wall, poked behind a sink, inspected an electronic panel with illuminated numbers. "Dr. Soames likes to use his own database in Minnesota," he said.

"We have excellent data sources of our own," said Armand Petrov.

"Please," said the assistant. "And he'll need a tall table for working. He never sits." Immediately, a nurse commenced to clear a metallic stand of its boxes of disposable white rubber gloves. A coiled blood-pressure cord, with its protruding black bulb, fell to the floor. An orderly raced down the hall, shouting and wheeling a bed.

Uncomfortably, Bill turned over, tangling the tubes in his arms, and stared at the bed next to him. A curtain surrounded its patient, but he could see a woman's hand hanging down and could hear her tortured breathing through an oxygen mask. A nurse floated into the room like a starchy ghost, went behind the curtains for a few moments, and disappeared.

There was a commotion in the corridor outside the room. Someone began speaking in a restrained voice to a nurse. A taxi was to be waiting at the Emergency circle in fifty minutes. Then Dr. Soames made his appearance, flanked by two nurses, his assistant, and Dr. Petrov. The Mayo specialist was dressed in a dark-blue pinstriped suit, as if ready to deliver his lecture in London at any minute. He smiled faintly at Bill. Then he proceeded at once to the table where his laptop had been set up, chest high, and went to work. Soames's assistant and Dr. Petrov peered over his shoulder as information surged through the modem, shimmered for forty-five seconds on his screen, and was printed out noiselessly on the attached laser printer.

After a few minutes, Soames said, "Bring me more paper." His assistant flew from the room and down the adjoining corridor.

"Has he touched you?" Melissa whispered to her husband.

Removing his jacket, Soames pored over the flitting images and data on his computer screen as if they were diagrams of enemy military installations. Radiology and neurology were not his specialties, but he wanted to have all the information available. His specialty, the assistant explained, was auto-immune diseases, in which, for unknown reasons, the body attacked itself, the body turned into its own enemy: lupus, where the body assaulted its connective tissues, causing painful joints, fatigue, a slow downward spiral; Guillain-Barré syndrome, in which the peripheral nerves became inflamed, particularly where they exited the spine, leading to numbness and weakness of the limbs, a sagging of the face muscles, difficulty swallowing and breathing, and eventually paralysis; multiple sclerosis, in which the immune system slowly destroyed the protective myelin sheath around the nerve fibers in the brain and spinal cord, causing tingling and numbness, muscle weakness, slurred speech, intermittent blindness, difficulty walking, and often death. Others: rheumatoid arthritis, myasthenia gravis, fibromyalgia, ankylosing spondylitis, Ménière's disease, Wegener's granulomatosis, Goodpasture's syndrome. Some could be treated.

Dr. Soames glanced at his watch and frowned. Hurriedly, he and his assistant now began laying out the reports and films at the bottom of Bill's bed, in columns and rows, as in a game of solitaire. "Sagittal plane: 500 milliseconds TR, 13 milliseconds TE, field of view 24 centimeters, matrix size

128 × 256. Axial: 3900 milliseconds repetition time, 17 and 90 milliseconds TE, field of view 24 centimeters, matrix size 192 × 256." Charts of blood and spinal fluid. Bill would have felt their fingers on the bedsheets, tracing the contours of curves, pointing to numbers, but he had no sensation in the lower part of his body. The Mayo specialist called for more light.

"I can find nothing definite," Dr. Soames said to Dr. Petrov. "The Sed rates and RF look normal." To Bill, it seemed that Petrov released a slight sigh of pleasure. Soames turned to his assistant, who nodded in agreement. "But . . . an ANA of 130 is suggestive. Yes, suggestive." Soames began tucking his laptop away in its black carrying bag. He put on his jacket and went to the mirror over the sink. "We'll need more blood work. I'd like to have tests for ACA, ssDNA, and another rheumatoid factor." Soames's assistant wrote down the orders on a slip of pink paper and handed them to Petrov. "And an autoimmune Western blot," added Soames, straightening his tie and collar. "I'll ask for additional tests later on. My opinion is that we may have some unusual autoimmune disease here. If so, the plasmapheresis may halt or even reverse the paralysis. We can follow with steroids."

"I'll be able to walk?" asked Bill, leaning forward in his bed. The specialist was probably lying, he felt, but he wanted to believe.

"Possibly."

A nurse appeared at the door and announced that Dr. Soames's taxi was waiting to take him to the airport.

Bill turned over again to face the wall. The needle in his arm entered just below a pink sliver of a scar left from long ago, diving off rocks at summer camp. If he held very still, he thought he could feel the blood move into him, a faint quivering. His eyes returned to the photograph of the nurses. Some were pretty. One had braided hair, a terribly sad smile. She was the only one who looked away from the camera.

After the plasmapheresis, Bill's condition seemed to improve slightly. The new blood and the steroids, which caused his face to puff up, had restored a slender mobility, so that on some days he could take a step or two before falling. His dead fingers sometimes tingled. These uncertain gains, guardedly reported, were greeted with immediate e-mails from Dr. Petrov and Dr. Soames and another specialist of some kind from the Duke medical school in North Carolina. Such was the doctors' interest, and even optimism to a degree, that Bill began to take seriously the hypothesis that he suffered from some autoimmune disorder, and he spent the morning hours at his terminal researching that condition. In the long afternoons, he often just lay on his bed, unable to nap, listening to the sounds of the house or dumbly staring at the ceiling. Sometimes he would summon the will to crawl across the floor and drag himself up to the window, braced against the wall, so that he might look down on the familiar neighborhood. Here he found a temporary peacefulness and pleasure in observing small things, the tiny splotches of white on the shingled roof, the way that the ribbon on the Cotters' mailbox slowly fluttered and waltzed, the glint of chrome on automobiles as they passed down the street, fallen leaves cartwheeling in a breeze, the red brick chimneys and the painted white chimneys, a kite caught in a tree, birds. After a time, however, a great sadness would sweep over him, a sensation that he was the only human on earth watching these things, and he could not bear to look through the window any longer. Then he would close his eyes and let his head drop against his raised arms until the impotent legs finally crumpled beneath him.

He stopped shaving, with the result that his swollen face became covered with a patchy growth of brown whiskers, white on the chin. Now, he hardly recognized the reflection of his face any more than the rest of his body. Day by day, his legs were visibly shrinking. His body was dwindling toward the nothingness he felt. He attempted to imagine the future. What would happen to his family? Melissa would have to get a money-earning job. Alex would have to go to a different school. They would have to move out of Lexington into a small house somewhere. It all seemed impossible, unimaginable. If only he could turn back the clock to the beginning of June, when he drove to the Alewife garage every morning, put in a full day of work at his company, ran sweaty and complaining on the treadmill in the Universe Health Club. It was not a bad life, it was a comfortable life, and he would give anything to have it again. As he sat with his limbs scattered on the divan, waiting for Melissa to bring him his tray, he pictured himself running on the Universe treadmill, his legs surging forward and down on the black rubber mat, forward and backward, as if he were a running machine, built for running, unable to do anything except run, run, run.

"Why sue only Plymouth?" Bill retorted to Melissa late one night as they gazed at the television, unable to sleep.

"What are you saying? Is your brain going, too?"

"Sue all of them," he said, trying not to jostle his head. "Especially the rows of dummies in Marbleworth's Communications Room. Sue the motorists who clog up the highways, sue the fax machines and telephones. Sue the televisions."

"Your brain is going." She got up from the bed, her nightgown a glimmer of dead white in the light of the TV, and trudged to the bathroom.

>> MAIL 50.02.04 << From: Petrov at MGH.HARVARD.EDU
====> Received: from TAR.HARVARD.EDU by HARVARD.EDU
with BFP
id AQ74078; Tues, 15 Sept 9:23:22 EDT
for WCHALM@AOL.COM; Tues, 15 Sept 9:23:38 -0400
Press * for message

>>> MAIL 50.02.04 <<< From: Petrov at
MGH.HARVARD.EDU
Dear Mr. Chalmers,
As you knnow, we have been consilting with Dr. Marjorie
Stebbins at the Duke Medical School. Dr. Stebbins is
an intenraltionaly known specialist in congenital
neuropathies. I received the following E-mail from her
over the weekend.
With good wishes, Armand Petrov, M.D.
  Attached file:

RE: Case MGH 384930
Dear Dr. Petrov,
I havae come to believe that we are not looing at an

autoimmune disease here, but rather a rare kind of congential neuropathy. I will send you a list of recommended tests t pusrue this hyoethesis.
Marjorie Stebbins, STEBBINS@DUKE.MED.EDU

———————————————————

THE ATTORNEYS

Late in September, when the summer heat had finally given way to a freshening of the air, Bill had his ninth session with Dr. Kripke. For a few moments, they sat silently in the psychiatrist's cramped office. Kripke had just administered a Rorschach test, having reluctantly agreed that the last month of Paxil was failing to produce any positive effects.

"There's plenty of anger here."

"What?" Exhausted from staring at one inkblot after another, Bill could hardly understand human speech.

"The anger is building," said the psychiatrist. "But it is too broad, unfocused and broad." He scribbled a few lines in his notebook. "Generalized anger eats away at the mind and the body. It's wasted." The psychiatrist then offered some metaphor relating Bill's anger to a Thoroughbred horse without any rider, such an absurd comparison that Bill found himself listening instead to the ripples from the noise machine on the wall. "In my experience," Kripke continued, "it is best to channel anger, if possible, to give it a specific target. Action is a mode of adaptation."

It was at this point that Bill realized he must sue Plymouth. How dare they treat him the way that they had, suddenly firing him as if he were temporary help. He had given Plymouth his lifeblood. Yes, he would sue the hell out of them, cut them off at the knees. And after that, he would sue his useless physicians, including Kripke.

"Do you see yourself as being in control of your life?" asked the psychiatrist, miles away.

Bill stared at the speckled pattern of light flowing through the single tiny window. "Control? I feel like I'm always being rushed. Rushed and pushed. I let myself be rushed and pushed."

"Like a cork in the ocean?"

"You're right!" Bill exploded. "You're right. I'm going to sue those bastards."

"That might be a healthy thing," said the shrink, suddenly standing, for their hour had run out. "After you've succeeded in releasing your anger, we can begin seeking its cause."

These last words Bill barely heard. Already he was banging into chairs and tables, wheeling himself as fast as he could toward the middle door, the one for exiting after a completed session.

On the afternoon of his appointment at the law offices of Thoreau and McCullough, Bill had worked himself into a healthy state of fury, which only intensified after Melissa had parked their car at a pricey garage at Beacon and School Street and begun pushing him up the sidewalk between the towering buildings of downtown Boston. Sue the bastards, Bill muttered to himself. The sidewalk teemed with people who scurried around Bill like ants dodging a crumpled leaf in their path. He imagined their eyes squirming upon him as they paused and stared, headsets protruding, then hurried on to their urgent appointments. How pathetic and helpless he must appear in his wheelchair. He scowled at each passerby.

Melissa gently placed her fingertips against his cheek. "Just tell the lawyers everything that's happened," she said softly.

"And be decisive. These high-powered attorneys appreciate toughness."

"Don't tell me what to do," snapped Bill. "Do you think I'm some cork on the ocean?"

They continued along Beacon, the crowds of pedestrians now laden with boxes and cartons and suit packs from their shopping expeditions on Newbury Street. It seemed to Bill that now, instead of staring at him, people avoided looking at him altogether. Which was worse? Was he not even worth staring at? Was he nobody at all? Plymouth had treated him like a nobody.

It was 3:15 when Bill and Melissa, heavily perspiring, disembarked from the elevator at the entrance to Thoreau and McCullough. Immediately Bill found himself squinting in the bright light. Looking up, he saw that the old plaster ceilings, with their elegant crown moldings and center medallions, had been completely covered over with fluorescent light tubes. Pale messengers squinted also as they boarded the elevator carrying armloads of documents. At the end of the hallway, Bill could discern a shining figure leaning over a desk. It was the receptionist, a sallow woman who appeared as if she hadn't left the building in days. Her hair hung like spaghetti down the sides of her thin face, and her skin seemed to have permanently taken on the pale milky white of the fluorescent lights. Wearily, she looked up from her computer screen. "Mrs. Chalmers. Yes. Thank you. Mr. Baker will be with you shortly." Then, with a wave of her hand, she gestured toward a waiting area, where one woman sat with her neck in a brace.

"Waiting, always waiting," Bill muttered loud enough for the receptionist to hear him. He hated waiting, he was always waiting for people. He was on time, even now, even paralyzed and in a wheelchair. Why couldn't the attorneys be on time? Bill angrily wheeled himself into the waiting area and wedged himself next to an antique commode bearing a porcelain lamp. A workman was installing a large acrylic painting on the wall.

"I'm sweating," said Melissa. "I'm going to the rest room."

"My husband wouldn't come with me," said the woman in the neck brace, carefully rotating her body to look at Bill. "But he wrote down a list of things for me to tell the lawyers." She took some pages out of an envelope, tore them in two, and let the pieces drop to the floor. "I'm sorry for you," she said and smiled sympathetically at Bill. "I hope you get something. I really hope you do."

It was 3:25. Bill rolled himself back to the receptionist. "We have a three-fifteen appointment," he shouted. "Look at me. Here. Look down. Do you see me now? Why do you keep people waiting?"

"I do apologize," whispered the receptionist. She was about to say something more when her telephone began beeping in short frantic bursts. Then another instrument on the desk began humming. Glancing past the reception desk, Bill could see a maze of bright corridors, legs fluttering back and forth. Lawyers in gleaming white shirtsleeves hurried down the hallways, sputtering into their telephones or recorders, stopping now and then to interrogate one of the secretaries who sat in little booths along the way. In a room straight ahead, a conference of some kind was in progress. Through partly open white shutters, Bill could see a half-dozen people, leaping up and down at a table, slanted sections of moving torsos and heads.

Just then, a handsome, tallish man rounded a corner and strode to the reception desk. He was dressed in a beautiful herringbone suit and silk tie. His curly hair had turned prematurely silver and reflected the hues of his blue-gray eyes, which gazed calmly from behind the polished lenses of his glasses. Altogether, he gave the impression of a man in complete control of all things, so that it was surprising to see that he held a tissue against his dripping nose.

"It's only a small cold," he said at once, his voice thick and cottony. "I'm Thurston Baker. Forgive me for not shaking your hand. I'm afraid I don't look well. But I feel much better than I look." He gave a little laugh and smiled pleasantly, glancing down at Bill and fixing him with his eyes. "We're going to try to help you, Mr. Chalmers."

"We've been waiting for that," said Bill.

Before further introductions could be made, a disheveled secretary ran up to Mr. Baker with a sheaf of fax pages and thrust them into his hands. "Is this really so urgent, Olivia?" he said, holding out the pages at arm's length as if Olivia would take them back.

"They're from Mr. Davidson-Chamberlain, and Mr. Kelleher," said the secretary, out of breath. "Mr. Davidson-Chamberlain just called and insisted that you respond to him today, by four-thirty. He said he'll take whatever you've got." She glanced helplessly at the receptionist and adjusted a tired-looking purple scarf on her shoulders.

Mr. Baker began coughing. It now struck Bill that almost everyone he had seen on the premises appeared ill. He could hear other coughing and sneezing coming from the hallways. Baker glanced at his watch. "Shall we go to my office?" he muttered through his tissue. "Where's Mrs. Chalmers?"

As they started down a bright corridor, ancient oak floors creaked under their feet. Lawyers and their assistants hurried by, each tossing a "Good afternoon, Thurston" to Baker as they flew past. Some of the office doors were open, and Bill could see people in shirtsleeves at great desks, typing at their terminals or talking on the phones.

Then they were in Baker's office, which smelled of old wood and new electronic equipment. On the wall were autographed photos of baseball players, glinting in the light from a large bay window. The attorney withdrew a fresh tissue from a box on his cluttered desk. "So you live in Lexington," he said and took off his jacket. Reaching forward, he moved the computer terminal a few inches so that he could clearly see Bill. "There you are." An odd expression moved over his face. "You look familiar to me, Mr. Chalmers. Have we met somewhere before?"

"I don't believe so," said Bill. Then the horrifying thought came to him that Baker could have been on the subway that fateful morning when he had made a fool of himself. In a flood of repressed memory, he recalled his panic at the unfamiliar subway signs, the vomiting on his tie and shirt, the stickiness and the smell and the disgusted stares of other passengers. Could Baker have been in that train? Or in the church, when Bill was on stage in the cash booth? Little by little, as imperceptibly as possible, Bill rolled his chair to one side so that the computer terminal again came between his face and Baker's.

"I must be mistaken," said the attorney, a slight note of doubt remaining in his voice.

"Yes," said Bill. Quietly, he slid down in his chair, further distancing himself from Baker's direct view.

"Well, then," said the attorney, "let's get the discussion of the billing out of the way." His charges were $300 an hour, he explained, with billing in five-minute units. Associate attorneys received $150 per hour and were used to as great an extent as possible to keep costs down for the client.

"How much time have we been billed for so far?" blurted Melissa.

Mr. Baker smiled. "As of yet, not a single second, Mrs. Chalmers." He began to say something else, possibly some further assurance that his new clients would not be excessively charged, when there was a knock on the door. A smartly dressed young woman entered, clutching a pad of yellow paper and faintly annoyed.

"This is Alice Stevenson," said Baker. "Alice is an associate in the firm and will be joining us in our meeting." Instead of taking one of the chairs, Ms. Stevenson installed herself on the windowsill, dangling her legs like a schoolgirl.

Although Bill could not see Baker's face, he imagined that it must be registering disapproval. Why did the senior attorney tolerate this kind of behavior from a subordinate? Baker stirred behind his computer terminal and called attention to the clock on the wall. It read 3:44.

Bill found himself staring in silence at the floor. He could think of nothing except the figure of $300 an hour. Plus $150 for Ms. Stevenson's services, which had been left in a cloud of uncertainty. Whatever her function, he had never asked for Ms. Stevenson. Thinking about her now, he grew angry. Shouldn't he have been consulted about bringing Ms. Stevenson in on the case? These attorneys did what they wanted. So now it was $450 an hour. He should speak up this minute and say that he didn't want Ms. Stevenson. That's what he should do. Why couldn't he speak up? So it was $450 an hour. His face contorted in mathematical calculations as he strained to compute the cost of each five-minute "unit." Unconsciously, he made a grunting noise as he thought.

"Mr. Chalmers."

Bill looked up at the digital clock and saw that the numbers had already advanced to 3:46. He had little choice. Blurting rapidly, in a manner that he felt was humiliating, he began recounting the chain of events following his episode on the subway. At once, Baker took up a gold pen from his desk and began taking notes, now and then asking to clarify particular details.

"My husband is ill," Melissa interrupted. "You can't fire someone for illness, can you? They can't do that."

Baker nodded sympathetically but without comment. Continuing his story, Bill glanced hopefully at Ms. Stevenson, to find her staring with apparent disinterest out the window.

As Bill neared the end of his narration, his wife suddenly burst into tears. "Melissa," he whispered in astonishment. He could not remember a time when she had allowed herself to break down in public. Tears came to his own eyes, and he reached for her hand. What misery she must be going through, what fear and concern for him. Despite all that was not right, she did love him. She did love him. How had he ever doubted that? He gazed at her tenderly, noticing the fragile curve of her neck, the whiteness of her. Then, remembering where he was, he looked away from his wife and at Baker, who silently offered his box of tissues. For some moments more Melissa continued to sob quietly, leaning against her husband. Then, she wouldn't let go of his arm. She dried her eyes with the back of her free hand, like a child, and put on her dark glasses.

"We will do all that we can, Mrs. Chalmers," said Baker, getting up from his desk. "I am at your disposal." He hesitated, waiting another few moments. How many people had cried openly in Baker's office, Bill wondered, telling their sad stories and tales of persecutions. He could see that the attorney, while sympathetic, was not allowing himself to become emotionally involved, any more than did Kripke. Baker was a perfect professional. Now the attorney had taken off his glasses and was cleaning the lenses. His eyes had that same calmness that Bill had seen earlier.

"There are certain issues," Baker said at last, in a gentle tone. "Mr. Chalmers, did Plymouth not fail to make any reasonable accommodation for your reduced manual efficiency?"

"Yes. I mean no." Bill stared at the attorney without comprehension, like a cow at a passing train.

"Were people at Plymouth aware of your condition?"

"Certainly," answered Bill. "They had to be aware. They could not have been unaware."

"Good," the attorney said and nodded with satisfaction. "That will have to be documented in our discovery."

At that point, Ms. Stevenson, who had remained silent from her perch on the windowsill, launched a series of incisive questions, brilliant in their simplicity. As Bill attempted to answer them, he could not help gazing repeatedly at the clock. Four twenty-three. Four twenty-four. Four twenty-five. "So we have a case?" he asked finally. It was 4:26.

"Maybe," said Baker. The senior attorney grasped the mouse of his computer and began clicking it randomly, like tapping a pencil. "I must tell you that medical matters are extremely difficult. The precise state of one's health is almost impossible to prove. But in your case . . ." He leaned forward and gestured to Bill's legs in the wheelchair. Click. Click. "It seems quite clear that you have a definite malady of some kind. Although, if I understand you, we don't know what it is. Even so, I remember a case several years ago, I seem to recall that the woman was from Woburn, or maybe it was Winchester, where she was missing a hand, but there was no consensus about whether she was disabled. The Americans with Disabilities Act of 1990 forbids discrimination against qualified individuals with a disability, but there was no agreement whether this missing hand, in fact, constituted a disability. You see what I mean." The senior attorney then went on to give a tedious summary of related cases and the various conflicting medical reports, clicking his mouse all the while.

Despite the importance of Baker's comments and the preciousness of each passing minute, Bill found himself gazing out the window and across to the Public Garden. How much he would like to be down in the garden with Melissa at this moment, in one of the green-bottomed swanboats that he could see in the distance, floating quietly beneath weeping willows. Or walking among the trees, which dabbed the criss-crossing paths through the park like colored balls of cotton. At the corners of each patch of velvety grass, he could see dots of red and yellow and orange, the marigolds still in bloom, reflecting the smooth autumn light. He imagined that he and Melissa were walking there now. They had no destination, no place they had to be, they could just stroll through the garden, stop whenever they wished, look at the water or sit on a bench. Fronds from a willow tree dropped in her hair. Wind blew against his face.

A buzzer exploded on Mr. Baker's desk, causing Bill to jerk his head from the window. The attorney whispered into an intercom on his desk and then, with a smile, said that he would have to excuse himself for a few minutes to speak to Mr. Springer just down the hall. He glanced at the clock and recorded the time in a little book in his shirt pocket. Then, sneezing and grasping a new handful of tissues from his desk, he hurried from the room.

"I don't feel well," whispered Melissa, releasing the grip on Bill's arm for the first time. "I think I'll go to the rest room and put cold water on my face. I'll wait for you in the reception area." She kissed her husband and left the room.

When the others had gone, Ms. Stevenson dropped from the windowsill, strolled behind the desk, and occupied Mr. Baker's chair. "I do all of his research and analysis for him," she said and leaned back. Bill regarded the junior attorney with amazement, uncertain what she would say next. She was an attractive young woman, with angular features, high cheekbones, and perfectly coiffured chin-length hair. "In my opinion," she said, her eyes wandering around the room in evident boredom, "you have a weak case, Mr. Chalmers."

"Why didn't you speak up earlier?" Bill replied angrily. Ms. Stevenson shrugged her shoulders. "Mr. Baker did not say I had a weak case," Bill said and glanced toward the half-open door through which the senior attorney had vanished. "He only said it would be a difficult case."

"He never says that someone has a weak case," said the junior attorney with a laugh.

Although he was suspicious of Ms. Stevenson, Bill found himself depressed by her remarks, and he laid his head back against the metal bar of his chair and stared at the wall. By now, much of his fury against Plymouth had uselessly dribbled away. Even Marbleworth. Who had the energy to fight him? "All I want is to get my job back," Bill said in a low voice, uncaring whether Ms. Stevenson heard him or not. "In another few months I would have been a senior partner."

"I understand," said Ms. Stevenson, the brashness gone from her voice. "I have ambitions, too. I want to be the youngest senior partner ever at Thoreau and McCullough. I want to argue cases in front of the United States Supreme Court." She got up from the desk and moved slowly next to Bill, quite close, placed her hand on his shoulder, and said softly, "Tell me what's really wrong with you. Surely you have some diagnosis after all of those doctors' reports."

Bill shook his head. He was thinking of Petrov's office with its steep cliffs of papers and reports.

"What does your wife do?" said Ms. Stevenson. "Or does she stay at home."

"That's none of your business," Bill said and wheeled himself away from her. He now realized that he could say nothing of a personal nature to this woman. Unwittingly, he had allowed himself to be vulnerable to her. From now on, he would confine himself entirely to the facts of the case. These attorneys were despicable and arrogant and smooth. Why had he come here? He looked at the clock on the wall. It read

5:02. Then he heard a flurry of coughing and sneezing, and Baker returned. The senior attorney seemed in good spirits from his consultation down the hall and went briskly to his desk.

"If you won't be needing me . . ." said Ms. Stevenson.

"Just a few more minutes." Baker went to his keyboard and began typing. "Mr. Chalmers," he said, "I will send you by e-mail a list of things to do next. In fact, we can have our next meeting by e-mail. That will save time."

"When will you know if I have a case?" Bill asked, his stomach in knots, his head beginning to pound. The words of Ms. Stevenson were going over and over in his brain.

"That's hard to say," said Baker. Bill leaned forward in his chair, trying to read what the senior attorney was typing.

"This will all come to you by e-mail," said Baker, continuing to type. "One thing is certain. It is critical that we have a diagnosis of your illness. We cannot do much without that." Ms. Stevenson picked up her yellow pad and went to the doorway, where she stood with one foot out and one foot in. "You must have a definite diagnosis," said Baker, "signed by a licensed physician. In fact, it should be corroborated independently by at least two physicians."

As Bill wheeled himself to the door, his head pounding, he was met by a chorus of coughs in the hall.

DRAWINGS

He lifts himself up at the window, sore from his sprawl on the floor. Although no one is home, he has sensed something stir. Overhead, a beam faintly creaks in the attic, a small motor groans in the distance. He leans against his wheelchair, feeling the cool metal against his back, again bends down to the floor.

On the floor, he is tracing the shadow of a leaf. It is the leaf of a sugar maple, just beyond his second-floor window, with a central pinnacle and two side lobes. Each of these partitions further into a coastline of sharp points and round gullies. When a breeze blows outside, the leaf shadow on the floor gently quivers and sways, and he suspends his drawing and waits. Then he begins again. Every hour, he makes a new tracing. In an hour, the shadow shifts by a hand's width, tracking the path of the sun. The first shadow each morning falls on the floor by his bureau. By midafternoon, when the day's drawings stop, when he can no longer resist the taunting stare of his keyboard, the shadow has crept to the red writing desk. After a week, his tracings spread across the floor. As if the different drawings were all connected, a single vine twisting over his floor, or possibly one giant leaf.

Melissa has pleaded with him to resettle downstairs, to stop the terrible trips down the steps, the confinement, but he prefers the hardship of their bedroom, the constant four walls of his illness. That is what he now calls it, no longer his problem but his illness. He is ill. He accepts that now. He is ill. His legs have become bones. His arms have become bones, miraculously still able to convey desires from his brain to his hands. Portions of his face have become numb. An ear, his chin, his left cheek. Daily, he prays for pain.

He grips his lead pencil as tightly as his mind will allow, for he wants his drawings to be perfect, he wants to record the exact shape of the leaf at this moment in time. Every tiny bend and indentation, every nick and turn. On one lobe, five points and six valleys, each slightly different from the rest. There is a small puncture in the leaf, a hole letting light through, and he lovingly traces that, too, an inner view. The right lobe is slightly larger than the left, almost imperceptibly, the left is lower and more shallow. He has found a lack of symmetry, more beautiful in imperfection. At times, the shadow seems to him a hand, or a small face, and he pulls back from his drawing, sensing that he has invaded some intimacy. Has he become a voyeur, peering through a window? Or a supplicant, offering himself? Even when the leaf seems a leaf, his tracing is an intimacy, he knows its contours so well. The central pinnacle erect like an army captain. Each curve like a water gully or a woman's breast. He knows the leaf so well that he can feel it despite his dead fingers, he can touch every crinkle and edge. He can feel its prickles against his cheek.

At night, he often dreams of the leaf and awakens to find his hand moving across the headboard. Sometimes, he awakens in a sweat. Then he has been dreaming not of the leaf but of his computer screen, his hand fidgeting on the headboard now become keyboard, jabbing at the keys, struggling to keep up, to keep up, sitting white-bellied naked in front of the screen while a thousand darts of information fly at his skin. Or driver ants devouring his flesh. He bleeds. Waking, he sits shaking and stares at the illuminated clock on the vanity.

As he drags himself about on his stomach, following the leaf shadow on the floor, it occurs to him that he is drawing a history of a sort. It is a history of the earth, a map of the movement of the earth. The earth moves in time, the shadow creeps across the floor. Nothing could be more simple. The earth moves, shadows move. Earth mother, the giver of leaves, the paradise, the blessing. He blesses the leaf and its earth mother, he traces and blesses. For he is seeing every detail in his history, he is observing every curve and movement. And is that not a blessing? He is a chronicler of small things, and big. Perhaps the universe resides in the leaf.

And as the leaf slightly changes its posture from one hour to the next, it occurs to him also that from his drawings, from their accuracy and sequence, a person might determine the precise time and place that the drawings were made. This possibility gives him pleasure, binding him to events far beyond himself. Lying on the floor, he soars. His drawings are both history and moment. With this enlarged frame of reference, he imagines other people at this instant, gas station attendants pumping gas, bank tellers counting out fives and tens, commuters hurrying down the sidewalk between buildings, people cooking cabbage in kitchens, drivers honking, the whole teeming heave, and he realizes that none of these people is looking. None of them knows of this history unfolding. He must record. He has a responsibility as well as a pleasure.

Observing the leaf shadow so minutely, he begins also to notice the floor. It is a yellow pine floor with wide planks, uncovered since he rolled up the rug, and its amber ridges swirl and wave in a variety of forms. In some places, the grain plunges down in long wavy streams, like paths of rain sliding on glass. In others, the grain thickens and radiates out from a warm center, like smoke rings around a fire, or amorphous blobs of amber whirling randomly within yellow seas. No two locations are the same. Patterns change abruptly from one plank to another, patterns glow in the sunlight and dim to Bach fugues in the shadows. Here and there, dark knots break the patterns, interlopers. This floor is a universe itself, he decides, faintly oily and moist against his good cheek. A world of infinite forms, with secret messages and meanings of its own. Undoubtedly also a history of the earth and living things. It is against this universe that the universe of the shadow leaf exists. The lead of his pencil creates the connection.

Then he discovers that he the observer has not observed well enough. When he stares carefully at the boundary between the universe of the floor and the universe of the shadow leaf, he is astonished to find that the shadow has its own shadow. The coastline of the leaf is not a sharp edge, but a slow gradation of dark changing to light. Around the inner shadow is a halo shadow, less intense, filamentary, mimicking the inner shadow yet breathing its own air. The halo shadow is the more delicate of the two, a piece of fine lace. So delicate, in fact, that it wavers slightly even when there is no wind. Its tiny filaments of half-shadow flutter like cilia of some exquisite sea creature. It seems to respond to the slightest of movements, even to anticipated movement, to thought. The halo shadow is the soul of the leaf. When he makes this discovery, he wonders if he can redo his drawings, add the slow lessening of dark. But the second shadow is too fine to trace.

To both shadows, he raises a blessing. And blesses himself and even his illness, for that is part of him also. Were it not for his illness, he wouldn't be here on the floor, dragging his dead weight but minutely seeing. He has become a seer, a historian of the life of a leaf. If only now he had pain. With pain he could feel the parts that are missing. He would see better with pain, understand more what has happened to him. With pain he would be complete. Is the leaf listening to this? Of course not, it is only a leaf, although it is also a universe. Why shouldn't he feel pain? What kind of illness is his, what kind of cruel disease that denies even pain, the clarity of pain? He will have pain, even though it is denied, and he cuts the places on his body still not numb, his good cheek, his chest, and he celebrates the pain and lets a few drops of blood drip on his tracings. Now, the drawings are even more beautiful, splotchy red like autumn leaves, and he wants everyone to see them, his minute observations, his silences.

```
>>> MAIL 50.02.04 <<< From: Petrov at
MGH.HARVARD.EDU
====> Received: from TAR.HARVARD.EDU by HARVARD.EDU
with BFP
id AQ74078; Tues, 14 Oct 11:18:32 EDT
for WCHALM@AOL.COM; Tues, 14 Oct 11:18:51 -0400
Press * for message

>>> MAIL 50.02.04 <<< From: Petrov at
MGH.HARVARD.EDU
Dear Mr. Chalmers,
The first musclar-skeletal ultrasound ddin't how
aything. I would like to do another at 10 MHz, which
can get to a much finere reslution of a few millimeters.
The office will be in touch with you.
   The PET examination is now scheduled for MOnday
```

October 27. We received a special allowance from your
HMO. IHae thought all along that PET would give us
imortnatn new information on metalboic activity. We wil
be using carbon 11 and nitrogen 13 radioisotopes. Let's
kee our fingers crossed.

Please continue your sessions with Dr. Kripke.
With good wishes, Armand Petrov, M.D.

_____

_____

>>> MAIL 50.02.04 <<< From: Stebbins at DUKE.MED.EDU
==> Received: from ALP.DUKE.EDU by DUKE.EDU with TBF
id ML43790; Tues, 14 Oct 15:31:48 EDT
for WCHALM@AOL.COM; Tues, 14 Oct 15:32:03 -0400
Press * for message

>>> MAIL 50.02.04 <<< From: Stebbins at DUKE.MED.EDU
Dear Mr. Chalmers,
Dr. Petrov has sggestjed that I correspond with yu
directly. The results of our first tests for
multifactorial genetic disorders were negative, but
there are many more genetic markers that we can look
for. Binding is not always guarantted even with
defects. I remain convinced that you suffer from some
rare congenital nueropathy, rather than from an
autoimmune disease as Dr Soames has proposed. Will let
you know soon about th next tests.

Pleae leat me know if yu have any pain, and where.
That would be an invaluable help.
Best wishes, Marjorie Stebbins, STEBBINS@DUKE.MED.EDU

_____

_____

>>> MAIL 50.02.04 <<< From: JO1SW at OLS.COM
==> Received: from RING.AOL.COM by AOL.COM with GOTP

id AQ06498; Tues, 14 Oct 18:52:29 EDT
for WCHALM@AOL.COM; Tues, 14 Oct 18:52:32 -0400
Press * for message

>>> MAIL 50.02.04 <<< From: Olswanger at OLS.COM
Dear Bill Chalmers,
Sorry you're not well. (I just heard.) You didn't
respond t o my messages of yesterday. The situtatio is
now urgetn. I need to hear from you by 10:30 EST
tomorrow morning at the latest. Thnaks.
Jasper Olswanger
_____

_____

>>> MAIL 50.02.04 <<< From: ACHALM at AOL.COM
==> Received: from RING.AOL.COM by AOL.COM with GOTP
id AQ06498; Wed, 15 Oct 17:01:36 EDT
for WCHALM@AOL.COM; Wed, 15 Oct 17:01:49 -0400
MESSAGE LOCK OVERRIDE
>>> MAIL 50.02.04 <<< From: Alexander at AOL.COM
Dear Dad,
I'm over at Brad's house. I came over aftre cshool.
HOw are you feelingl today? I'd like to stay
here for dinner. Is that all right with you
and Mom?
Love, Alex
_____

_____

>>> MAIL 50.02.04 <<< From: Baker at THORMCCULL.COM
====> Received: from THORMCCULL.COM by NETCOM.COM
with BFP
id BZ48693; Thurs, 16 Oct 10:11:08 EDT
for WCHALM@AOL.COM; Thurs, 16 Oct 10:11:32 -0400
Press * for message

```
>>> MAIL 50.02.04 <<< From: Baker at THORMCCULL.COM
Dear Mr. Chalmers,
Ms. Stevenson has keot me informed of her
corepsoncdence with you. We are continuing our
discovery process, but let me say onc agin that here is
very little we can do withouh a diognosis of your
ilness. I don't want to interfere with whatever tests
you are doing, but I might recommend tht you speakk to
Dr. Francis Emory at Deaconess Hoptitsl. She is a
specialisin neurological disorders and, I am told,
quick to make diagnoses.
   Your wife has been enquirign about our billing.
Please tell her that you will receive shortly a bill
for the period September 24 to October 10, and
thereafter bills every two weeks.
Yours truly, Thurston Baker, Esq.
```

When she entered the bedroom, Melissa had some letters in one hand and a glass of scotch in the other. She glanced at the half-empty lunch tray on the bed, glanced at Bill working laboriously at his computer terminal, then sank into the chair by her vanity and sipped silently at her scotch. A woman was speaking on the television: *When I decided to have the latest hydrogel and natural oil implants, I wanted to know if I would be treated in a fully equipped hospital or some clinic designed only to perform cosmetic surgery.*

"Henry called," Melissa said. "He's getting married."

"What?" Bill turned and stared at her, his eyes red and stretchy the way they got when he'd been sitting at his terminal. His whole face was beginning to get stretched out and loose now, with the puffiness of the steroids and the lack of any physical activity.

"Henry's getting married," she said again with no emotion. Her voice was almost drowned out by the raspy drone of a gasoline engine across the street.

"After all this time. Good for him. I had no idea." Bill turned back to his screen.

"Neither did I. To someone named Maureen McClaran."

"Sounds Irish. Or Scottish."

The telephones began ringing. For a moment, the phones sounded like they were coming out of the TV on the bureau, from the hospital that gave the woman the new breasts. Bill froze, jarred, then Melissa grabbed the remote phone on the bed. "That was Virginia," she said after hanging up. "She wants to know why you never answer the phone before four o'clock in the afternoon. She's left three messages on the tape."

"There are eight messages on the tape," said Bill. "From Virginia and other people. I've stopped answering the phone before four o'clock."

"She knows that. Why don't we put something on our tape message that says to call after four? What am I saying? I don't know what I'm saying." Melissa swayed in her chair, her head sank on her shoulder. "A little courtesy, I say. You should put a courtesy message on the phone if you're not going to answer it. People know that you're here."

"A lot of people don't know I'm here."

"I think we should have a courtesy message."

"How about I start answering the phone at 3:30. Will that make you happy?"

"Henry says he feels guilty, getting married while you're like this." Melissa stood up and swallowed the rest of her scotch in one gulp. "And how are you today?"

He rolled in his wheelchair from the desk to the bed, closer to her so that he could gaze into her eyes, see the look that he didn't want to see. "I hate it when you ask me every day how I am."

"Please don't take out your anger on me," said Melissa. "I'm going downstairs to get another scotch." As she went to the door, she stared down at his drawings, then looked at him to see him looking at her.

"I like your drawings," she said, holding herself against the door frame. "I never knew you could draw." She rubbed her forehead and sighed. "But I don't understand. It's crazy. You've gotten crazy, Bill."

"Look at them."

"I am looking. I said they were nice a week ago." She paused and rubbed her forehead again. "But why are you doing this? You're wrecking our floor. No, wait. I'll help." She got a lipstick from her vanity and drew a leaf on the wall, red and smudgy. "There, that's another one." Then, with three tiny steps, she sat down on the bed, pushed her glass back and forth against the bedpost like she was trying to pull off a scab. "I'm so happy for Henry." She began crying and went out of the room, closing the door behind her.

"Alex," she called as she went down the hallway. "Go look at your father's drawings."

"I've seen them," yelled Alex from his room. "What's for dinner?"

"Go see them again."

She was mocking him, Bill thought. She was drunk, she was out of her mind, and he was out of his, too.

A small knock at the door. Alex came in, rumpled, his hair in a bowl shape where he had cut it earlier that afternoon. How was his homework going? Bill asked from his wheelchair. Fine. Alex stood by the door, hanging back low, making his small body even smaller, and Bill looked at him and loved him. Alex kept his eyes on the bureau, away from his father. How wonderful he looked, Bill thought to himself, he had boy all over him, and life and imagination, except that he was pale, he spent far too much time in his room. What a sensitive, pale boy. Bill wanted to hold him forever just as he was now, to keep him from disappointments and tragedies.

"Come over here by me," said Bill. He sat by the window, the light flowing in smooth now.

Alex walked slowly to his father. When the boy got to the wheelchair, he put his hands to his face.

"I love you, Alex," said Bill. He leaned forward in his chair and touched the boy's shoulder. "Come closer, I can't reach you."

Alex kneeled to the floor and put his head in his father's lap.

"I love you," whispered Bill. "I've made a mess of things. But I love you."

"Please don't die."

"I'm not going to die."

Alex tried to say something but couldn't. "Do you promise?" he mumbled.

"I'm doing everything I can."

Alex raised his head up. His face was wet from tears and shone in the light coming in from the window. "I want you the way you used to be," he said.

"I'm trying. I'm trying to get well. Do you know how much I love you?"

Alex nodded his head yes. After a few moments, he stood up and dried his eyes on his shirt. "I'm going back to my room."

Bill watched as he left and closed the door.

He lies on the floor, tracing the leaf. Many leaves have fallen but his leaf is still there. It has been three weeks now, and he notices the shadows tilting and moving further back from the window, the sun lower in the sky. Seasons advance. New aspects have been revealed. The altered shapes are the same leaf and yet different, like a person who has gained weight, or grown older. It is almost as if he has been tested, to see if he can render the slight changes without copying himself. But he has noticed, he is minutely observing, and he traces the new shadows as if they were the first. He wants his mind to be empty, to see each new thing as it happens, to be ready. These are his first drawings, he imagines. Here is the first pinnacle, the first side lobe, the first point and valley. He pretends that he has never seen the leaf before in order to see it more perfectly at this moment. He must record it exactly because no one except him is observing the leaf. No one except him is seeing. This thought brings him sadness, but it also propels him. He has never felt so alone in his life.

He is alone but not quite alone. Because as he draws his leaf-shadows on the floor, he listens to sounds and he hears the ubiquitous hum, the low hum beneath everything else. He cannot get it out of his head. He closes the windows, he turns off the television and computer, but the low drone continues, a buzz, a vibration. What is it? What is it? He claps his hands to his ears, but the sound will not cease, the sound goes into his bones, the sound fills up his body, destroying muscle and blood and silence. What is it? He feels his pulse. Hum and pulse beat together, canceling each other. He gulps air, he wants to hear himself think between breaths, but there are no silences between breaths, the hum swallows the silences, leaving no room to breathe. Damn you, he shouts. Damn you. He heaves, he gasps for breath. The hum only increases in volume, a whine, an electrical vibration, a moaning in his brain. He slams his chair into the TV. I'm going to break every machine on this planet. The billions of cell phones and fax machines and computers and automobiles and TVs and other machines without names. I'm going to rip the phones out of the wall.

———

In late October, a few days before his scheduled PET examination, Bill's leaf tracings began to lose accuracy. Not because of his hands but because of his eyes. Nothing had enough light. When he propped himself up at the window, leaning crooked against the wall and looking out, the houses across the street appeared a hundred miles away. Color went first. From the other side of the room, the bed appeared to be a dim white barge, indistinct. Words on his computer screen gradually faded, then became scratchings. He continued his drawings. Now they were wild and roaming, even partly up a wall.

"Oh no. No." Melissa bent down and pressed her lips against his right cheek. "You need a nurse. How can we afford a nurse?"

"I don't need a nurse."

"You're bumping into things, you're spilling your food."

"I can see well enough."

"No. I'm staying home now. I'm not going to leave you here alone. I shouldn't have left you before."

"Melissa. Don't you listen?"

"I'm staying home, Bill."

VISITS

Bill was sitting by the window of his bedroom when he heard Peter and his mother come in downstairs. They had arrived in a rented car from the airport so quickly that he was still in his bathrobe, with his wasted white legs dangling out, and he just had time to hide the latest "get well" card to keep himself from appearing as pitiful as he felt. However, he could not conceal the many containers of flowers, lending a funereal atmosphere to the room despite the bright colors and smells. He debated about whether he might be able to wheel himself into the closet and struggle into some trousers, but then came the heavy footsteps on the stairs, undoubtedly Peter's, and the tentative knock on the door. He wanted to see Peter and dreaded seeing him at the same time.

"Peter?"

"Yes. I'm by myself. Melissa thought your mother should rest awhile downstairs before coming up, give you and me some time."

When Peter saw Bill in his wheelchair, he winced. Then he walked over and hugged him.

"Excuse the way I look," said Bill. "These steroids don't do much for my face." He gave a little smile and squinted at his friend, whom he hadn't seen in two years and could now only dimly make out. A big hulk of a man as always, with wiry red hair beginning to come loose at the crown and a limp from an old football injury. And a way that he filled a room, took control without letting you know he was doing it, except that at this moment he seemed off his mark, upset by Bill's condition and the perfumy odor of the room. Peter made no comment but placed his jacket on the vanity table and sat down on the divan.

"Melissa tells me you're spending all of your time up here."

Bill nodded and sighed. "I'm glad you came."

"Shit, Bill. What a goddamn shitty thing. I wish I'd come sooner. I should have come sooner." Peter looked at Bill by the window, then glanced around the room, trying not to let his eyes rest on anything too long. If he noticed the drawings on the floor, he gave no indication. He grinned at Bill. "Lisa Bell sends her good wishes." He paused. "You remember her? She's been married and divorced twice. Went back to the name Bell."

"Lisa Bell." Bill recalled a pretty girl with rosy cheeks and curly blond hair, quiet but walked down the hall like she was hoping somebody would kiss her. A million miles away. He didn't care about Lisa Bell. "Tell her hello for me."

"Well, she sure wanted to make sure I told you hello for her." Peter gave a gruff laugh. "She's still good-looking. I run into her once in a while, having lunch with some guy or other in Chinatown. She's starting to sag a little, but she's still real cute and she remembers you."

"I remember her."

"I'll bet you do."

"Thanks for bringing Mother."

"Happy to," said Peter. "I told her we were coming to visit you."

"Did you tell her I was sick?"

"No, I didn't tell her that."

"I'll tell her."

The phones began ringing and Peter immediately reached for the cell phone on his belt, then relaxed when he realized it wasn't his. "Goddamn the phone," Bill suddenly shouted. "Rip it out. Rip out the phone." With a jerk of his body, he began wheeling himself to the nearest phone, on the writing table. Peter stared at him, startled. Someone picked up the phone downstairs and it stopped ringing.

"Want me to unplug the phone?"

Bill's blood was striking in his ears. Then he heard what Peter had said and shook his head slightly, no. He should have ripped out the phone.

In the silence afterward, they listened to Melissa talking downstairs and a radio coming from a car on the street. It had been a warm day for the last week of October, Indian summer, and the windows were open, letting in sounds and air and the smooth autumn light.

How was Alex, Peter wanted to know, must be in high school now. He hoped he could see the boy before he left, maybe later this afternoon after school. No, he wasn't staying the night, too much going on for that, he wouldn't impose. And the Philadelphia Eagles were having an excellent season, with the usual injuries and bone breakers. Bill knew nothing about the Eagles, never had, but he and Peter always talked about the Eagles when they got together, especially in recent years, it was one of the things they did. Peter had played high school and college.

"So, is Melissa taking good care of you?" he asked.

"Melissa's tired."

"She looks tired. I didn't want to say it. Maybe you need somebody else to help out. Maybe you need a nurse."

"No, I don't want a nurse. I'm okay."

"You're not okay. Don't tell me you're okay when you're not okay. I'm your friend." They looked briefly at each other.

Despite his difficulty seeing, Bill felt bombarded by every-

thing around him, the presence of his friend, his mother waiting downstairs, the air, his own skin, smells, especially smells.
A vase of stargazer lilies on the writing table was pounding out fragrance in high frequencies, like someone blowing
too hard through a piccolo. And beneath, his own cowardly
stench.

"Melissa's a good woman," said Peter. "You've got yourself
a good woman. Hang on to her." He shifted uncomfortably on
the divan. For a few minutes, they sat in silence. The drapes
rustled with an occasional breeze, the draw cords slapped
lazily against the window frame.

"I brought something for you," said Peter. Standing up and
again expanding into the entirety of the room, he fished an
envelope out of his jacket and grinned. On the writing table
he spread out a half-dozen old photos, faded and creased. "I
was planning on blowing one up and framing it, but I thought
I'd let you pick which one. I already got the frame."

Bill leaned forward in his wheelchair and stared at the
photos. "Describe them to me. I'm having trouble with my
eyes."

"What? When did this happen?"

"Started a few days ago."

Peter hesitated, confusion and then embarrassment washing over his freckled face. "What a piece of shit," he said and
let out a long groan of air. "I should have come sooner. I'm
sorry, Bill."

"Describe them to me. I'll pick one and you can frame it.
I'll put it on the table beside the bed."

"Shit." Peter put up a hand and covered his face for a
moment. "All right. All right." He pointed at one of the photographs and said, "We're sitting at the counter at Zeppi's. Both
sixteen, I'd say. I can't remember who took it. You've got on
that ragged Phillies T-shirt you used to wear, looking like a
goofball that Lisa Bell wouldn't touch with a ten-foot pole,

and I've got a big mouthful of hamburger or something, hand-some though."

In his mind, Bill was back there at Zeppi's, watching that lean chef with the veins popping in his arms as he grilled onions and hamburgers behind the counter. Smell of hot oil and cheese and french fries, burgers hissing on the grill. And that chef with the veins had eleven things going at once, hamburgers with cheese, hamburgers without cheese, ham-burgers with grilled onions, maybe some bacon going for a BLT, maybe some pancakes for somebody who thought it was breakfast time at one o'clock in the morning, flipping burgers here and there like they were platinum 45s, just perfect, scooping onions and hash browns when they were golden, drawing a Pepsi or Coke in between, just to the point where the fizz started to crawl over the sides of the glass, and that chef moved from item to item with the grace of a ballet dancer, never making a wrong move, never messing up, per-fect timing, and he had his white chef's hat cocked back on his head like he knew he was being watched and admired. Chrome metal going up the walls behind the grill, chrome sliding drawers, all sparkling clean, scrubbed-looking, six stools in front of the counter with red vinyl tops, three or four tables in back but nobody sat at the tables, a front wall of solid glass with "Zeppi's Grill" in red curly letters, nobody knew who Zeppi was. But the chef, the one they came to watch, was named Frank. And there was nothing finer in life than to sit eating one of Frank's medium-rare burgers in a toasted and buttered sesame-seed bun after they'd watched him perform for a half-hour. Maybe before that, they'd been to a movie downtown or walking by the river or out at Clear-pool at a party. It would be a Friday or Saturday night, one o'clock in the morning. And they'd sit eating their burgers and fries and turn around on their rotating thrones and stare out through the glass wall at their kingdom, the endless black night, endless like they were, stretching down Roosevelt Boulevard past streetlamps and parked cars and side streets, past closed stores with fronts lit up in neon, past houses and apartment buildings, their own three-story rowhouses with their harmless parents sleeping in their rooms, past the homes of girls they might visit later that evening. Or they might decide to sit in Zeppi's until dawn, maybe talk one of the red-eyed customers into going across the street and buying some beer for them, not too much nuance at this hour of the night. Or they might just get into Peter's '63 Triumph with its burgundy upholstery and cruise, make a tour of their dark domain, let the burgers and fries and their own natural body electricity work on them while they popped and whizzed and grew bigger than mountains. They could do all of it, and it was all theirs, all theirs.

Bill's remembrance was so hard and strong that it ached in him, but at the same time it had a terrible distance, greater than displaced time and space. Maybe it was his illness. And his friend, Peter, his best friend in the world, had the same terrible distance from him even though he was ten feet away.

The yellow freesias on the blanket-box chest were smelling like damp honeysuckles, and Peter was describing another picture, one of him and Bill lying bare-chested on top of his Triumph, and Bill remembered the afternoon they slammed into the rear end of a Pontiac Firebird turning in front of them at Broad and Columbia, Peter knowing he could slow down but also knowing it was the other guy's fault and hitting him anyway just to prove the point. Not a life-threatening hit, just a good clip of the tail feathers to prove his point. The other guy was definitely a herbivore. They used to classify people as either carnivores or herbivores. A herbivore with a brain too big for his own good. And then they felt responsible and offered to pay for the whole thing, even though it was the other guy's fault for turning in front of them. When was that?

Junior year? No, the summer before college, when they shot themselves out of cannons. Now this distance, greater than displaced time or space. What was it? What could he say to Peter? How could he explain that the world was suffocating itself. That he watched and did nothing.

"Which one you want me to frame?"

"You pick."

Now Bill heard Virginia downstairs, talking to Melissa near the front door. And his mother shouted something. Was she calling for him?

"The photo's for you," said Peter. "You pick."

"You pick."

Peter sighed and collected the photographs, gingerly, one at a time, and put them back in the envelope in his pocket. He looked sad. Even though Bill could not see much, he knew that his friend looked sad.

"All right," Peter said. "I'll pick. I'll send it to you."

"It'll go on the table beside my bed. How's the med center?"

"I hate administration."

"Why don't you get out?" said Bill.

"I can't get out. I'm making too much money."

There was more noise from downstairs, shuffling and voices. "Rosalie wants to come up," Melissa shouted.

"Does she know I'm here?" Bill shouted back.

"I don't know. She just wants to go up the stairs."

"Maybe I should go out for a few minutes," said Peter, "and leave you and your mother alone together." He moved slowly toward the door, limping slightly. He paused. "You still don't know what it is?"

"No."

"What a goddamn shitty thing. You've got the best doctors. Maybe if they can't find anything wrong, it'll go away just like it came, huh?"

"Maybe."

"I'll just be downstairs. I'll be back." He gave Bill another hug, unable to look at him, and went out the door.

Moments later, Rosalie entered the room a little uncertainly, her dyed blond hair still up in the scarf she had worn in anticipation of a cool New England fall day. Bill had sent her a scarf for her last birthday, and he peered at this one, trying to see if it was his gift, a billow of fabric on her restless shoulders. And something swung near her hips, a purse or an umbrella.

"Delphinium," she exclaimed at once in her lilting voice and went straight to the flowers on the bureau. "Two-toned. Witches' hats. And snapdragons. Where did these come from? I can't get snapdragons this time of year." She turned and gazed at the door from where she had come, as if she might want to go back out again, then at Bill for the first time. Her jowly face with flirtatious mouth, expectant even when she didn't know what she was expecting. She looked at him and through him. Suddenly he heard her voice in his mind: "I love you oodles and caboodles," what she used to say to him. Now she was looking at the door again.

"Sit down, Mother," said Bill. "Sit at the vanity. It's a good chair." She looked at him with faint suspicion, as if unsure whether she should be following his instructions. He could smell her damask rose powder, the same powder she'd been using for forty years. The powder in his nose along with the stargazer lilies. He wanted to kiss her, but he found himself unable to move, a thousand miles away. She was a dim setting moon. "Do you know who I am?" he asked.

"Yes, I know who you are."

"You're looking beautiful." He lied, matching her lie.

"Thank you. I don't feel beautiful. I don't get out anymore. They don't let me drive. I'll have to talk to Ted about that."

"You haven't been driving for ten years."

"Ten years?" For an instant, her face decomposed, turning into a blob of pink putty. Then it was her again, at least what he could see dimly, and she looked at him and nodded. "It's been ten years since I was driving. I haven't been driving for ten years. What do you think of that."

Driving. Memories flooded over him. Out on the Schuylkill Expressway, seventy-five miles per hour, eighty-five miles per hour, passing other cars as if they were motionless, reflector disks careening past like bullets from a machine gun, air sucking hard at the half-open window, her hair flying beautiful, her left gloved hand on the steering wheel, her right holding a cigarette. This is when she talked to him, took him driving with her to talk. She loved to drive fast more than anything in the world, and she took him because his father, her husband, wouldn't go with her, was afraid to drive that fast. You'll kill yourself one of these days. Ninety miles per hour, and she would ask him about school, his friends, his girlfriends when he got older, his entire life because she didn't want to miss any detail about her son, she wanted to savor everything about him. She was the one who listened to him. She was the one who made him feel like he was worth something. She was his biggest cheerleader, always. Shouting back and forth, to be heard over the howl of the wind. It never occurred to him to ask her about her. He was frightened, of course; he could have had the safety of his father, but he went with her because he wanted the closeness, even when he was fifteen and sixteen, the smell of her perfume, her aliveness behind the wheel, her joy of life and of him. With her, he took chances. She had such strong likes and dislikes. Nothing was neutral. Hot fudge she loved, so much that she would eat it right out of the can without wasting it on ice cream. Flowers of all kinds she liked. Other women she rarely liked. Books she hated, she didn't have the patience for sitting days and weeks reading a book, she would far rather see a good film, be thrown into laughter or tears on the spot. Singing. She could have made a career as a singer, and even when she gave it up for marriage she sometimes sang at a cabaret in town, into her mid-forties. And she loved speed and fast cars. Once, she had just bought a new sports car, a red convertible, and she roared up to the house at great speed, spewing gravel, and knocked down a lamppost by the front door. Then she pretended that nothing had happened and made no comment about the gash in her car and drove it around like that for a year.

She was saying something now about the weather in Philadelphia, always a safe topic. No names, no contradictions. Bill nodded, trying to hear the person he knew in the rise and fall of her voice, word choices, minute inflections and pauses. Who was this woman? How could she still be here, miraculously, after she had faded away? He wanted his mother, his real mother. He was burning. He closed his eyes and tried to see her as she had been, wearing her white cable-knit sweater, sometimes a flower in her hair.

When he opened his eyes, Rosalie was staring at his legs.

"You've injured yourself," she said. "You're in a wheelchair."

"Yes." He returned her gaze, looked into her eyes. Did the eyes make a mother? He wanted his mother back, he wanted his mother back. He shoved hard against his brain, trying to remember the way she was, things she had said to him, moments. Talk now was futile. He loved her even like this, he had to love her. He wanted her to know. No, he didn't want her to know anything. He should wheel himself into the bathroom and wash. "My legs have become paralyzed." Help me, help me. Mother.

"I'm so sorry, young man," said Rosalie. She continued to look at him, at his legs, and she smiled sympathetically. "I can't drive, and you're in a wheelchair. What a shame." She sighed. "Ted is always breaking an arm or a leg or something.

I don't know how he does it sitting in that office all day, but he does and then he comes home and expects to be coddled. I tell him that I don't coddle and he sulks. I can't stand sulking men. They're not like people." That's her, he suddenly thought to himself, and he clenched the metal bars of his wheelchair so tightly that his hands turned white. Yes. That was his mother speaking. *I can't stand sulking men. They're not like people.* Tears came to his eyes. Rosalie, embarrassed and puzzled, looked away. Then he saw tears in her eyes, too. She was crying softly, even though she didn't know why.

The telephones were ringing again, absorbing light and air. As soon as his mother left, he would rip them out of the wall. "It's Alex," Melissa shouted from downstairs. "He says he won't be able to read your e-mail messages for you tonight, he's going out with Brad. Why did you ask him to do your e-mail? He's got homework."

"Excuse me," he said to his mother and turned to the open door. "I didn't ask him," Bill shouted back to Melissa. "He volunteered. He wanted to do my e-mail for me."

"I'm sorry," he said to his mother. "This shouting."

"Oh no, I'm interrupting," said Rosalie. She dried her eyes and shifted on her chair, gathering herself up. She searched around for something. "If you could just ask that nice man downstairs to come get me. The one who brought me. He drove me in his car." She looked blankly at her son.

"Peter."

"Peter. Is Peter still here? He said he would come and get me." She stared at the door.

"Please stay a few minutes more."

"Peter knows where I am?"

"Yes." He was burning. There was no way to begin over. His life had dwindled to this tiny cupful of air, this moment. He wheeled himself to her and held her hand and imagined her hand as it was, her left hand, the hand she placed on the steering wheel in his mind. Looking down, he saw milky veins, splotches of brown.

"What a shame about your legs," said Rosalie, flustered but allowing him to keep hold of her hand. "We get used to things." She looked around the room, at the window, the four-poster bed, the bureau, as if wondering why she was here, and then at the door again. "She was rude downstairs. She told me I couldn't come upstairs. Is she calling me? Tell her I'm not ready."

NURSE

The visit from his mother had unleashed memories. When she went back to Philadelphia, Bill could not stop thinking of her as she once was, in motion, flying down highways and expressways, oblivious to the needle of her speedometer. Indistinct shapes of furniture in his bedroom turned into parts of her automobiles: curving hoods, mirrors, exhaust pipes, flywheels and crankcases, even herself, sometimes standing in that impatient manner of hers, sometimes leaning over the dashboard. On the floor he drew pictures of her driving her car. Jumbled lines barely connecting, resemblances only in his imagination. He could only vaguely see his drawings, they happened more in his mind. There, in his mind, he imagined himself standing over a painter's easel, brush poised and ready, his mother posing reluctantly. Each movement of his imaginary hand on the imaginary canvas sent a wisp of an electrical impulse to his actual hand on the floor, so that he didn't have to see his hand move on the floor, he could just watch the imaginary hand in his mind. This twice-removed invention was another history of a kind, a history not of the movements of the earth through space but of the movement of his memory through time. He remembered other things: playing gin rummy with her late in the night, massaging the back of her neck with safflower oil when she asked, rubbing her knobbly shoulder blades so hard he feared they would crack.

But what he drew mostly was pictures of her driving at great speed, with trailing lines to show the whoosh of the wind.

These new pictures on the floor, recognizable to no one but himself, overlapped leaves, images of dogs, hypothetical animals and plants. When he estimated that the floor had been covered in its entirety, he moved to the lower sections of walls. Then to the front of his bureau, the headboard of his bed, anything he could reach. It seemed to him that he must be recalling details of his mother that he had never seen before, seeing them for the first time in his memory. And yet he was filled with the same sense of distance, excommunication from a world that was hurtling further and further away into heaven, or hell, unbending in its frightening trajectory.

A moment came, the Saturday after she'd gone, when he could no longer give movement to his hands. In his mind, the imaginary hands at the easel came to rest, and so did those on the floor. It was 3:12 in the afternoon.

He was almost relieved. He'd been wondering what would be next. Now, complete paralysis of legs, arms, and hands, an orderly progression. From the beginning, it had seemed odd to him that he could move parts of his body that he could not feel. Now all was in accordance. What did not feel did not move. Finally, his limbs had deserted him altogether, leaving brain only, dim images on the optic nerve, sounds spiraling in auditory passages, smells. Vocal chords. He could ask Melissa to wheel his brain from one side of the room to another. Shout at her. That was living now, to shout at her, and then listening to her shouting back, or weeping hysterically. That was life now in these four walls of his illness, his prison, the box that enclosed what was left of him. Windows taunted with glimpses of another world, people walking under their own power, moving bodies. Look what his awareness had gotten him. He was magnificently aware and unable to wiggle his little finger. Some people were born like this, he thought to himself, totally paralyzed from birth, nothing but brain stems. He hated them all, for living. For thinking that this paralyzed existence was life. "Bill, I love you. What can I do?" What was that? Some auditory sensation of his brain, emanating from a dim shape that might be his wife. "You promised you wouldn't die." Another auditory electrification of the brain stem, possibly even an illusion. Maybe the world was all imaginary. How would he know? And when he had to eat or piss or crap, totally helpless to relieve himself, those urgent sensations in his petrified body were nothing but his imagination at work, errant electrical currents running through his brain stem, floating in nothingness like signals to cell phones, his brain flagellating itself out of pure boredom.

What were his drawings now? Final histories of the earth? Or were they, too, only illusion. Wasn't this all punishment for his failure.

The nurse, Dorothy, was huge, and indeed she needed her muscle and bulk to lift him onto the toilet or into the tub.

At first he was shocked to have himself heaved around naked by a strange woman, his white belly, his penis and testicles dangling under a sheet. A detestable intimacy, thrust upon him at $16 per hour, all Commonwealth Health would pay for, not even a nurse but a home health aide with an emergency beeper strapped to her huge hips. But he deserved no better. The food that Melissa or Virginia fed him three times a day as they sat by his wheelchair was wasted. The bony legs, the stomach, the white buttocks in the bathroom mirror were not body but merely numb things attached to his brain stem.

Dorothy handled him like a sack of potatoes, but she was not unkind. Ruddy-faced, she smelled of hand lotion, sweat, and alcohol from disposable towelettes. She had worked for a paralyzed woman, she told him, who recovered completely from some disease that started with a g. "Love is important," she said, lowering him into the tub. "I sense a lot of love in this house." "Don't bullshit me, Dorothy," said Bill. "What I don't need is bullshit." "All right," said Dorothy. Bill had limited things he could do with his body, but he began licking his lips with his tongue and rubbing his head hard against the back tiles of the tub. "Take it easy," said Dorothy. Something silver glinted and swung around her neck. Was it a cross? Was she religious, too? He squinted but could make out only the red blob of her face hovering over the tub. "Why do you do this kind of crap?" he asked. "I like it," said Dorothy. After a few moments of washing him, she said, "Your family loves you." "I don't want to talk," said Bill. A sense of humor was important, she said. "You're not eating enough, don't you want to look like me?" Then it would be 5:30, the end of her shift.

Hopeful calls and messages from the attorneys and physicians arrived at accelerating rates as the PET examination approached. Competing theories could be tested. A dozen e-mails a day, sometimes two dozen. "Have informed Dr. Petrov of the analyses that I would recommend. My assistant Dr. Cunningham will be in touch from Paris tomorrow evening." "We have received some cooperation from the

principals at Plymouth Limited." "Please return below enquiries before 4pm today. Thank you." The shrink Kripke had
taken to e-mailing too. He was writing up Bill's case for the
Annals of Psychosomatic Disease and needed to be kept up to
date.

All of these communications were received by Alex, who
logged on with his father's password and then read the printed
messages to Bill in the evening. The boy like a ghost at the
foot of the bed, his T-shirt in white billows. He was losing
weight. "Dad," he kept saying.

As Bill listened to his messages, he thought: What are
these grunts from the other world? And then it would be necessary to grunt back. Alex had developed a streamlined set of
replies, so that Bill had only to dictate a few critical words
and his son could send off an appropriate response within
minutes. One boilerplate for the lawyers, another for the
doctors, another for the occasional business associate who
still wrote to Bill with project proposals. Alex had also created
a new Web site, www.paralysis.aol.com/achalm, a clearing-
house for information on paralysis, with each entry coded by
its origin and moment of transmission. After reading the day's
messages, Alex would return to his room, where he remained
more than ever, fixed to his terminal beneath the swinging
Stademeir speakers.

Bill should have ripped out the wires when he had a
chance. He could hardly imagine that he once had a body,
volition, movement. Twenty messages a day.

"They're playing games with us," Melissa murmured as she
lay motionless and drunk across the divan. "Screw them.
Haven't they done enough? What do they think, that we've
got money? Is that the hell what they think?" She spilled her
drink and stared bloodshot at Bill. He stared back at her, dim
and wet on the divan. "You know something?" she said. "I

never believed our life was real. I always knew we were going to lose what we had. I knew this was going to happen. I never told you, but every day when I woke up, for years, even when we were first married, I wondered if this was going to be the day." She drank the last swallows from her glass. "It was too good to be true. I never believed it. Henry said I'd be all right. That's what he said when I got married. And you acted like everything would be all right. I never believed you. Why did you act like that?" She paused. "When I was in high school, I knew the rich girls, the ones from the rich families. I knew I would never be like them. I didn't want their money. That's the God's honest truth. I didn't want their money. I just wanted . . . I wanted to feel safe. Was that too much to want? Just to feel safe. Aren't I entitled to that? Why can't I be safe. What do I have to do?" She dropped her head and let her arms fall limply over the sides of the divan. "People treat me like I'm an ignorant southern bitch. Maybe that's what I am."

Somewhere, as if inside cotton, a clock ticked. No, it was too irregular for a clock, an erratic clicking and clacking, but far away, muffled, entering the empty spaces between Melissa's breathing. Bill opened his eyes and peered through the dark room, faintly illuminated by a night light in the corner. What was it, two o'clock in the morning, three o'clock? He found himself propped against the headboard. His neck ached. Thirsty. Should he wake his wife for some water? Was he awake himself? Or half sleeping, dreaming that he was lying in bed, the smell of Dorothy's sweat still on his shoulders, Melissa beside him in her Valium sleep.

There were sounds in his head. Fear swirled in him. Possibly he could no longer distinguish between waking and sleeping. If sound was imagined, then why not his heartbeat as well. He could imagine his heart out of existence. As he listened, the sounds became more distinct, clearly intentional. They came from the other side of the hall, Alex's room. A clicking, as if from the keys of a keyboard.

POSITRON EMISSION TOMOGRAPHY (PET)

Bill hoped to feel something, maybe the tiny subatomic particles exploding inside him. He closed his eyes.

The invisible Armand Petrov said to some invisible technician: "I'll want a kinetic tracer analysis on each ROI."

"No problem."

"This is an amazing machine," said Petrov. "Mr. Chalmers, I know you can't see anything from where you are, but you're getting the best."

"You want to see it coming in, Dr. Petrov?" said the technician.

"Yes, I'd like to see."

"Here. I've split the screen into twelve sections. Here's twenty seconds' worth on each section."

"The PET is the first and only application of antimatter physics to medicine," said Petrov. The technician did not reply. "Mark that region of interest."

"Okay," said the technician.

"Twenty-fifty."

"Yes. And there's the blood count for comparison."

"Bill, are you all right?" said Melissa. "I'm standing right here."

"This is completely painless, Mrs. Chalmers," said Petrov.

"Bill, are you okay?"

Although his eyes were closed, Bill could sense the thing around him, the coils of photocells or wires or whatever they were wrapped around him. It felt in his mind like a giant clasped hand. He was being held by a great hand, maybe it was trying to squeeze the bile out of him, he could sense the thing's own heat, its own blood pumping through in electrical currents and subatomic particles. The doctor was saying something again, Melissa was speaking, but he was drifting off. He was playing golf with Edward Marbleworth on a rolling, swirling golf course, grass waving in wind. An unspoken friendship lay between the two of them. Bill was now in the inner circle, taken into Marbleworth's confidence, and he felt the glow of it, the power. Marbleworth hit a golf ball into the trees, lost, then immediately a second swing, a ball going out fast and strong, making a high, perfect arc in the air and landing on the distant green. Now it was Bill's turn. He swung at the ball and missed it, didn't even touch the ground. Swung again and got only air. Swung again. His club seemed to have shortened. He swung again, getting only air. His club had dwindled to three feet. Now it was only two feet. He dropped to his knees and swung again, still missing. People behind him were shouting. He'd made a fool of himself. "You're finished, Mr. Chalmers." "What?" "Finished."

"We're finished," said Petrov. "Mr. Chalmers. You can go home now, as soon as we take the arterial line out of your arm. We have a facility for him, Mrs. Chalmers. Maybe he should stay there for now."

Bill felt dribble on his good cheek, underneath the face mask.

"I'll take him home," said Melissa.

"I've marked six ROIs," said Petrov. "They should give us a lot more information. You'll be hearing from me."

"You wimp," said Bill.

SICILY

Read aloud by Alex to his father:

On the morning of the sixteenth day of the month of Elaphebolion, Anytus wandered out of the Melitides Gate toward the harbor. He needed some destination.

He had not slept since Pyrrhias awakened him before dawn and delivered his bad news of the assassin, had spent the next hour slowly pacing the perimeter of the court in his bare feet, watching the rain splatter on the statuary. Finally, he had returned to his bedchamber to lie beside Pasiclea. Her breathing was remarkably simple and untroubled, like waves rolling in. I am your wife, the breathing said. I am your comfort, so breathe with me, let me bring comfort, breathe with me, say yes, then say yes, I am the sea that rolls over you, I am the green and your comfort, lie with me lie with me. Anytus listened and still could not sleep. He studied her, lying so lovely on her back. What did she know of his insides? He told her little, and what he did tell her were lies. He told her little because she would always love him even when he should not be loved. I am the sea that rolls over you, I am the green. He listened but could not be lulled by her waves.

When Anytus reached the Melitides Gate, it was still

raining hard, the rain fell like little cold arrows. Able to see nothing, he numbly followed a path beside the ruins of the once great North Wall, which led to the harbor. Several paces behind shuffled Pyrrhias, out of breath, carrying a small traveling lamp that glowed feebly in the damp. Pyrrhias had also brought a drinking cup, an oil flask, an extra lantern, a brush, a wrapped loaf of bread, some papyrus, and an onion, all of which were attached to a rope about his waist. Both men were soaked. Their mantles were heavy with rainwater and hung like bricks from their shoulders.

Anytus was silent and brooding. The eyeless rage of the storm, savage Boreas, was come to punish him. He imagined the old sophist at this moment, enjoying a breakfast of bread and fruit in his dry cell, casually conversing with his friends and confirming their hatred of him, Anytus. Perhaps the old sophist, on his last mortal day, would set Aesop's fables to verse and sing them to those sitting around his couch. Curse them all. Let them all wallow in bird shit.

"What will we do at the harbor?" panted the slave. Anytus was submerged in his thoughts. He walked ahead in the pouring rain, hardly noticing as he trod past the hilly Necropolis, City of the Dead, its rolling stone slabs like gray faces afloat in the sea. For well over an hour now, the two men had been slogging through the rain and the mud. They were halfway to the Piraeus, two misty silhouettes in the rain. They'd passed no one.

In the distance, the faint sound of a cithara moved like a small animal. Then a trumpet, then only the steady hiss of the rain and the thud of rain into mud. Moments later, music again, wafting in and out like the tides, and voices. Then only rain.

The tanner decided he was conjuring things. He felt feverish. He reached behind him and touched Pyrrhias's arm, he wanted to feel another human body. Ahead, between the gray beaded curtains, outlines of people slowly formed in the wet air. Heads. Arms and legs swinging. A procession of some kind. Chanting. Beardless young men reciting the oracles. Dancing girls twirling, flute girls attached to each other by rope made of hair. In moments, everything faded in the wet and was gone.

Anytus thought to himself: Could this be the overland return of the Sacred Festival from Delos? The final procession to the city, in this weather? No, it couldn't be. He was hot and exhausted. Movement again. Dim chanting figures passed in the rain. Gray women and men, dressed in gray wavering robes. A priest of Apollo, wearing a headdress of tiny earthenware bottles. The containers tinkled and clattered against each other as he walked. Musky odors of frankincense and myrrh and lystria. Riderless horses with erections, and dogs. An old woman with paint smeared on her face wailed to Apollo and chewed on something that wriggled in her hand. The ashen figures appeared, then dissolved in the gray rain, then appeared again, soft and unfocused. Anytus reached out to one of the spirits, but his hand met only air. He called out. No one answered. Figures seemed to float only several feet away. He looked back at Pyrrhias. The slave was glancing frantically this way and that, trying to follow invisible motions with his eyes. Half puzzled, half frightened, he stared imploringly at his master. "By Zeus," he said softly and clutched the tanner's hand. "Great Laphina. Zeus help us."

"This is the Sacred Procession," said Anytus. "It is the end and the beginning of the end. We are honored. We have made the city safe for the procession. Democracy has won out." He sat down in the mud. The procession continued, over his head. Spirit robes brushed over his cheeks. Men stood on each other's shoulders, drinking wine from dark vessels. Flutes played strange melodies. Three bald-headed old women limped by, moaning prophecies. Anytus strained to hear their foretellings but heard only mutterings, swallowed in the rain.

"Master, please rise. We must get out of the storm."

They found shelter in a farmer's storage cabin standing on a hill next to a fig arbor. The wooden door of the cabin fell off its hinges when they opened it. Inside, the single room was close and dark, and the rain pelted the flat roof like a low drum roll. Smell of corn huskings, hay, linseed oil, mule. High lattices let in a spray of gray light and mist.

Pyrrhias built a fire on the dirt floor, guarding the small flame in his lamp like a heart. He took hay and pieces of a broken wood stool that he found in a corner. The slave helped his master undress, undressed himself, embarrassed by the thick rolls of flesh around his waist. Wrung out the wet clothes and hung them on sticks. The two men knelt near the fire, their skin bristled and clammy. Pyrrhias looked at the naked white of his master, the curving white belly, and unconsciously began massaging Anytus's shoulders and neck. Under his touch, the skin warmed and melted. Anytus closed his eyes.

I will tell you about Sicily.

Many times Pyrrhias had heard stories of the War. He had heard of the slaughter in his native town Scione in Pallene, from which he was taken and sold to Anytus's household before his tenth birthday. With Sicily, only fragments, as if Anytus wanted to tell and didn't want to tell at the same time.

I was a human anchor.

It was the nineteenth year of the War. A grappling hook, hurled at my ship by a Syracusan galley, buried itself in my thigh. They reeled me in, dragged me across the prow of my boat into the sea. The water was on fire. There were hundreds of ships. You could hear them crashing into each other, you could hear men screaming.

One of the lattices in the cabin flew open with wind and let in a gush of rain. Pyrrhias found a stick and closed the lattice, then broke the stick into pieces and fed the fire. He squatted down again beside Anytus.

When the hook was removed, my leg was an open red mouth. The Arcadians bled me, applied sponges and olive leaves. One man, I never knew his name, changed my bandages every day and washed me. They carried me across plains and between mountains to Gela. No, that was later.

First, I sank toward the bottom of the harbor. I was content that my men not see me like that, pierced and caught on a line. I was willing to go to the bottom. I wanted to die a soldier's death. I didn't want panic. Oarsmen are like dogs, they can smell fear in your voice. I didn't want my men to see me pierced, I wanted to sink to the bottom. But the Syracusans wouldn't let me sink, kept pulling me, hauling in on the rope. The curved iron was lodged deep and would not come free. With the pulling, it went only deeper. It held my weight. I was part metal, part flesh, a sacrifice to Hephaestus. I was a blood prayer.

It was the nineteenth year of the war with the Peloponnesians. Amphipolis had fallen. Cleon and Brasidas were dead. The Sicilian campaign had already been two years. At Epipolae some of our infantry leaped off the cliffs, some thrust arrows in their throats for fear of being taken as prisoners. Then the Syracusans tried to burn our fleet. They drove our ships against the shore of their harbor, set fire to an old merchantman filled with faggots and rotting pine wood and let it drift down the wind toward our ships. We should have escaped days earlier, when the harbor was open.

Master, how did you survive when you were dragged overboard?

What? Yes, survive. Anytus sat up and traced the long curling scar on his thigh with a finger. He turned to look at Pyrrhias, only a few years older than the son he could not talk to. The cabin had become warm from the fire, and the slave's fleshy arms were wet with perspiration.

Why didn't they kill you?

I was a blood sacrifice. They thought I was dead. From the prows of their ships, Dorian archers and darters looked down at me, half anchor and half man, one rope of twine and another of blood. They cut me loose and threw me back into the sea. The water was thick with floating corpses, bobbing facedown, tangled. Athenians' legs over arms of Syracusans. Allies and enemies. Dead Lemnians, Camarinaeans, Chalcidians, Styrians, Aeginetans, Corinthians, Iapygians, Eretrians, Himeraeans. I was an offering among them, a red anchor unloosed from its rope, the iron curving out of my body. Arcadian mercenaries, fighting for Syracuse and Sparta, found me raving in the water. They were my enemies. They didn't know who I was. Later, they didn't care. They were sick of the war and wanted to go home.

The Arcadians took me ashore and poured burning wine on my leg. They left the iron hook in for a day, debating how to remove it. One of them was a bronzeworker, another a potter. Should I be hammered or worked moistly like clay? They built a litter out of tent poles and canvas and carried me to their camp. At first, they planned to sell me to the highest bidder. I should have killed myself then, in my dishonor, but I didn't. I could have killed myself, I had a knife. That first night, we Athenians were surrounded, waiting to be butchered in the morning. I should have called out to my men. They were desperate and they had no food. But what could I say to them?

I never saw any of my comrades again. A few days later they were trapped in a valley and slaughtered. The Arcadians didn't sell me. Instead, they built a litter for me, let the blood run, then sewed up my thigh with tent stitchings. They cleaned the wound with powdered linseed and boiled leaves of fig, also olive, horehound, epipetrum. Wrapped my leg in a cloth soaked with boiled lentil and wine and trefoil. They carried me from camp to camp, slowly making their way across the Sicilian plain to Gela, where they hoped to find a friendly ship back to the Peloponnese.

I remember his smell, the man who fed me figs from his hands.

Anytus had stopped talking and stared at the dirt floor. Pyrrhias stood up and slowly moved around the cabin, naked and white. More wood for the fire. Outside, the rain was letting up. The low drum roll on the roof had diminished.

They carried me across the plains to Gela. We ate dried figs and what we could find in the plains, small animals and plants, lizards, birds. It took us five days. They intended to sell me back to my family when we reached the Peloponnese. One morning, at dawn, I heard chimes. We went through a valley shaped like an eagle. In Gela, the Arcadians boarded the first ship traveling east and, in their haste and exhaustion, left me lying on the floor of a lampmaker's shop. I promised the owner a half-talent of silver, and he fed me for a week. An Eretrian vessel took me to Sunium.

When I got back to Athens, dragging my bad leg, the city greeted me as a hero. They believed nothing I said about Sicily. They did not believe that Nicias and Demosthenes had been killed. They did not believe that fifty thousand men had been slaughtered or captured. A hundred Athenian ships lost. They believed nothing except that I was a hero. After a while, I wanted to be what they wanted. Prodicus, a small boy then, marched around the house with my shield and begged to sail with me against the Chians.

Anytus spit out a thin hollow laugh. He removed a burning stick from the fire and held its glowing sharp point just above the scar tissue on his thigh. Pyrrhias quickly snatched away the stick. He could not look the other man in the eyes.

"Can you believe that Prodicus once thought I was a hero?" said Anytus. "Now he despises me. I hardly know him. He's a grown man now. I hardly know my own son, Pyrrhias. He is my flesh and blood."

"Master." Pyrrhias paused. "I wish I had been with you in Sicily."

Anytus smiled sadly. He listened and heard silence. "The rain has stopped. What do you suppose is the hour?"

THE EXECUTION

It was early that evening as Anytus reclined on one of the couches in the men's dining room of his house, drinking from a painted earthenware cup. He was alone. Next to his elbow sat a table of inlaid wood and pink ivory, bearing a large bronze vessel of undiluted wine. He had finished his dinner, without company, and the fish bones and fruit peelings still littered the marble floor. Slowly, his chin sank to his chest, his grip on the cup began to go slack. A trickle of wine spilled on his chest.

He was gazing up at the painted designs on the ceiling, bright from the light of a dozen oil lamps, when Pyrrhias returned from the prison. The slave entered the dining room and stood anxiously in front of Anytus. "He is dead."

"Were you seen?" asked the tanner.

"No, Master, I was not. I hid in the cell next to the sophist's. I could see through cracks in the walls."

"Tell me everything."

Pyrrhias bit off a piece of bread that was his supper and began talking rapidly. To begin with, there was no trace of the Twine. No body, no blood on the floor of the prison. Possibly, some of the sophist's followers had secretly taken care of everything. Attendants discovered the night jailor lying on the stone floor and carelessly attributed his death to a drunken fall.

The executions took place just before sunset. There were two. The Eleven sent a message that the Megarian should drink the poison first. He refused. When an attendant entered his cell with the cup, the prisoner burst out of the room into the corridor, pleading his innocence all over again. He was a handsome, fierce man with the build of an athlete and a trimmed beard. He demanded to see his wife and young son, who had been standing outside the prison all day in the rain calling his name, and the prison attendants let them in, and they also pleaded his innocence. The wife had cut off her hair, as if her husband were already dead. Seeing his family, the prisoner became distraught and shouted, tried to rip off his clothes, struggled with his chains. The child, a little boy, began wailing and rushed toward his father. At this point, the Megarian tried to escape. He was stopped by an attendant and subdued with a great blow to the back. When he fell to the floor, his wife and son began wailing even louder, promising anything, promising to sell themselves if he could go free. The prisoner struggled to his feet and cursed everyone, he swung his chains at the air, he shouted profanities. No longer did he recognize his family, who stood back from him, crying. Finally, the prisoner drank the poison. Then the jailors chained him to a ring in the middle of the corridor and escorted his sobbing family out of the prison.

The Megarian did not let the poison work gently. He banged on his chains, shouted continually for his family. He twisted and turned and jumped up and down in anger and madness. He began foaming at the mouth and started to shake in convulsions. One of the younger jailors vomited himself. The prisoner continued to shake and to twitch and to drool at the mouth. Finally, he went limp.

After that, one of the attendants prepared the drink for Sokrates and took it into his cell. The old sophist had just returned from a bath and reclined on his bed in a clean tunic and mantle. His friends and supporters stood and knelt around him and wept. Sokrates greeted the cup as easily as if it had been filled with red wine but did not quaff it immediately. Instead, he held it in his lap, carefully, so as not to spill any drop of the liquid, and sat talking a few moments longer. He was taking pleasure in describing part of his system of the world: "The earth, when looked at from above, appears streaked like one of those balls that have leather coverings in twelve pieces, decked with various colors." He chastised his friends for crying like women and urged them to take courage.

Then he smiled at his weeping friends and drank from the cup, swallowing four times. Rising from his couch, he began walking around the room, round and round, walked for some time until he claimed that his legs had grown heavy and dull. At that point, he lay down quietly and covered his face with a cloth. However, he continued talking, occasionally asking questions. One of his friends touched his feet and ankles, as he had been instructed, and the sophist reported that he had no sensation there. A few moments later, the same for his groin. The poison was slowly moving up. He made some kind of a joke about his head being in his feet. Then, with the most gentle sentiments, he thanked his friends for their friendship. They asked him what should be done with his ashes, and he said to scatter them wherever they liked.

Anytus stood up from the couch, his lips curled in mockery. "What kind of fool is that, unconcerned about his final resting place. What else did he say just before the end, Pyrrhias?"

"That's all I remember, Master."

Anytus began pacing the room, holding his half-full cup of wine. "Did he curse anyone? Did he curse me?"

"No, Master. He did not seem angry."

Anytus filled his shallow cup with wine, drank, and continued pacing. "He must have been frightened. Did you see his eyes?"

"He looked calm, Master."

"How could you see? You were looking through a crack."

Pyrrhias didn't reply. He swallowed uncomfortably.

"Did you see his hands? Were his hands gripping the edge of his bed?"

"I didn't see his hands, Master. He said that death is only the separation of the soul from the body. After that the soul is pure and free. He said that men who fear death love the body, and probably power and money as well."

Anytus threw his cup to the marble floor, where it shattered into a thousand pieces. He sat down on the couch, staring at the curtains on the other side of the room. He placed his sandaled foot down on a shard of his cup and slowly pressed until it crunched. Finally, he said in a low voice, "I want you to take twenty minas to the dead sophist's house and leave it at his doorstep. Pronapes will show you the way."

"Master?"

"Are you hard of hearing?" shouted the tanner.

"No, Master," said Pyrrhias. "I will take twenty minas to Sokrates' house."

"I am going out for the rest of the night. Have Penelope tell my wife that I will not be home until tomorrow. Better yet, have Penelope tell her that I will be with Calonice tonight." Anytus abruptly rose from the couch and moved toward the doorway.

"Master," Pyrrhias called anxiously. "Please. Do not do this thing to your wife. Master." But Anytus was gone, and the curtains rippled and swayed like the ocean.

THE JOB OFFER

When he finished the reading, Alex remained sitting near his father, staring at the last page.

Bill peered toward the foot of the bed. He had never seen his son so exhausted, so serious, bearing weight. His illness was taking an awful toll on the boy, and the Anytus story was tragic, too tragic to be read at this time. Why had he allowed Alex to continue reading to him so late at night, when the boy should be in bed? And he was still losing weight.

"You look worn out," Bill said.

Alex turned away from the lamp on the vanity, placing his face in half-light. His hair was auburn and fine, like his mother's. "I'm okay," he said after a pause.

"Are you getting enough sleep?"

Alex nodded. "What happened to the Megarian's child?" he asked.

"I don't know."

Alex seemed to be trembling, almost in tears. Bill should never have let him read the story.

"I wish Anytus sent money to the Megarian's family, like he did for Socrates."

"Why would he do that?" asked Bill. Now, he could hear Alex's sniffling, tiny rivulets of sound that merged with the trickles of Melissa's shower in the bathroom. How he wished that he could comfort his son, his dear son. But who was he, to comfort anyone?

"For the child," said Alex. "What will happen to the child?"

"I don't know. I don't think Anytus really cared about any of the children. He sent the money to Socrates' family out of guilt. Anytus wouldn't do anything from the goodness of his heart."

Alex stood up from the bed and began walking toward the bedroom door.

"I don't want to hear any more of the Anytus story," said Bill. He found himself suddenly angry. "Is it finished?"

"There's one section left."

What was that look on the boy's face? Bill squinted to see, tried in vain to move his head higher against the headboard. "Go to bed now, you need to get to sleep." Bill moved his head into the pillow; he wished he could fall asleep himself, deep in some dreamless sleep.

"Wait," said Alex. The boy turned and hurried from the room in a determined manner, as if he were going to bring something of importance to his father. In a few moments he returned and placed a piece of paper on the bed. Then he stepped back. What was this piece of paper that Alex seemed to regard with such significance? Bill squinted at his son and thought he could make out a pleading look on the boy's face, a look of pleading combined with childish pride.

"What is this?"

"An e-mail I got from Dr. Soames. I printed it out."

"Addressed to you?"

"Yes."

"An e-mail to you from Dr. Soames? Read it to me."

It was a job offer, to do transferrals of medical informa-tion on the Internet, part-time. Dr. Soames had been very much impressed with Alex's "facility on the Internet, and your promptness at replies to messages, your conciseness, and your Web site www.paralysis.aol.com/achalm, which has come to my attention." Alex's face lit up as he read the letter. When he finished, he placed it carefully in his pocket and gazed expectantly at his father. He had received the message several days ago, he explained, and had not known what to do with it, how to respond, and had hid the printed copy in his room. Now, he looked again at his father with pleading eyes, almost embarrassed.

"Maybe I could help out," Alex stammered, "make some money. While you're . . ." He didn't finish the sentence and stared painfully at the floor.

Poor boy, Bill thought and felt his son's distress. Alex must be so conflicted, to receive such an endorsement of his abilities at the same time that his father lay useless and paralyzed. Bill could see the hesitation in his son's body, the embarrassment at displacing his father. For even though the job could not be a great deal of money, Alex would consider the offer as usurping his father. What a triumph this letter might have been. The boy had hidden his treasure for a week, probably first elated and then embarrassed, but now he had come out with it, possibly to prove his worth to his father, to show his father that despite his small physical size and fleeting hobbies he had achieved something of meaning in his father's world. Asking Bill's permission to take the job and at the same time apologizing for it. All of these things Bill could sense in Alex's tender face, the slump of his shoulders. How grown up the boy had become.

"You should take the job if you want it," Bill said. "Take it." He wanted to praise and congratulate his son, he should have congratulated his son, but Alex's embarrassment and confusion had spread to himself, and he could say nothing more.

Alex nodded. But Bill could tell that his son would not accept the offer, would tuck his treasure away in his room, never to mention again but to look at privately from time to time. Alex gazed once more at his father.

"Good night, Dad."

"Good night."

THE MALL

The next morning, Saturday morning, Melissa took Bill and Alex to the Burlington Mall. They both should get out of the house, she said, some air, a change of scenery, and the mall contained miles of walkways for the wheelchair. And she needed them out of the house, she needed the house to herself. They were all drowning in the muddle of visitors, Dorothy's shifts, Virginia coming and going with her children, and Petrov's constant updates on the results of the PET.

What an absurd excursion, Bill thought, to go to the mall in a state of paralysis. He would be on parade. As Dorothy carried him down to the waiting automobile below, he let his head flop back on her shoulder and stared at the ceiling. It bobbed up and down with each step, just as he remembered when his father carried him to bed as a child. A wave of nostalgia passed through him. His father would have been a young man then, considerably younger than Bill was now, his future lying in front of him as he crossed the narrow hall of the rented house. Bill strained to remember the sound of his father's steps as Dorothy thudded heavily down the stairs. In a mental diversion, he imagined that each of her steps was five years. Five years, ten years, fifteen years. So quickly his life had gone by, from infancy to marriage to this acutely aware forty-year-old brain stem being carried down the stairs.

One step for every five years, until this. His pants bulged with the double diaper beneath.

Outside, Bob and Silvia Tournaby stood in their driveway and called hello while he was being loaded into the car. Not too close, as if they might catch whatever mysterious disease he had, but a sympathetic wave of the rake. Silvia had brought chicken pot pie once a week. A wave of the rake. Across the street, a dim form that looked like Olivia Cotter slid out of her house and also waved. Bill could see her from the corner of his eye. "Olivia," he suddenly shouted, wanting to hear a definite loudness in his ear, something definite in the midst of this cowardice.

The parking lot of the Burlington Mall was a hundred acres of gray asphalt and cars, thousands of cars, half of them speeding in every direction, plowing through intersections and traffic lanes without slowing, honking impatiently, a constant danger to other cars and to pedestrians. Two-hundred-odd stores stacked together like toy blocks. The Election Day Sale. Everyone was rushing to get to the double glass doors of an entrance before everyone else, to buy quality merchandise cheap while it lasted, Ralph Lauren shirts and slacks, Ann Taylor blouses, sweaters at Banana Republic, Liz Claiborne separates, suits at Jones of New York, shoes by Enzo Angiolini, exercise machines and cameras, microwaves, blenders, computers and calculators, digital alarm clocks, bedsheets and towels, CD players, robot swimming-pool cleaners, humidifiers, rugs and carpets, virtual-reality helmets, skis and ice skates, televisions and stereos, cosmetics, jogger clips measuring speed and calories burned, correct-posture dog feeders, lamps and pens and end tables, spray paint, automobile accessories. It was all here. Bill could sense the frantic urge to stay current, the eagerness to buy and consume, the sobs of desire caught by the churning bodies and the spastic blasts of automobiles moving through the gray, teeming swamp. He hated the mall the same way he hated himself, except that he hated himself more because he was a part of the mall and he knew it. With a struggle against his dead weight, 175 pounds and climbing, even though his legs had dwindled to nothing, he was hauled into his wheelchair by Alex and Melissa. "Alex, you take care of him." She would return in two hours. Watches were synchronized.

Inside, the air exploded. Colors from sale signs and banners. Shouts and grinds of machines being tested, smells of perfume and pizza and chocolate chip cookies. It was a city, an indoor metropolis, older people, young people, children with mothers, teenagers in love. Escalators jagging and glass elevators with their umbilical cords dangling. Fountains spewing from sunken pools. Bill felt sick to his stomach. Why was he here? His insides were sending tumultuous signals to his brain. Why was he here? "I want to see the new pet store first," Alex said and he pushed the wheelchair as fast as it would go, Bill's arms and legs shaken loose with the speed and splayed over the wheels. "Brad said they've got some good stuff." Wheels squished as they rolled over an Egg McMuffin lying on the pink tiled floor. "Hey," a man said as he walked past with a package in his arm. "They've got motorized wheelchairs you can operate with one finger. Or with eyeblinks if you can't move a finger." The man hurried on. "I want to see the new pet store," said Alex. "After that, Radio Shack. I saw their new stuff advertised on the Net." Stores pounded the corridors, one after another. People laughing and eating, hoarding their purchases, visiting on benches, kids flying past on rollerblades. New cars for sale sprawled in the middle of the floor. "Made in America." Bill could hear dissatisfied customers arguing with store managers. "The automatic shutter delay was advertised as fifteen seconds." "You can have a store credit." "I don't want a store credit." A great wall of merchandise vibrated and pulsed. Clothes, shiny surfaces

of metals, small unidentified objects. One store after another, kaboom, kaboom. A giant plaza with intersecting corridors, enameled benches and white columns. "That way," Alex
shouted, caught up in it, and flew around a corner, jerking
the chair. To Bill, Alex seemed suddenly a wild dog unleashed,
all of his quiet and hesitancy gone as he ran from one store to
the next, wanting to buy everything, already looking at his
watch to see how much time they had left. "I want to go
home," said Bill. He tried to close his eyes, to escape into his
brain stem, but the motion disturbed him, the air rushing by,
the legs and arms bumping into the chair. Shouts and radios
blared from hand-held CDs. "Can you call Mom? I want to
go home." "Oh, Dad. We just got here." Alex looked at his
watch, a Casio with alarm that he'd bought at this same mall
six months ago. "We've been here only ten minutes." Ten
minutes, Bill wondered, coughing on the scent of somebody's
perfumed soap. Living trees sprouted suddenly from the
middle of the floor, their trunks descending through holes cut
out of the pink tiles. Could there be real earth here? Bill stared
down and then up and saw the dim forms of second-floor
shoppers scurrying along glass walkways with mirrored sides.
Now the glitter was multiplied into doubles and quadruples.
Maybe he would spend the rest of his life in this mall, maybe
he would die here. "Excuse me." Someone had bumped him, a
woman with shopping bags.

Then they arrived at the pet store, nestled next to a giant
banner reading: "Celebrate American Leadership in the New
Millennium." It was an advertisement for the throbbing entirety of the mall, in letters so big that even Bill, half blind,
could read them. Now every glimmer of light, every molecule
of air bombarded him. An orange necklace screamed. A smell
of beef jerky diddled his nose. Someone's hot breath. Maybe
it was his paralysis, intensifying other senses and peeling back
the few nerve endings he had left. The mad crazy rush of the

world, the world bent on self-suffocation—all of his exquisite awareness, his precious self-righteous sensitivities were now focused like a laser dot onto his sensory input. A child crying was a fire engine. Scents of perfume were knife blades. His senses so painfully acute that he could feel each molecule of smell, one atom of air against his stretched eardrum. He wanted to unplug. Anything to escape the push and the heave. Was that a humming he heard? *Celebrate, celebrate, celebrate.* The filthy hum.

They were in the pet store. Smells of hamster food and hamster turds, stench of fish tanks, chirps from parakeets. In front of his chair, a remote-controlled plastic mouse skittered over the floor. A grinning salesman pushed buttons on a transmitter shaped like a hunk of Swiss cheese. "Entertain your cat. You, sir, do you have a cat?" Aisles of merchandise like city blocks. At the cash register, people stood in line with arms of premium dog and cat food, pet magazines, pet cages, an electronically timed cat feeder. Bodies shoved against his chair.

"I want to go home," Bill moaned, his throat dry. Alex had hurried off to the pet toy section and left him near a crate of plastic bones in the center aisle. Every ray of light, every molecule of air. Above the front entrance, a cardboard Lassie spun on a twisted string, jostled by each person who came in, her cardboard tail brushing people's hair. Music pounded from ceiling speakers. Bill's stomach churned. "Calm down," a woman said from the next aisle, "you probably left it in the car." Who was she talking to? Bill felt like he could not endure another sixty seconds. He began counting. One, two, three. He had to urinate and released himself into his diaper. Four, five, six. He could not endure. People walked by, talking loudly. Seven, eight, nine. Now he could smell himself. Urine. Was he not receiving what he deserved? Forty years of heaving and rush, and now this, sitting paralyzed in his piss in a mall. Seven, eight, nine. He would count until . . .

A man and his teenaged daughter entered Bill's aisle. They were evidently in a hurry and pulled one item after another from the shelf, yet a certain calm and composure hung about the man. He wore a suit and held several packages easily under his arm. "It was here before," he said. "Just give me a minute." "I've got to go," said the girl. "Shelley is waiting at Macy's."

With a painful twist of his neck, Bill turned and squinted at the man and was astounded to behold what seemed to be the same fellow he'd seen on the subway months ago, reading his *Wall Street Journal* in magnificent serenity. This would be the perfect store for such a man's pet, the most advanced pet store in the world. Bill wondered what kind of pet this man might own, maybe some pedigreed cat or rare fish. As Bill stared at him, he again marveled at how easily the man moved amid the hubbub around him, unperturbed, in perfect synchrony with the mall. The perfect modern man was also a mall man, of course. The mall was clearly the most efficient way to shop, the maximum product in the minimum time. The rush was all part of it, an easy good rush. What were those packages in his arms? The man came closer and Bill imagined he could see his quiet blue eyes and pale skin, just as he remembered. Were those tassels on the shoes, as before? How satisfied and oblivious he was. Didn't he feel the noise and the crush? Why couldn't Bill adapt like the mall man adapted? He hated him. He strained to see into the mall man's dim face. Surely, some sign of arrogance would show in the face. Yes, was there not a slight curl of the lips? Despite his poor eyesight, Bill imagined he could detect a slight curl of the lips. A man so superior would have to have some physical defect on which he could be called. Bill continued to squint as the man spoke to his daughter, and he became more and more convinced of the slight curl in the lips.

Then another thought occurred to Bill. By accident, the mall man would eventually bump into his wheelchair. The aisle was narrow. And that would be it. That would be the opportunity Bill had been waiting for. How dare you, he would shout at the man. Don't you watch where you're going? How could you be so careless? And shoving a paralyzed person. You should be ashamed of yourself. An opportunity had presented itself. A fortunate confluence of circumstances had brought him and the mall man together at this moment in time, in this particular spot of the mall. With this discovery, Bill almost felt pleasure. He began rehearsing what he would say. He would begin softly, but then he would shout, for he had a true grievance against the man, forty years of grievance. He would scream. How he hated this man. If only the mall man would brush against his chair. Bill didn't require a large shove, just the smallest brush would do. Just the slightest nudge, a careless turn of the elbow, a knee, a foot. If he'd been able, he would have repositioned himself. They were very close now, the man and his daughter, talking to each other, examining merchandise, moving back and forth past his chair. He prayed for the accident, just the slightest miscalculation.

"Can I help you with something?"

"What?" Bill sputtered. Incredibly, the mall man had spoken to him.

"Is someone with you?" The mall man bent down. Was he smiling? "It must be tough to be stuck in that chair. Please, let me help you. Are you alone? Would you like to go somewhere?" He laid down his packages and placed his dim face next to Bill.

"No thank you," Bill whispered. "I'm waiting for my son." What had gone wrong? He was suffocating. The mall man was smothering him with his kindness, mastering him with his total superiority. The ultimate insult. And that nauseating faint curl of the lips.

"Are you sure?" said the man. "I would be glad to help you with something."

"I'm sure. Thank you." Bill wanted to scream. But what would he scream about? The man had not bumped into his chair. Would he scream about the man's self-satisfied superiority, his obliviousness to the world, and now, finally, his abominable niceness? Bill could do nothing. Leave me, Bill howled in his mind, take your success and your splendid oblivion and your superiority and get out of my sight.

But the mall man would not leave. He stood there talking to his beautiful daughter, examining items from the shelf, and now and then he glanced at Bill. Could he smell Bill's urine, his stink? Was that it? Was that why he had been so polite, hiding his disgust so that his superiority might shine even brighter? Other people came and went down the aisle, but the mall man remained. Voices in Bill's ear. Now, the aisle was throbbing, shaking, and the mall man kept glancing at him. Wasn't he glancing? He had smelled Bill's filthy body, and he was smiling, remaining nearby to rub in his superiority, to grind it in, grind it in. Bill closed his eyes. Twelve, thirteen, fourteen. He wanted out, he wanted out of the mall, he wanted to go home. Where was Alex? How long had it been? Bill could not see his watch. What time was it? How long? Something itched on his face, and he struggled to shift his head, to scratch skin against the metal of the chair. Fifteen. He could not endure. He could not endure.

"You've got to see this," suddenly came Alex's voice.

Bill opened his eyes and squinted. Alex was pushing him down the aisle. Indistinct shelves of merchandise rolled past, sounds of yips, then the next aisle.

"You've got to see this, Dad."

"Alex, take me home." Bill was dizzy and spent. Smells burned into his face. Shelves of wires and antennae, the remote-controlled pet toys.

"It's only twenty-four ninety-five," said Alex. "It's the coolest thing I've ever seen. For Gerty. Gerty will love it."

"Please, Alex. I want to go home. Take me out."

"Dad. We can't go home now. It's only eleven o'clock. Do you have to go to the bathroom?"

"Alex, stop. I don't want to see it, whatever it is." Aisles tumbled past, moving things, open mouths on shelves, people shoving around his chair.

"Dad."

"Stop. Stop." He found himself screaming, and the boy suddenly stopped and stood against a shelf. "Stop. Stop." Bill continued screaming. Other people in the aisle stared and moved away.

"Have you stopped now?" Bill shouted at his son. "Have you stopped now?"

Alex was silent.

"Have you stopped?" Bill screamed again.

"Yes," Alex whispered, almost inaudibly.

"You shouldn't shout at him that way," said a woman at the end of the aisle.

"It's none of your business," Bill barked at her. His mouth was working now, ugly and twisted. His cheek was wet from the spit and saliva. "Don't you see what's happening?" he shouted at Alex. "Don't you see what you're doing to yourself?"

Alex stood speechless against the shelves.

"You're becoming just like me."

The boy started to say something but turned away from his father.

"Look at me," shouted Bill. "Look at me. What do you see?

Look at me. I am a paralyzed man. Look at me. I can't move. I'm paralyzed."

Alex hid his face.

A man ventured into the aisle and began speaking angrily to Bill. "Get away," Bill screamed. "Get away, I'm talking to my son."

"Do you know what's happening, what'll happen to you?" he said to his son's back.

Alex remained slumped against the shelves, turned away, hiding his face. "I'm sorry, Dad," he whispered. "I'm sorry."

"I'll tell you what's going to happen to you," Bill shouted. "You'll get a good job, probably paying big bucks. Maybe you'll work downtown like I did, in one of those skyscrapers with a view of the ocean. Then you'll be in your late twenties and married, you'll start to get indigestion."

Another man was approaching Bill, a man talking to someone on a phone. A crowd of people stood behind him.

"But you won't realize what's happening," Bill continued shouting to Alex. "You'll be making more and more money. You'll live in a big house, you'll have nice cars and suits. You'll be promoted and taken to dinner at Locke-Ober's by the top brass. And you won't be able to stop because you won't notice, you won't realize what's happening. And even if you did realize, you won't do anything about it because you're a coward. And when you're in your forties and fifties you'll gradually lose your mind. But you won't notice. You'll just lose it, until you've gone from a rat to a little jiggling blip on a screen. Or you might get a little too far behind, and they'll fire you and have you in a coffin before you know what's happened. You think—"

"Stop it," said Alex. He was sobbing. "Stop it. Stop it." He ran down the aisle.

For a few moments, Bill's mouth continued twitching, as if

he were still shouting. Something was burning in his body. He squinted at the lights overhead and at the crowd of people huddled and whispering at the end of the aisle. Then he stared across at the shelves where Alex had been and felt loathing for himself. What had come over him? What demon had taken hold of him? He twisted his head, straining to see where Alex had gone, and his heart broke.

"Alex," he cried out, but the boy had fled from the store. How could he have said such things to his precious Alex, his dear Alex? Is this what he had finally become, a monster who devoured the person he loved most? He threw his head to one side. Where was Alex? Where was his son? Forgive me, Alex, forgive me.

In minutes, he convinced a woman with a straw hat to push him into the main corridor. "I must find my son," he said. He offered her ten dollars from the wallet hanging around his neck. No, she could not take money for aiding a paralyzed person, she said. She was a Christian woman. Where did he want to go? They went back toward the fountains and the new cars for sale, glancing hurriedly into stores. She was not as strong as Alex and struggled with the chair. Now the roar of the mall seemed far away. All he could think of was Alex. Tender images of his son cut into him, Alex as a child holding out his hands, tucking Alex into bed in his blue-wallpapered room. How could he have said those things to his son? He would beg forgiveness. What could he say? There, over there, is that him? No. Faster. Please, faster.

It was 11:48. The woman took him out of the mall. She explained that she wanted additional help, her legs were starting to ache. When they had wheeled through the south doors and down the walkway, he saw Alex sitting on the sidewalk.

"Don't come near me," said Alex, standing up.

"Alex." Bill pleaded with his eyes. He could hardly talk. "I didn't know what I was saying."

"I'm going to get more help," said the woman in the straw hat, and she went back into the mall.

"Alex," said Bill. "Please forgive me, Alex." He was ten feet from his son.

"Why did you say those things to me?"

"I didn't mean what I said."

"Why?"

"Alex. I love you. I'm so upset about everything. I'm not thinking straight. I say things I don't mean." Tears were sliding down Bill's face.

"You called me a coward." Now Alex was looking at him hard.

"I didn't mean it, Alex. I'm the coward. I was taking everything out on you. I'm out of my head. Please, Alex, please forgive me. I love you. I'm so proud of you. Will you forgive me?" He began coughing and rubbed his wet face against his shoulder. "Please, Alex. You're my son. I love you."

Alex walked over and put his arms around his father.

NEWS FROM MR. BAKER

He had been dressed for a very long time and waited without interest for the arrival of Thurston Baker. A blanket covered his legs. A steady hiss from the bathroom.

Listening to Melissa shower, he thought of their first time alone. She had taken off from work and made lunch for him at her apartment, lowering the shades so that no one would know she was home. He remembered a patch of light on the sill beneath the shade, oblong, the cries of birds. Neither of them could eat. After sitting in silence at the table, he had stood up, and she stood up, and they walked toward each other, to a distance just beyond touching. Every cell was exploding. He remembered shadows on the wall, objects on tables.

He had been dressed for a very long time now. Beyond his room, from downstairs, he could hear the voices of Virginia and her children, Alex, Peter Harnden. What time was it? He was deviled now by never knowing the time. His final curse.

Melissa's voice from the bathroom: "I'm not going to make it. He's going to be here in ten minutes. I can't find anything."

Alex's voice, muffled, behind the door: "Dad. Aunt Virginia wants to know what you want for your birthday."

"A tie." He had not drunk anything since lunch, and his throat was dried up. He felt like all the air had been sucked out of his body. In his mind, he thought again of their first time alone, her standing against the lowered shades.

He heard her now, out of the shower and moving about in the closet. All the delicate sounds of her getting dressed. A silky breath that must be her slip against her skin, the flutter of a blouse moving over her shoulders. Her heeled shoes on the floor making little clatters, then a comb on his head. He felt her hand trembling.

"Bill, you look so . . ."

"What?"

"Do you need anything?"

"Water."

The telephones began ringing. He bit his lip until the phones stopped. The comb against his head, her hand on his cheek. Breathe slowly, breathe slowly.

He asked her if she was wearing the necklace he gave her, the gold chain with the small gold pellets. Would she put it on for him, so that he could imagine her in it? Yes, she said.

Then he felt her head resting against his chest.

"Bill. My darling. You've got to go to a hospital now. In a few days. Okay?"

"I want to stay here."

"I promise I'll come the first thing in the morning and stay until you go to sleep at night. We can't take care of you here anymore."

"I know this room."

She stood up. He could hear the rustle of her clothes. She started to cry, and he knew she was crying partly for him. That was what was left now. He asked her to take his hand and to press it against her body.

"Where is my hand now?" he asked.

"Against my lips."

"Against your lips."

"Yes."

For a few moments, he listened to her breathing. The smell of invisible flowers, white casablanca lilies, her skin.

"Melissa," he said. "Suppose that none of our lives before now had happened."

"What do you mean?"

"Suppose we just met."

"You can't pretend things like that."

"Try. Suppose we're just meeting for the first time now."

"Oh, Bill," she whispered. "I can't pretend that everything that's happened hasn't happened." She hesitated. "I'm doing all I can do." He felt her fingers touch his cheek.

Gerty began barking and the doorbell rang. The sounds of many footsteps on the stairs, a knock on the bedroom door.

Thurston Baker's voice: "Nice house. Hello there, Bill. Mrs. Chalmers."

Virginia's voice: "I've left my children downstairs watching TV. I don't think they should be in here."

Peter's voice: "I'm not sure I should be, either. I'll wait downstairs."

"Stay, Peter," said Bill. He imagined Peter, his red hair and his largeness. He imagined Thurston Baker, dressed in a fine suit and gazing from behind the polished lenses of his glasses. The attorney's footsteps stopped just past the bedroom door.

Melissa's voice: "Sit down, Mr. Baker. We have coffee."

Bill sensed a hesitation. People had come into the room, he heard movements in corners, chairs, but no one was speaking. Undoubtedly, Thurston Baker and Peter were shocked by his appearance. He knew what he must look like. His skin pallid, his head lolling about on his chest as if unattached. His legs shaking with occasional spasms. Everyone must have been frightened to look at him, to contemplate his suffering. What he did not tell them, what he alone knew, was that complete incapacity was the easiest thing in the world. For months, he had been fighting his growing incapacity, his powerlessness. But now it was easy.

Virginia's voice: "Cream, Mr. Baker?" A pause. "Didn't your firm handle that suit with the Japanese factory a few years ago? Where was it? Reading?"

Baker's voice: "You mean the Worcester case."

Virginia's voice: "Yes. I saw you quoted in the *Boston Globe*."

Baker's voice: "That was Jason Weatherhill, one of my colleagues. I don't speak to the papers."

Melissa's voice: "What is it you came here to tell us, Mr. Baker?"

Bill heard a movement from Alex's direction. He had a mental picture of where everyone was sitting, and he imagined his son on the edge of the bed, wearing his Nike shoes with the shoelaces untied. Then he heard Alex's footsteps quietly moving toward him, he felt Alex's arm on his shoulder. "I'm here, Dad," Alex whispered.

Baker's voice: "I have some possibly good news." A stirring. Plymouth Limited was beginning to talk about a settlement. No one had expected anything so quickly, certainly not in the absence of a diagnosis. Evidently, Baker said, Plymouth's attorneys had calculated that it would be cheaper for them to settle now rather than later.

Virginia's voice: "Thank God almighty." Her heavy footsteps on the floor. "Thank you, Mr. Baker. Thank you. We've won."

Baker's voice: "We have no idea how much they might offer. I want you to understand that. We'll begin discussing the details after Ms. Stevenson returns from Ohio next week. I don't want you to get your hopes up. Still, I thought this news might cheer you a little. I wanted to tell you in person."

Melissa's voice: "It doesn't seem possible."

"They feel guilty," said Bill. He thought he would react more strongly, but he felt very little, he felt as if he were looking at a small dot in the distance.

Peter's voice: "Assholes."

Bill imagined everyone moving toward the door. What time was it, he wondered. He wanted everyone the hell out of his room. What time was it?

CALONICE

When Anytus arrived at the hetaera's small stone house on a narrow street in the Limnae, the air had cleared and the moon hung full over the city, casting shadows from fountains and vestibules into the dirty streets below. The tanner approached Calonice's door and knocked.

After a few moments, the door was half-opened by a male slave whom Anytus had never seen before. "What is your business, sir?" the slave said unpleasantly. "The lady of the house has retired for the evening." The porter squinted at the man standing in the moonlight, rudely dragging his gaze up and down Anytus as if he were a servant himself.

"Please tell the lady that Anytus is here."

"Do you have an appointment, sir?"

"An appointment?" Suddenly, Anytus got a sick wormy feeling that he might not see Calonice tonight. And he needed her terribly. "Calonice," Anytus shouted into the house, "it is Anytus." The slave slammed the door shut.

Anytus stood outside the closed door, anxiously pondering what he should do next. Sounds of a cithara floated through the street. The instrument was sad and beautiful, a voice of the sad city. Then the door opened again. This time it was Calonice. She moved forward and embraced him, kissing him on his eyelids, then long on his lips, then his eyelids again.

He wrapped his arms around her and held her and they stood that way for a time before she pulled him into the house and closed the door. Her scent of sandalwood was all over him.

"I'm sorry about Simmias," she whispered. "He won't venture out of his room again tonight. He is a frightening creature, isn't he. But he does his job. You should have told me you were coming." She spoke perfect Attic Greek, although one could hear the musical lilt of her faded Corinthian dialect. She stooped down and began unfastening Anytus's sandals in the dark entry.

Anytus leaned against the wall, overcome with relief. "I don't like your new servant. Peleus never treated me like that."

"You should always tell me when you are coming, my dove. Let me look at you." She stood back, then softly cupped his cheeks with her hands and gazed into his eyes. "It's hard to see you. Let's go into the court where I can see you better."

She reached out her hand, but Anytus did not take it. He continued standing against the wall, his feet cold on the stone floor. "I was . . ." He started and stopped. "Why is it so important that you know in advance when I'm visiting? So that you will not be with someone else, isn't that it? Do I need appointments like your other men?"

A wounded look came over her face, but she soon smiled and reached again for his hand. This time, she held his hand firmly and led him into the small rectangular court, with its smell of perfumes and soap and the flaking limestone statue of Callisto in the center. They sat down on a pillowed bronze couch.

In the good light, he could see that she was wearing a flowing silk saffron gown, sleeveless, fastened at the left shoulder with a lavender brocade. Her black hair was unpinned, and the dark beauty of her native Corinth was accented by kohl tastefully applied to her eyelids and lashes. He looked at her face and her hair and buried his head against her bare shoulder. "Calonice," he whispered. "Calonice. I can't bear it that you entertain other men. You know that I can't bear it. You must stop. I'll give you anything, whatever you want. You have no need of their money."

"Is it fair to say such things?" she said softly, stroking his neck with her fingertips. "You have a wife, a woman you sleep with every night. How do you think that I feel about her? I cannot even say her name. I try not to imagine. We should not talk about these things. You know that I love you."

"And do you love the others as well?" he said, his face still pressed against her shoulder.

"I love you. When you are here, there are no others."

Anytus sat up and studied her face. "That is no answer to my question." He took a strand of her long hair between his fingers and played with it.

"Please, Anytus, must we quarrel? Let's talk of other things."

A puff of cool air tumbled in from the night sky over the courtyard, and Calonice shuddered. She gently moved Anytus's head from her shoulder and stood up. "Let me look at you. I will have to get you out of those silly clothes. What is this?" She pointed to a small yellow bruise on the underside of his arm. "This wasn't here the last time I saw you. You've hurt yourself." She bent over and kissed the spot with her lips. "You look tired, Anytus dove. You're worried, I can see that. Tell me what worries you. Can you stay the night?" Anytus nodded. "Good. I will have you all to myself. I have missed you, it's been two weeks."

Anytus put his arms around her, drawing her toward him. He ran his hands lightly over her breasts, then kissed her on her mouth and her neck. "You are so beautiful," he said. "I want to stay with you forever. Don't let me leave." He closed his eyes, holding her. "I feel quiet here. This is my home."

"You must not say that, my dove. It will make both of us unhappy."

"I want to be still. You are my stillness. Don't let me leave." He held his cheek against her chest, listening to her heartbeat.

She placed her palm against his cheek. "Is it Prodicus?" she said. "Has he been insulting you again?"

Anytus shrugged his shoulders. "No more than usual. Prodicus is a grown man. He does what he wants." Anytus picked up a jeweled brush and began brushing her black hair, which glistened in the lamp light.

"Your son should be more like you," she said softly.

"No, not like me. Not like me."

"Oh, Anytus my dove, my sweet nightingale." She looked up at the dark square of night above the stone head of Callisto. "Hasn't the weather been strange? Pouring rain and gray for a whole day, like winter, and then suddenly at dusk the rain stops and the air clears and shines. Who can understand the blessed Immortals."

At these remarks, Anytus's hands trembled, and she felt it. She took the brush and kissed his fingers and studied his face. "Promise you will talk to me. You will tell me." He nodded. "I will remember that promise," she said. "But we have all night. First, I want to make love to you." She took his hand again and led him to the back of the court and through the vermilion curtains to her bedchamber.

Later that night, after she had fallen asleep, he lay next to her and stared at the ceiling. They had left one small lamp burning. Its flickering light caused shadows to shift on the ceiling, darting at each other like attacking armies. Or like unfolding vines, struggling to climb down the walls. Below, the room smelled of spring lilies and perspiration. He sprawled naked on the bed, wanting to wake her and talk. He felt empty and full at the same time.

No longer could he look at the ceiling. His eyes wearily circled the room. On a chest near the door lay dim combs and brushes, on another a dark perfume vial shaped like a bird. He closed his eyes but the shadows continued to dance on his eyelids. He turned on his side. His body would not relax and let go. Undulations of strain flowed down his legs, constrictions of muscles in waves. He tightened and loosened his fists. He let out a deep breath and turned to his other side, opening his eyes in the flickering light, then closing his eyes.

From somewhere outside, the cithara again, insinuating its way through the walls of the house. The cithara in the middle of the night, some sleepless person plucking its strings to take revenge on all those sleeping. But he was not sleeping. The sound was not beautiful now but metallic and sharp, cutting the stillness. He found himself waiting for the spaces between notes, between sharp knives cutting into the vast empty dark. How jagged the night had grown, tall and pierced in its great empty rooms. The cithara became louder and bigger until it was voices screaming, an evil chorus chanting some sharp and metallic chant. He had never before heard such voices. He could swear they were coming from the next room. He would get up and go to the courtyard to stop them, but he found himself unable to move. He looked down at his own body and saw that his hands were gripping the side of the bed. He turned and looked at Calonice, the thin skin on her throat, her bare arms and legs.

The cithara stopped.

He watched the shadows, darting ceaselessly back and forth, and the ceiling seemed to descend and descend and he closed his eyes but felt the ceiling lowering further, continuing its descent. He opened his eyes and saw that it was one foot away. In response, he stretched his body as flat as it would go. The world had become two horizontals, near-ly touching, the bed and the ceiling. How could Calonice sleep? He raised his arm, expecting it to crash into the upper boundary of the world, but nothing happened. He could not be hurt. Was he not Anytus, former general in the Thirty-Year War against Sparta, defender of the democracy? He turned to Calonice, beautiful and rapturous Calonice. Or was it Pasiclea? In dim light their bodies were similar. They both loved him, did they not? Anytus, distinguished citizen of Athens. Where was this room, this bed? Could it be Pasi-clea who lay with him now? She would forgive him every-thing. Or Calonice? Wasn't that Calonice's brocade on the wood chest, glinting in the flickering light? She would also forgive him, had already forgiven him. She was his quiet, his stillness.

He turned over and over, kicking the sheepskins to the floor, and finally settled on his left side in an uneasy chasm, half asleep and half awake. He opened his eyes to look at Calonice and saw that she had also opened her eyes. They were red and inflamed. She turned toward him and smiled, but her smile was a horror. Blood dripped from her tongue, and a rotting smell jumped out of her mouth. She began coughing a deep hard cough, like stone against stone. Yellow and brown liquids trickled from her body and soaked the bedsheets. Plague. He sat up, sweating. "Anytus dove," she said. "Where are you going? You cannot leave me now. No matter what's happened, you cannot leave me now." She began retching and shaking, and the lamp seemed to get brighter, and he saw that small pustules and ulcers had formed on her breasts and her stomach and legs. Her breath smelled of decaying flesh. Still smiling, she reached out to touch him with swollen red fingers. "Anytus dove."

She wiped his face with her dripping hand and he screamed

and she sat up. "Anytus, what is the matter?" she said. "Are you all right?" She got out of bed and lit a second oil lamp. Her pustules and ulcers were gone. "Are you ill?"

"No, I'm all right."

"Are you sure you're not ill?" she said, her lilting voice rough around the edges with irritation. "You frightened me, my dove. I am sorry, but I need my sleep. I need my sleep."

"Yes. I'll be quiet. I'm all right."

She extinguished the lamp and got back into bed and put her arm around him. Soon she was asleep again, but he lay awake, listening to her breathing.

After Melissa had finished reading the story, the room fell into silence. Bill waited for Melissa to say something, to move from her seat on the blanket chest, but the only sound he could hear was the soft clopping of a hot-water pipe. It was late, after midnight. Far away, a car engine coughed. He listened again and heard her breathing.

"I've done a terrible thing to you," she whispered. He heard her rise, go the bureau and pour herself a scotch and drink in swallows.

"Melissa," he said.

"I've caused everything. I'll never forgive myself."

"What are you talking about? Come here." She remained by the bureau, sipping her scotch. "Please come." Her feet softly clapped on the floor. She would be barefoot, he knew, wearing her turquoise silk robe. He imagined her in her robe, her delicate nose and mouth.

"I've done a terrible thing," she said. Her sleeve brushed his cheek, her fingers.

"I don't want to know," he said.

"But I have to tell you."

"I don't want to know. Whatever it is. Just touch me." She put her glass down on a table.

"Oh, Bill . . ." She paused, the glass moved again.

"Do you love me?" he said.

"Yes. Yes. I feel like we're in a nightmare. Isn't this all a nightmare? I do love you." He felt her hand on his forehead, heard her sigh with exhaustion. Her silk sleeve touched his eyelids.

"Alex has stopped losing weight," she said. "He's been drinking some milkshake supplement. His first match of the chess tournament is on Wednesday."

"Good."

"He'll be getting out to matches. He needs to get out." She paused and slumped against him, resting a limp arm across his chest. "Isn't it amazing that we made him," she said, slurring her words now. "We did that together. At least that's something."

Her body moved, and he heard her fall across the bed.

"I'll take care of you," she mumbled. "I'll take care of you. I will."

Then he allowed himself to slip down into the dark of his illness. Vague sensations of shadow and light flickered across his blind eyes, the errant pulses of nerve endings. The body had its own memory. His fingers were tingling wires, his legs vibrated like echoes in vast canyons, his stomach throbbed with each pulse of blood. Waves traveled his arms. A tear slid over his cheek. For a few moments, he wondered what Melissa had wanted to confess. He envied the sharp point of her guilt. Then the familiar black bile stirred in his stomach. Peter. How despondent and spiritless his friend's voice had been that afternoon. The pressure of his existence, the chase and the emptiness were slowly crushing in on Peter. He had no center. One of these days he would collapse completely, lose his job to a less used man, end up sitting on the couch in his house in Drexel Hill, unshaven and watching television all day. Or maybe he would just slowly fade, never knowing. And Bill had been unable to warn him, knew it with certainty and could do nothing. Bile, all bile. Bill wanted to escape his body, he wanted to spill it, to shed it, to slough off the cowardice and rot.

Soon he could hear the deep breathing of Melissa in her sleep. In his mind, he could see her lying there on the canopied bed in her silk robe, her hair tangled, her shoulders rising and falling with each inhale and exhale. How many times he had lain there with her, how many years. As if regarding their lives through a telescope, he wondered if he could ever have made her happy. Possibly during the first year, when they lived on Anabel Circle. They both thought it was the prettiest street, with a lilting name. A lifetime ago, gone in the drop of a leaf.

Now he would not wake her to get him into the bed. He would spend the long night in his chair. His pulse was throbbing, the night was pulling at him, the night would not let him sleep.

He listened to her breathing, to his own breathing, and he realized that he was wheezing. He could hear himself wheezing. Were his lungs beginning to fail? In the morning, Melissa would try again to make him go to the hospital. Petrov would order another round of examinations for him. But he would not oblige.

Melissa shifted in the bed, and his thoughts returned to her. He wondered what she would do. He could not imagine her living alone. She would remarry quickly, maybe to someone he knew now, or an old boyfriend. In a vision, he saw her in another house, standing by a great window, her hair longer than he'd ever seen it. Had he gotten some glimpse of the future? He strained to see her face, to see if she was contented, but the image dissolved into the curve of her shoulders. Maybe she would move back to Fayetteville, take Virginia and her children with her. Then he imagined Alex. At college in his new dormitory room, putting photographs on the wall with thumbtacks. Alex's eyes dark and dewy, his sincerity. Light from a leaded glass window. Alex might live a life.

He listened again to the shallow pantings of his breath. The world had diminished to the most feeble red light, stray thoughts in his mind, inhales and exhales. Pieces of letters formed with his breathing. Inhales ascended with the start of a vowel or consonant, exhales fell with the turning. Slight swirls were *c*'s, longer flat breaths were *b*'s, or *w*'s, or *t*'s. A world in the breath. His breathing in counterpoint to hers, letter by letter, word by word. What message could he be writing with his breaths? No message. Only intricate turnings, drowning gasps and pants. His breath had almost succeeded in sloughing off his body, now he was a thin line, a thin column of air. Hers, the sharp point of guilt, his the dull edge cutting jagged. And as he listened to his labored breathing, he resolved more than ever not to leave this room. He would remain here in this room. Then there rose in his mind the memory of lying on the hospital bed beside the cellseparator machine. He could see his blood flowing through the clear plastic tube, into the machine and back to the blue vein in his arm. He could hear the thumping and thumping and the doctors standing over him discussing his brain scans and blood counts.

Suddenly a fury ran through him and crushed his chest muscles and twisted his mouth. He screamed, "No." The scream did not seem to come from his lips but exploded out of his body. The scream rang in his ears, the scream rang through the silent house, Melissa moaned in her sleep. No. His heart pounded. His lungs sliced raw and bleeding. He gasped for air. The invisible room had punctured and collapsed on itself, the ceiling had dropped until it hovered just inches above his head. No. In his last remaining days, his life would be his, his spirit would be his. He was not a cork in the sea. He could act, even if only for himself. He could act.

For a few moments, his body jerked and quivered. Then the terrible grip of his chest began to subside. His muscles slackened. Slowly, slowly, air returned to his lungs. The pounding of his heart slowed to throbs, his blood slackened. His quivering distended to sighs and thinned to a slight tremble and dissolved in a last gentle sway, and then a calm began spreading over him. He would have his dignity. He would have his dignity. He would have this small space of stillness. In his calm, in the stillness, he listened again to his breathing. He listened to sounds, unable to measure time or the hours remaining in the night.

After some moments, he heard rain. He could hear a soft splattering on the roof, a fluttering and tap at the windows. In the distance, shutters creaked in the wind. His neighbors might be listening also as they lay restless upon their beds. He imagined the drops of rain outside his window, small and gray in the night. He imagined the rain moving in slants to the ground, leaving a silver glove on each branch and leaf, washing the sidewalks and streets, washing the blue-shadowed lampposts and the metal fenders of cars and the vast stretch of highway leading to Boston. Rain would be dripping softly on the windows of the Marbleworth Building and on the Prudential Center and, further east, making dimples in the dark sea along the coast.

ACKNOWLEDGMENTS

For help with legal, medical, and other technical matters, I thank Neil Arkuss, Isabelle De Courtivron, Robert Kane, Karla Kanis, William McClaran, Ross Peterson, Chris Sawyer-Laucanno, James Suojanen, Sherry Turkle, Alice Whitehill Wiseberg, and the Harvard Medical School Library. I take responsibility for all factual errors remaining in the novel. Thank you, Robbie Bosnak and Janet Sonenberg, for your guidance at a critical juncture.

While Anytus and Socrates are historical, as is the general narrative of Socrates' trial and execution, the "Anytus Dialogue" presented here is fictional. Particularly useful texts for me in re-creating ancient Athens and its characters included the *Dialogues* of Plato, particularly *Apology* and *Phaedo*, the plays of Aristophanes, Thucydides' *History of the Peloponnesian War,* and the writings of Hippocrates on disease and medicine. For additional consultations on ancient Greece, I thank Zeph Stewart, Ted Lendon, and Rob Loomis.

I am grateful to Don DeLillo, Richard Goodwin, Ilona Karmel, Leo Marx, Agnieszka Meyro, Annie Proulx, Janet Silver, Michael Rothschild, Peter Stoicheff, Dan Terris, and Rosalind Williams for commenting on the manuscript in progress. Thank you, Jim Leahy, for many readings at the early stages and for your support.

A deep appreciation to LaRose Todd Coffey, exacting teacher of long ago, insightful critic, and friend.

Loving gratitude to my wife, Jean Lightman, who has patiently nourished me through the many years of writing this book.

Finally, a special thanks to Dan Frank, for his perceptive and sustained editorial suggestions, to Jane Gelfman, for her encouragement and friendship over many years, and to Liz Calder, for her readings and advice in the last stages.